# Maa

**Anurupa Devi** (1882–1958) was a pioneering woman writer of Bengal, many of whose novels were made into films and/or stage plays. She won several awards for her novels, including the Kuntalin Purashkar, and the Jagattarini and Bhuvanmohini gold medals. She wrote 33 novels, many short stories and essays, and *Sahitye Nari: Sroshtri o Shristi,* which was a collection of the Lila Lectures delivered at Calcutta University, an amazing feat for a woman who had received no formal education.

**Sanjukta Banerji Bhattacharya** is Anurupa Devi's granddaughter, and has a keen interest in literature. She has a BA degree in English, an MA in History, and a PhD in International Studies from the School of International Studies, Jawaharlal Nehru University. She recently retired as professor of International Relations at Jadavpur University, Kolkata, and has numerous books and articles to her credit. She is currently associated with several universities and academic institutions in various capacities. Her complete academic profile is available at https://jadavpur.academia.edu/SanjuktaBhattacharya.

# Maa

## ANURUPA DEVI

*Translated by*
Sanjukta Banerji Bhattacharya

Published by
Rupa Publications India Pvt. Ltd 2024
7/16, Ansari Road, Daryaganj
New Delhi 110002

*Sales centres:*
Bengaluru Chennai
Hyderabad Jaipur Kathmandu
Kolkata Mumbai Prayagraj

Originally published in Bengali in 1920
Edition copyright © Rupa Publications India Pvt. Ltd 2024
Translation copyright © Sanjukta Banerji Bhattacharya 2024

This is a work of fiction. Names, characters, places and incidents are either the product of the author's imagination or are used fictitiously and any resemblance to any actual person, living or dead, events or locales is entirely coincidental.

All rights reserved.
No part of this publication may be reproduced, transmitted, or stored in a retrieval system, in any form or by any means, electronic, mechanical, photocopying, recording or otherwise, without the prior permission of the publisher.

P-ISBN: 978-93-6156-566-3
E-SBN: 978-93-6156-036-1

First impression 2024

10 9 8 7 6 5 4 3 2 1

Printed at India

This book is sold subject to the condition that it shall not, by way of trade or otherwise, be lent, resold, hired out, or otherwise circulated, without the publisher's prior consent, in any form of binding or cover other than that in which it is published.

To
My grandmother
Anurupa Devi
who broke glass ceilings when Bengali women were not even
aware that glass ceilings existed

# Reintroducing My Grandmother Anurupa Devi

By Sanjukta Banerji Bhattacharya

Anurupa Devi was well known for her iconic novels portraying the inner world of the Bengali *bhadralok samaj* even fifty years ago. However, as happens with books written in vernacular languages, her works remained confined to Bengal, although some of her novels were made into Hindi films. Today, she and her contemporary pioneering women writers from Bengal are slowly becoming postscripts in history. Yet, their contributions to literature as well as their independent thinking on women and their position in society hold immense historical value. The present translation is an attempt to recreate her characters, revive interest in her writings and bring at least one of her novels before a wider audience as it is a labour of love. She is my paternal grandmother, and this is something I have always wanted to do ever since I first read this book many decades ago.

Most urban Bengalis know the meaning of bhadralok samaj and bhadralok culture, a society of gentlemen or genteel folk, a kind of new aristocracy that arose in Bengal under British rule. However, few people are aware of a corresponding *bhadramahila* society in the late nineteenth and early twentieth centuries—daughters of bhadralok families who were exposed to the discourses of their fathers, brothers and husbands, and began to think for themselves. Most were schooled at home, others were sent to school for a few years between the ages of nine and fourteen for some formal education before getting married. But given the patriarchal nature of even the most progressive Bengali families, most bhadramahilas grew up against the backdrop of the contradictory pressures of tradition and modernity, and only few were able to defy social norms. But there were some who took up the pen despite little formal education and restrictions on women's learning, and proved that the pen had an edge too by writing stories that openly critiqued patriarchy, which imposed innumerable burdens on women.

My grandmother, Anurupa Devi, was a product of those times; the contradictions of the bhadramahila samaj echo in her novels, with *Maa,* written over a hundred years ago, being a classic example. This is not a feminist novel (Anurupa Devi was not a feminist in the modern sense), but it is certainly an anti-patriarchy work, if one can use that word, with the entire plot hinging on decisions made by the patriarch, thus affecting the women characters who are the objects of patriarchal diktats and correspondingly their families.

Anurupa Devi's *Maa* was considered an iconic novel in undivided Bengal. It was read by thousands and made into a movie in 1934 with some of the finest actors of the time in the cast, like Kanan Devi, Manorama Devi and Bhaskar Dev. The popularity of *Maa* is evident from the fact that a Hindi version of the film was released in 1936 starring, apart from Kanan Devi (who won the best actress award of that year for her role), two of the best known actors of the contemporary Hindi screen of the time, Jal Merchant and Zubeida. It is, in fact, a period piece, and to understand a period piece, one must put the period within a context, both in terms of person and time. Anurupa Devi was writing at a time when (a) few women were educated enough to have an independent understanding of what was going on in the country, let alone write novels, and

(b) the country, particularly Bengal, was in a state of political turmoil and intellectual churning, the effects of which must have infiltrated the women's world, especially in educated, influential bhadralok families. The Bengal Renaissance—a fluorescence of intellectual and reform activities, the offshoot of a combination of Western education and a revival of Eastern scholarship—also had its impact on women of the bhadralok samaj, who still lived in the *andar mahal*, or inner sanctum of the house, but were exposed to some amount of education and the discourses of their male peers, which perhaps prompted them to think independently on matters that concerned them. However, being confined to the house and household matters, women writers rarely wrote of politics, nationalism or the outside world the way their male peers did, having much more exposure. Their stories and novels deal with the internal politics of the home and the andar mahal, although they very often offer a strong implicit commentary on patriarchy and reflect an intense psychosocial and analytical understanding of women's lives.

Anurupa Devi was no exception. She was comfortable with what she knew first-hand, that is, women's lives and psyche under the multiple pressures of patriarchy, tradition, exposure to modernity, progressive education, poverty, convention, and so on. She did not dabble in affairs that she did not experience but had only read or heard of. Interestingly, she did not do much in-depth analysis of male characters either; she preferred to describe women's and children's mental make-up and reactions to events in great detail, something she observed, experienced and understood well. Her women characters were strong and self-willed, and this attracted women readers. I believe she had a very large women fan-following, which also reflected women's feelings about fellow women and patriarchy.

Anurupa Devi had a strong persona; she was a grande dame in more than one sense and had an overwhelming aura, even in her old age, from what little I can remember. She commanded a presence in the public sphere as much as at home. She was tall, fair and aristocratic, and dominated the scene not only because she was such a well-known writer—that Bengalis, born literature lovers, were in awe of her—but also because she had a strong authoritative personality to match her appearance.

She was born on 9 September 1882 into a famous Hindu Brahmin family: her father was Mukunda Dev Mukhopadhyaya, and her grandfather Bhudev Mukhopadhyaya was a doyen of Hindu intellectualism and learning in nineteenth-century Bengal. He had been awarded the title of Companion of the Order of the Indian Empire (CIE) in 1877 by the British rulers for his services to the British Empire in the field of education, but he never became a lackey of the British. He aligned his Western education with traditional learning, set up charitable institutions like schools, ayurvedic and homeopathic dispensaries, a college in Rajshahi, and Bishwanath Chatuspathi—a Sanskrit school in Hooghly in the name of his father—and also formed the Bishwanath Trust Fund (1894) with his own savings to provide scholarships to deserving but destitute students. In some of his essays, for instance, 'Paribarik Prabandha' (1882), 'Samajik Prabandha' (1892) and 'Achar Prabandha' (1895), he endeavoured to spell out ideas regarding the reform of Hindu customs and family laws in keeping with the needs of his times. In various interviews, Anurupa Devi has claimed that this grandfather directed her early education and shaped her childhood thinking, which obviously impacted her later life.

Equally important, though almost unknown today, was her maternal heritage, especially from the point of view of her writing style, which had an inherent theatrical element. Her maternal grandfather was Nagendranath Bandopadhyay (1850–82), a well-known novelist of his time who dabbled in amateur acting and is said to be one of the pioneers in organizing community Durga Pujas (*barwari pujo*), which also showcased amateur theatre much as is done even today. He was secretary of the National Theatre (founded in December 1872), the first public theatre in Bengal. In 1873, he co-founded the Hindu National Theatre and the Great National Theatre; he, in fact, became the manager of the latter. Moreover, he founded a touring theatre group called the Great National Opera Company in 1875. Among his literary works are *Pherar Dak*, a book of poems; stage plays *Lilavas, Hazrat Abubaker, Kamyakanan* and *Sati ki Kalankini*, which was the first opera produced in Bengali public theatre and was staged by the Great National Theatre in 1874. It is interesting that many of Anurupa Devi's novels were adapted into stage plays and movies, and she had a say in the adaptations.

Her father Mukundadev Mukhopadhyaya was a deputy magistrate and her mother Dhara Sundari was one of the earliest Bengali women to be adept in the English language. After getting married, she received piano and English lessons from a memsahib, Mrs Collins, who was the sister-in-law of Bengali poet and playwright Michael Madhusudan Dutta's daughter, Sharmistha. Coming from such a background, Anurupa Devi must have developed an artistic and literary sensitivity as well as a social consciousness in her childhood.

Among Anurupa Devi's siblings, her elder sister, Surupa Devi, better known as Indira Devi (1880–1922), was also a well-known contemporary novelist. Anurupa Devi did not receive any formal schooling; whatever education she received was given at home till the age of 10, when she got married to my grandfather, Sikharnath Bandopadhyay, a brilliant student with record marks in mathematics at the master's level and a lawyer. Their ancestral house was and probably still is at Uttarpara's Banerji *para*, unless it has fallen victim to modernity. From what I can deduce from family tales, my grandfather's household was intellectually advanced, sending male members abroad for further studies, but strongly traditional where women were concerned.

My grandmother later told my mother, Subrata, that when she first entered the household, women were not allowed to take a postprandial afternoon nap in their bedrooms, although the men of the house could do so if they wished. The women rolled out *madur*s on the verandas surrounding the central courtyard and either slept, or did some minor, easy household tasks, like sewing or repairing old clothes. Reading novels, magazines or newspapers was frowned upon if not totally banned because of the superstition that women reading novels would bring *akalyan* on their husbands.

A child of ten or twelve could not be expected to sleep in the afternoons, and my grandmother, who was innately creative, had been encouraged to read whatever she wished to in her paternal home. In fact, she had attempted writing stories before she got married; the first titled 'Samadhi' was never published. Instead of sleeping away the afternoons at her in-laws', she read what she could lay her hands on without arousing anyone's ire—and this happened to be the yearly almanac, the *panjika*, which is a staple in every Bengali middle-class household. She claimed later that this helped in broadening her vocabulary apart from giving an insight into all kinds of rituals, ceremonies, annual forecasts based on the stars, etc. Very soon, she began writing a novel, hiding her endeavours from her elders and peers, even her husband, until it was complete. She was about fourteen or fifteen at the time. When Sikharnath wanted to see it, Anurupa Devi was too shy to share it with him; she became so embarrassed at his insistence that she ran off to the Ganges, which flowed close to their house, and threw the entire manuscript into the river! She related this incident to my mother, with whom she became quite close as she grew older. Did this sacrifice of her first novel earn her the blessings of the Holy River? One can only wonder.

My grandfather moved to Muzaffarpur shortly afterwards because of health reasons and that is where my grandmother's career took off. She wrote a total of 33 novels, but many more short stories, essays and plays. Her first published story, titled 'Mukti', was written under the pen-name Rani Devi; it was published in the *Kuntalin Purashkar Granthamala* in 1904 and won the Kuntalin Puraskar. Her first novel, *Tilakuthi*, was published serially in the periodical *Nobarun* under the pseudonym Anupama Devi, beginning in the same year till 1906. It was Swarnakumari Devi, daughter of Maharshi Debendranath Tagore and editor of the journal *Bharati,* who persuaded her to write under her own name and publish her works in *Bharati.* Whether she met Swarnakumari Devi through her cousin, the well-known writer Sourindra Mohan Mukhopadhyaya, or through her friend and neighbour Madhurilata (Bela), who was Rabindranath Tagore's daughter, is unclear, but the fact that she called Swarnakumari 'pishima' or paternal aunt is suggestive of the latter, because Swarnakumari Devi was Madhurilata's paternal aunt.

Anurupa Devi's first novel to be published serially in *Bharati* from 1909 to 1911 was *Poshyoputro*, which was later published as a book by Gurudas Chattopadhyay and Sons in 1912. This novel won her the highest of accolades and brought her at the forefront of women novelists of the time. Her next novel *Bagdatta* was also published serially in the same periodical, but she simultaneously began to publish serially in other well-known contemporary journals, like *Bharatvarsha* and *Basumati*. Many stories flowed from her pen: *Mantrashakti* (1915), *Jyotihara* (1915), *Mahanisha* (1916), *Ramgarh* (1918), *Pather Sathi* (1918), *Rangasankha* (1918), *Maa* (1920), *Patha Hara* (first published in 1922; the second edition published in 1955 was dedicated to my father, Asoka Nath Banerji, whom she addresses as 'Major', a post he had held till 1947 before he joined the Indian Administrative Service), *Gariber Meye* (1926), *Bibartan* (serially published in *Basumati* in 1939, and published as a novel in 1940), *Praner Parash* (dedicated to her childhood friend, well-known writer Nirupama Devi, and published in 1953), *Krouncho-Mithuner Milan Katha* (a book of short stories, 1956), *Stree* (1964), and *Chitradeep* (a collection of fascinating short stories written and published earlier in various periodicals and dedicated to her elder sister Indira Devi) are some of her famous works that placed her at the pinnacle of fame.

She also tried her hand at writing plays, such as *Vidyaratna* (1919), *Kumaril Bhatta* (1922), *Natyachatusthay* (a collection of four short plays, 1933), etc. Some of her novels like *Poshyoputro* and *Mantrashakti* were made into plays, and she in fact helped draw up the transcripts for the dramas. These were so popular that they ran for months in famous theatres like the Star Theatre. I am the current proud possessor of an inscribed gold pen that was gifted to her by the producers on the completion of the hundredth successful performance night of *Mantrashakti* at the Star Theatre. The drama edition of *Poshyoputro* is available online now. In the foreword written by the director Aparesh Chandra Mukhopadhyaya, he mentions that most novels cannot be adapted for stage performance; it is only because Anurupa Devi's novels had that special quality that made them adaptable, such that two of her books could be made into plays. Some of her novels were made into films in Bengali and Hindi. *Maa* was filmed in Bengali in 1934 and in Hindi (Bombay Talkies) in 1936; *Mantrashakti,* produced by Harendra Nath Chattopadhyaya and directed by Chitta Basu, was released in 1954. It had a star cast comprising Uttam Kumar, Sandhya Rani, Asit Baran and Bhanu Banerjee (a perfectly good version is available on YouTube). *Gariber Meye*, directed by Ardhendu Mukherjee, with Sabitri Chatterjee, Chhabi Biswas and Anil Chatterjee in the star roles, was first screened in 1960 after the death of the writer.

Anurupa Devi also wrote poetry, and some of her poems got published in *Bamabodhini Patrika* under the pseudonym of Anupama Devi. Towards the end of her life, she had also undertaken an autobiographical work, *Jibansmriti Lekha* (roughly translating to *Memories of My Life*), but this remained incomplete as she passed away on 19 April 1958.

About her writing, Anurupa Devi herself said that it was Swarnakumari Devi who had inspired and encouraged her to write. She told her to first lay out a broad plot and then develop the story slowly whichever way she saw fit, as she published it monthly in serial form. Here, an interesting episode about her serial writing may enlighten the current-day reader about women and writing in those days. The plot may have been in place, but emotions could shape outcomes. Anurupa Devi told my mother that she and her elder sister, Indira Devi, often confided in and consulted each other about their stories. There was a character called Shanti in *Poshyoputro*, which she was serially writing for a journal. According to the initial plot, Shanti was to die at the end. But as the story progressed every month, Indira Devi felt that the character should live, while Anurupa was adamant that she should die. Using emotional blackmail to upset the plot, Indira Devi, who was expecting a child, named her newborn daughter Shanti, and wrote to Anurupa Devi triumphantly, 'Now let me see how Shanti dies in your novel!' And sure enough, the plot was changed to accommodate the turn of events—Shanti almost dies but recovers in the last pages of the book!

In fact, the 'serial' nature is amply observable in Anurupa Devi's novels. It seems from her writings that she published one long chapter or a couple of short chapters per month. There are chapters in *Maa* that are descriptive in nature—one chapter could be a vivid portrayal of storms and thundershowers that are metaphors for the internal tempests buffeting the minds of the characters in the novel; the next chapter could be just dialogues, with hardly any descriptive paragraphs, and the exchanges carrying the plot forward. Therefore, sometimes the modern-day reader may find the novel jumping forwards and backwards, but the story always flows towards the goal that was presumably set earlier. The titles of her stories (novels, short stories, plays and the Lila Lecture essays, 'Sroshtri o Shristi'), are interesting in that each one of them portrays the essence of the story. For instance, both her novel *Maa* and the short story titled 'Maa' are about motherhood, the yearning for motherhood, and the sacrifices that a mother has to undergo. *Mahanisha* has a blind woman as a central character, a person for whom life is one long, dark night. *Mantrashakti* is about the power of nuptial prayers that can reverberate in a woman's mind and draw her to a husband she has been forced to marry.

All her stories are woman-centric. She wrote about what she knew, and what she knew well enough to write about was the lives of women and consequently children. She was well aware of the social evils of the time, the agents of which were men, and for which women had to suffer the consequences, be it the dowry system, polygamy, the impact of poverty, the deprivations of widowhood, or the legal system that was designed to benefit only men. Although the word 'patriarchy' was not widely prevalent at the time, educated middle-class women were well aware that it was the machinations of men that adversely affected women.

In *Maa*, Anurupa Devi clearly stated that it was the greed of men that compromised women and they could do little about it. In each of her stories, she lashes out at the patriarchal system of the late nineteenth and early twentieth centuries, without once calling it 'patriarchy'. In fact, many of the prominent women writers of the time, like Nirupama Devi, Rokeya Sakhawat Hossain and Shailabala Ghoshjaya, used the pen to portray women's social problems and their lack of agency in a world driven by patriarchy; their stories make for a fascinating read for not only those who enjoy excellent writing but also for many who seek insights into women's issues, women's history (there should be an equivalent in women's studies to subaltern history, that is history seen from the eyes of women), the sociology of women's lives, and literary developments.

Anurupa Devi was not only a writer but also a social activist. In Muzaffarpur, along with her friend Madhurilata, she started a school for girls that they named Chapman Girls School, since they received help from the wife of the then district judge, a Mr Chapman. This was the first of several schools she set up and endowed, one of which I visited as a child in Calcutta (now Kolkata). She was also involved with the Hindu Mahilashram, Arya Vidyalaya and Matrimath of Benares, and the Banipith

Nari Kalyan Ashram and the Hindu Mahila Ashram in Calcutta. Interestingly, she was apparently also involved in the political upheavals of the time. There is an account by Shiboprosad Chattopadhyaya, a writer and early resident of Salt Lake, in which he talks of an agitation during the Civil Disobedience Movement in that area in 1930, where people from villages around the Kestopur Canal gathered to make salt on the banks of Bidyadhari River in defiance of the British monopoly on salt, and a number of the satyagrahis were arrested.* Some well-known Bengali personalities, including Jatindranath Sengupta, his wife Nellie Sengupta and Acharya Prafulla Chandra Ray, visited the area. Chattopadhyaya writes, 'Well-known writer Anurupa Devi came. She started making salt herself.'**

Anurupa Devi received due recognition during her lifetime for her writing. In 1919, Shri Bharat Mahamandal gave her the title of 'Dharmachandrika' in praise of her knowledge of religion. She, who I repeat, had no formal education or degrees, was designated as a member of the panel of paper-setters and examiners for the I.A. (Intermediate in Arts) Bengali literature paper of Calcutta University from 1920 for the next several years. Amazed at her scholarship in Bengali and Sanskrit as well as subjects like ancient history and Islamic culture, Pandit Jadebshwar Tarkaratna, her contemporary and a doyen of Vedic studies and logic, gave her the title of 'Saraswati'. Other scholars gave her the designations of Bharati, Ratnaprabha, and so on. Calcutta University awarded her the two most prestigious gold medals of the time for writers, the Jagattarini and Bhuvanmohini

---

*'Freedom Cry in Salt Lakes', *The Telegraph*, 14 August, 2015, http://tinyurlccom/5fszkvfe.
**Ibid.

medals in 1935 and 1941, respectively. Between 1931 and 1938, she was extended several invitations to preside over the Prabasi Banga Sahitya Sammelan, the main literary conference for Bengali writers. In 1944, Calcutta University honoured her again by inviting her to deliver the Lila Lectures for that year, and it was the university that published the compiled lectures later. The content of the lectures is so erudite—covering the history of women's literature (the creator as well as the creation) from Rig Vedic times to 'modern' times, that is, till the 1940s (including then upcoming authors like Ashapurna Devi), as well as discussing women writers or women characters from ancient Greece and ancient Rome, to Africa, Europe, America and Japan—that it is quite mind-boggling. It is not surprising that she was given the title of 'Sahitya Bharati' by the Jessore Sahitya Sangha in 1946.

*Maa* is a period piece in the sense that it is a story set around the turn of the nineteenth and twentieth centuries, painting a picture of the lives and customs of people at different levels of society back then, providing a glimpse into what it was like to be a woman around that time. Anurupa Devi used her pen to draw difficult emotions and convoluted personalities with complicated psychological make-ups. Each character, be it man, woman or child, is a distinct individual, reacting to situations in a distinctive manner—and the writer made them all natural. There is nothing in this novel that seems out of place or pretentious. She knew the inner sanctum of a woman's world in an upper middle-class household, called a *bonidi* home, very well, and she was equally familiar with women's psychology. This is apparent from the story and the characters she has drawn. Her descriptions of the decrepit areas of a small town, the splendour of the capital city, as well as life under colonial rule, where the lifestyle of the European master was copied and simultaneously held in contempt by middle-class Bengalis, bring to life an age that we hear about but have not experienced. And what I found fascinating is the flow of her language. Very few writers, even today, have such command over the Bengali language—and what is surprising is that she had no formal education at all and was completely self-taught! It is not surprising, given her own experiences, that she believed that women earn their rights through their own actions, and she was a living proof of that.

I still remember when I saw her last: my father was her younger son, and after my grandfather's death in 1956, she spent much of her time with us in Durgapur, where my father was the first deputy general manager of the Durgapur Steel Plant, which was under construction. She insisted on accompanying him to Calcutta where he was to spend a couple of days at work and was reluctant to take her. After reaching Calcutta, she spent the night with two of her sisters in Ramtanu Bose Lane, and the next morning my mother got a call that she had suffered a cerebral stroke and passed away. She had always wished that her ashes be immersed in the Ganges (something that would not have happened if she had remained in Durgapur) after her death, in the hope that she would acquire *gangaprapti*. This wish of hers was fulfilled. After having lived life on her own terms, she also died on her own terms—being a remarkable and self-taught woman who used her own agency to rise to heights unimaginable for women writers of the time. My attempt at translating one of her novels is not only my tribute to my grandmother but also the desire of an academic to revive interest in women's history during a period when feminism did not exist in India, but when there were conscious women who, through their pen and activism, tried to influence the public and make them conscious of social evils that 'un-empowered' women.

# Chapter I

The lovely Manorama was busy in household work when her mother Durgasundari Mitra returned from the neighbouring Ghosh household and called her: 'Monu! Come and listen to this—your father-in-law passed away.'

Manorama hurriedly descended the stairs and asked, 'Really, Maa? Have they sent a letter?'

Her mother sniffed, 'Keep your dreams to yourself! Have they ever written? Nitai returned home this morning and informed his mother, and she told me.'

Manorama was as sweet-natured as she was beautiful. She remained silent while memories flooded her mind and then asked, 'When did this happen? Did Nitai-da say what ailed him?'

'He died three days back. He was unwell for some time, but Nitai does not know what happened at the end.'

Mother and daughter both reminisced quietly for a while. Perhaps they were reliving the unpleasant past. Durgasundari finally broke the silence: 'Our relationship is not superficial. He was your own father-in-law, your son's grandfather! They may not have done their duty by you, but we should not shirk ours. It is too late to bathe Ajit now; just sprinkle some water from the holy Ganges on his head, but *you* go and bathe. Remember, no normal meals from now on. Today you will only drink milk and holy water from the Ganges; from tomorrow, you have to burn the *malsha*. Their behaviour is despicable, but you have to follow your dharma. Go, it is already late.'

Manorama was still lost in her thoughts as she began to unwind her hair. She sighed and said, 'I feel sorry for my mother-in-law. After all, my father-in-law was not such a bad person.'

Her mother exploded, 'Really! If he was *good*, why would your condition be what it is today? I thank heaven that God has not created too many men like your father-in-law!'

Red-faced and hurt, Manorama bowed her head and continued contemplating her past... This woman, beautiful as a dew-drenched lotus, soft-natured and pure, was an unfortunate wife abandoned by her husband.

ಙ

## Chapter II

Mrityunjay Basu, popularly called Mrityun Basu, a well-established lawyer of Bhagalpur town in undivided Bengal, had passed on to the next world after a long, successful life. His practice had brought him great wealth—people said that he had saved up a considerable sum of 50 lakh rupees. He had begat two sons: the younger one had died in childhood; the elder son, Aurobindo, who had two wives, had failed to pass the law examination several times and had taken up a well-paying government job in Calcutta. At twenty-eight or twenty-nine, he was well-respected and professionally successful. Some of you might find it unbelievable that an educated young man of our times could marry twice! It is unfortunate that even though Aurobindo was born towards the end of the nineteenth century, when bigamy was disfavoured among the educated Bengali bhadralok class, he was a victim of his fate.

Mrityunjay had died a few days back and the family was in mourning, but being high up in the social order, they had to perform a number of social duties as per the conventions of the time. The patriarch had been a rich man and the post-cremation rituals had to be befittingly grand. Tomorrow would be the fourth day, the propitious traditional day when married daughters paid obeisance to their father and absolved themselves of their debt to the parent. His elder daughter, Saratsashi, a rational person who realized that death was the culmination of life, reluctantly began preparations for the ritual despite her grief. However, nobody could give solace to the younger daughter, Ushabati, who had been her father's favourite.

The patriarch had died at a ripe old age, but he had left his wife behind, a companion of almost a lifetime whose balding pate still carried signs of the *sindoor*, the insignia of a married woman, which she had religiously applied to her sparse hair-parting every day for many decades since the time she got married as a child. She, who had always dressed in wide-bordered saris and worn the auspicious red, white and gold bangles of married Bengali women, now appeared in the unfamiliar stark white garb of a widow with no jewellery. As she lay listlessly in a corner, her heart and mind were equally blank, like a deserted, derelict house. Seeing his mother thus, Aurobindo, who had always viewed his mother as an ageing Goddess Lakshmi, with her sindoor, bangles and red-bordered saris, felt tears stinging his eyes. He said, 'If you lie around like this, Maa, what will *I* do?'

She answered softly, 'What should I do, son? My life is over. Fulfil your duties, take Sarat's help.'

Aurobindo replied, 'Maa, father's gone, but we have to keep up appearances. What have Sarat or I ever done around the house? Have we ever borne any responsibility? I am so afraid...'

A mother can never ignore her child's helpless appeal. She forced herself to get up despite her broken spirit and take over the reins of her household. But where was that mental strength, that willpower, that desire to do things just right? All that seemed to have evaporated with the death of her husband, never to return. Now, life had to be lived because she was still alive; work had to be done because it would otherwise remain incomplete.

Meanwhile, utensils that would be required at the *shraddha* ceremony—earthen pots, plates, cups, bamboo trays, etc.— had arrived by boat from Calcutta. Putting these away in the storeroom, Saratsashi, perhaps expressing her own inner wish, replied to a question from a relative, 'Of course, the first wife will *have* to come. This is such an important ceremony!'

The relative nodded, 'That is exactly what we were all saying—she *is*, after all, the elder wife, the mother of Aurobindo's only son—if she does not come, what will society say?'

Ushabati was quietly mourning in a corner. Hearing this exchange, she flared up, 'Didi! How dare you! Don't you remember Baba forbade the first wife to ever be allowed to re-enter this house? She will *not* come.'

Sarat asked, 'I would like to know what *she* has done that she cannot come here?'

'Baba ordered her not to come.'

'If Baba erred in his anger, should we ignore our own dharma and continue to follow his diktat?'

'Yes! We *have* to! Living in *his* house, partaking of *his* bounty, we *have* to accept his mistakes. If anyone *dares* to disobey him—' she did not complete the sentence.

'What will happen? Why did you stop?'

Usha silenced herself with great difficulty and turned her back on her sister. Whimpering, she said through tears, 'She can *never* come! I had no idea that Baba's words would be ignored so soon after his death.'

Sarat said curtly, 'You exaggerate everything,' and left the room, acknowledging defeat. Usha had been much pampered by her father. There was little that Sarat, who was closer to their mother, could do to go against Usha's whims.

Meanwhile, seeing the disarray around him, Aurobindo asked Sarat irritably, 'Where is your Boudi? I don't see her doing any work!'

Sarat snapped back, 'When have you ever seen her doing any work?'

Aurobindo replied, 'Why don't you call her? Everyone must lend a hand...'

'I don't dare! *You* call her if you have the courage!'

Annoyed with this reply, Aurobindo went looking for his wife, Brajarani, and found her in their bedroom, lying on the bed with unkempt hair splayed on a pillow, reading a novel. Angry at this sight, Aurobindo said in an uncharacteristically rough tone, 'Is this the time to hide your face in a book? Is Sarat expected to do everything alone?'

'Alone? Someone else is expected, right? *She* will help her when she arrives.'

'Who is expected? Remember, this is *your* family—is it proper that you should remain indifferent to everything, Rani?'

'*My* family indeed! Who am *I*, pray? The real householder is *that* woman, the mother of your *son*. When *she* is coming, why bother me?' With this, she began turning the pages of her detective novel as though it deserved more attention than what was happening outside. Aurobindo's face reflected emotions that we can only guess at; despite wanting to, one did not have the courage to look at it—what if Brajarani saw it too?

But his voice reflected his feelings, 'Who has been feeding you these ludicrous ideas?'

Without lifting her eyes from the book, Brajarani replied, 'Are you saying that the person who told me should not have done so?'

'People who go around spreading rumours should be—'

'Don't curse anyone, dear. I am not a simpleton. I live in this house and I hear things.'

'No, *you* are certainly not a simpleton, *I* am. Whatever! Stop thinking rubbish and go help Sarat. Maa is no longer strong enough to take control.'

'Oh, does that mean *she* will come only after all the work is done? If she is coming, she should come *now*, and why should I care?' With this, she threw her book on the bed and said, 'I shall write to my father or elder brother. One of them will come and take me away on the very day that she arrives.'

Added tension! Aurobindo left the room in despair.

ಇಲ

## Chapter III

The rooftop was awash with the smell of night blossoms wafting from potted plants lining the four sides—mallika, juhi, bel and rajnigandha. The newly widowed matriarch lay on a mat mourning her dead husband as the sun went down—long lost memories wedged themselves up from forgotten corners of her mind, filling her eyes with tears. Her grandchildren, Sarat's sons and daughters, had milled around their Didimoni for a while, demanding stories, but had left disappointed. She knew that time was a great healer but was not yet ready to accept her bereavement. Her old maidservant Kadam, companion of a lifetime, came upstairs to massage her legs, refusing to accept dismissal. The roof was dark when Aurobindo came looking for his mother. He sat down beside her and began massaging one of her legs while enquiring after her well being. Replying that she was well, she asked, 'How many more houses are you yet to visit? Remember, no friends, acquaintances or relatives should be left out. People will not come if you don't invite them personally.'

'I have invited our relatives in Bhowanipore, Salkia, Kashipur and a few other places in Calcutta but not those outside the city. There are many more left, Maa.'

'Have you visited Sarat's mother-in-law? Usha's in-laws?'

'Yes. Sarat's mother-in-law was very upset—she said she will visit you sometime.'

'Did Usha's father-in-law say anything?'

'As usual, he used the occasion to censure us. But Manin is a good person—he expressed his condolences and said he will come.'

'Why did Usha's father-in-law criticize us? What did he say?'

'Oh, don't bother…in-laws are always critical. He said that Father gave his daughters only 10,000 rupees in dowry, what else?'

The matriarch had enough experience of in-laws and their comments. She dismissed the maidservant and asked Aurobindo to sit close to her, enquiring whether he had had some water to drink. He answered in the negative, saying that he would join her when she ate.

'What? You have been out all day and must be dying of hunger and thirst! Kadu, go tell Saru and my daughter-in-law—'

'Don't blame them Maa, Sarat wanted me to eat; it was *I* who told her that I will have my meal with you.'

'My dear boy, go and eat, please… I am neither hungry nor thirsty! Please…'

Kissing his fingers, she stroked his head to persuade him, but he remained adamant, 'No Maa, tomorrow is *ekadashi* and you will fast. If you don't eat something now, I too refuse to eat… Kadu, make me a bed here, I will lie down.' Saying this, he put his head down on his mother's lap.

The old maidservant, who had reared him as a child, raised a hue and cry, 'What nonsense is this! All you have eaten today is some rice and raw bananas mashed together in the malsha that you burnt over the fire yourself, and *I* know how much of that you could eat! And you have been out all day without food or water! Oh Maa, if he refuses to eat without you, please join him!'

The mother was touched by her son's blissful torture of love, and caressing his head, she told Kadu to ask Sarat to get some food ready. Sitting down to eat, she poured most of the milk from her glass into Aurobindo's, and transferred over half the fruits on her plate to his dish. This was the dinner-fare of the newly widowed mother and bereaved son; the next day was ekadashi, when widows did *nirjala upabas*, fasting without food or water.

Aurobindo protested, 'You are old Maa, you have to fast tomorrow, please eat properly now.'

'Nothing will happen to me if I fast. Just think of those thousands of child-widows who fast like this their entire life! Poor children, they almost die from hunger... I am old and do not need much food.'

Sarat said, 'Maa, the young can withstand a lot. It is the elderly who need care.'

'No Sarat, I will be fine—what is left of my body in any case that food will improve?' She then changed the subject and asked Aurobindo, 'Aru, have you gone to your mother-in-law's?'

'Of course, I visited Bhowanipore yesterday.'

Sarat asked, 'Did you go to Burdwan, Dada?'

Aurobindo replied, 'Sarat!—Bring Maa some water!'

Sarat said, 'That silver vessel is full of holy water for Maa. Dada, have you visited them in Burdwan?'

Aurobindo tried to change the topic again, 'Have you checked the things that have arrived against the lists? Don't tell me later that some items are missing!'

'Yes, I have. Please answer my question,' Sarat remained adamant.

Aurobindo concentrated on chewing a stick of sugarcane, but seeing his mother's enquiring eyes, he finally said, 'No.'

Sarat asked, 'Is that appropriate? Maa, shouldn't Dada go and invite them personally?'

This thought had been worrying their mother too, but she had been hesitant, perhaps even afraid, to say anything. Now that her daughter had broached the subject, she nodded vehemently and said, 'Of course! He should go! Why don't you bring them back with you, Aru?'

'Who, Maa?'

'My daughter-in-law and grandchild.'

'What are you saying, Mother?'

'I haven't said anything wrong, have I? People are coming from all over—why should only *they* be left out? And don't you know our Hindu customs? All of us should be together for the shraddha.'

Aurobindo didn't want to upset his mother but insisted that it was impossible. She persisted, 'Why not, Baba? You *have* to bring them home! Otherwise she, who is innocent, will forever have her reputation besmirched before society. Besides, the *heir* to this household is also in Burdwan! And he has some important duties in the rituals!'

'Maa, Baba has just left us. *You* want me to rebel against *his* wishes? You did not have the courage to say anything while he was alive—on what grounds are you telling me to do what he forbade, now that he is no longer with us?'

'He acted wrongly on a whim. You are his worthy son—if he committed a mistake, it is your *duty* to correct it! You will only be helping his departed soul find peace. I have felt this all along but never said anything out of fear!'

'Then don't say anything now. What I couldn't do while he was alive—which you, out of fear, never asked me to do—please don't ask me to do today. I have to perform his funeral rites in a few days. If I do what you say, how can I face his soul during the rituals? What if his soul refuses the water that I offer? No, no Maa, I can't do it.'

The vehemence with which this was said could not be refuted. Both mother and daughter fell silent as Aurobindo finished his meal. But Sarat remained adamant; she made silent pleas to her mother, who tried again, 'She is not guilty of any sin but is the victim of someone else's wrongdoing. Can your father's actions be justified? Tell me, where is *your* sense of duty? Will God tolerate the tears of an innocent woman forever? If there is any sin in what I am asking you to do, it will be *my* sin, not yours!'

'No Maa, I cannot do it. Father gave his word to the Bhowanipore in-laws; Sarat had tried her best to persuade Father to bring her elder Boudi back even then. Have you forgotten his reply so soon?'

The mother did not know of Sarat's attempts or her husband's rejoinders. In response to her mother's enquiry, Sarat replied, 'Father continued to say what he had always said—he will *not* give permission, since he will then be reneging on his word to my younger Boudi's family.'

Aurobindo said, 'So Maa, what will you say now?'

'What *can* I say? Do what you think is your dharma. But let me tell you this, *she* is totally innocent. I don't know what sin I committed in which previous life to be born as a woman in this country, this Bharatvarsha...'

She sighed deeply as Aurobindo silently left the room. Sarat said helplessly, 'What can *he* do, Maa? He is more scared of his younger wife than of Father. She comes from the Dutta family—*you* know what *she* is like!'

Her mother sighed deeply, blaming fate, 'Everything is preordained. My son decided to marry Manorama and your father reluctantly agreed, although he was unwilling to accept her from the outset because she was from a poor family! But *she* was very happy here from what I could gauge—then her mother suddenly began to pine for her daughter! Manorama's father was a good person; he tried his best to give whatever was demanded in dowry despite his poverty! Ultimately, your father made this an excuse to pick a fight with him and threw this innocent girl, the goddess of this household, out of our house forever!'

Unlike her mother, Sarat refused to blame fate for the grave wrong done to her gentle, ingenuous sister-in-law. She had always protested against the injustice done to Manorama whom she had befriended. She said heatedly, 'I want to know *which* gentleman worth his salt will accept the kind of verbal abuse Father showered on Boudi's father and his family going back to fourteen generations?! He may be the bride's father, his guilt maybe that he presumed to marry his daughter into a family with more wealth than he ever possessed, but what did his forefathers do to elicit such abuse? Dada is making a mountain out of a molehill—the two protagonists who brought about this disaster, *her* father and *our* father, are both no more.' Making no attempt to hide whom she blamed *now* for not attempting to right a wrong, she shouted after her absent brother, 'You had nothing to do with what happened, so why are *you* afraid?' Her voice woke her child who was sleeping in the next room; hearing him cry, she quickly left the dining room to look after him.

## Chapter IV

Dinanath Mitra's house, in a remote suburban corner of Burdwan, was currently in shambles. However, it was clear from the quality of the structure and facade that the owners had been quite well-off in the bygone past. An unkempt Chandi temple stood in the yard surrounded by large pillars, and a big iron-studded gate spoke of better times. These served no purpose now except as a reminder of a wealthier time long ago.

The owner of the house had passed on some time back. His widow Durgasundari was now the mistress of this destitute household. Apart from the house, she possessed a few acres of rice-producing land and a small kitchen garden containing some fruit trees and vegetable patches. The land produced sufficient paddy at the time we speak of to keep her and the other members of her family—her abandoned daughter and grandson—sufficiently fed and clothed. There were also Rakhu, the peasant who worked the fields, a cow Mungli, and her calf and a pet parrot. This was the household of humans, animals and birds who resided in and around that now-dilapidated house.

This portion of Burdwan was somewhat deserted, with a looming jungle threatening to engulf the neighbourhood. Some well-built houses could be seen in the distance, but *this* particular area had few inhabitants: Chhidam the cobbler, the potter's wife Haari Bou, Aghor Pod the tiller and Aduri the milkmaid lived in mud hutments close to Durgasundari's house. There were three other comparatively better built houses visible in this weed-infested corner of the town. One of these belonged to a family of the same caste as the Mitras, another to the Brahmin

Chatterjees, and the third to a Muslim family descended from royal origins. The story was that they were close relatives of Tipu Sultan of Mysore who had been vanquished and killed by British conquerors; his family had been banished to Bengal from Seringapatam in 1799 and, deeply impoverished, had spread over Calcutta and its neighbouring cities.

But we are talking of present times here. It was the hot season and the cries of cold drink vendors could be heard all over Calcutta. But in Burdwan, the plaintive wail of a solitary thirsty bird spoke of sadness and want. Manorama had just finished her meal of rice and raw bananas semi-boiled in an earthen pot as per the custom of recently bereaved Hindus; after washing the dishes, she came to stand with unwashed hair in the walled yard of her house. Her childhood friend from the Muslim household, Rabeya, entered the yard and asked, 'What are you doing, Manu?'

Nasiruddin, the head of that Muslim family, had two wives; Rabeya, the same age as Manorama, was the elder daughter of his first wife. This beautiful girl had been married into a very wealthy Muslim family at an early age, but her husband had died soon after and she had returned home, a hapless widow. Rabeya was calm as moonlight, gentle as a sapling, bright as a streak of lightning—God had given her a lot but fate had had other plans. Manorama smiled and said, 'I have just finished eating. Why have you not visited me all this while?'

'My younger daughter was unwell; Khuki too had fever. I heard that your father-in-law has passed away?'

'Yes.'

'So now I suppose our angelic fairy will be freed of her curse and will return to heaven?'

Manorama blushed as she replied, 'I don't know.'

This was a topic that the Mitra household had not dared to broach, although it was foremost in everyone's mind. When Rakhu the peasant had laughingly told Manorama's son Ajit, 'My young lord will take up the reins of his kingdom; I will leave the plough behind, go to town with him and be his phaeton-driver,' the innocent child believed him. Filled with youthful simplicity, he had dreamt up scenarios of a wealthy paternal house, and only *he* had spoken of 'going home'. His worldly-wise grandmother had bitten her lips and refrained from commenting; she had grave doubts whether 'going home' was an option. She had heard of the patriarch's death from a third party and not from the family; this had dimmed whatever little hopes she had had. She was almost certain that her son-in-law, who had abandoned Manorama at his father's behest, would continue to follow his father's diktat even after his death. She burnt with hidden anger at this thought and blamed Aurobindo with renewed vigour. The two fathers-in-law had quarrelled; the son-in-law had not been involved, so how could he wilfully insult his legally wedded wife, the mother of his only son? But Durgasundari had a glimpse of hope lighting up her daughter's face and had kept quiet. She had watched her despair-filled features with anguish for the past seven years. Now, viewing a glow of anticipation, she realized that her daughter still hoped to return to her husband. She sighed and thought, *My darling daughter, do not expect so much...*

Manorama's hopes too were tinged with doubt and that is why she had been evasive with Rabeya. The mourning period was about to end, and she had not heard from her in-laws yet. Her neighbour Mrs Ghosh had learnt from someone who worked under Aurobindo at the Bengal Secretariat that the Basu family were planning a huge shraddha ceremony where many gifts and donations would be made to the poor, but what of Manorama and Ajit? She had heard nothing.

This 'someone' was Aurobindo's college friend who had brought him to Burdwan to find a match for another classmate. He had seen Manorama here and become besotted with her beauty. This friend had connived with Aurobindo to partly convince his outraged father to accept his choice, and he had married Manorama. But his father had made it clear that Aurobindo had married against his will, and it was *he* who would decide whether Manorama would be allowed to stay on in the family home. Unable to withstand the mental agony and other pressures from his father, Aurobindo had ultimately succumbed to his will; after having spent a year together, he had been forced to forsake Manorama. He thus kept his word despite the pain of separation and did not meet her subsequently, thus appeasing his father's ire. And what of the innocent victim of this appeasement? Did anyone ever think of *her*? Well, she was just a girl, and that too from a poor family, so what was the point?

Rabeya was intelligent. She understood Manorama's dilemma and harboured doubts about her friend's future. She simply asked, 'Has Aju's father come?'

Embarrassed, Manorama said, 'No, not yet. Maybe he is too busy...'

'Has he written?'

'No, no.'

Rabeya's lotus-like face turned grave with misgiving. She knew that Manorama was too innocent to be suspicious even when faced with hard facts. She was still devoted to her erring husband and had full faith in the world. Mistaking her friend's silence for grief at the impending parting, Manorama said,

'You will miss us a lot, Reba, won't you? I too will miss you. We have never been apart except for that year I spent at my in-laws', right?'

Rabeya smiled brightly and said, 'And the time we went to Ajmer? No, I am not thinking of your departure. Someone once wrote, "True love emerges from separation." Now let us see if our love will emerge as pure gold after passing through the fire of separation—Aju! You are home already?'

A seven-year-old boy, gleaming with sweat, clutching a slate and a few dog-eared books, entered the house with dust-encrusted feet. The child was charming and fair-skinned. He was wearing a wrinkled dhoti, had a bright face and fawn eyes with dark pupils—his face shone with intelligence. Quickly depositing his slate and books, he hugged his mother, 'The school closed early.'

Rabeya said, 'Oh, today is Saturday! Hamid must have returned, too. I must leave, Manu. Aju, don't forget us when your father takes you away—write to Hamid sometimes.'

'Mashima! Has father come?'

'Not yet, but he will, soon.'

Aju, excited, ran to Rabeya, 'When Mashima?'

Manorama, a bit disconcerted, tried to temporize, 'Come, Aju, let me wipe the sweat off your face!'

But he was not to be sidetracked; Aju fixed his exquisite eyes on Rabeya and asked again, 'When is he coming, Mashima?'

Rabeya was taken aback by the deep yearning in the boy's eyes. He had never met his father. His innocent eyes now revealed his passionate desire to see him! She felt a deep foreboding—what if the heartless man did not come? No, he *had* to come! Why should Allah deprive this sinless child of his father's love? No, Allah was kind! He would never accept such human cruelty!

Stroking the sweat-soaked locks of the child, Rabeya said, 'He is sure to come in a day or two. Aju-moni, you will not forget us, will you?'

'No, I will never forget you! Just wait, I will write every day!'

'I am sure you will not find time every day, but you must write once in a while!'

'Certainly! Maa, when are we leaving? Let me tell Didimoni.'

With that, Ajit, emulating a train, let out a whistle and ran out of the courtyard. Manorama, who had allowed herself to dream, came back to earth at the mention of her mother. Her smiling face turned dark with apprehension as she said, 'Ajit, listen to me!'

But Ajit had already reached the first floor and had woken his grandmother from her afternoon slumber.

## Chapter V

Manorama had anticipated that her mother would be furious but was relieved to find her relatively calm. Earlier, when Ajit had repeated stories she had related to him about his father, he had either been rebuffed or faced silent indifference from his grandmother, and Manorama was subjected to an unspoken reprimand that left her blushing with embarrassment. Her mother hated the name of her husband and his family who had abandoned her and Ajit for no fault of theirs. Aware of this, Manorama rarely spoke of the unpleasant past. But it was not as if others did not bring up the topic, so Manorama had to face her mother's rage time and again.

Although Manorama expected today to be no different, Durgasundari only asked her whether she had made *sandesh* for her son when she brought some snacks for him. But he was not interested in eating anything. Instead, he was trying to gather his things together and reach a kite hanging from a nail on the wall. He requested, 'Didimoni, please help me pack. Maa, bring all my clothes into this room.'

Meanwhile, Shyam's paternal aunt, a next-door neighbour, had come visiting. Durgasundari smiled and addressed her, 'Just see, Didi! This is my reward for looking after him for all these years! But what can be expected? He is, after all, from *that* family.'

The neighbour empathized, 'Don't you remember the saying: "Your own child eats your food, and looks after your house;

another's child eats your food and leaves for the forest."'* But no one joined her when she laughed at her own witticism. Meanwhile, Ajit had dragged his belongings from all over the house for his grandmother to pack into trunks or bundles; he then ran off to tell everyone that he would be leaving soon.

His first stop was the cowshed where the peasant Rakhu was cutting hay. Seeing him, the boy shouted, 'Rakhu-da! I am going to Bhagalpur!'

The old man smiled toothlessly, 'Have they written?'

'No, Baba will come himself!'

'Of course, he will! Will you take me, too?'

'Yes! Yes! You will go! I will go! Maa will go! Didimoni—'

The old peasant laughed enthusiastically. 'How can your grandmother go, you crazy boy? It is not our custom for the mother-in-law to visit her son-in-law's house! You and Maa will go, and I, your servant, will put my walking stick on my shoulder and follow you like this,' saying that, he began to parade around hoisting a thick stick on his shoulder, leading to peals of laughter from both.

Ajit said, 'Oh Rakhu-da, you look like a royal sepoy!'

'Really, Dada? My spine is bent—I would make a perfect sepoy if I could stand straight!' And with that, he pulled the child onto his shoulders and began dancing and singing a nonsensical impromptu verse, 'My "Kanu" will reign in Mathura! This ends the Vrindavan *lila*! Dada, jewel, take me with you! I will pluck my tooth, so that fish-bones cannot stick like glue!'

The child was embarrassed, 'Aah! Put me down! What will

---

*'*Ghorer chhele khaay, ghorer paane chaay; porer beta khaay, aar bon paane dhaay.*' This is a Bengali saying implying that no matter how much you care for another's child, he is not yours, and his eyes are always focussed elsewhere.

Baba say if he sees me like this? He will think that I am still a small child! Oh Mungli, why are you shaking your head? Rakhu-da, who will feed Mungli after we leave? Who will milk her or drink the milk?'

Rakhal had not thought of this. The simple man worried what would happen to the cow after they departed. He deliberated, 'But that should not prevent us from going. Another peasant can milk Mungli and feed her and her calves. But who will drink the milk?'

Ajit considered the situation, 'Then what can be done? Didimoni does not drink much milk. Okay, we can give it to Hamid, whose cow is somewhat dry!'

Rakhal did not want to donate the milk, but finding no other solution, he accepted the idea.

Ajit said, 'Mungli-moni! You are only a stupid cow, but I hope you understand. Father will take us home. Rakhu-da, go pack while I tell Hamid, Chhotu and Bishu-da's little daughter that Father will come and take us back, and nobody will see me here again!'

'Tell them that I will be going, too!'

'Certainly!'

And with that, Ajit jumped over the fence and ran away like the Punjab Mail train in full steam. Rakhu stood smiling at the small disappearing figure, happy at the boy's pure joy. He thought, *Now my prince will become the king of Ayodhya. Maa Janaki will complete her exile and return to her kingdom, O Madhusudan, you are the Truth!*

That day, there was no human or animal in that small neighbourhood who remained ignorant of the news that Ajit's father was coming to take them away. Hamid's cow Romjan, their pet bird Punti; the one-and-a-half-year-old granddaughter of the Ghosh family, Souravi; the maidservant of the Chatterjees; the mother of blind Gadai who sold puffed rice door to door; the cobbler Chhidam's daughter-in-law—Ajit visited them all. It was dark when he returned home hungry and tired. His mother, still carrying his snacks, was thinking of sending Rakhal to look for him when she heard his voice. Ajit was in his element; ignoring her, he ran to the flowering champa tree near the doorway where a hidden cuckoo was singing plaintively. He addressed the invisible bird, 'Oh, Koo, Koo, Koo, my father is coming! When we leave, who will you sing to, you black ghost!' Manorama had prepared to upbraid the child, but hearing this, a tremor ran through every sinew of her body. When he called out, 'Maa', all she could do was kiss his tired face.

## Chapter VI

Three days passed. A few neighbours came, curious about the projected departure of the mother and son. On seeing Durgasundari's expression and hearing her despondent answers, they left dejected. Some had even arranged to invite Ajit for farewell meals. One neighbour brought a few koi fish, another some puffed rice; Hamid had plucked four unripe pineapples from his garden, reasoning that if Ajit's father took him away suddenly, he would never taste their favourite fruit if he waited for the pineapples to ripen.

Mrs Ghosh and Mrs Chatterjee arrived together one day and one of them remarked, 'Manorama will be leaving but we can't treat her because of the mourning period! We cannot even put *sindoor* in her hair-parting. She will return to her in-laws' looking like an ascetic! Her mother-in-law should have sent for her before the cremation—then she would not be returning dressed in an unwashed red-bordered sari with unwashed hair... We have seen a lot in our lifetimes, but I have never seen anyone as callous as Manorama's mother-in-law!'

Durgasundari refused to take part in such conversations; she kept her comments to a minimum. Mrs Ghosh and Mrs Chatterjee were disappointed that she would not join them in criticizing the in-laws. Durgasundari, trying not to offend them, broached another favourite topic: 'So Mrs Chatterjee, what did you cook today?'

Now, *this* appealed to them! Mrs Chatterjee touched her diamond-cut gold ear-hoops and pulled her sari over her head quite unnecessarily before replying, 'Oh nothing much! What can one cook in this weather? Just something to stuff in one's mouth! First, I washed some golden lentils and made dal, then I fried some bitter gourd, potatoes and soaked gram into a dry dish; after that, I made a curry of pumpkin stalks, watery gourd, jackfruit seeds and shredded coconut, and added some fried coconut slices. It was delicious! Okay, this was all vegetarian. After that, I cooked some fish: first, some lobsters with potatoes and *potol*, and then I made a hot and spicy large-sized bata fish curry. And you know how my husband cannot eat without a tangy fish dish—so I also cooked some small fish with tamarind and sugar. I also made a chutney of unripe mangoes with molasses. My daughter-in-law is pregnant and is avoiding fish; she eats her rice with mango chutney. Satish doesn't like bony fish, so I cooked two pieces of *katla* for him. What can I do, I have to cater to everyone's taste buds!'

'The mangoes are ripening, right?'

'Yes, of course! About two hundred mangoes were plucked from our trees yesterday. But our children refuse to have a simple meal of rice, milk and mangoes! No, they are not like ordinary children!'

Then Durgasundari turned to Mrs Ghosh: 'And, Nitai's mother, what did your daughters-in-law cook?'

That started Mrs Ghosh off with her saying 'nothing much'. She then launched into a long list of dishes that had been cooked, ending with 'I have to do everything, otherwise my daughters-in-law will make a mess of even the rice. I am just a poor widow, what can I eat? Just some fried spinach and vegetables, dal, a bit of sweet and sour chutney, a curried gourd or vegetable curry with bitter gourd; that is enough for me!'

After her friends left, Durgasundari pulled out a rough *kush* mat and sat down to meditate with her rosary beads. Manorama too had finished her morning's work when Ajit asked, 'Why is Baba taking so long to come, Maa?'

Manorama quickly put her hand over the boy's mouth, 'Don't say "*ashbe*", use the honorific "*ashben*". When he comes, don't make this mistake!'

Ajit was embarrassed and repeated 'ashben' several times before asking, 'So when will he come?'

'Soon, there is so much work, he has no time... Ajit, what will you talk to him about and how will you address him when he comes?'

He had not considered this; in a rather sad voice, he said, 'I? I will call him Baba.'

Manorama kissed her son, 'Don't be shy, Aju. Go close to him and touch his feet. What will you say if he asks you your name?'

'I will tell him my name.'

'And that is?'

'I will say my name is Sri Ajit Kumar Basu, my father's name is Srijukta Aurobindo Basu mahasay, my grandfather's name is...'

Manorama laughed and said, 'No, not the genealogy, just your own name. What else will you tell him?'

'I will tell him my mother's name is Srimati Manorama Dasi, my grandmother's name is Srimati Didimoni—that's not right—what is Didimoni's name, Maa?'

'Crazy boy! Don't say all that!'

'Then I will say, "Baba, when will you take us with you?"'

Manorama became serious. She said, 'No, Aju, please don't ask him that. If he wants to take us with him, he will. If he is unable to do so, then why should we hurt him needlessly?'

Unhesitatingly, the boy began to recite a Sanskrit verse, '*Pita swarga, Pita dharma, Pita hi paramangtapah—Pitari* *pritimapannay priyante sarvadevata!*[*]

Manorama pulled the child to her breast—her teachings had not been futile. Her son had realized his deity, and that was the biggest victory of her wasted life.

∞

---

[*]Father is my heaven, my dharma—my ultimate penance; if my father is happy, all deities are pleased.

# Chapter VII

As evening fell, Manorama lit an earthen oil lamp at the base of the *tulsi* plant in the yard, and came to sit by her mother who was chanting mantras and counting her beads. It was a stiflingly hot summer evening, too suffocating to stay indoors. Ajit was sitting nearby doing his homework; he asked Manorama to test him on a poem when they heard a male voice at the doorway, 'Kakima, see who I have brought with me!'

Half-visible, their neighbour Mrs Ghosh's elder son, Nitai, was standing at the gate with another man. Who was he? His features were not distinguishable in the semi-darkness, but his height, fair skin and spotless white *dhoti-chadar* made it clear that he was none other than who he announced himself as: 'Ill-fated Aurobindo Basu'.

Durgasundari looked up at Nitai's voice and stared at the bare feet and borderless white dhoti of the newcomer—it was obvious that she recognized him, but nothing in her demeanour suggested that she was aware of Aurobindo's presence. She continued to count her beads, totally ignoring what was happening at her doorway.

On the other hand, Ajit was overtaken by a feeling of dread at the sudden appearance of this strange white-clad tall apparition in the looming darkness. The man was barefooted, had long, unwashed hair, and had not shaved for many days as customary for mourners, but Ajit could not connect the dots. What he saw seemed to him the scary presence of a ghoul. The local amateur theatre had put up a play a few days back, *Naramedh Yagna*, in the backyard of Nitai Ghosh's house in which there was a scene that depicted the weeping phantom spirit of a character called Nohush. Ajit's unexposed mind saw that same spectre in this still, unkempt figure. He became immobile with terror and goosebumps appeared on his arms, although his horrified eyes remained fixed on Aurobindo. He could not understand why Nitai Uncle had brought Nohush's ghost with him to their house!

But the most affected was unfortunate Manorama. Over the years, she had imagined this moment when she would see her husband again, but now that he was standing at their door, a flame seemed to have desiccated the garden of her memories. His arrival was too sudden—she could have laid her head at his bare feet and ended the curse of their separation in a moment of reconciliation. Instead, she continued to stare frozenly at his feet with tear-filled eyes. She could not even stand; she was too paralysed by contrary emotions to even breathe or look up at her husband's face. But the turbulence within her was not visible outside—she remained seated, seemingly calm, while a storm of emotions raged within her.

Aurobindo too was swayed by long suppressed feelings that he had never been able to express. Now, he could not endure the unnatural stillness that seemed to have immobilized the three figures before him. He too found it impossible to look at the wife he had abandoned; but how could he ignore the beautiful face of a young boy with large, starry eyes who was watching him with fearful apprehension? He glanced at the boy fleetingly, like a murderer looks at a person he has just slaughtered, and then looked down at his feet with guilt-ridden eyes. After a moment's awkward silence, he moved forward and touched the ground in front of his mother-in-law's feet with his forehead in a semblance of salutation, and then recited in one breath, 'My father left us on 19th Baisakh. It is my duty to inform you so as to be free of my social obligations.' He did not wait another second after this and walked rapidly out of the main gate. He stood outside for a moment.

The road was empty at this hour. Only the cuckoo in the champa tree, which Ajit had called 'black ghost', plaintively called, 'Koo, Koo, Koo'. Across the road, the field was covered in a shadow of darkness that had spread from branch to branch of the now obscured trees. From somewhere within those trees, a group of jackals let out a loud, cheerful howl. Aurobindo peered in that direction as though some sudden memory had stirred within him. He quickly retraced his steps towards the station without waiting for Nitai.

He had a flashback of another night in the same place eight years back when the jackals had let out a similar cry. But that was such a different night—as he had stood at the gate, a shehnai in the wedding band had played a happy welcoming tune. This broken-down house had then been filled with joyful guests; it had been lit up with wedding lights and there was so much laughter. But today? Darkness! Inside and outside, only darkness! Oh, such darkness!

Nitai, meanwhile, had been stunned into silence by his friend's behaviour. Aurobindo and he had arrived on the same train from Kolkata in separate compartments. It was only in Burdwan when Aurobindo had descended from his first-class compartment and looked towards the third-class compartment for his servant that he had seen Nitai, who immediately volunteered to accompany him. They had stopped at a couple of houses where Aurobindo delivered sweetmeats and invitation cards for the shraddha ceremony. As dusk was approaching, he had turned into a lane leading out of the city and summoned Nitai: 'Let us go!'

Nitai had said, 'Sure! But it is too late for Monu and Ajit to accompany you back tonight.'

Aurobindo had walked on without saying anything. The servant, Kartik, had already been sent back to the station despite the old-timer protesting, 'Let me join you and we will bring young Khoka-babu, your son, back with us!' But his freshly deceased master's son, his new boss, had shaken his head in a familiar manner reminiscent of his father's, meaning there could be no further argument.

Nitai had said, 'This means that you won't take them today. If you wish, I will bring them to your house tomorrow. Why don't you leave your servant behind to help me?' Aurobindo had replied curtly, 'Let me see.'

Nitai was a simple country boy. He had not understood the intent of those words. Had Aurobindo's actions so far not amounted to procrastination, tantamount to insulting that helpless family? Generally a charitable person, Nitai felt that Aurobindo's behaviour was becoming intolerable. That an outsider, filled with the pride of wealth and position, should assault the dignity of these powerless women was unacceptable. Nitai felt that he could not be party to such abuse. He knew very well that Manorama's family had never really thought of Aurobindo, who was so much above their station in life economically, as a prospective groom. They had only asked Nitai, who studied in a college in Calcutta, to look out for a suitable match for their daughter. With Manorama's extraordinary beauty in mind, it was *Nitai* who had thought of his fellow student and friend, Aurobindo, as an appropriate husband for her; it was *he* who had lured him to the Mitra house on the pretext of viewing a prospective bride for another friend. Aurobindo had seen the exquisite Manorama and become besotted; he had made a silent offering of his heart to the young girl, whose silver anklets tinkled melodiously on her henna-decorated lotus-like feet. God alone knew what kind of moment that was—it began so well but ended so disastrously. Although both families were initially unwilling for different reasons, Nitai had acted as a go-between and the marriage had been settled. Nitai had been thrilled to the core of his heart, but as events unfolded and Manorama the guiltless, guileless bride had been returned home after a year, he was unable to show his face to Durgasundari. When Manorama's father died, he had stood at the doorway, hiding his face with a corner of his dhoti. And today? He had accompanied Aurobindo with great hope that Manorama and her son would finally occupy their rightful place in Aurobindo's house! But now, as he watched Aurobindo walk away, his disappointment knew no bounds.

He was about to follow the malefactor angrily, when he happened to glance at the two women who had been subjected to grave insult all over again. He was astounded to see that Durgasundari had not moved an inch and was still counting her beads with the same peaceful look she had had earlier. Nitai did not have the courage to look at Manorama—he only saw her trembling fingers indicating something to the boy who continued to sit in the same place with a bewildered, frightened look. Taking all this in, Nitai felt infuriated and hurried out of the house in pursuit of Aurobindo. He knew that his friend had not rejected his wife—it was his father who was responsible; but *he* had no business insulting these helpless women and would have to answer to him!

He had just crossed the next house when he heard the soft jingle of a bunch of keys in the darkness behind him. He was about to stand aside to let the person pass, when he heard a voice from the Mitra doorway, 'Nitai-da!'

'Who? Monu?'

'Yes, where are you? Please don't leave our house just now, Dada.'

Nitai said with growing wonder, 'Why not, Didi?'

'Because—you will not be able to restrain yourself.'

Nitai angrily retorted, 'There is no reason why *I* should remain silent.'

Manorama replied calmly, 'That is why I am telling you not to leave.'

Her voice remained composed, without any shadow of the blows she had suffered seeming evident. Nitai, buffeted by opposing emotions, tried to penetrate the darkness with his eyes to gauge her feelings, but all he saw was a hazy tranquil figure standing in the deep, murky dusk. In a dull voice, he said, 'Then, do we have to bear this affront silently? Hasn't he lost all respectability?'

Manorama replied in a small voice, 'You have borne a lot of abuses for my sake, Dada!'

'Yes, but that was only because I continued to hope. I will not allow that rascal to return home after this. He will either take you back with him with due respect, or I will—'

'Nitai-da!'

Nitai, furious, had every intention of pursuing 'that rascal', but hearing the pain in her voice, he became still. The two continued to stand in their own separate places as the night deepened and the buzzing of mosquitoes increased. Finally, Nitai composed himself and said, 'Come Monu, let us go and see Kakima.'

Manorama said, 'Please don't tell Mother what we talked about.'

'Okay.'

When they entered the courtyard, Durgasundari had finished her prayers. She was sitting with her grandson, who was asking her, 'Didimoni, why did Nohush's ghost come to visit us? I was ever so afraid!'

Manorama leaned against the wall and looked away.

# Chapter VIII

Aurobindo reached home past midnight. The town was silent and there was no one in sight except for a few night guards and some drunks returning home from inebriated sprees. Aurobindo's gatekeeper, Chhottu Singh, was reciting Tulsidas's *Ramcharitmanas* while he waited for his master. He greeted Aurobindo with a salaam as he opened the door.

'Everything okay, Chhottu Singh?' Aurobindo enquired.

'Yes, but the elder Maa was unwell earlier.'

'Maa? What happened to her?'

'I heard that she was feeling feverish.'

'Kartik, go and see if she is asleep, but don't wake her up!'

Aurobindo entered his personal sitting room with the help of Chhottu Singh's hurricane lantern. He unbolted a south-facing window that opened onto a garden. A passing breeze wafted the dense nocturnal scent of jasmines and magnolia flowers into the room. Aurobindo felt as though a cool hand had caressed his brow. He wiped the sweat off his face with his *chadar* and turned his troubled eyes towards the deep, dark star-filled sky. Meanwhile, Chhottu Singh had opened all the other doors leading to this room. Kartik returned and said, 'Mother is asleep and well. Your sister is waiting for you to come and have dinner.'

'Go and tell her that I don't want to eat anything. Bring the carpet from the next room and lay it under the window. I am going to sleep here tonight.'

Kartik was amazed. 'Won't the mosquitoes eat you alive?'

'There are hardly any mosquitoes here, just a lovely breeze.'

'This place is full of bugs—is there any shortage of breeze upstairs? Didi-thakrun will be very angry if you don't eat.'

'No. Please lay the carpet here, will you!'

'It is full of dust—it hasn't been aired in ages! Let me get you the silk carpet from upstairs.'

'Stop arguing and do what I say—that carpet will do fine.'

Kartik pulled a long face and brought the dust-filled carpet from the drawing room and said, 'What Kartik says is for your own good. This is the summer season, there may be scorpions here and more—those things should not even be named at night. When Ma-thakrun hears of this, will she not blame Kartik? Is Kartik a new servant that he cannot advise you?'

After making a makeshift bed, Kartik went upstairs again to tell Sarat. He returned sheepishly after a while, 'Di-than jumped on me and said, "Just bring him here. Whether he eats or not is *my* business."'

Aurobindo replied sleepily, 'Go tell her that I am too tired to go upstairs. Don't bother me, I am going to sleep.'

'Di-than doesn't listen to me, what will I do?' Kartik continued to mutter to himself, 'Ever since he returned to the platform, our young master looked exhausted—he walked like a drunken man! How can he endure such backbreaking work? Has he ever done any hard work in his life? Kartik is not today's servant—I have seen it all!'

'Kartik, please switch off the light.'

'Okay, but I will sleep in the courtyard outside. You get up early no matter how late you sleep. Kartik knows this household only too well!'

After Kartik left, Aurobindo lay face down on his stomach, cradling his head in his arms. No one knew whether he slept, but one could hear quick muffled intakes of breath and deep sighs for a while. As dawn approached, long moans and intermittent exhalations were audible as though some unhappy spirit was drifting around the room spreading sorrow and pain. Kartik, sleeping outside, heard the groans and began to quietly chant, 'Ram, Ram, Ram.' The house was old and he was well aware that old houses were haunted. But did the young master believe in ghosts? Thank God, he had put a steel knife under the carpet—iron and steel warded off evil. He was not a new servant like Chhottu Singh who was now snoring on his charpoy. Kartik could not sleep properly that night.

Early in the morning, some extended family members arrived; the women entered the house and immediately there were sounds of wailing. The men collected in the drawing room and subjected Aurobindo to commiseration at his father's death, along with much advice on future courses of action. He was his father's much-beloved only son. He had accepted his father's love and commands with equanimity. Now he was the head of the household and had inherited its problems and responsibilities. His mind was in a maelstrom as he tried to weigh what was just in the eyes of man and God. So far, he had followed his father's diktat without protest and had not allowed himself to judge what was right and wrong. A soldier knows that it is easier to serve under a commander than to *be* the commander; the responsibilities of the commander of the household were no less than those of a battlefield commander.

In the morning, Brajarani came down to supervise breakfast for the children and found a basket of sweetmeats that were the speciality of Burdwan. She was too upset to talk directly to Kartik who was close by. Using a little girl as an intermediary, she said, 'Ask him, what time did they return last night.'

Kartik immediately replied, 'Very late, Bouma—after midnight, close to 1.00 a.m., I think.'

'Ask him, where did these sweets come from?'

An aunt-in-law, who had taken temporary charge of the storeroom, replied, 'Can't you see these are from Burdwan—*khaja, motichoor, sitabhog*. Aurobindo bought them himself.'

Kartik assented, 'Yes, Bouma. Can one get khaja this delicious anywhere except in Burdwan? Mamima, do you remember when Bouma got married, her father had sent a whole wooden plate full of khajas—'

Meanwhile, Aurobindo's sister Saratsashi had entered the room and begun to upbraid Kartik for failing to bring her a couple of bamboo baskets that he had been sent to fetch. Embarrassed, Kartik said, 'I had come here for that but Bouma was asking about these khajas—'

'Well, where are the baskets?' Entering the room, she understood the cause of Brajarani's discontent, and said, 'How are the khaja and sitabhog to blame, Bou? Why are you upset?'

Brajarani stood by grimly while the aunt-in-law replied, 'No, no, nothing has happened. Bouma was just asking where these came from.'

'She doesn't know Burdwan sweets?! How childish!'

In irritation, Brajarani said, 'Who says I don't recognize sweets from Burdwan? I don't come from a poor family! I was just asking who brought them.'

'*You* know very well that Dada brought them—you are quite aware that he went to Burdwan yesterday.'

'How would I know? Does he consult me? And so what if I asked?'

'You make me mad! Why, is it wrong to bring even sweetmeats from Burdwan?' Sarat gave two small baskets to

Kartik and quickly left the room without a glance at anybody.

She did not wait to see Brajarani's eyes flash with anger. Such fights were not new between the two. When Braja had walked into the house years back, Saratsashi had pretended to be suffering from a stomach ache and had not come out of her room; she had not welcomed the new bride along with the other women of the family, with honey and water in which a gold item was dipped, signifying that the relationship between family members and the new bride would always be as sweet and smooth as honey and as unadulterated as gold. She had taken to her bed in tears and howled at anyone who came to call her, 'I am dying of a stomach ache—I don't want to do a thing!'

Many relatives had sympathized with her, thinking that the pain was real. Her mother had come to persuade her, carrying some sago milk and adding that it was inauspicious to fast on a propitious occasion. But Sarat had refused to eat or drink, or leave her bed, saying that she just could not welcome *this* bride. Her mother was frightened thinking what kind of misfortune would *this* bride bring to the house. Wasn't it ominous that her daughter, who was fine till then, had taken to her bed in such pain that she could not drink even a spoonful of water the moment the new bride had crossed the threshold? The elderly aunts nodded wisely and were also fearful.

Sarat lay alone as dusk descended. Someone silently entered the room, but she was too upset to look up or question who it was. If an unfamiliar girlish voice had replied, she would not have been able to bear it! This intolerable pain...! Others could accept this marriage, *she* certainly would not! Then she heard her brother's voice, 'Sarat!'

'Who? Dada?'

She leapt up—the pain of her frustration with the wedding

that she had been unable to prevent or conceal seemed to disappear within a moment. But, as Aurobindo said, 'Why are you hurting yourself? Get up and eat something,' the anguish returned, and she lay down again. She muttered, 'I will die if you make me eat.'

Aurobindo said, 'I know how distressed you are but there is nothing wrong with your stomach.'

Sarat said angrily, 'You think I am just pretending?'

'Yes. What I am saying is that you don't have to look at that "someone's" face for the time being.'

'Have you come to *fight* with me on *her* behalf?'

Aurobindo smiled briefly, 'No.'

This made Sarat even angrier, and she shouted, 'You are *smiling*? Uff! What kind of a person are you, Dada?'

Aurobindo replied in a toneless voice, 'Sarat, have you finally realized what kind of a person I am? Then let me tell you something else—last night, at the wedding reception following the ceremony—'

'You sang?'

'Yes.'

Sarat said quietly, 'Please go.'

'Yes, I am going, but please eat something.'

'Leave right now—'

'I am going, but first get up.'

'You won't listen to me? Then *I* am going! You are my elder brother, I will touch your feet in obeisance, but how can I ever look at your *face* again?' Sarat cried out but hid her tear-stained face in that same 'cruel' elder brother's lap.

This was the introduction to the relationship of the two sisters-in-law. Sarat continued to claim that she was very unwell on the few days that she spent at her father's house following the wedding. Relatives advised the new bride to enter her room and attend to her well-being. Sarat turned her back on her every time she entered her room. Brajarani was not unintelligent. She understood that Sarat did not like her but failed to comprehend what wrong *she* had done to be treated so. One day, she expressed her feelings to her younger sister-in-law, Usha. 'She gets irritated when she sees me, so how can I keep going into her room?'

Usha, who was about the same age as the new bride and had found a new friend in her, asked with surprise, 'Why, does she scold you?'

Picking at her diamond bangles, Brajarani said, 'No, but she is angry with me. She always asks me to leave.'

'Then *don't* go.' With that, she took Brajarani to her playroom, and if anyone came to ask her to go and sit with Sarat, Usha defended her by saying that her sister scolded Brajarani, which is why she would not go.

Brajarani was a bit scared about what the consequences of this could be and said, 'Don't put it that way, sister; they may get angry with me.'

But Usha was adamant and established a kind of right over her sister-in-law's friendship; Brajarani too soon learnt how to create a rift between the two sisters. Aurobindo was upset with what was happening; he told Sarat one day, 'She will never forget your behaviour.'

'What behaviour? Has she been complaining to you?'

'Not really, but she did say...'

Sarat laughed angrily and said, 'Stop! I have no wish to know what goes on between you two. But since you have come to talk to me on her behalf, tell her to keep her distance if she doesn't like my manners.'

Seeing her infuriated face, Aurobindo smiled and said, 'Why are you so needlessly hurt?'

'There is nothing I can do. I happen to be what I am.'

She was about to leave in a fury when her brother asked, 'Is it good to unnecessarily cause such disturbances within the family?'

Sarat cried out, now totally angry, 'If I am causing trouble within your family, why don't you ask me to return to my in-laws'?'

'You are very obstinate. How can you blame *her*? *We* brought her here as a bride.'

'Just tell me, was the other one to blame? Did *she* come to this house of her own volition?'

'But that is not the point—your new Boudi did not get rid of her. *I* married her and brought her home—'

'So, perhaps you did only a *nikah* with the other one!'

'You are turning every word on its head! Why don't you stop talking about *her*? Why don't you try to imagine that she never existed...as though it was just a dream...'

Sarat was livid with hurt and anger. She said, 'You horrible, horrible person! Are you at all *human*?' and stuffed the end of her sari into her mouth to muffle her sobbing.

But all this had happened a long time ago. Now, Saratsashi was the mother of five children and seven to eight years had passed. With time, her anger had dimmed and the enmity against the second wife had lessened. But the early disagreements had left their mark on their relationship and neither viewed the other with much affection. Sarat had never been able to forget Manorama—nobody else nurtured as much desire for her return and re-establishment in the household as her. And she had influenced her mother to think along the same lines.

## Chapter IX

Brajarani's father, elder brother and other family members arrived at the Basu house the day before the shraddha. Braja called her brother into her room. He looked grim when he stepped outside after a while.

This was the shraddha of a wealthy person and all the rituals were on an appropriately large scale. Brajarani's father went around the house viewing arrangements and commenting on this and that; he finally turned to his son-in-law and said, 'Don't misunderstand me, Aurobindo, but your family is part of my extended family and my paternal feelings are involved here, so I *have* to broach this subject, however objectionable it may be—do not misunderstand, I have complete faith in you—'

Aurobindo asked with due humility, 'Please command me?'

'No, no, this is not a command. I am just remembering something from the time of your wedding. Everyone had advised me against this marriage. You must have heard that your mother-in-law had taken to her bed in tears when our daughter Chhutki's wedding was arranged. She had said that it was better to drown her in the Ganges than to marry her to someone who was already married. But she is a stupid woman, and women anyway have no intelligence—I, for one, never pay women any heed. But it is true that everyone held the same opinion except *me*. I told them that since Mrityun Basu had given me his word, he would never go back on it. But you know what they then said: "But what if the son does not keep his father's promise after his death?" It was then that I told them, "Why are you worried? He is the son of Mrityun Basu. There is a saying: A son is like the horse of a sepoy; they maintain the same discipline. Those who are the real sons of their fathers will never allow their father's promises to be broken. Aurobindo had abandoned his first wife at his father's behest—will he shame his father and bring her back after his death?" But then your mother-in-law is a foolish woman. Hearing of Mrityun's death, she has stopped eating or drinking. She is saying that if there is any chance that Chhotku will now become a co-wife, God knows she may one day decide to hang or drown herself. You understand, this is a mother's love speaking! She is her only daughter, much beloved; but you know all that, Baba—'

Aurobindo asked quietly, 'Have you noticed anything that demonstrates that I intend to break my father's promise to you?'

His father-in-law Mokhhodacharan replied agitatedly, 'No, no, you don't have to explain anything to me! But these brainless females—who listens to them anyway? I have already given them my assurance, and now I will go and tell them again that Mr Basu has died, but his word has not died with him. Why are you women so small-minded? Oh Chander, go and see whether the children are in the carriage? I am expecting a client in the evening. Okay then, I will be seeing you soon!'

After that, Aurobindo went to sit with his mother for a while. She enquired whether he had visited 'them'. Getting an affirmative nod, she asked, 'Are they well?'

'Yes.'

'Did you see the little boy?'

'Yes.'

'How big is he now?'

'He has grown.'

'Whom does he resemble? You or my daughter-in-law?'

'I don't know.'

'Didn't they want to come?'
'No.'
'Did he say anything to you? Did you pick him up?'
'No.'
'Oh Aru, why didn't you bring him back with you? I could have at least seen my grandson's face for the first time!' She burst into tears, 'Oh, what a heartless person I bore in my womb! I thought that once you see the boy, you would not be able to contain yourself! But I was wrong to expect anything from a cold-blooded person like *you*!' Aurobindo quietly left the room.

That night, Brajarani was surprised to see her husband, who had been sleeping in his mother's room since Mrityunjay's death, lying on their bed. She asked, 'You are sleeping here tonight?'

He had been staring at the blank wall in front of him, and without turning around, he replied blandly, 'There is too much of a ruckus everywhere.'

Hearing this, Braja felt exasperated; he did not desire her company, he needed a quiet place to brood! However, she decided against any sharp repartee because her father had given her the 'good' news that her 'rival' and her child were not expected to return. She sat down on the bed and said, 'You did not eat anything last night. Did you eat at their house?'

'Yes.'

'Oh, that is why you were so late.'

'Yes.'

'But Kartik did not say anything about having a meal there?'

'He is not crazy like you.'

'I am not crazy.'

'Yes, you are.'

'Maybe. But why do you think I am crazy?'

'Don't you know that I cannot eat or drink at just any

place during the mourning period? You are crazy to think that I will eat anywhere.'

'Their house is not "anywhere"!'

'What is the difference for me between "anywhere" and that house?'

Brajarani understood the concealed irony behind her husband's words and said with equal sarcasm, 'There certainly is! However small that difference—' She did not complete the sentence.

'I did not hear you. What?'

'On what other day have you arrived home at 1.00 a.m. and stayed downstairs crying all night?'

'Crying?' Aurobindo's voice seemed to come from afar.

Brajarani was starting to get infuriated. '*Yes*! Crying! Kartik lay outside your door and spoke about hearing heartbreaking sighs from some demigod—and *who* was that? Don't I know that *she* still reigns in your heart, mind and soul? Do I occupy even a *small* place there?'

Aurobindo did not deny this accusation but quietly asked, 'Have I ever neglected you—have I not cared for you?'

'There is a big difference between love and care!' With that, she came and stood before her husband. The balmy moonlight pouring in through the window lit up her eyes, which were flashing like two freshly burnished steel knives. She burned with envy as she declared, 'If I say that you neglect me, may my tongue fall off! It is true that you have taken care of me and my whims. But I have *never* felt the essence of that "care". You have bought me endless books, perfumes, jewellery, saris... You have never spoken harshly unless I provoked you. But is that *all*? I don't care for your dry *concern*! If you knew that you could never really love me, then why did you marry me? Isn't it a huge deception—loving someone else but setting up house with another woman? Isn't it a *sin*?'

Aurobindo said quietly, 'I never asked you to marry me, Rani. Our respective fathers decided that we should marry. What is the point of crying over what *they* arranged? Now go to sleep, it is quite late.'

Brajarani was not appeased. She continued to stand where she was and said bleakly, 'I know very well that you married me at your father's behest. I also know that you courted her and married her for love, even going against your father's wishes. But what *right* do men have to bring home a wife they know they can never love? What right do you have to hurt me so much?'

'Don't be childish! Nobody has wronged you! Think—if you are constantly jealous, the fault is only *yours*!'

'It is *not* my fault. I know that she is *everything* to you even now! I am a beggar so far as your heart is concerned!'

'Rani, this is too much! Are you people not satisfied even after making *that* poor woman worse than a beggar? And what proof do you have that your constant accusations are correct? Have you ever seen me lacking in humanity towards you?'

'Your words reflect your true feelings—they are filled with so much love and care... I don't blame you. You had loved her, so how can you forget her? Is it possible to love someone else in the same way?'

'Rani, I am dying for want of sleep. Take pity on me on account of my tiredness for tonight...'

'Fine, go to sleep. Why should I hold anyone culpable? I can only blame my own fate!'

Aurobindo began snoring within a few minutes, but Brajarani kept sitting by the window, softly shedding tears and thinking, *Maybe it would have been better if she was here. We could have fought and I could have cursed her. The present situation is impossible to cope with—I have no one to censure, no one to reproach! The way things are, she is being wronged, but then I too am being hurt. Yes, we are being wronged equally, but does that mean I can allow* her *to come here? No! Not while I am alive, no! Oh Maa, why do people marry their daughters to men who already have a wife? Isn't there enough water in the Ganges? Why don't parents drown them instead?*

༃

## Chapter X

Usha was born in Bhagalpur and had been tended to by a Bihari maidservant who lovingly nicknamed her 'Kabutari' or female pigeon; this name had stuck to her and her mother still called her Kabutari sometimes. Brajarani often teased her saying, 'Come, my little pigeon, my Kabutari,' making pigeon-like clucking-gurgling noises. This irritated Usha and she retaliated by calling her sister-in-law by her nickname 'Chhutki'. But, Brajarani pointed out that there was a world of difference between 'Chhutki', roughly meaning 'small one', and 'Kabutari'. Usha had complained to both her parents; her mother had laughed it off but her father, who could not tolerate even the childish pranks of children, declared that Brajarani's mother had taught her bad manners. This had infuriated Brajarani; she brought some paddy from the storeroom and strewed it all over the backyard. Looking at the sky, she pretended to call imaginary pigeons, 'Come, come, ti-ti-ti...coo...coo...'

Usha ran at her in rage and Braja replied with equal vehemence, 'Are you a pigeon? Then come, eat this paddy!' After that incident, the sisters-in-law had maintained temporary peace and the name-calling had been dropped. But today, Braja called her by the same name lovingly and said, 'Sister Kabutari, can there be any iniquity worse for a woman than being made a co-wife?'

With time, the two had grown very close to each other. Turning serious, Usha said, 'Of course! To fight with the co-wife twenty-four hours of the day—isn't that a sin?'

Braja laughed at this, 'My mind is in turmoil because the

two wives are always at loggerheads within me—you may not hear their arguments but I am fed up! I tell you Chhoto, those who, out of sheer greed, marry their daughter to an already married man are the worst enemies of women! Look at you! You do not have to go through this kind of mental torture!'

'You are jealous! If you like him, you can have him!'

'Fine, I am ready to exchange!'

'Go to hell! Fie on you!'

Braja teased, 'So, that is love! There is an English saying: "Out of the frying pan, into the fire." Why, is your elder brother *so* bad that I should desert him for *your* husband?'

'Go on! Die!'

'That would be fun! *I* die, and my co-wife returns and takes over the household!'

'Tell me Boudi, if you really were to die, how would you stop her from returning?'

'Don't speak such ominous words! They say that one can give one's husband to the God of Death but not to a co-wife. I will never share him—I will become a ghost and keep him in check.'

Usha shuddered and stared at the resentment imprinted on Brajarani's face. 'Oh God, are you really *that* jealous?'

Instead of displaying remorse, Braja recited a childhood poem, 'Can he who is content, even in illusion, envisage the sadness of another; how will he know, the poison of pain, if he has not tasted poison himself?'

Usha sighed, 'I don't know.'

Braja now heaved a deeper sigh, 'Of course you know. Just imagine for a moment that your husband is enjoying himself with someone else on your bed...that your husband is making love to her—'

Usha didn't let her finish—she aimed a small fist at her sister-in-law and said, 'Go to hell!'

'Why are you hitting me? Wasn't that a pretty picture?'

Usha admitted that she didn't like the 'picture' at all and asked, 'Tell me something. We cannot stand *one* co-wife, but our ancestors had hundreds of co-wives, how did *they* co-exist? I have heard that among Kulin-Brahmins and Kayasthas, especially Kulin-Brahmins, men married up to 108 wives! In fact, my mother herself had three mothers-in-law!'

'What did *they* have to tolerate? Were the men marrying or conducting business propositions? Did they bring their wives home? In fact, did they actually have households? They would visit each in-law's place twice or thrice a year pretending to favour them but actually collecting gifts from each, and in the process would spend a couple of nights with the wife. They probably hardly knew any of their wives or vice-versa. Who would be jealous under those circumstances?'

'But what about women like my grandmothers? Three of them lived in this house, and nobody was a virgin. I think the women those days were far more tolerant!'

'Is there proof that they never quarrelled? In fact, Bengali novels characterize such women as always hostile to each other.'

Usha had no answer to this. But it was Braja's favourite topic. 'Our epics do not depict even a single woman as being broad-minded about co-wives. Look at Draupadi; she had five husbands, and yet when Arjun married Subhadra, she refused to greet her with the traditional *barandala*. She also fought with Hidimba, Bhim's other wife whom she met only once. Also look at Suniti–Suruchi, Devjani–Sharmistha—there are many instances in our ancient literature.'

'...also in the Puranas. In the Ramayana, the co-wife Kaikeyi was no less... But in the revered Bankim Chandra's novel, *Bishabriksha*—'

'What? Did Surjamukhi favour her co-wife? It was because of her that the lady had to leave the state!'

'But what about Nanda and Sagar?'

'You think Nanda liked her co-wife? She suffered because she was overly dutiful. If you remember, it was through her that the author said, "It is good if the co-wife dies, *but*..." That "but" reflects her intolerance of her co-wife!'

'Okay, accepted. But Sagar-bou? She was almost a child and she herself brought a co-wife for her husband.'

'How many women can be like Sagar? There are many female characters in novels, but there is only one Sagar!'

'So you are like that owlish Nayantara?'

Braja finally laughed, 'Oh go on! Am I that dark or do I have buck-teeth?'

## Chapter XI

Manorama had spent only one year in her husband's home post-marriage. Though a small drop in the ocean of her life, for her, that year was so wonderful that it seemed like an aeon. She would never forget the marvellous memories of that year and it was these that helped her overcome the deep gloom of the present; they lit up the long, unending night of her separation from Aurobindo like a galaxy of twinkling stars that sparkled and saved her from despair. Her mother-in-law had accepted her affectionately; her elder sister-in-law had become a bosom friend; and so far as her husband's love for her...Manorama wondered whether even Goddess Lakshmi, Lord Narayana's wife, was so lucky! Aurobindo had treasured and protected her.

His mother had been shocked at the few gold and silver ornaments her parents had adorned her with; too poor to afford anything better, she had brought only a single silver coin with her. And of course, Aurobindo's father's fury knew no bounds when he realized what little dowry they could offer his highly accomplished, handsome son. Manorama's parents had sent only a small amount of sweetmeats as gifts for the in-laws' family. The many relatives, retinue of servants, and hangers-on of Aurobindo's family were irritated and cursed the bride's family for their poverty. But Aurobindo had been besotted with his wife and did not care about dowry. He had ignored his father's ire and the disapproval and disparagement of relatives and family and sycophants, and pursued the object of his love, his beautiful young wife, trying to get to know her better.

Child marriage was the custom in those days, but Manorama

was not really a child at the time of her wedding. Because of their poverty, her father had been unable to find a suitable match at the 'acceptable' age of nine or ten. Perhaps Manorama was grateful to Aurobindo for enabling her father to fulfil his religious duty of 'gifting' his only daughter in marriage to a deserving man; *kanyadan* was, after all, considered to be the holiest of obligations of a father, the most sanctified of all obligatory *daan*s that a 'good' Hindu male is expected to make during his lifetime.

In her in-laws' house, there was her sister-in-law, Saratsashi, who had befriended her from the very beginning. But Aurobindo's father remained furious. He used the pretext of his son's upcoming law examinations to separate the couple at the approach of summer, and sent his son to stay alone in an outhouse to study. Sarat then came to the rescue of the pining couple; she arranged for Aurobindo to come into her room on some pretext, after which he would use the excuse of a headache to remain there at night. Sarat would then exchange rooms with Manorama, so that she could sleep with her husband. She would either wake them up at dawn or they would get up by themselves and return to their respective rooms. Aurobindo's father's ploy of reducing their passion through separation did not work; instead, it added fuel to the fire. In fact, Aurobindo soon took to visiting the house anytime the desire to see his wife overtook him, be it morning, noon or night. His father, a law advocate with a flourishing practice, left for the High Court in the morning; Usha too left to attend school; the matriarch lay down for her afternoon nap—and in any case, she would not bother about her son's presence within the house; she would remember her own youth and smile indulgently. The newly-weds were at the peak of their happiness when events suddenly took a terrible turn.

At the time of the wedding, Manorama's father Dinanath Mitra had promised Mrityunjay Basu he would send 15 or 16 grams of gold jewellery, a part of the dowry, later. Dinanath had been overjoyed when the wedding was arranged and had spent a lot on Manorama's dowry: the mandatory wedding bed, chairs, table, silverware and, of course, the wedding feast. As a result, he had been unable to pay the goldsmith his full due and a few ornaments demanded by the groom's father had remained undelivered. Dinanath had explained all this to Mrityunjay, who at the time, putting on the act of the wealthy man that he was, had waived it off. However, he had sent his family accountant, Bidhubhusan, to count and compare the ornaments on the bride with the list that he had demanded of Dinanath. It was found that a set of earrings and eight gold butterfly-shaped hairpins were missing. Dinanath explained with embarrassment that these ornaments had not yet been delivered, and promised to send them to Mrityunjay's house with the rest of the dowry on the bridal night. Mrityunjay was busy conversing at the time with his rich friends, one of whom was a famous social reformer whose views against dowry were well known. On overhearing Bidhubhusan's report, he remarked angrily, 'What is this, Basu? I had heard that you were not demanding any dowry?'

Mrityunjay was furious with both Bidhubhusan and Dinanath for letting the cat out of the bag, but controlled himself, 'Yes, of course! Otherwise, do you think that I would bring Aru to get married here?' He looked around him scornfully to show that Dinanath's house was far below his expected standards.

Mrityunjay's friends were all well-placed and wealthy—none of them would have entered this dilapidated house to even wash their feet. They were attending the wedding out of deference to Mrityunjay Basu; they considered the bride's father well below their social class. One of them spoke up, 'You don't have to explain, Mrityunjay. Your son is like the handsome God Kartik without his peacock—prospective fathers would give you 10,000 rupees in cash and cover the bride in gold, diamonds, emeralds and rubies! And here he is getting only 1,000 rupees in dowry! Why, even blind or maimed boys fetch more dowry these days!'

Another gentleman, who had earlier tried to negotiate a wedding for his granddaughter with Aurobindo, but whom Mrityunjay had rejected because he had requested a reduction in the demanded cash dowry from 8,000 rupees to 5,000, now said sarcastically, 'We are poor people and cannot afford much, but even we will be embarrassed to give a dowry of less than 7,000 or 8,000 in cash and jewellery!'

Another so-called gentleman exclaimed disgustedly, 'Can anyone call this a wedding venue! Basu, you have strewn pearls in a pigsty!'

Some guests, however, praised him: 'But you *have* to admit that Basu is humane. *Who* shows so much kindness these days, especially in our Kayastha society? You are an example!'

'The news should be published in all the popular journals, *Bengali*, *Basumati*, *Sanjivani*!'

Mrityunjay intervened, apparently embarrassed, 'No, no, don't do that. I have just done my duty!'

'What you have done is great! Many fathers of prospective grooms force poverty-stricken people to sell their houses and land for a few thousand rupees to provide dowries—the richer they are, the more they demand! Fathers fall into terrible debt to get their daughters married; many such are serving jail terms for indebtedness! Others commit suicide, unable to repay debts! And you! You are so rich, and your handsome son has a Master's degree—you are marrying him willingly to a girl from an indigent household…what is nobler than that?'

The social reformer friend spoke up at this moment, 'But what is this I hear about some paltry jewellery? If a person is rich, it will not hurt to take 40,000 rupees instead of 10,000 in cash from him! But it is immoral to put pressure on this poor household by demanding even a few ornaments!'

Someone said acerbically, 'Why do the poor want to pick fruits from boughs that are too high up for them? Why can't they maintain their own social position?'

The social reformer retorted, 'Which parent would not want his daughter to be happy and to live well? I don't blame a girl's parents for wanting their daughter to lead a comfortable life. If the wealthy desire to make money from their sons' marriages, they should never agree to matches from poor families, otherwise you will be raising the hopes of the unfortunate father and then slowly strangling him by the throat.'

Manorama's father shamefacedly came to tell Mrityunjay that the auspicious moment had arrived, and if he kindly gave the permission… The latter glanced at him with strong dislike and replied mockingly, 'Do you think we have come here for a picnic? Permission is given.' It was evident that he had been forced to consent to this marriage because of his adamant son, who now stood up to receive the wedding garland from his bride.

But the thread that held the garland together was perhaps weak, or maybe it was not threaded at all. Whatever the reason, the strand broke and the garland, ominously, fell to the ground. Mrityunjay was livid. However, he had no option but to bring the new bride home. Throughout the journey, he continued to assert that he had been compelled to accept this wedding and had no intention of ever allowing Manorama to return to her father's poverty-stricken house. When the bride's dowry arrived on the second day following the wedding, on the newly-weds' honeymoon night, he distributed the sweetmeats and other gifts among his lowly servants at the doorway itself and sent off the dowry-carriers with offensive words instead of customary tips.

Later, many important people from Burdwan were invited to the Basu household for various feasts, but Dinu Mitra, the bride's father, never got any invitation. And why should he? Had this man given his daughter expensive gold and diamond ornaments? Had he sent a hundred servants bearing the wedding dowry? Mrityunjay's mind was poisoned against him and although he could not have cared less, it made life impossible for Manorama's father. During Durga Puja, he sent some customary gifts, all of which were rudely returned. The clothes that were sent for Aurobindo were given to his servant. Only Manorama received the sari sent by her father. Dinu's neighbours, who had brought the gifts, had expected tips or return gifts, but instead received abusive words. They repeated these to Durgasundari on their return, claiming that Manorama's in-laws were scoundrels and they had felt so insulted that they would never return to that household for any reason. Manorama's father-in-law was an untouchable *chamar* so far as his behaviour was concerned!

Durgasundari was shocked at hearing this and tearfully asked her husband to bring their daughter home: 'They must be constantly humiliating my poor girl. Please bring her home!'

Dinanath did try to bring Manorama home on several occasions but was unsuccessful. He had met Mrityunjay personally before the pujas and given him 150 rupees of the 300 or so still due for the yet undelivered ornaments, and had requested him to send Manorama home on a short visit. But Mrityunjay had not budged from his earlier decision to not allow her to return. He was a tough one! His one joy in life was to collect debts and interests on debts from his clients—and here Dinanath still owed him 150 rupees, not to mention the interest! He had also not sent customary gifts to the entire family on various ceremonies.

Mrityunjay suppressed his anger but refused to allow his daughter-in-law to visit her parental home. He did not allow that 'shameless scoundrel', Manorama's father, to enter his house during Durga Puja. He pretended that he had no say in matters regarding Manorama, 'You know, Dinanath, my son is a grown man now, he chose his own bride; he doesn't want his wife to go back with you. And my wife too says, "This girl is from such a poor, vulgar household that she was never taught the ways of a refined family; she has so much to learn that she has to remain here. We are old; she has to learn everything while we are still alive, otherwise people will laugh at us!" You know, Dinanath, our family is reputed! My son and wife both feel that one may possess beauty, but you cannot judge a girl's upbringing from that. Well, what has happened has happened. Now we have to mould her to our way of life.'

Dinanath scratched his head and said hesitantly, 'You are certainly right, but the girl's mother...she is our only child, you see—'

'You have understood nothing! A wife of the Basu household never travels by train if it is not in a first-class reserved compartment. Can you afford that?'

Dinanath said after a minute of silence, 'Yes, if you say so. When will you send her?'

'Oh! I see you have a lot of money now! Then first repay your debt!' Mrityunjay re-entered the house, leaving Dinanath standing outside, unable to do anything to change the former's decision. The house was teeming with people, but no one paid any attention to the unimpressive, badly dressed, indigent man.

Dinanath waited. As dusk fell, Aurobindo, dressed in fine clothes, smelling of an expensive perfume and chewing on a betel leaf, emerged from the door for an evening of revelry. He stopped, astonished to see his father-in-law squatting at the doorway. Dinanath, at the sight of his son-in-law's handsome face, greeted him happily, 'How are you, son?'

Aurobindo cursorily touched his destitute father-in-law's feet after a furtive glance around him and said, 'Fine.' He looked as though he had committed some kind of transgression and slipped away. Dinanath no longer trusted himself to wait and meet his daughter and thus left for home.

Durgasundari was not told about the details of this meeting; she still kept pestering her husband to bring Manorama home. She had deep misgivings, especially since Aurobindo too did not keep in touch. Did they even give her daughter enough to eat? She had heard stories of mothers-in-law beating daughters-in-law if they so much as talked back. Although they were poor, Manorama had never suffered any abuse before marriage. Maybe her beautiful features were now tarnished with worry, tears and starvation? Maybe, one day news would come that she was grievously ill due to neglect and then... Oh God! Is it for this that they had indebted themselves to get her married to a wealthy person's son? If only they had chosen someone of their own circumstances, the girl would have been spared this humiliation! God forbid! We women are always obsessed with the worst thoughts although we are capable of so much goodwill!

Meanwhile unexpectedly, Aurobindo, though always a good student, failed his law examinations. His mother blamed

Manorama for having brought bad luck. His father was imaginably furious, and his ire was totally directed at his daughter-in-law. Entering the inner sanctum, he addressed his wife, 'Get rid of that rogue Dinu Mitra's wretched daughter! The daughter of that rascal has lowered the prestige of this house! I lost an important case that would have fetched me 50,000 rupees the day she entered this house! And see what has happened today!' The ranting continued for a long time.

Manorama met Aurobindo with Sarat's connivance on the stairs to the roof. She burst into tears on seeing her husband's wan face. Aurobindo was shocked at his own failure, but his wife's tears surprised him. He tried to comfort her, 'Don't cry, Mano. People do fail sometimes. I am sure I will succeed next time.'

But Manorama was inconsolable; she sobbed, 'It is all because of me!'

'Because of *you*?' Aurobindo pretended to be surprised. 'I see, so *you* set that difficult question paper? Or, perhaps you were the examiner who gave me low marks? Or, you sat on my shoulder like a "*dustu* Saraswati" and made me write the wrong answers! What exactly did you do, tell me?'

Manorama smiled through her tears at his loving features. Hiding her face in her hands, she answered shyly, 'Don't laugh at me! Don't you know that I have brought you bad luck? If you hadn't married me—'

'Then some fortunate person would have married you who would not have failed the law exams, right Monu?'

Aurobindo crushed his blushing bride to his breast as she replied, 'You speak such nonsense!'

Lifting his beloved's face, Aurobindo said in an adoring voice, 'Wasn't it *you* who said that good things would have happened if I hadn't married you? You wouldn't have remained unmarried if I hadn't come along, right? Your family would certainly have found a perfect match!'

Manorama pulled out of his embrace and said vehemently, 'Impossible! And *you* call yourself *learned*!'

'Learned!' Aurobindo laughingly retorted. 'Does a learned person fail? Well, Muniya, what is impossible? Don't tell me that there is no other jeweller who would have recognized the gem that you are?'

Besotted with her husband's tender words and caresses, Manorama said many loving things that evening! She made it clear that apart from this 'semi-believer, who had got only a semi-education in Western institutions,' no one in this entire world could have become her husband; their match was made in heaven, preordained, and their relationship had spanned aeons—they had been a couple in every birth! Whether he accepted the idea of rebirth or relationships across births could not be discerned from his adoring face that was now filled with bliss, hearing her words. He was a bit of a sceptic regarding such things, but he had no intention of hurting her and did not dissent.

## Chapter XII

Mrityunjay had a friend from his college days who was an advocate in Punjab, where he had accumulated immense wealth; he had retired recently and returned to his ancestral home in Bhowanipore. He had a daughter who was now beyond the customary marriageable age. He thus penned a letter to Mrityunjay, reminding his friend of a promise made to each other in their youth about getting his daughter, Brajarani, and Aurobindo married. He wrote that preparations had been made and only a date had to be set for the wedding. Mrityunjay sighed deeply and again targeted that 'scoundrel' Dinu Mitra for his ill-fortune. He also cursed his son: 'These shameless modern boys see a pretty face with a dangling nose-ornament and get besotted! I always knew that Mokhhoda Dutta would remind me of our commitment some day, but my son could not wait! He had to bring me this daughter-in-law from the dregs of society—I should say the *lowest* of communities, those who clean cremation grounds! *Now* I will miss out on at least 40,000 rupees!'

Nobody dared to counter the patriarch when he was angry. His wife, in an effort to calm him, said, 'But our daughter-in-law is one in ten thousand! I doubt that anyone can find such a beautiful and accomplished girl these days!'

Her husband flared up, 'Oh! What does beauty and accomplishment count for if her father is a *beggar*? Just look at Mokhhoda Dutta—he is rich and reputable! I would have been proud to say that I am connected to him through my daughter-in-law! You talk *nonsense*!' From that day, his hatred for Manorama increased a hundred-fold, and Aurobindo's life became miserable as he became the target of his father's fury.

Around that time, Durgasundari fell seriously ill; she repeatedly pestered her husband to bring Manorama home. At the end of his tether, Dinu Mitra had somehow managed to arrange for 200 rupees in lieu of the pledged ornaments, along with money for a first-class reserved compartment. He took these to Mrityunjay's house and squatted in a corner of his chamber, not daring to utter a word. He realized that this would possibly be his last attempt; his wife was at death's door, and it was probably the hope of seeing her daughter that was keeping her alive. However much he dreaded the encounter, he *had* to try one more time... He was immobile with fear lest this attempt too failed.

He watched as four or five clients entered Mrityunjay's office. He charged money from all, accepting the larger sums while disdainfully throwing smaller amounts on the floor. He glanced haughtily at some papers, others he returned to clients, ordering them to return after a few days despite their pleading and coaxing. Mrityunjay Basu was a reputed lawyer; clients came back even if he abused them. Dinu Mitra watched in appalled fascination; he was reminded of the hundreds of well-mannered lawyers he had met in his lifetime...

After Mrityunjay had finished talking with his clients, Dinanath quietly placed the bundle of notes at his feet. He said hesitantly, 'I came to give you this money, and if you kindly permit...'

'You could have sent the money through insured post. Why did you come?'

Dinu Mitra replied in a small voice, 'My wife is very unwell, maybe dying. She desires to see her only child just once more.

If you permit a visit of just one week, my wife will die happy.'

Mrityunjay smiled grimly. He said, 'This is a new ploy, Dinanath—I am too old to be fooled. I have been dealing with scammers all my life! You have been sitting watching these rascals flooding me with money to help them dodge misdeeds—they are all cheats. *Your* tricks will not work with me!'

Dinanath's fair skin reddened at the implied insult; he said with suppressed anger, 'I am not a trickster! I have never conned anyone ever!'

'Really? On the contrary, you and your ancestors up to fourteen generations are swindlers and cheats! Didn't you trick my son into visiting your house and trap him into marrying your elderly daughter? Isn't *that* a swindle? And taking a year to pay me the negligible dowry! What a rip-off! And even after I have thrown you out of my house, you use the false pretext of someone's illness to take your daughter home—you *bastard*! You and your forefathers are all charlatans!'

Dinanath now stood up. 'I have committed a grave sin by giving my daughter in marriage to this household, and I have listened to your abuse in atonement. You can call *me* a cheat, a swindler, a conman, whatever you like, because I am poor and it was beyond my means to carpet your courtyard with dowry! But don't you *dare* abuse my forefathers—my father Haranath Mitra, my grandfather Surnath Mitra were gentlemen of great standing. Don't you *dare* call them charlatans!'

'Really? Isn't it surprising that a swindler like you should be born into the family of great men? In that case, perhaps your mother...'

Dinanath could no longer restrain himself, 'Watch your tongue!'

Mrityunjay acted as though he was magnanimous enough

to ignore this. He said with a twisted grin, 'Will you leave now or should I call the doorman?'

Dinanath restrained his anger and said, 'I will leave on my own. I will tell my dying wife that Mano will be doing her last rites here—'

Mrityunjay coldly cut in, 'Do you think that your daughter has any place in *my* house after this insult? Call a carriage or walk back with her. She is no longer my daughter-in-law; from now on, she is *your* daughter only. Oh, Chaturiya...' he shouted, calling the doorman.

Dinanath was stunned! The ground beneath his feet seemed to open into an endless chasm into which his whole life was being vacuumed in, like matter into a black hole! His anger was replaced by dire foreboding as he understood Mrityunjay's plan. He ran and fell at his feet and cried out, 'What crime has my daughter committed? I will *never* bother you again. She will never hear our names again!'

He rushed towards the door. He would have taken any train anywhere, just to leave before Manorama was affected in any way. But Mrityunjay's harsh voice stopped him. In despair, he berated himself, 'Wretched man that I am! Fool! Sinner! Is *this* the outcome of my visit? Why was I carried away by the tears of a stupid dying woman? I have caused momentous harm to an innocent girl!'

His mind was desperately seeking ways of escape, when Mrityunjay addressed him sternly, 'Dinu Mitra! It will be better if you take your daughter with you. *You* have displaced her from the Basu household! If you do not take her, maybe she can meet her needs by getting a job as a maidservant somewhere, or if she has learnt anything from *your* mother, perhaps she can take to the streets! I don't care—*I reject her!*'

Helpless and hopeless, Dinanath flopped down on the floor and somehow whispered, 'Then I will certainly take her with me.'

The young bride, not more than a child herself, had no inkling of what had happened. She was told that her father had come to take her home and was joyous at the thought of returning after a year, but why was everyone so grim? The women in the inner sanctum had no idea what had taken place between her father and father-in-law in the latter's chamber. The servant Chaturiya had hurried in and announced, 'Bouma's mother is grievously ill; her father will take her home by the 11 o'clock train. Babu has ordered her to get ready quickly, but she should not take any ornaments except the ones she brought from her parents' house.'

Sarat was not pleased. She asked her mother why her father had forbidden Manorama to take any jewellery given by them. Her mother too did not understand the implications of that command. She said, 'Someone is grievously ill there; also, Manorama will be travelling alone in the carriage and the jewellery is very expensive. But Bouma, do take a few nice rings, earrings, the pearl bracelet, that neckpiece. Your mother hasn't seen these ornaments—she will be happy. If she dies, she will never see them!'

'If she dies!' Hearing these ominous words, tears coursed down Manorama's cheeks. She said, 'No Maa, Baba has forbidden it. Let my mother improve. I will take them with me next time to show her.'

Her gentle mother-in-law empathized, 'I sincerely hope that your mother gets well soon. Your father has no one else!'

Sarat had slipped in some expensive jewellery along with the cheap ornaments from her parents' dowry, and when Manorama tried to take them out, she said, 'Don't! Your face doesn't look half as pretty without that tiara, and you can't wear those huge gold ear-danglers all the time! Take this diamond earring and a couple of small ones!'

Manorama was tempted, but she took them out and gave them to her mother-in-law saying, 'Not this time, Baba has said "no".'

Sarat made a face, but her mother-in-law was touched, 'Has anyone ever seen such a good-hearted, obedient girl?'

Manorama drew her sister-in-law aside and said, 'I will write a quick letter. Will you send it to him?'

Sarat nodded sadly, 'Of course.'

'You will write to me every day?'

'Yes.'

'But I will not be able to write to you every day!'

'I understand!'

'Maa is unwell; I will have to care and cook for her. Oh no, are you angry? Okay, I will write every day—somehow!' she embraced Sarat and said again, 'Don't behave like this when I am leaving! My sweet Didi! I don't know when we will meet again!'

She had learnt the phrase 'my sweet Didi' from her husband, who often addressed his sister this way although she was younger than him. Now, Sarat too began to cry.

## Chapter XIII

Aurobindo lived in a third floor room at Eden Hindu Hostel when he had been a student at Calcutta's prestigious Presidency College. He continued to retain the same room when he later enrolled as a law student in Ripon College; that is where he was at the time that we speak of. Apart from embarrassment at having failed, he also realized that his father blamed his wife for the failure and *she* had to bear the brunt of his ire.

He was determined to do well next time and had moved into the hostel to avoid distraction. But despite the effort, he could not concentrate on his books as he lay on his uncomfortable hostel bed; visions of a nose ring on a perfect straight nose, a pair of shapely eyebrows with a small black dot right at the centre enhancing the beauty of her enchanting eyes, and rose-pink lips that curled like lotus petals into an endearing smile floated through his mind like puffs of harmless pretty clouds across a September sky. Could his dry law books compete with such pleasant thoughts? His neighbours could sometimes hear him pause muttering as he tried to memorize cases, and peeping in, they would see him lying with a heavy volume before him, staring unblinkingly at a large framed photograph of a beautiful young girl on his cabinet. They also observed that this brilliant boy, a first-class BA Honours in Sanskrit and a first class first in MA, spent a lot of time re-reading a letter written on a perfumed light-blue note-paper. It did not matter that it was smudged, full of spelling errors, and that the letters crazily wavered across the paper—to him, it was no less than Kalidasa's Sanskrit mega-poem, *Meghdoot*. Maybe it reminded him of images from *Meghdoot*: the surprised eyes of a fawn as the chariot flew by, hidden by feathery clouds; a beautiful dew-sprinkled lotus; the heavy dark clouds of the first day of the rainy season; the moon seen through a veil of clouds. Each image reminded him of Manorama, her shy sparkling eyes, her soft dewy skin, and her beautiful long dark hair. The pain of separation was intense; he was sure that she missed him and cried secretly—the thought of two lines of kohl streaking down her cheeks troubled him no end.

But his room was not an isolated hill where a person was all alone surrounded only by wild nature, like in *Meghdoot*; this was the Hindu Hostel in populous Calcutta, full of noisy students, and he himself had to memorize tomes of cases and finish reading a large number of books before the examinations. This left him little occasion to indulge in reminiscences of his wife's fawn-like eyes and dew-sprinkled lotus-lips. He cursed himself for having failed—had he succeeded, this separation could have been avoided. But the way he had indulged himself with her prior to the previous examinations, it was bound to happen! He told himself that this was atonement for his sin of not paying attention to his studies over the past year. He promised himself that there would be no repetition! Meanwhile, there was always the post. It was cheap and all that was needed was some paper, a pen and a few coins. This was such an advancement from *Meghdoot*'s time, when the poet wrote of the pain of separation and messages being thrown to the clouds to be carried to the beloved!

One morning, he was surprised to receive a slightly crumpled envelope addressed to him in Manorama's hand, after having heard from her only the evening before. He reckoned that she had perhaps posted two letters at the same time and one had remained undelivered. He felt happy—*what a sweet girl my* maina *bird is, look how she has surprised me by writing two letters*! But looking closely at the envelope, he found that it bore the Burdwan post office's stamp. He was not worried; in fact, he felt happy because Burdwan was near Calcutta and he could make a day trip any time. Tomorrow being Sunday, he could go and return by an early train on Monday morning to attend his classes. He decided to do so and opened the envelope:

Dearest!

I have reached here today. Calcutta is not too distant—will you please come? My mother is seriously unwell—I am scared. How are you? I am fine.
Please let me know when you can come.

Yours
Manu

For once, Aurobindo was not upset at the brevity of the letter; he placed the letter on his desk and went to take his bath. After breakfast, he filled a bag with some clothes, a pair of extra shoes, soap, aftershave lotion, etc., and then went out to buy gifts. He returned to his room around three in the afternoon, carrying packets, books and whatnot. There was a loop train at 3.40 p.m. for Bhagalpur; his plan was to take that and get off at Burdwan. He was in high spirits; he skipped lunch, and taking two stairs at a time, he quickly reached his room on the third floor. But his friends followed him, seeing him with so many packages—obstacles always follow when one wants to do something good! Aurobindo coaxed them, 'I have no time today! I will return tomorrow or the day after and answer all your questions! Okay?'

'Oh! Are you sure?' They laughed and said, 'Look at him—he is jumping with joy! So where are you going? Your wife is still a prisoner of your father—have you found someone new? At least tell us where she lives!'

He retorted laughingly in kind and managed to escape. After quickly changing into fresh clothes, he dropped all his purchases into his small bag and was ready to leave. Just then, the hostel boy, Suryaprasad Tiwari, was seen delivering letters to the hostel inmates. Aurobindo had already received Manorama's note in the morning and a letter from his father a day earlier, and thus was not expecting any further mail. He was trying to squeeze past Suryaprasad when the latter pulled out two envelopes and thrust them at him saying, 'Two for you, Sir!'

Aurobindo was surprised, '*Two* letters!'

Suryaprasad smiled, 'There must be some good news! Two letters yesterday and then again two today! I deserve tips!'

Seeing his father's handwriting on one envelope, Aurobindo said, 'I am sure it must be good news, but I have no time now; I will make you happy later.'

Suryaprasad laughed and left to distribute the rest of the mail. Aurobindo opened the first envelope and read:

Bhagalpur,
Friday

Blessings!

Aurobindo. I have broken all relations with your wife. If you consider yourself to be my son, you will follow my command and sever all relations with her. If you do not obey my order, I will reject you even though you are my only son.

Yours
Sri Mrityunjay Basu

Both letters fell from Aurobindo's senseless hand. Despite the afternoon sun, his eyes saw only darkness. All around him, the atmosphere was filled with the careless joy of youth exulting in their everyday happy lives. But Aurobindo was not aware of his surroundings; he could not hear their clatter, their laughter—nothing was audible as his mind struggled to understand the implication of what he had just read. His father's letter, he felt, had brought him news of his own death.

## Chapter XIV

It is often observed that what occurs in life is just the opposite of what is desired. For instance, when rain is needed for crops to ripen, there is drought, and just when a spell of dryness is required for harvesting, unwanted rains flood the land. Something like this happened to Durgasundari. Many Bengali women, struggling with uncertainties, burdened with unwanted responsibilities, are not too enamoured of a long life. Mano's mother's desire to live diminished further as a result of what had just happened; it was like digging up a poisonous snake while looking for snails! That Manorama's father-in-law would *reject* her permanently was beyond her wildest imagination—she wished for death! She thought that if she died, Manorama's in-laws would sympathize and recall her. But where was death when she so deeply desired it.

One day the *kaviraj* checked her pulse and declared that she was improving. Manorama smiled after days of fretting, but Durgasundari refused to accept the doctor's verdict. However, there was no denying that she had been brought back from death's door. The kaviraj, nodding vigorously, extolled the marvels of traditional medicine, how various men and women had recovered from grievous illnesses; why, one patient was now 67 years old but looked 50, and felt healthy enough to marry again! The more he tried to lift Durgasundari's spirits with such stories, the more depressed she became. As she realized that she was improving, she was filled with self-disgust. She continued to harbour hopes of death and felt relief at any sign of weakness. At the least indication of sweat, she would tell her husband,

'Look, Manu has to do her four-day rituals after my death—please take her back to her in-laws after that!'

Dinanath had been too distressed to reveal the details of his encounter with Mrityunjay to either his wife or daughter. But the truth always comes out. Manorama had begun to develop certain doubts as she had received no mail from her husband; he had sometimes written two letters a day from Calcutta, replete with expressions of love and longing, but now he had not sent even a single line! She had also received no mail from anyone at her in-laws' house, not even Sarat! Despite her mother's illness, she had initially looked forward every evening to the mailman, but it was fruitless. She would leave the sickroom in the evenings, bathe and comb her hair, put on a fresh sari, all in the hope that her husband may suddenly appear. Knowing that he would be uncomfortable in their badly maintained house, she took the utmost care to keep up appearances by sweeping the yard, stitching up holes in the mosquito net, dusting the rooms, filling fresh drinking water in a new earthen jar to keep it cool, folding betel leaves dipped in *attar*... Nobody knew of these efforts, but He who sees all must have sighed in compassion. Forever hopeful, women water the plant of desire with care, not aware that the roots may have dried up forever. Is God so cruel that He, who is all-discerning, can smile at the expectations of those who are ignorant of the future? Perhaps not, but He certainly remains unperturbed. What *else* can He do? Can He overrule fate? Can He go against the very law that He has Himself proclaimed, overturn that which He has Himself preordained?

## Chapter XV

As the days went by, Manorama's anxiety slowly gave way to despair. Deep lines of worry appeared on her young brow, dark shadows underlined her eyes, ageing her far beyond her teens. Surely 'something' must have happened, but *what*? Her parents-in-law must be fine, otherwise they would certainly have sent word. *Then, had 'something' happened to* him? *No, that could not be—he would definitely have written. Then, then—Oh God! No! Has any harm befallen him? Why doesn't lightning strike my head! But then, maybe he was too busy studying? But a couple of lines? Let him not come, but a short letter to his 'Monu'?*

Meanwhile, Durgasundari began to recover. It took her three months to get out of bed and eat some rice. She urged her husband on that same day to prepare for Manorama's return to her in-laws. But their neighbours, the Banerjee and Ghosh matriarchs, berated her: 'What kind of a woman are you, Manu's mother? This is a *jora maash*, a "sick" and inauspicious month, and therefore this is not an auspicious time; there are bad omens, haven't you noticed? We have been suspicious for a long time but Manu just smiles—'

'In that case, she cannot go next month either, Didi—she is the *jestho* wife, and she should not travel during the *Joshti* month—'

The Ghosh matriarch recalled more such popular superstitions, 'And *Ashar* will be the eighth month. *Athhe kathe chorena*. So, it seems like she will have to go during *Sravan*—it will be time for her *saadh* by then.'

The other neighbour interjected, 'Why, the saadh can be

held here—she can give birth here too, and return with a child in her arms! Teach your stingy, miserly father-in-law a lesson, Manorama!'

Dinanath was overjoyed to hear the news of Manorama's pregnancy—her father-in-law would surely not reject Manorama now that she was with child! He quickly penned a letter to him, but the envelope was returned unopened. He remained determined and said, 'So what if it is an inauspicious month; let me take her back to her in-laws.'

Her mother did not agree, 'Don't even think about it! This is an ill-omened month; suppose something bad happens? Then there will be no end to our regrets.'

That year, *Jamai Sashti* fell early in the summer month of Joshti. Dinanath sent a registered letter to Aurobindo inviting him for the ritual feast and reminding the family of the saadh that should be celebrated in the seventh month of pregnancy. Both parents felt that this time the letter (and news) would be received; however appalling their behaviour, they could not possibly turn a blind eye to the coming child after hearing of Manorama's pregnancy! Even if they did not reply, Manorama's parents had done their duty—they had informed their son-in-law who, hopefully, possessed a conscience!

But the registered letter was also returned with a single word, 'Refused'.

The family pundit was consulted and he declared the third of Sravan to be an auspicious day. Dinanath decided to travel with his daughter to Bhagalpur. But Manorama developed high fever the previous night. She was diagnosed with pneumonia and remained in bed for over 15 days. The best kaviraj was consulted; he said that Manorama would recover but did not hold out much hope for the unborn child. He advised complete rest and no travel for the child to survive. Dinanath despondently accepted his fate: 'That means she will go only after the child is born.'

His wife retorted, 'What do I care whether *they* are angry or happy! My daughter is my first priority! What if she dies?'

Dinanath had sent letters to Mrityunjay and Aurobindo separately informing them of his daughter's illness but, needless to say, these too were returned unopened.

Manorama gave birth in mid-September. All her sorrows were washed away as soon as she saw the beautiful face of her newborn son. Mental states often regulate the body's responses; her doubts and unhappiness had decimated her desire to live. But now the yearning to care for this puny, helpless life infused her with a fresh longing to survive, and she began to revive. She stared at the child's face as though it contained the wealth of the world! When others were not looking, she would plant an affectionate kiss on his cheek. A weak loving smile played on her bloodless lips as she watched the baby curling his lips in sleep or twisting his body, with tiny fists clutching at the air as he woke up.

Knowing that it would be useless to send a letter to inform Manorama's in-laws about the birth of her son, Dinanath had sent the village barber, Behari, with the news. When he returned, he spat out curses against the Basu family. They were certainly not Kayasthas, he said; they were like Chamars by caste, *Kasai*s in business, and *Dom*s in behaviour—in fact, *Muchi*s were better spoken than they! What would they do with a girl as perfect as Manorama? She had been rejected because she would never be able to indulge in butchery like the Basus!

Dinanath had no wish to hear the details of what Mrityunjay had told Behari, but the latter ranted on. Among other things, Mrityunjay had said that neither he nor his family would accept the newborn child. He had ordered his son to stay separately from his wife when the child had supposedly been conceived, and nobody in the Basu household had the guts to defy him! Moreover, the news of pregnancy should have reached them within a week of Manorama becoming aware that she was with child. Since that had not happened, he assumed that both the child and his mother were *impure*! The child was certainly not *his* grandson, and he rejected them both!

During the sixth day of Durga Puja, Manorama somehow gathered the courage to ask her mother, 'Maa, isn't it time to return to my in-laws?'

Her parents had been discussing this over the past few days. Her father favoured her return; her mother opposed him. She said, 'After all that has been said, how can you even *think* of taking her back? Especially since our son-in-law too seems to be on his father's side? Will they even accept the child? Don't you see, Manu is alive because of the baby?' This made sense to Dinanath; he no longer broached the subject.

At her daughter's words, her mother angrily told Manorama, 'How can you go back now? You have not fully recovered from your illness!'

'But if we don't return, what will happen to this child?' Manorama began to cry. Her tears fell on the baby and he too began wailing. Seeing her so distraught, her father went once more to her in-laws' house in Calcutta but to no avail. He was slighted and abused and turned away once more. It finally dawned on him that Mrityunjay had not rejected Manorama because of the small disagreement between him and her father-in-law—he had been seeking an excuse all along and their quarrel had provided him the opportunity. He was now stigmatizing his innocent daughter and adding insult to injury by insinuating that his son was not the father of his grandchild! Dinanath castigated himself: *Oh God! Are these people not part of your creation? Father, mother, son—do none of them possess even the slightest bit of conscience? And Aurobindo? Educated, charming, privileged offspring of an affluent family! Why did you not choose a rich girl who would have suited your so-called status? What momentary desire made you want to play with my daughter—she is our only wealth, the life that runs through my veins, and you only wished to amuse yourself with her! You had fun and discarded her like a rag doll once your craving was satisfied! You have nothing to lose; your millionaire father will find you a new bride from an equally affluent family! Why? Because you are the well-educated, 'moralistic' son of a well-heeled father! But the damage that you have caused—is there anything to undo the harm that you have done to this poor girl? No-no-no! This is the punishment for my sin of greed! Yes, I have been greedy in wishing the best for my daughter! I should not shed tears! I have been told, 'Why don't the poor behave like the pitiable people they are?' Why should we wish for a better life for our children? It is because of me that this disaster has occurred!*

In the month of *Aghran*, Sriman Aurobindo got married to Srimati Brajarani, the daughter of Srijukta Mokhhodacharan Dutta. When Dinu Mitra heard the news via local gossip, he had already taken to his bed with an unidentified illness. It did not take him long to die thereafter. He had asked his daughter to forgive him for his failures before he died. Manorama had burst out crying, 'Baba, how many fathers do as much for their daughters as you have done? It is *my* ill-fate, *my* misfortune!'

Shortly after that, Dinanath closed his eyes forever—perhaps, just perhaps, her words had brought him some peace.

But all this happened a long time back. Let us take a look at what was happening in the present.

## Chapter XVI

The Raja of Burdwan was getting married and the city was abuzz with celebrations. The entire population spoke of nothing else; the groom's attire, the wedding feast, dance performances, these were the topics of discussion from roadside tea stalls to the court's offices. School and college boys too wished to take part in the revelry, and were distracted from their studies.

It was past four o'clock and the last bell had sounded. Schoolboys were returning home in groups, happy because the schools would be closed for a few days in honour of the wedding. Some boys headed towards the royal palace, some towards the station and others walked towards the areas of entertainment like public dances. Some of them were interested in literature, and a few even tried their hands at poetry! These budding poets had a different idea from the other boys. The Raja was an amateur litterateur and had invited some well-known contemporary writers. The train carrying them was due at the station a few minutes past six o'clock. The boys wanted to welcome them at the station with banners. There was a good-looking young boy—a child, actually—who was standing on one side, ruminating on a school book. One of the older classmates called to him, 'Okay, you donkey! That history of England will not fly off like a rocket—put your book aside just for today!'

This boy who had been called a donkey was in no way comparable to any animal! He was the 'first boy', that is, the topper of Class VIII, and had come first in every examination so far. In fact, he had got a double promotion once and was younger than his classmates. He had no other interest apart from his studies. He looked up in surprise and hesitantly said, 'I am going home...'

The other boy now caught him by his collar, 'Nobody goes home on a day like this, rascal! No excuses!'

Another boy held him by the hand and said, 'Oh come on! Don't go home—let's go and see what is happening in the Punjabi area!'

The young boy said mildly, 'Maa will worry if I don't go home. Tomorrow morning perhaps?'

'Oh, we had forgotten that *you* have a mother and we don't! He is a *good* boy,' they teased, 'and we are discarded children! Gopal is an excellent boy; he eats what is given him, wears what is given to him—' And they began to chant a childish nursery rhyme.

Another one taunted, 'Go and drink your mother's milk! See how dry his throat is—oh, you poor boy!'

Just then, another group of boys was passing by. Someone from the present group called out, 'Where are you going?'

'To the station.'

'Why? Who is coming?'

'We hear that the writer-friends of the Raja have been invited.'

'Is Aurobindo-babu coming?'

The young boy, who had so far been trying to evade his classmates, pricked up his ears.

'Which Aurobindo? Aurobindo Ghosh of the Indian Civil Service?'

'No, Aurobindo Basu—haven't you read his English essays and poems in the *Bengalee* and *Amritabazar*? He writes Bengali poetry occasionally, in *Pradip* and similar journals. He is a good friend of the Raja.'

'Oh, *that* Aru Basu? You call him a writer? There is a saying: "A cockroach is a bird; a crocodile is a covering basket!" Similarly, Aru Basu is a poet! I'd be damned if I go!'

'Why brother, Aru Basu is not a bad poet! There is flow in his writing.'

'Birds of a feather flock together! Go carry him on your shoulders! I will not lend my shoulders to such humbugs! Well, if it was Mr Tagore, I would lay down my head before him!'

The young boy from Class VIII jumped up and joined the Class X boys. Eyes bright with curiosity, he approached the boy who had praised the writings of Aurobindo Basu and asked, 'Do you know him?'

The boy did not understand and queried, 'Do I know who?'

The young boy replied hesitantly, 'This Srijukta Aurobindo Basu mahasay?'

'Oh, Aurobindo-babu? No, I have not met him, but I have read some of his works. Why? Do you like his writing?'

He replied haplessly, 'No, do you have his poems?'

'No, I cannot afford monthlies or weeklies—my elder brother buys them.'

The young boy sighed disappointedly. Meanwhile, another acquaintance, seeing him in the company of the literature fans, said, 'What, Aju, since when did you become a litterateur? Oh, look at boys these days—they still spurt milk if you squeeze their cheeks and they think they are writers! My mother used to say: "All those wild boys, decided to become folk singers—broke up their scythes to make cymbals!"'*

---

*'*Joto chhilo nera bune/sabai holo kirtone; kaste bhenge goralo kortaal* (All the shaven-headed weavers and tillers became *kirtaniya*s [folk singers], and broke up their scythes to make cymbals).' The inference is that people who do not have the talent for a job take it up.

Ajit ignored the jibes and joined the group. A train had just chugged to a stop and a number of persons descended from the first- and second-class compartments. They were greeted by royal servants and duly taken to various guest houses. The group of boys raised slogans praising the literary Raja and literature in general and left. Ajit too unwillingly returned with them—what bothered him was which one of the 13 royal guests was Aurobindo? Ajit cursed himself for failing to recognize the coveted person he yearned to see and know, with whom he wished to identify. It was as if a sleeping dragon had awakened within him; the desire to identify his father and make himself known to him was intense—it crushed his small breast, making it almost impossible for him to breathe. He didn't dare ask any of his fellow students. He was considered the teachers' blue-eyed boy, but as happens with 'blue-eyed boys', his fellow students were not too friendly towards him. So he felt inhibited about asking anybody which one was Aurobindo Basu.

Manorama was waiting anxiously at the door. The sun was sinking and shadows were spreading across the field when Ajit returned home. She asked him angrily, 'Why so late, Aju?'

Instead of replying, the boy hugged her. This had never happened before! He had never hidden his face against her if she scolded him; he used to stiffen in fear or humility and stand meekly like a statue until she smiled again. She was even more astonished when she found his cheeks to be wet; she soon realized that he was crying. The mother understood that these were not ordinary tears. He never cried silently unless he was intensely hurt, unless some terrible sorrow overcame him! *What was this sorrow?* She held him tightly and kissed his face.

Later, she noticed that Ajit had become deeply depressed; his dark, tormented eyes reflected a passion well beyond childhood fancies. *What* was worrying him? It was true that the boy had a lot of future sorrow in store, but *that* time had not arrived as yet! *That* day was hopefully far off; she wanted him to enjoy at least a few more years of innocent happiness!

The next day was a school holiday. After lunch, Ajit suddenly pulled at the corner of Manorama's sari in which she tied the household keys. He said, 'Maa, I want your keys for a short while.'

'Why?'

Pulling the knot free, he replied, 'I need them.'

'No, no, don't mess up my things.' Manorama pulled at the key ring with her left hand because she had not yet washed her hands after feeding her child.

On any other day, Ajit would have felt hurt, but today he insisted tearfully, 'I need it, Ma—I promise I will not mess up anything.'

Manorama was bewildered at his distressed look. Aju's face lit up like summer lightning when she gave him the keys; he was gone in a minute.

There was a photograph of Aurobindo in Manorama's trunk; it was a customary photo of a young graduate in graduation robes with a mortar board hat taken years earlier at his graduation ceremony. Aurobindo had presented it to her because he possessed no other good photo of himself. He had promised to get himself photographed again for her, but she had had to leave the house in unexpected circumstances before he could do it. So, she only had this rather out-of-focus photo as a memento for the rest of her life. She had wrapped it in newspapers and put it at the bottom of her trunk, but took it out occasionally to gaze at in secret. Her son too must have viewed this photo at least a thousand times since his childhood. Yesterday, he had been unable to recognize his father and was deeply ashamed. It was true that he had never seen his father in person, but he was well acquainted with this photograph! Why could he not remember his features from this photograph? What happiness there would have been if they had recognized each other at the station! His father would have picked him up surely and kissed him! But who, among the royal guests, was Aurobindo Basu?

He rushed to his mother's room with the keys—all his doubts would be cleared if he looked at that photograph carefully once more. But what was this? The photograph showed a handsome, smiling young man with a narrow moustache...his eyes shone with pride and happiness; there was no one in that group of writers who resembled this man! Everyone there had careworn faces; none looked so fresh, idealistic or youthful! Ajit felt despondent; the photograph had been his last hope, and now there was nothing! On entering the room silently, Manorama found her son sitting like a statue of Buddha. He looked so immersed in himself that she laughed. He tried to hide the photo but she pre-empted him. She now understood the cause of his dejection; maybe someone had said something, or he himself may have had some unhappy thought? Aju must have realized that there was something wrong in their relationship with his father. But when had he learnt to hide his feelings from his mother? These thoughts flitted through her mind and she realized that it was only since last night that she had noticed a change in her son's behaviour. Why had she not instinctively understood? She pulled the child onto her lap and, caressing his face, said, 'Why did you not tell me, Aju?'

Ajit felt relieved that everything was out in the open. Indicating the photograph, he asked, 'How can I recognize my father by looking at this photo? I see no resemblance—'

Manorama was taken aback but smiled and said, 'How do you know there is no resemblance?'

Ajit nodded like a wise man, 'I know! Didn't I go last evening to greet the group of writers? That is why I returned home so late!'

'Where did you go to greet whom?'

'I went to the station to meet the group of litterateurs.'

'What has that to do with this photograph?'

'Huh! How can I identify my father if I don't examine this photograph? Have I seen him? Maa, you don't remember *anything*! He was supposed to take us home when grandfather died, but you said he was overloaded with work and couldn't come? I have *never* seen him, so how could I recognize him at the station last evening?'

Manorama's fingers ceased playing with Ajit's curly black hair; she asked in a quiet voice, 'Aju, who did you not recognize at the station yesterday?'

'Maa! You don't know anything! Hasn't Baba come as a guest at the Raja's wedding? Is he not a writer-friend of the Raja?'

Whether Manorama's ears were able to convey the meaning of the words to her brain is not certain. She continued to sit inert with her hand on her son's head. Ajit was still a child and could not comprehend her stillness. He continued, 'Did you know that Baba writes English essays in papers like *Amritabazar* and *Bengalee*, and his Bengali poems are published in *Bharati* and *Pradip*? Have you read anything, Maa?' Manorama remained silent, so he added, 'How will you read his writings? We don't subscribe to these monthlies! Maa, we have to buy them! I want to read Baba's writings! If I can identify him, I will request him to give me some of his old essays and poems—right, Maa?'

Manorama stirred, 'What?' She had heard only the last

word of what the boy was saying.

'His old writings!'

'Who will give whom?'

'Maa, were you sleeping? If I ask him, will Baba give me his earlier essays and poems?'

'Yes, Ajit.'

Manorama's listlessness ultimately had its effect on Ajit's innocent mind. A sudden doubt flitted across his consciousness and he asked, 'What?'

'Are you sure that he is in Burdwan?'

'Who, Maa? Who?'

Manorama felt that she was at the end of her tether. She said sharply, 'What a stupid boy you are! You just told me that you could not recognize him, and now you have forgotten who!'

'Oh, Baba? Yes, yes, he has come! But I couldn't recognize him. He looks so different in this photograph, perhaps because of this terrible-looking cap!'

Like a small stream flooded with incessant rain, Manorama's immense patience had reached its threshold. In a desperate voice she pleaded, 'Aju, can you show him to me just once? Please take me there!'

'You! How will *you* go there, Maa? It will be full of unknown people—you never appear before strangers!'

But Manorama's craving was like the thirst of a dying person for a few drops of water—it would not be assuaged by anything other than the sight of her husband. She implored, 'Take me there somehow. Aju, think of something! I have not seen him in ages; he *did* come that night but what happened? I was so inept!'

Ajit had never seen his mother so disturbed. Her innermost thoughts had always remained hidden. She had always concealed the agony of rejection deep inside her and put up a brave smiling face to the world. Now the ache in her voice stunned Ajit. He raised his bright eyes to her tortured ones and smiled. Tenderly embracing her, he said with childish assurance, 'Okay Maa, I will certainly bring him and show him to you.'

Manorama returned his gaze with half-believing eyes and said, 'You will? How?'

'I will not tell you now—all I have to do is show him to you, right?'

Manorama, like a child, wanted to believe Ajit. She accepted his words and smothered him with kisses on his cheeks. She became so engrossed in thought that she did not realize when Ajit quietly slipped out of her embrace. Like the ever-thirsty bird, *chatak*, she had craved for one sight of her beloved, but like the legendary thirst of that bird, hers too had not been assuaged. However, now she would see him again! And joy of joys! The one who would bring them together would be Ajit, who had been her life, who had kept her alive during this interminable interval.

## Chapter XVII

Ajit soon realized that fulfilling his promise would not be easy. There was one young man in the writers' group who was quite good-looking, but he could not have been more than twenty-two or twenty-three years of age. Ajit was ten or eleven at the time; he did a quick calculation and to his childish mind, it seemed *possible* that *this* man could be his father. He had heard so many good things about him from his mother that the boy's image of Aurobindo Basu did not fit any of the others. He began to hover around the young bespectacled gentleman trying to catch his attention. Just as Aju was about to give up, the man turned and noticed his lovely fawn-like eyes trying to desperately catch his own eyes. He told his friends, 'Why are you confusing yourselves with your heavy verses? Instead, let us acquaint ourselves with this attractive child. What is your name, boy? I think I have seen you off and on throughout the day—do you live nearby? In which class do you study?'

Sweat lined Ajit's forehead like pearl beads and his heart beat fast as he stepped into the room. He wanted to rush into the man's lap and shout 'Baba!' but the room was full and he felt constrained as he replied to the questions in a trembling voice and finally announced his name: 'Sri Ajit Kumar Basu.'

But what was this? The name made no impact. The gentleman continued puffing on his cigar with semi-closed eyes. He was about to turn away, when the man spoke again, 'You are so small and you are already in Class VIII? How old are you?'

Ajit looked down to conceal his eyes that were filling with frustrated tears, and replied, 'Ten.'

'Only ten years! Very smart! You must be the "first boy" of your class?'

'Yes.'

'Why are you leaving? Come let us chat awhile. Tell me, apart from the royal palace, Shyamsagar and Krishnasagar Lake, is any other place worth visiting?'

Ajit came forward and, leaning on the back of a chair, talked about Burdwan's attractions and many other topics. When he returned home, he still did not know the stranger's name, but assuming him to be his father, his heart was filled with joy! Yet, one thought nagged at him: why had the gentleman not asked who his *father* was? If he had asked, he would certainly have accompanied Ajit home. And what kind of a boy was *Ajit*? Poets were a different breed—too engrossed in creativity to think about home and hearth. Maybe Ajit's name had not struck a chord in his memory. So, why did he himself not volunteer to announce his father's and grandfather's names? He would certainly have made the connection then! The gentleman had called him intelligent—but Ajit had acted so stupidly!

On returning home, he was too ashamed to tell his mother anything. How could he relate that he had spoilt everything through his own stupidity? He shrank like a thief under his mother's enquiring gaze, but he was surprised that his mother did not ask him anything. Her face was akin to a cloud-masked inscrutable sky. Ajit thought that perhaps she was annoyed with him, and vowed to return to the gentleman first thing in the morning and declare that his father was Aurobindo Basu and his grandfather's name was Mrityunjay Basu.

But the next morning, his friend Hamid took him away to fetch a doctor for someone who had taken ill at their house, and then, he was sent to the pharmacy to buy the prescribed medicines. It was noon by the time he returned. So, it was not till early evening that he was able to go to the royal guest house. When he reached the place, he found that luggage was being loaded onto a carriage. Some of the writers had already climbed onto their seats; the lazier ones were still loitering around. Ajit's heart jumped to his mouth—oh, what an idiot he was! What had he done! He was momentarily stunned, but then he rushed towards the carriage and looked desperately inside—where was *he*? Had he left already? Would he never know who Ajit was? He had called him 'intelligent', but did he know that actually he was the greatest ignoramus there was? Ajit had told him nothing about himself.

'You there—you all are worse than women! We will miss the train!'

'Coming, coming!' Two or three guests emerged from the main door, among them the much-sought-after gentleman! Ajit rushed forward, clasped the stranger's hand and said breathlessly: 'I am Ajit Kumar Basu. My father's name is Sri Aurobindo Basu!'

'Really? Aurobindo Basu is your father! Which Aurobindo Basu; he lives here obviously?'

Ajit was taken aback, 'Baba lives in Calcutta. He is a poet.'

'Oh, you are Aru Basu's son? Why didn't you tell me earlier? I know him quite well! When I see him next, I will tell him that I met you…'

'Sujan, stop your childishness, we will miss the train for sure,' said another gentleman from the carriage. The gentleman who had just been called Sujan gave Ajit a friendly pat on the head, smiled and quickly climbed onto the carriage. The coachman whipped the horses and sped off.

Ajit's tiny face looked like the moon during a lunar eclipse—he was bewildered. The person he had thought was his father was someone named Sujan! He stared at the dust left behind by the carriage. Looking at him, many would have thought that the whip had descended on *his* shoulder instead of the horse's back.

ॐ

## Chapter XVIII

After the death of Mrityunjay, his wife had lost all interest in housekeeping. She had been a child bride and losing her near-lifelong companion perhaps overwhelmed her. There may have been another reason. Mothers can bear a lot, but what is insufferable is the sight of a son becoming a slave to his wife. Although Brajarani did not misbehave, she was totally indifferent towards her mother-in-law. She had always been independent but had become more so after the death of her father-in-law. On a sudden whim, she would call for the family carriage and leave for her parents' house without thinking it necessary to inform her mother-in-law; she no longer covered her head with her *pallu* before her mother-in-law's friends and neighbours, and conversed with them on an equal footing; she would talk to the servants without bothering to keep them at an acceptable social distance. These neighbours and servants were taken aback by her 'shamelessness'—she did not appear to care any longer for time-honoured social customs or norms.

Her mother-in-law felt shamed and hurt but said nothing. Instead, she defended Brajarani before her friends: 'What can she do? She read tons of English books and novels at school. She was not taught how to conduct herself in the conventional manner of bonidi families.' In truth, Braja did not have to pay any special attention to her mother-in-law; it was the old maidservant, Kadam, who took care of all her needs, providing *paan*, bringing the water, towel and clothes, massaging her legs—she heeded all the requirements of her mistress of many decades. As was the practice in those days, the wealthy Basus had also given shelter to many poor relatives, especially widowed women; there was no dearth of ladies in the house to cook for the matriarch who, as per the old Hindu custom, would not eat anything except food cooked by Brahmins or Kayasthas. She possessed everything, yet she felt slighted if Brajarani ignored her.

The days somehow went by without any confrontation—the only problem was Sarat. Braja and Saratsashi barely tolerated each other. It was quite usual to see Sarat's carriage entering the driveway from one gate and Braja's carriage leaving from another. If Braja *had* to remain home for any special reason while Sarat was visiting, she would hole up in her room with a book or some embroidery work. If they chanced to bump into each other, arguments and cold words were common.

During the first Durga Puja following the patriarch's death, Braja decided to buy all the clothes that would be gifted to relatives. So far, the matriarch, in consultation with her daughters, had always chosen the saris. The weaver-woman brought a large bundle of saris and dhotis and was proceeding towards the matriarch's room when Brajarani called her, 'Let me see what you have brought, weaver-auntie.'

'Okay Bouma, I will show them to you.' And with that, she unloaded her bundle in Braja's room, realizing that from now she would have to deal with the daughter-in-law and not the mater. It made no difference to her—all she was interested in was selling her products. In fact, she knew that young people were better buyers than fussy, old, widowed women! That day, Aurobindo had entered the room and been astonished, 'You seem to have brought home all the goods from Burrabazar! Tell me, how many years will it take you to finish wearing these saris?'

The new householder fluffed her lips and said, 'Are they for me? Don't we have to gift saris to many people during the pujas?'

'But Maa has been doing that all these years!'

'It was time for her afternoon nap, so I decided to do the buying! Any harm?'

Aurobindo's voice sounded irritated as he replied, 'No, what harm?' And he left the room.

Next day, the weaver-woman came directly to her room saying, 'Where are you, Bouma?' But Brajarani pretended not to have seen her.

Usha, who was with her at the time, said, 'Do you want to look at new saris?'

Brajarani stretched lazily on her bed and muttered, 'I? Why should *I* look at saris? Let her go to Ma's room.'

The weaver-woman was a bit taken aback but proceeded to the mater's room. She returned a few minutes later and announced, 'Boudi-thakrun said that she is no longer interested and sent me back to you.'

Brajarani made a face and said, 'I am sorry I can't select saris!' And she lay down again and picked up a book from a side table.

But Usha would have none of that. She snatched the book from her hand and said, 'You are acting pricey! Does Maa have to do all the work here eternally? She is old, tired... Oh Aunty! Why are you standing there like a clown? Open your bundle!'

A bit of budgeting had to be done in the household following Mrityunjay's death because the in-flow of money had slowed, but the expenditure on clothes that year exceeded earlier years. Not everyone was happy about this. On *sashti,* the first day of the pujas, all but Sarat wore new clothes. If anyone commented, she would wipe her eyes and say, 'Maa is widowed and *she* is not wearing anything new. Have you forgotten that Baba passed away not too many months back? Let those who have become *happier* this year dress up!'

Brajarani heard the comment and bit her lips; she could not tolerate this sister-in-law but was terrified of her sharp tongue that knew no bounds.

Several other festivals followed Durga Puja, an important one being *Bhai Phonta,* where sisters ceremonially wished their brothers a long life. Sarat had always taken the initiative for this festival. This year, too, she arrived with her children on the day before Bhai Phonta. She saw the family caretaker entering the house accompanied by a labourer carrying a big bundle of dhotis meant for Brajarani's brothers and family members. Sarat insisted on seeing the dhotis and bought the ones she liked, including a silk *punjabi* ordered for Braja's seven-year-old younger brother. The *sarkar*, Bidhubhusan, worriedly said, 'Didi, the punjabi has been specially ordered by Bouma—what if I cannot get another one like this?'

Sarat spoke sharply, 'You think that you will not be able to get a silk punjabi in this huge city?'

Bidhubhusan scratched his head and said, 'I am sure I will find something—but an exact match?'

'The Mahabharata will not become impure[*] if you do not find an exact match! Don't worry, Sarkar-da, you will not get hanged! If she says anything, tell her that *I* forced you! During the pujas, she gave many expensive things to her mother, aunts and nieces—during Bhai Phonta, her male relatives can get something less!' With that, she bundled up her purchases and dared him to say anything more. But of course, he did not.

---

[*]*'Mahabharat asudhha hoye jabena'* is a Bengali saying. When someone tries to make lame excuses for not doing what he is being asked to do, this phrase is used to coax him into doing the task. The implication is that no harm will occur if the deed is done.

Everyone in the household was afraid of Sarat's tongue, but equally respectful of her generosity and love.

Although Bidhubhusan did not repeat all this to Brajarani, such things cannot be kept secret in a household. Braja returned the dhotis saying she did not like them and, pretending to be unwell, took to her bed. She took out her anger on Aurobindo, and resumed preparations for the festival the next day, blaming everyone else for things left incomplete. Brajarani's brothers had been invited to a feast at their house, which would be preceded by the ritual of putting *tika*s on the brothers' foreheads and chanting mantras to ward off evil; she was afraid of calamities befalling them if the ceremonies were not conducted properly. So, she got busy making sweetmeats, etc.

The carriage went to fetch Usha in the morning for the ritual that was meant to wish for the long life of a brother and praying for his immortality. Sarat had already put the required sandal paste tikas on Aurobindo's brow and completed her rituals, but Aurobindo was continuing to fast because Usha was late, and she had to complete her part before he could eat anything. When she arrived, Usha began chatting with Braja instead of coming to Aurobindo; the two then went to the storeroom, still talking. Irritated, Aurobindo called her, 'Ushi, you seem to have no time for the rites! Who will you put the tika on if I die of hunger?'

Usha returned with a small silver bowl with sandal paste in it, and replied, 'What can I do? It is so late and Boudi's things are nowhere near ready! Her brothers will be arriving any time! I was helping her remove the moulds from the milk sweets in the storeroom.'

Aurobindo said, 'Why can't she do it herself? Here your *own* brother is starving, but you go off to help arrange gifts for someone 'else's brother!'

After completing the ritual, instead of touching her brother's feet in the customary mark of respect, she touched the floor in front of Aurobindo in annoyance, and while tying his gift of a gold guinea, a traditional blessing in a rich household such as theirs, to the end of her sari, she angrily said, '*We* are not so small-minded! Is there a difference between brothers—this one is mine, that one is yours? All brothers are equal! Maybe it would have been better if I thought that only *my* brother mattered to me, but *I* am not like that!'

Aurobindo laughed sarcastically, 'Is that correct, Ushi? Everyone's brothers are equally important to all sisters? Good, good! You have become all-knowing! May your new-found *Vaikuntha* be indestructible! But poor me! I think I will rot in hell because of my small-mindedness!'

Just then, Saratsashi entered with two big plates of fruits, sweetmeats and savouries, and addressed her brother, 'Dada, it is noon already! Do you have any intention of eating?' Usha too carried a plate filled with all kinds of sweets and savouries, but Aurobindo ignored her and began to eat Sarat's offerings. Usha looked at her elder sister with displeasure and stamped off in annoyance. It was not that she had accepted defeat; Brajarani had expressly told her to return immediately after the ceremony to help arrange delicacies on plates for her own brothers.

## Chapter XIX

*B*rajarani's brothers arrived, and after completing the rituals, she invited them for the special feast, but they felt that they could not begin till their brother-in-law and host, Aurobindo, joined them. He was about to do so when Sarat entered and said, 'Come Dada, lunch is ready.'

He replied, 'I am coming,' and got up.

Sarat then said, 'Not that way! We have arranged lunch in Ma's quarters.'

When Aurobindo reached his mother's veranda, he found that only one place had been laid. He enquired, 'Where are the guests, Sarat?'

'In their sister's room. You sit here—it is quite late!'

Aurobindo hesitated, 'Maybe we should join them—'

'You need not worry about them today. This is *my* special day for *my* brother, it is *our* exclusive day. Why don't you ignore *her* brothers just this once? Now come on—sit down, please!'

He smiled in embarrassment as though being scolded by an elder sister, which Sarat was not, but he sat down for lunch. Brajarani had meanwhile come to her mother-in-law's storeroom looking for a lemon to serve with the food and had heard everything. She was furious and left in a huff.

Once lunch was over, Braja, her two younger brothers and Usha began to play cards in Braja's room. Aurobindo came in looking for something when Sarat too entered with a parcel and called, 'Dada! Where are you?'

'Yes, Sarat, what can I do for you?'

'Please give me your special seal—Sarkar-babu said this seal is not clear and the parcel will not be accepted at the Post Office. If I send it from my house after I return, it will be delayed by another day!'

Meanwhile, the atmosphere in the room cooled considerably with Sarat's entry. Brajarani, who considered it uncivilized to cover her head in the conventional manner even before sarkar or male outsiders or elders, leaving her face brazenly exposed before all, now pulled her sari down to her chin before Sarat, who was just four years older than her. Usha sat up, disgruntled, and even the two young boys who had so far been laughing over the card game looked grave.

Aurobindo said, 'Give it to me, I will do the needful.' But his hand froze when he saw the address written in bold black ink—the words seemed to jump out and strike him like a poisonous snake. But why was he simultaneously fascinated? His heart thudded as he stared at the name in the address: 'Dearest Sriman Ajit Kumar Basu, may he live long...'

Sarat held out the packet in such a manner that the two other women could also see the name. If Brajarani's gaze could burn, Sarat would have turned to ashes. Usha frowned disgustedly and got up to leave. One of the young boys called out, 'Usha-di! Don't leave now! The game is incomplete!'

'I don't want to play! I have a headache!' She stormed out of the room, her anger evident.

Sarat said, 'Dada, can I not expect this bit of courtesy from you? Lend me your carriage then—I will return to Taltala, seal it and send it from my house. It is quite late—my little child won't be able to wear new clothes today!'

The room remained silent even after Sarat's departure. However, it is not expected that two small boys will remain quiet for any length of time; they discarded the card game for a game of dominoes and invited Braja to join them. She had forgotten about the sari pallu, which now covered her entire face, and was sitting still in soundless fury. Appearing to suddenly wake up, she looked cripplingly at her husband and said, 'I am not interested. You two play.'

The two children then asked the mute Aurobindo, 'Then *you* join us, Jamai-babu.'

He appeared lost in his thoughts, 'Join you for what?'

'Will you play dominoes with us?'

'No.'

'Okay, if not dominoes, reverse, draft, *bisti, golam-chor*—anything? Didimoni, please be nice, join us too!'

Aurobindo smiled, 'Not me—I don't know how to play any of these games. Ask your Didimoni, she loves to play games—'

As he was about to leave the room, Brajarani sprang up from the bed and addressed him sharply, 'Why does your sister insult me whenever she likes?'

Aurobindo answered from the doorway, 'She doesn't consult me. If you really wish to know, ask *her*.'

'I am asking *you*—your family promised my parents to have no connection with *that* household, and yet, behind our backs, you and your family continue to have relations with them. You don't need to add insult to injury by flaunting your association with them in front of my brothers' and my eyes! You *have* to answer me—I seek an answer from *you*!'

Aurobindo retorted, 'Why *me*? Why do you blame *me* repeatedly?'

'Can you tell me with a clean conscience that you haven't encouraged her?'

Aurobindo opened the door without replying. But Brajarani was not going to let him go so easily. She again observed heatedly,

'You have *no* answer! I am not the daughter of a farm-labourer—my father has used his brains to earn lakhs of rupees! I am *his* daughter and I am certainly not a *fool*! You think I don't know—clothes were sent as gifts during the pujas, and again today! I say you are complicit! Do you deny this?'

Aurobindo stepped out and said, 'I have no wish to argue with a mad woman like you!'

Brajarani called out, 'Listen, please don't leave! If I am so stuck in your throat that you can't swallow me or spit me out, tell me! I will leave of my own accord right now with my brothers, Hitu and Nitu. I can't stand this everyday insult any longer!' She began to cry in desperation and distress.

Aurobindo re-entered the room and smiled, 'Rani, you are still a child! Didn't you realize what Sarat was like when you arrived here as a bride?'

'Of course, don't I know what she is? I want to retort to everything she says, but she is my sister-in-law! And she is older! If it was anyone other than me—!'

What 'anyone' other than Brajarani would have said or done to Sarat remained unsaid because just then who should return to the room but the person she was berating. Sarat said, 'Dada, Maa is looking for you.' But she had heard the last sentence and her face had reddened like the autumn sun hidden by a dark cloud. She sneered, 'If it was anyone other than you, she would have beaten her elder sister-in-law out of the house with a broom, right? Well, why should you deprive yourself of that pleasure? And Dada, you were listening to your wife's complaints with such indulgence! If you wish, I will never visit your house again! I have seen many characters in my lifetime, but I have yet to meet another person like you! When your wife criticizes me, you listen raptly like you are hearing verses from the Vedas or the Koran!'

Aurobindo laughed, 'Why not, Sarat? Tell me, what do your husband Jagadindra's words sound like to you?'

'No, no, Dada, we are talking about the husband paying attention to the wife; *my* words to my husband should sound like Chanakya's Niti Shastra to him and he should listen enraptured!'

Sarat was amused at her own wordplay, and fearing that she would burst out laughing in front of the 'enemy', she turned aside and said, 'Maa has to say something urgently to you. Come if you wish, otherwise sit here and conspire with your wife on how to behead your wretched sister—'

Sarat stomped out, closing the door with a bang behind her. Aurobindo was in no mood to listen to his wife any further; caught between Sarat's badmouthing and his wife's anger, he proceeded to leave. Glancing at his wife who was speechless with hurt pride, he mildly muttered, 'Yes, "wretched sister" indeed! We really have to think of some way to behead you! Jagadindra has pampered you too much!'

Aurobindo said this with so much affection that it had just the opposite effect on the person the words were meant to mollify—Brajarani doubted whether her husband had ever spoken to her so affectionately! She also heard Sarat's reply—and that too was full of affection: 'She is learning from you, Dada! Poor thing—does she have an option? It is written in the Shastras, "The path that great men tread, that is the path to follow—"'

Brajarani was livid with humiliation and suppressed fury. Her fair face darkened as the evening sky with mortification as she lay down where she was.

## Chapter XX

Usha was two years younger than Brajarani, but when she reached the age of sixteen and had not conceived despite several years of marriage, her mother-in-law tied some flowers from Tarekshwar Shiva Temple around her neck and began to call on the gods for the blessing of a son. When this effort was not rewarded, the matriarch began to berate her daughter-in-law and her family in no uncertain terms. She threatened her son, 'Listen to me, Moni, if your wife does not beget a son within a year, I swear that I will not drink water until I get you married again next summer. We, the Bowbazar Mitras, have been tricked into bringing home a barren palm tree! What do you take us for? Are we low-caste Doms that you two go around as freely as sahibs and bibis enjoying yourselves? I want a grandson and I will not rest until I get one!'

Moni was as scared of his mother as he was of a tiger. Instead of retorting, he fled her presence and tried to placate Usha, who was in tears, 'You silly girl! Why do you listen to my mother? Who is marrying again? Not everyone is like your Dada!'

'Don't speak badly of Dada—he is different. Why didn't you reply? Maybe you agree with her and will marry again!'

'Yes, dear, yes! Of course, I will bring another wife home! And as if I will tell you beforehand! Now listen, why pick a fight with Maa? It will only make matters worse. And *you* have not crossed the childbearing age, have you? Why are *you* so afraid?'

Basking in her husband's love, Usha soon forgot the fear of

a co-wife. She had been hearing about the horrors of having a co-wife from Brajarani for so long that she was mortally scared. *My God, it would be better to die!*

But as the days went by and she did not conceive, she started becoming even more depressed. One day, she told her mother, 'My mother-in-law said the other day that those who have brought home a second wife for their son and made her life miserable, aren't they afraid that the same thing could happen to their own daughter? Let them do what they can for their daughter now, I will *not* wait after the end of this year. I am the daughter of "so-and-so" Dutta—I have sworn to keep my word and I *will*!'

Her mother was irritated, 'Why, is your childbearing age over?'

'They have no wish to wait any longer, Maa! I have heard that there is a place—Koralo or something—where they give you some medicines. Do you know if these things work?'

Her mother sighed deeply; perhaps she was thinking that her daughter's barrenness was the consequence of some sin she had committed earlier. She said thoughtfully, 'No harm in trying. Why don't you ask your Khuri-ma to accompany you?'

Khuri-ma was the wife of Mrityunjay's father's younger brother and was the matriarch's aunt-in-law. The maidservant Kadam, who was plucking grey hairs from her mistress's head, cackled, 'Who doesn't know that place? It is not far from our Banshberey village. You get off at Hooghly station and proceed to Korla-Sidhheswaritala temple. Come Didimoni, I too will accompany you. And Maa, why don't we take our Boudidi with us—she is two years older than our Didimoni—and your family too has no heirs! Didi here, God bless her, has a younger brother-in-law at least. Our house has nobody!'

Usha thought of this as an excellent proposal. She remembered Braja's intense desire for a son and felt grateful to Kadam. As for herself, she had no immediate yearning for a son; she was petrified because of her mother-in-law and the fear of a co-wife.

But Aurobindo's mother was annoyed at Kadam's words. She said, 'It is true that our house is empty, but that does not mean that there are *no* heirs—there *is* one!'

Kadam replied quietly, 'That is true, Maa.'

Aurobindo's mother continued, 'Women come here and advise—give your daughter-in-law this or that medicine, give her sacred amulets. Just the other day, Bouma's mother told me, "You know so much about charms and religious blessings, but have you done anything for my Rani? Don't you want a grandson? *I* yearn to hold a grandson in my arms!" What does she think? I would like Bouma to have many children! But what have *we* done to the one we have? We have offended God by insulting this family's heir. With what face can I ask God for more? The One who creates gave us an heir without asking and we rejected His gift!'

She sighed deeply and two tear drops coursed down her dry cheeks. Usha was furious at her words and tears, and shouted, 'You are wrong, Maa! The moment anyone mentions Boudi, you shed tears and bring up the old stories. Tell me, if you cannot forget the other one, why did you bring this one home? You are being one-sided!' And with that, she stomped off. Her mother, thus rebuked, despaired silently. But was it possible to suppress her feelings all the time and hide the sparks from the fire burning inside her?

Subsequently, both Usha and Brajarani went to visit the holy shrine of the goddess at Sidhheswaritala. Braja had not objected, although she did say, 'Is it absolutely necessary for me to go?' Usha had requested her mother to persuade her personally.

Sarat had commented with a tight smile, 'As though she waits for mother's permission to go anywhere!'

Usha said, 'Forget that! It is *our* requirement and Maa *should* request her!'

'It is *her* requirement and she knows that very well! She will certainly go whether Maa requests her or not.'

'You don't want Dada to have children?'

'Dada already has a son—but no harm if the younger one also conceives.'

Usha was aghast, 'Didi! How can you call *that* boy his *son*?'

Sarat looked up and said in a calm voice, 'You amaze me, Ushi! Should I call his son a daughter?'

Usha could find no words to counter her sister. However, the mother-in-law did instruct Brajarani to go to the temple. Both Usha and she were given holy amulets to wear. After seven or eight months, they were all invited to the pregnant Usha's saadh at the Mitra household. The following day, Braja threw her amulet away.

## Chapter XXI

Time flew by like the fast currents of a mountain stream and before she realized it, Brajarani was twenty-one. In Bengali society of that time, there was a saying, 'Twenty is plenty!' Since child marriage was the norm, childbearing was presumed to be completed by twenty-four or twenty-five—at least one child was certainly expected by that age. Brajarani and her mother became despondent. Both her paternal family and in-laws were families of lawyers, and even the women knew that a childless Brajarani had little claim to her husband's immense fortune. On what grounds could they stop the son of the co-wife from inheriting his wealth? This was what was called an 'embarrassment of fate'—whose would be the last laugh? Braja's birth chart had indicated that her life would not be too happy; her parents had even consulted charlatans and conducted rites involving black magic before her marriage to improve her prospects. But her marriage had been arranged through deceit—she had entered the household through conspiracy between the two fathers.

Braja often felt guilty about what had been done to the 'other' woman to get her married. But she simultaneously wondered *who* the lucky person was. Apart from a few close relatives and friends, everyone sympathized with the rejected wife. In fact, Brajarani herself would have empathized with the 'other' if she herself was not one of the main characters in this drama! Had she been sitting in a reserved box in a theatre, she would have cried at the co-wife's plight! If this had happened to a neighbour, she would have commiserated with the wronged person. But she was a principal character in this real-life drama! This was about *her* happiness! If one were to judge the situation from *her* point of view, would one not sympathize with her? Would questions not be raised regarding what her family had done to get her married? But then, was she not a victim too? Brajarani's mind was in turmoil—being essentially good-hearted, she was pulled in two opposing directions.

In fact, if one were to judge taking everything into consideration, one could not blame this girl entirely. Before her wedding, many close relatives had declared that it was better to drown the girl than to get her married to a married person. Much had been said between her parents, many fights had taken place, all ending with her mother in tears. But her father had been adamant; there was much at stake—money, status... During a wedding, there is a ritual where the bride and groom look into each other's eyes for the first time; during this *subha dristi*, when Braja looked at Aurobindo's grave, emotionless countenance, her thumping, expectant heart turned ice-cold. Following the wedding, when the couple sat side by side in the post-nuptial room, the *basar ghar*, where women are given the freedom to tease the groom, he did say a few words in response to questions by Brajarani's female relatives; he even sang a song at the repeated entreaties of her cousins, but Braja shivered in apprehension whenever she stole a glance at him through her richly decorated veil. He looked like a mourner on his way to the crematorium, sombre and solemn like God Shiva, who dwells in cremation grounds. He looked like an inert clay idol indifferent to the fact that he was sitting beside his newly-wed bride; Braja had seen the story of Bluebeard screened on a magic lantern—he was so grim that she was frightened to imagine what life had in store for her. What if this man turned out to be like Bluebeard; what if he married women, took them home and murdered them?

Her mother-in-law, wearing a new Varanasi sari, had come forward to welcome her in the traditional manner at the groom's house, but Brajarani noticed that she wiped her eyes several times using the pretext of managing the new slippery silk. Despite Mrityunjay Basu's strict command that the 'other's' memory had to be wiped out, she realized that many relatives were unhappy, especially Sarat. Brajarani felt insulted. She was beautiful, educated, accomplished; her father was extremely wealthy, and he had paid a handsome dowry to her father-in-law. She could not understand why she was not being put on a pedestal and treated as someone special! She could certainly not complain about Aurobindo's behaviour—he was extremely polite and a perfect gentleman, but the relation between husband and wife is not expected to be constricted to the norms of genteel politeness only.

On the nuptial night, Braja lay on her bed, lonely and wallowing in wounded self-pride. Aurobindo did not look at her but could feel her restlessness and knew that she was crying—he appeared to wake up from a tormented sleep and said, 'You haven't slept yet? You are crying? Please don't.'

Brajarani was not stupid; in any case, after her marriage had been arranged, her mother, aunts, grandmothers and other older and younger relatives had doused her with advice on how to tackle the bull by its horns on the first night itself. This kind of coaching would have trained even a jungle animal—and Braja was only a human. Still weeping, she slid closer to him, touched him softly and sobbed, 'I am not welcome in this house.'

Aurobindo trembled at her touch, but Braja was too engrossed in herself to understand anyone else's distress and perhaps interpreted it as something else. After a while, Aurobindo began to gently stroke her hand and said calmly, 'They will come around, Rani. Since my father has decided that you will be my wife, can anyone neglect you?'

'But my elder sister-in-law refuses to even look at me!'

After another moment of silence, Aurobindo cleared his throat and said, 'She is very unwell. She cannot even get up from bed.'

'Her suffering is mental. Your younger sister has told me everything. She had cried desperately when our marriage was arranged. She didn't want to stay for the wedding but is terrified of your father. I have also heard that she has vowed not to even *see* my face in this life!' She dissolved in tears.

'*Chhee*! Do you *have* to believe everything that is reported to you? You are being childish!'

Brajarani now slid even closer to Aurobindo, pressed her breasts against his side and, placing her mouth close to his, said in a husky voice, 'And you? What will you do to me?'

Aurobindo trembled all over again. His tormented heart tried to push back certain cherished memories to the remotest corners of his mind. Like a small bird in the clutches of a large animal, his throat was constricted and he could not speak. He looked at his new bride several times and saw the combination of hope and despair in her eyes, the yearning in her touch, the desperation to be accepted in her looks, and he gained control over his feelings and pulled her to him, saying with great effort, 'I will not neglect you.'

And Aurobindo kept his word. No one, not even Brajarani, could ever say that he had neglected her. In fact, he looked after her so well that his friends nicknamed him 'uxorious'. He gave her the freedom to do whatever she wished. If she wanted to go to the theatre, she did not have to ask for his permission. If she asked him capriciously to accompany her on a sudden whimsical visit to the Botanical Gardens, Aurobindo would abandon all plans for the day, even if a big chess game had been planned with his friends. However, as long as Mrityunjay was alive, Brajarani could not make too many such demands, but Aurobindo fulfilled her wishes to every extent possible. If she liked an ornament in Labhchand's new catalogue, she would send a request through Usha to her husband, and the ornament would arrive the next day. Once, in fact, Brajarani had asked for a diamond spray brooch. Aurobindo, lacking sufficient funds, pawned his gold watch chain to buy it for her. One of his friends castigated him, 'Couldn't your wife wait a few days? Why did you have to pawn your watch chain? Such devotion to your wife does not look nice, Aru!'

Aurobindo laughed, 'She wanted that diamond brooch, why should she not get it? She might have lost interest if I delayed.'

'So? She has plenty of other jewels! You know what the women in my house say: "What the King's rani does not possess, Aurobindo-babu's Rani possesses."'

Aurobindo responded laughingly, 'Why, it was for *that* very reason that her father married her to me!'

Another time, another friend exclaimed, 'She is your wife, not your courtesan—why do you indulge her every whim?'

Aurobindo had laughed at that remark as well and said, 'A second wife is far more important than a courtesan!'

'Why?'

'Firstly, the Shastras decree that a second wife doesn't get the status of a life partner. Secondly, they are not given equal significance to the first wife in women's rites and rituals. Moreover, my wife's condition is such that—'

'What?'

'Nothing. My great-grandmother, who was the third wife of her husband, used to sing, "The first wife eats from the husband's plate; the second wife sits by his side and eats; the third wife sits on his shoulders and eats!'"

The two friends burst out laughing at this depiction of the privileged status of a third wife. Then, like a good barrister, his friend attacked him again, 'This one is not your third wife! Don't let her climb onto your shoulders! Double promotions are not allowed in schools nowadays.'

Aurobindo smiled, 'My condition is worse than a man with seven wives. Instead of shoulders, if she wants to climb onto my head, I will have to submit!'

Despite the attention showered on her by Aurobindo, Brajarani was desperately unhappy; she realized that she did not attract him in any way and was deeply jealous.

But who was responsible for this? Perhaps no one. Maybe it was just her imagination—maybe her husband had placed her in his heart and that is why he bowed to her whims. He had lived with his first wife for only one year after all, and that too many years ago—memories fade with time. Perhaps her memory had been obliterated altogether? Instead, perchance it was Brajarani, his beautiful, intelligent second wife, who now reigned in his heart? She had thought about all this several times but had not felt reassured. The harder she tried to believe that things had changed, the more she doubted her assessment. Aurobindo had himself chosen his first wife, she was his first love—and she had been tricked into leaving through conspiracy. One who could forget such a person, what could he *not* do? Did he at all have a heart if he could simply wipe her out of his memory? No, this could *never* happen! She realized that Aurobindo had already given all his love to Manorama, and Brajarani was sailing in an empty barge. Tears, haughty behaviour, fasts would not bring her Aurobindo's love. And even if it was possible that he loved Brajarani, there was no way to measure it with his love for Manorama.

She was very interested in finding out from her peers how much their husbands loved them, how often they fought or how they made up—she would query them for intimate details. She would compare her findings with her own circumstances and conclude that her suspicions were correct. And then she would pick a fight with her husband again, accuse him of mental infidelity and break down in tears.

One evening, after returning from the wedding of a paternal aunt's granddaughter, she lay down on a couch in her sitting room without changing out of her heavy Varanasi sari or taking off her ornaments. She alone knew what had upset her, but it was evident that she had cried all the way from Kalighat to Howrah. Whether she had actually cried or whether she had been on the verge of tears is of no concern to us, but we have to find out why she was now flooding the sitting room with buckets of tears.

Aurobindo returned home late in the evening and found the muted rays of the setting sun filtering into the room through open windows. He saw a sky-blue sari embroidered with tiny stars, in gold and silver thread, lying on the couch—this too had turned a strange violet in the evening light. But what was this? From the folds of the fine tissue, wasn't that a hand, a very fair hand, laden with diamond bracelets, pearl bangles, a gold armlet, and multi-patterned emerald, ruby and sapphire rings on shapely, tapering fingers? And there, amid the crumpled creases of the sari, wasn't that a fair tear-stained face surrounded by jet black wavy hair? No—this was not just Rani's discarded sari; Her Excellency was herself sheltered within that sari! Aurobindo approached her with misgivings, 'I hope nothing serious has happened!'

That was enough to make Brajarani break down in uncontrollable tears. She said in between sobs, 'What else is left to happen! Now, I am just waiting for the fisherwomen and potters' wives to call out, "It is not auspicious to see a barren woman's face first thing in the morning! How dare you go around showing your face so brazenly?" If I hear this, I will have no other option but to hang myself!'

Aurobindo cradled her face lovingly and joked, 'If you hang yourself, you will become a ghost, Rani. And you are so scared of ghosts!'

'I am a living ghost—is my life any better than that of a ghost? What else can I become?' She was so upset at her own words that she became hysterical.

Aurobindo watched her silently for a minute and then asked quietly, 'Why did you return from the wedding so soon?'

'I have a headache.'

'Oh, so you took this recourse. Fine!'

'I did the right thing! First they invite me, and then they humiliate me! Do I not have any feelings?'

Aurobindo did not want to ask who had humiliated her or how. He knew that this woman was so imaginative that if the breeze blew too strongly on her face, she was sure to find fault with someone. Realizing that he was not going to pursue the matter, Brajarani decided to tell him herself. The essence of what she said was this:

Brajarani had some knowledge of painting and was adept at *alpana*, the art of decorating the floor with rice paste for auspicious occasions. At weddings, there is a custom of seating the bride and groom on alpana-decorated wooden boards called *pirhi*s. Brajarani took these boards into a room and applied herself to drawing designs on them. Feeling proud of the outcome, she took them to show to her aunt, whose granddaughter's wedding was scheduled for the evening. The aunt clutched at her face in what Braja thought was surprised pleasure. But her mistake was evident the next minute when the aunt angrily addressed her elder daughter, 'She may be young and doesn't remember our customs, but how could you, Chapala, allow her to do the alpana on the pirhis? You know that *she* should not do any of these auspicious tasks! Now, look how late it is—go and wash off the alpana and do it again!' Chapala-di, the bride's mother, replied that Brajarani had been adamant, and how could she be rude? Braja was old enough to know that although married women had a special position at weddings, her position was not equivalent to that of other married women because she was a second wife; the implication was that if *she* did such auspicious tasks, the new bride could be burdened with a co-wife like Brajarani.

Feeling absolutely humiliated, Braja called for her carriage and, pretending that she had a headache, left before the ceremony. The aunt tried to persuade her to stay but finding Braja resolute, she addressed Brajarani's mother, 'What can we do, Bouma? If Rani insists on acting stupidly despite being intelligent, let her do what she pleases. She is a second wife— why does she have to touch auspicious things, does it bode well? Don't you know your bad fate may touch the newly-weds? Do you want these other girls to have co-wives, just because you are ill-starred enough to be one? You have managed to ensnare your husband and make him into a slave—but others may not be so successful, what then?' And it went on.

Addressing Aurobindo, Brajarani said through her tears, 'This is the respect I get! And soon, people may start calling me barren! I wish to die!'

# Chapter XXII

Sarat's eldest daughter's marriage had been arranged; she was sitting with the weaver-woman at her home in Taltala selecting saris when she suddenly had an inspiration. Her husband, Jagadindra, was a simple, goodhearted person; apart from his office work, he never took interest in any family affair. The everyday management of the household was left to Sarat even though her mother-in-law was still alive; she too was besotted with Sarat's good nature and efficiency, and thus left day-to-day household chores to her. Jagadindra, on returning home from work, would eat, take a nap, and then recline on his couch with his hookah and watch indulgently as Sarat bustled around. After hearing Sarat's proposal, he let out a slow stream of smoke, which curled upwards like an extraterrestrial being, and said, 'That is a *capital* idea. Why don't you go to Burdwan yourself?'

Meanwhile in Burdwan, Manorama sat in her destitute house with a needle and thread, mending a bunch of well-worn clothes. Her friend and neighbour Rabeya, who was knitting a magenta-coloured sweater, entered the yard and said, 'I am knitting this for Ajit. Tell me, is it long enough?' Saying that, she unwound the rolled-up part and measured it with her hand.

Manorama looked at her gratefully and answered shyly, 'It is long enough. You are so fast at knitting, sister! You began it just the other day and it is almost finished despite your housework!'

'Knitting is easy! Today I will have to go—Hamid has been promoted to the next class; he has invited some friends over for snacks.' She rolled and pinned up the completed part with a safety-pin, and got up to leave.

Manorama, who had threaded the needle to embroider Ajit's name on a new dhoti, pouted and said, 'When do you ever have time to chat with me?'

'What can I do, sister? Ever since Maa died, all the work has fallen on me. Chhoto-ma is always unwell. So I have to look after Father, my brothers, and then there is the housework...'

Manorama said, 'Yes, that is true. Your whole life has been one long workday. But tell me, God has given you so much beauty—are you going to simply waste it like this?'

'Whatever Allah wills!'

'I don't understand His will! Rabi, I have always hesitated to ask you something. Please don't misunderstand me, I am asking you only because widow remarriage is a part of your customs. Tell me, why do you behave like a Hindu child widow and remain a "priestess"? Your cousin, Tasir, your uncle's son, is keen to marry you—such matches are considered good in Islamic society. His parents, too, have no objection. Then why—?'

Rabeya's lotus-like face drained of all colour. Bending over her knitting, she said, 'Mano, why don't you do another nikah yourself?'

'Our customs are very different, Rabi! It is allowed in your culture, not ours.'

'Would you have done it if your society permitted it?'

Manorama's features reddened like a red hibiscus. She hid her face with the corner of her sari and said, 'Shame! No, sister, forgive me for raising the topic!'

Rabeya came close, embraced her, and laughed, 'Mano, can I ever get angry with you?' She continued more seriously, 'Listen, every society has certain customs, but that does not mean they should be blindly followed. There is a class system in every society; in *your* society, you have upper and lower castes. If you did not distinguish between those from the lowest castes in your society, like the burial ground workers, the Doms or *Bagdi*s, and treated all castes equally, this would not result in their temperaments changing overnight, would it? You and I belong to the same social class, although you are a Hindu and I a Muslim. There is no difference in the temperaments of a Hindu or Muslim wife in our section of society. Mano, it ill behoves *you* to speak like this. How can I forget my lineage in the pursuit of desire? Or will *you* forget the social standing of my family and urge me to do something that does not suit my social status?"

'You may be younger than me, Didi, but you are like a guru to me when it comes to knowledge!'

'No, Manu, we are both ill-starred women! But even if fate has not treated us well, does that mean we should not live up to our ideals?'

Manorama took a deep breath and said, 'You are right, sister!' But something continued to irritate her like the sting of a wasp. She realized that she should not have spoken of remarriage to Rabeya, *she* who came from such an elite household and so staunchly upheld the dignity of her family name! It was true that God had not created every one equal. There were upper and lower classes, upper and lower castes; people were born into these and each class and caste differed in terms of custom and behaviour. Was it possible for everyone to behave in the same manner regardless of their station in life?

She was immersed in these thoughts when Ajit interrupted her, 'Maa, read this letter. I would have shown it to you earlier, but you were busy cooking.'

'Letter? Who has written to *you*, Aju?'

'Pishima. She has *invited* me! Let me read it: "*Chiranjibeshu*

Baba, darling Ajit..."—Mamoni, Pishima writes in such a peculiar manner!'

'Don't feel shy Aju, she is your aunt and loves you!'

'Why? She has never even *seen* me!'

'No, she has not seen you, but she loves you all the same. Well, what has she written?'

'"I have not received any letter from you in a long time and I am worried. My dearest child, my Gopal! Your Didi is getting married. You will come to see her husband along with your mother, won't you?" Maa! Has something happened to you? Why did you suddenly sit down like that? Now look at what you did, my lunch is strewn all over the place! But don't worry, I am not hungry today—good thing that the food fell on the floor!'

Wild, conflicting emotions swept through Manorama when she heard that Sarat was inviting them to come to her house for her daughter's wedding, after so many years of utter neglect; the plate she was holding fell from her lifeless hands! She was still sitting stunned when they heard some footsteps outside. Soon a young boy of about ten or eleven, holding the hand of a toddler who was barely a year old, and an Oriya servant carrying a big container of food, entered, followed by a woman around the same age as Manorama. The mother and son stared at her. The lady came closer and wiping her eyes with the end of her sari, said, 'Aju, my darling boy! Guess who I am?'

On hearing her words, Ajit gazed in wonder at the lady and said, 'You are my Pishima!' He rushed up to her and bent down to touch her feet with his forehead in salutation.

'What are you doing, my darling? Your head touched my dirty feet!' She pulled him up and hugged him as tears coursed down her cheeks.

Manorama and Sarat finally met after a long stretch of eleven years! So much had happened during that period that the two were uneasy about talking directly to each other; they resorted to using Ajit as a medium. Sarat said, 'Well, Ajit, how did you know that I was your Pishima?'

She had pulled the uncomfortable child onto her lap; he was a Class IX student now and eleven years old—how could *he* sit on anyone's lap? The boy felt embarrassed—thank God no one was around to see him! Would his school friends, who called him 'mother's baby', leave him in peace if they saw him now? He slowly eased out of her lap and smiled, 'I knew that you were my aunt!'

'Tell me how, Baba?'

Ajit laughed, 'You speak in just the same way that you write!'

Sarat was amazed at his acumen and looked at his grandmother Durgasundari, who had joined them on hearing of their arrival, with astonishment. Sarat said, 'The boy is so intelligent! Even old people would not think of this, Maa.'

Durgasundari sighed deeply, but blessed Sarat when she touched her feet as per custom, and asked politely, 'I hope everything is fine?'

It was evident from her tone that she had no interest whatsoever in the visitor. Sarat realized her indifference and she said in a small voice, 'Yes, Maa.' They sat quietly for a while, at a loss for words, until Durgasundari left after asking Manorama, 'Mano, have you arranged for some snacks and cool drinks for them? Oh my God, what is this food on the floor? Has the boy eaten nothing yet? Is there anything left for lunch or will Aju starve?'

Manorama had been so excited by Sarat's sudden appearance that she had totally forgotten about the spilled food. The others had also been too keyed up to notice the mess on the floor. Ajit quickly addressed the retreating back of his grandmother, 'Didimoni, I am not hungry today, I will eat supper later when the rice is cooked. Pishima and Mohit-da, come see our garden. Seven sunflowers have bloomed today, and isn't it amazing, they stay erect all day and follow the sun, but droop when evening comes? You cannot touch them—they sag if there is a strong breeze. Today, our teacher was saying—Mohit-da, you too are in Class IX, have they suggested any book for Botany? Our teacher explains the subject so well that we don't need textbooks!'

Meanwhile, Sarat had taken the container from her servant, Jagua; she took out some special *talshansh* sandesh, milk sweets from Bowbazar's famous sweetmeat shop Bhim Chandra Nag, and called Ajit, 'Come and eat, Baba.' Manorama still fed her son with her own hands as though he was a toddler. But he felt embarrassed when his Pishima, whom he had just met, wanted to feed him.

'No, no, Pishima, I am not hungry!' He pulled Mohit to his feet and said, 'Come Mohit-da, let me show you my study.' Sarat too got up and pushed a bit of sandesh into his mouth. She said sadly, 'Don't feel shy, I am your Pishima!'

Ajit smiled and said, 'Then give some to Mohit-da, too!'

'Sure, let him eat—Bou, you give him a sandesh. And Jagua, don't stand around like a clown! Find the pond and go wash your hands and feet. Place the baby here on my lap.'

Manorama had controlled herself, but any observer could see her hands and feet trembling when she reached inside the container. Heaven knows what was going on in the deepest recesses of her mind where human eyes cannot penetrate! What blows and counter-blows of joyful and painful memories were pounding in her heart! It had been a long eleven years or more since the two had last met! Memories fade or retreat to the darkest corners of the mind where no light penetrates. Why this sudden reawakening of memories? Why this sudden light in the darkness of her life? Was this just a spark or could she expect more?

# Chapter XXIII

Sarat wept silently all the way home. She related everything to her mother-in-law and her husband, Jagadindra, on returning, and told the latter tearfully, 'Dear, I met a goddess in Burdwan today. This was truly a pilgrimage! I have heard that in Kalighat, they have kept a little finger of Goddess Kali in some locked-up trunk, but I saw a living goddess made of flesh and blood. She has kept her promise, her word, despite all hazards—she is the real Sati.' She wept some more and said, 'My Dada is star-crossed! My God, *why* did I go there today?'

Jagadindra slowly pulled at his hubble-bubble and nodded, 'No doubt about that! So, where is she? Let me also purify my soul before the goddess.'

'Is she here that I can call her? Did she come?'

'She didn't come? Why?'

'You were not listening! She didn't wish to upset Dada and feared that *others* may take issue with him, so she did not come. Her mother, of course, was against it, but *I* could have persuaded her mother. Boudi *herself* did not wish to come.' Sarat's eyes had shrunk into slits with all the crying and rubbing.

Jagadindra commiserated, 'Well, the two could have met if she had come.'

Sarat answered gravely, 'Don't you understand, *that* was the reason she did not wish to come? Three years back, Dada had visited them for a few minutes to inform them about Father's shraddha—she says she understood by just looking at him how deeply upset he was at seeing her. She said, "Since Father compelled *him* to reject me, I have to spend my present life like this. It is my karma. I do not blame anyone. I must have hurt Rani grievously in some past life; I have to pay her back in this life. And have I not received so much love? You gave me your love—it is like untarnished molten gold to me! And above all, my *son* is my king's treasure—I cannot tell you how grateful I am to God! But yes, if I did not have the gift of this child, I would certainly have reason for tears." Now tell me dear, have you seen any woman who forgives all who have wronged her, happy with the little that she possesses?'

Jagadindra had become so engrossed in the story of poor Manorama that he did not realize that his hubble-bubble pipe had fallen to the floor. He drew a long empathetic breath and said, 'No! This is magnificent! She is truly a Sita, Rama's ideal consort!'

'No, Sita had a certain amount of pride—this one has *none*! She added, "Didi, *why* should I harm him needlessly? It is true that I could have seen him with my own eyes for a moment if I came with you, but that moment may cause him a year of remorse. I *know* in my heart that he has not forgotten this wretched unfortunate woman even today. I see his happy carefree face when I close my eyes. Why should I go and make him miserable?"'

'Wonderful! You should learn from her!'

Sarat's tear-drenched face lit up momentarily as she laughingly retorted, 'What should I learn, dear? You haven't abandoned me for another wife!'

Hearing her familiar mocking tone, Jagadindra smiled, 'Yes, you are right about that! If you don't have a co-wife and if you haven't been rejected, then where is the necessity for wifely devotion? Our Puranas, Upapuranas and mythologies all point to that conclusion, what say?'

'I am so upset and you are laughing at me! Your hair is turning grey, but you still remain the same! Always joking!' And with a laughing rebuke, she went about her work. The wedding was just a couple of days away—where was the time to brood?

Ajit had never travelled beyond Burdwan till he accompanied Sarat to Calcutta. This was his first train journey. He looked around in wonder as station after station flew by—goods trains, passenger trains, mail trains... He was struck by the vastness of Howrah station, and then the magnificent city of Calcutta itself! Ajit stared in awe at the milling crowds, the city lights. Today was Saturday and it was already evening. Ashima's *gaye-holud* was on Monday and the wedding was on Tuesday; he was due to return home on Wednesday. Apart from missing school, he felt that he could not stay away from his mother for too long, and his mother too would miss him—perhaps the last two reasons had made him decide to return home right after the wedding. Moreover, his grandmother had been reluctant to give permission. When Sarat had not been able to persuade Manorama to come, she pleaded, 'But do allow Ajit to come with me!'

Manorama's eyes had flashed for an instant like summer lightning in a still sky, before she said, 'How can I object? But I am wondering whether this will burden you with the sin of violating your father's orders?'

'Let his orders affect those who appear duty-bound to follow them! I am not bound by those commands. And remember—if I *don't* accept him as my nephew, I will be undoubtedly bound for *jahannam*!'

Manorama forced a smile, 'Then let the relations between him and his paternal house depend on that thin thread! How can I deny the little that he is at last getting? But—'

By this time, Manorama had twisted the end of her sari into knots. Sarat had been leaning against her friend like in earlier, happier times. She jumped at the 'but—' realizing that *that* word contained Manorama's constraints. She asked, 'But *what*?' When Mano remained silent, she pulled her to her breast and whispered into her ears, 'Do you want me to convey anything to Dada?'

Caresses...too much love! Manorama could not bear any more! Like a stormy sea, with wave upon larger wave creating mayhem, her heart had been in tumult all afternoon. She clasped her friend to her breast and broke down in a torrent of tears. Neither one could speak—all they understood was that their friendship had survived years of sorrow and now they were together again! But they also knew that *he* who was at the centre of their friendship—he who had brought them together—was not part of their reunion. Therefore, this meeting contained more regret than joy. There was always this 'but—', this hesitation-filled 'but'!

For a while they sat clutching each other, lost in thought. Then Sarat dried her own tears and her friend's, and again asked Manorama if there was anything she wanted to tell her husband. But Manorama said, 'If you have the chance, let Ajit get a proper glimpse of his father, but his father should not see him. The father does not know his son—can there be any greater shame?'

Sarat retorted, 'You don't have to tell me this! Sujan-babu, Dada's and my husband's friend, had come for the Burdwan Raja's wedding and Aju had met him. He told them about him when he returned; he also said, "Aurobindo's son seemed to be a total fan of his father. He could hardly bring his father's name to his lips—so very devoted!" I was desperate to see the boy, especially since then—'

Manorama seemed surprised but merely added, 'Please remember, neither his *family's* nor his own peace of mind should be disturbed in any way because of Aju's presence! Dear sister of mine, there should be no problem because of this minor weakness on our part!'

Sarat answered tearfully, 'Didi, you will never be the cause of *any* unrest in anyone's life! Does anyone understand your value?' After this, not much was said, but Sarat again asked when she was leaving, 'Is there anything you want me to tell him?'

Manorama hugged her and said, 'No! Maybe—just tell him—I pray that I am his wife in my next birth and that I do not lose him in that life like I have lost him in this!'

# Chapter XXIV

Ashima's future father-in-law was a famous advocate who practised in the Hoogly judge's court. Her husband-to-be, a third-year college student, was the third son of his father. His two elder brothers were already working and earned good salaries. About 25 persons bore the gaye holud gifts from the in-laws' house. They arrived around 3.00 p.m. claiming that they had missed the earlier train. They said that the barber, who plays an essential role in these rituals, could easily have jumped onto the running train—which they had missed—with the bowl of turmeric and the yellow sari that had to be worn by the bride for the occasion, as he had been instructed to do, but he stood around stupidly while the engine gathered speed. Who listened to anyone these days?

The eleven-year-old bride, Ashima, had fasted since morning for the ritual as per the accepted custom, and was famished. Her father Jagadindra, who was incapable of anger, muttered, 'What kind of selfish inconsiderate in-laws have we found for our daughter?' And not finding anyone who could clean and fill his hubble-bubble, he found another hookah, scratched his head and pulled slowly at the pipe. The bride's mother was irritated and finding faults with everyone. The invited guests, embarrassed at the state of affairs, sat around quietly or murmured among themselves about other weddings where the ritual had been delayed because of unforeseen circumstances. Just when people were losing patience, the sound of conch shells floated in from the doorway. Visitors and family members rushed towards the sound and found that Ashima's gaye holud ritual items had arrived! The distantly related women sat down to examine the gifts, while the close female relatives crowded around Ashima and applied the turmeric brought from the groom's house on the bride-to-be's forehead and cheeks, before running after each other playfully to smear it on their faces and clothes. In the midst of this happy commotion, Brajarani, after attending the rice ceremony of the six-month-old third son of her second brother, arrived to grace her sister-in-law's elder daughter's pre-nuptial rituals.

Where was Ajit all this time? He had been drawn into a circle of young boys more or less his own age but felt hesitant to join in their games. He felt like a misfit and also missed his mother. He was uncomfortable with the noisy celebrations and yearned for the peace and quiet of his own usual surroundings, but did not wish to hurt his Pishima's feelings by wanting to return to Burdwan. Moreover, he had not seen his father yet—and it was *this* desire that had actually brought him so far from home!

Finding his aunt alone one time, he had approached her, and she had asked, 'Aju, where are your cousins?'

'I was with them—but Pishima?'

'Yes, Baba?'

Sarat had been looking for something in a cupboard but, hearing something in his tone, she turned towards him and found him looking listless. She came closer and asked, 'Tell me Aju-moni, do you want to see anything? You went to the zoo and the museum yesterday—do you wish to visit the theatre today?'

Ajit shook his head. She kissed him and smiled, 'Then where do you want to go?'

Sarat realized that his fingers were trembling. Surprised, she hugged him and asked, 'Baba! Are you missing your mother? Do you want to go home?'

Ajit hid his face in her hands and said softly, 'How can I return? I have not seen my father yet!'

Sarat did not know how to respond. She kissed him again and said, 'You will certainly see him, my jewel! Your uncle has told me that he will go and bring him in the evening.' She added with a bit of displeasure, 'I had invited him last night too, but he sent word that the son of his uncle-in-law was going abroad and had invited them to a farewell party, and that they would be annoyed if he did not attend. I have never seen anyone so devoted to his in-laws!'

'I can go and visit him at his house with Pishimoshai. May I, Pishima? What if he can't find the time to come today too? His house could not be far from Howrah station—if someone accompanies me, I am sure I can walk—'

'Oh my God, how can you walk there, you crazy boy! Wait, I will just go and give these sacred threads... I will be back.' She used the excuse of delivering the sacred threads somewhere to get a momentary respite from the boy's questions, giving him semi-assurances that she herself did not believe in. How could she tell him the truth: 'There, in your father's house—your father whom you revere so much—*you* have no place; your paternal home is forever closed to you.' She pondered, *Why make the boy aware of the real situation when he is here for only a couple of days. He will get to know the truth inevitably, but why rush things.* Sarat felt that she could not stand it anymore. Was Aurobindo entitled to such fidelity? He was stealing the affection of his son without doing a thing in return! He was a thief!

But she did introduce Ajit to his paternal grandmother. She was old and not likely to live much longer. She had hankered to see the heir to the Basu name at least once before she left this world! And now, look, she was sitting smiling, wet-eyed, caressing the boy's head and face!

Brajarani meanwhile entered the house and found that the gaye holud rites were not yet over. She had tried to avoid it by going to her nephew's rice ceremony even though she knew Sarat would be irate at this. She laughed to herself thinking of the old saying, 'The evening falls, where the tiger strolls.'[*] She had planned to steer clear of the gaye holud rituals lest her presence was seen as a bad omen! What was the point in attending these rituals if people considered her ill-starred, someone whose bad luck would rub off on others. She could always come later.

She evaded the ritual site and went towards Sarat's younger sister-in-law's room. On the way, she came across a group of women, including the bride's maternal and paternal aunts, Brajarani's friends Usha and Bina, their hands yellow and oily with turmeric paste mixed with mustard oil. They laughed at her, 'Oh you! The bride's Mami! Why so late? You could have fanned your husband to sleep and then come peacefully!'

She retorted laughing, 'Peacefully? Suppose he awakens and feels scared in the empty house?'

'Oh! This woman is shameless!'

'Alright, let us put some turmeric paste on you! Although you have come after lighting the evening lamps at home, we haven't finished with the paste!' The bride's paternal aunt, Bina, whose room Braja had been heading towards, now displayed her yellowed hands. Braja pulled her expensive violet Varanasi

---

[*]Derived from the saying '*Jekhane bagher bhoy, sekhane sondhey hoy*!' It roughly means whatever one is scared of will happen; if one is scared of tigers, they will find themselves in a tiger-infested jungle just when evening is descending.

sari embroidered with a gold leaf pattern tightly around her shoulders, and retreated a few steps. She cried, 'I beg you! This new sari will be ruined!'

'So, why did you wear it today? Didn't you know that the bride's aunts rub this auspicious paste on each other to reinforce their own marriages? And if we don't, the new groom will not love his bride!' They all broke out in peals of laughter.

Usha, Sarat's sister and the bride's maternal aunt, protested, 'Don't drag me into this! I have taken a certificate from Didi that I should be exempted! My baby has a fever and I have to avoid taking a bath this late!'

'Oh, *just* today—if it means that the girl's husband will love her, why not?'

Braja complied laughingly, 'Okay then! If my sister-in-law hears that I didn't do something that will bring blessings on her daughter, she will thrash me with a broom!'

Bina, the bride's paternal aunt or Kakima, raised her hand in mock attack but wiped it on her own sari and giggled, 'Okay! If the girl's Kakima is rubbed all over with turmeric today, then all will be fulfilled!' Both Braja mami and Usha mashi were happy that Bina had volunteered to be rubbed with the turmeric paste in their stead, since their saris had been saved from the ravages of the indelible stains of the paste. Usha too wiped her hands on Bina's back and said, 'Good for you, Chhoto-bou! Mamis and Mashis can love the girl, but only the Kakima, who is tasked with welcoming the groom, can make him into a sheep following the bride's every command!' There is a custom called *stree achar*, where the married women of the family carry out various rituals when the bride and groom exchange garlands. The bride's paternal aunts, sisters-in-law and others also do a bit of pleasant ragging of the groom, trying to make him bleat like a sheep, the inference being that he will later listen to his future wife's whims.

Bina smirked teasingly, 'But look at Braja-didi! Have we been capable of making our husbands bleat like Dada?'

Braja reddened with embarrassment and pinched Bina's arm. Sarat was hurrying down the corridor on some errand and saw the three young women bent in laughter! She raised her voice and said, 'Chhoto-bou! Ushi! You should be dressing the bride, displaying the gifts and dowry from her in-laws, looking after guests—! And here, you are behaving like invitees, all dressed up, enjoying yourselves!'

The three stopped laughing. Usha was sent to oversee the bridal make-up, while Bina took Brajarani with her to arrange the display of the gaye holud *tatwa* from the groom's house. Braja, who was good at doing make-up, had been given the task of dressing up the bride, but she refused saying, 'I am not supposed to do that.'

'Why? Oh, I see! But Mamis are not bad omens!'

Braja was, however, adamant: 'No, I will not do it. One of you dress the bride.' Seeing her turning to leave, Bina said, 'Okay, let Usha-di do it. Help me in arranging the display of the tatwa gifts.'

Braja asked, 'Am I allowed?'

Bina got irritated and said, 'No, you are not supposed to do anything! Is Dada a potter and you a potter's wife that you should not touch anything?'

Braja laughed, 'No, your Dada is a high-caste Kayastha *Kulin*'s son, *and* he is a male. Why should high-caste males be guilty of anything? It is I, a woman, who am a low-caste Bagdi!"

'So, if Dada is a high-caste Kayastha and you a *bagdidni*, does that mean you have another—'

'Fie! Your mouth does not stop at anything! What dirty talk!'

'Why, you yourself said...now you put the blame on me!'

'What nonsense! As if I said *that*!'

'Okay, you explain,' Bina teased, 'you belong to one caste and Dada to another, now what does that imply...'

'You are shameless! And look, Didi is coming this way again! I don't have the courage to face her—you wait here and get scolded!'

ಬಇ

## Chapter XXV

After sitting with his grandmother for a while, embarrassed but basking in her affection, Ajit joined a group of boys who had decided to go on a quick excursion of the city. The sights that he saw were bewildering to his inexperienced eyes; he used to think of Eden Gardens earlier as the paradise where Adam and Eve had roamed free until Satan's jealousy ousted them—was this garden *that* garden? Poor Adam and Eve!

Next to Eden Gardens, which did not turn out to be paradise, was the majestic Ganges River—what a mesmerizing view! He watched the swift flow of the waters, the changing hues, the playful moods and the massive breadth of the river, totally engrossed. The quay was filled with frolicking visitors, merry-makers and idle onlookers. He had seen a few Europeans earlier on Calcutta's streets but was amazed to see so many white men, women and especially children enjoying the river breeze. The latter were dressed in colourful clothes of varied designs; they were like a bunch of butterflies flitting around! He watched fascinated as European couples walked hand in hand, immersed in each other; there were young, unchaperoned Indian men and women too, obviously from a different, independent-minded class; and the songs, the music, the lights on the riverfront! All this was too much for the boy from a village-like place, practically the backwaters! And after that, they went to the bioscope to watch a silent movie. The funny antics of the silent actors would impress any child and Ajit was no exception; he was thrilled and dumbfounded at the same time. How beautiful was this city, this Calcutta! Living here would take so much good karma! He thanked God that he had the good fortune of having a loving Pishima!

By nightfall, most of the wedding invitees had returned to their respective homes, but Sarat's house was still bustling with people and activity. Feasting was in progress even now, and groups of people simply sat around gossiping about the new in-laws. The general opinion was that there was more show than content in the gaye holud tatwa—more trays than items, more people to carry them than goods. Some said, 'Look how sparse the items are on each tray! And the bearers—one person for every tray to get more tips from the bride's family! And oh my God, see how thin these milk sweets are! We have to praise the *handiwork* of the bride's mother-in-law—these sweets will fly like kites if you blow on them!' These gossips also decided that the pearl choker sent for Ashima was worthless—the pearls were small and crooked, and the gold hairpins were underweight! Three pins would not weigh even 33 grams! 'We must find the goldsmith,' they sniggered. 'Maybe he will be useful to us in the future!'

Bina remarked, 'But the Parsi sari is expensive. Only if it was a lighter colour—their taste is very rural!'

Brajarani added, 'Have you seen the outlandish colour of the blouse? Chemise, petticoat, white blouse, they have sent everything, but all of them were probably bought at the cheap Chandni market! None of them are—'

Someone elderly retorted, 'I think the dowry is fine. In our Kulin families, how many in-laws give this much? When *we* got married, they used to send the turmeric paste and a short *sari*, the border dipped in turmeric, probably cut from a piece of cloth by married women; it didn't even have a complete border!'

'You are talking of the age of Mandhata, grandmother! Your

fathers too never gave their daughters anything more than a five-stringed gold necklace and a few gold bangles. They didn't have to give you bangles weighing over 100 grams and silver dinner sets, suits, watches with gold chains, 2,000 rupees in cash and more for the groom! Your parents were not subjected to today's dowry demands!'

'That is true. If a bride was lucky, she got a colourful Varanasi sari or a Baluchari veil, perhaps a heavy silver anklet, a necklace, or a couple of bangles, a five-stringed necklace and maybe a gold bead hairpin from her parents' house! If the in-laws were rich, the father-in-law would present the bride with a cowry-shell-embedded case for sindoor, a nose ring, a sanctified amulet, and blessings for an eternal marriage! And if they were poor or from the middle class, just a pair of auspicious red wax bangles and a thin nose dangler—that was all!'

'What did your in-laws give *you*, grandmother?'

'Oh, Jagat's grandfather, my father-in-law, was the *dewan* in a sahib's bungalow in Serampur. He gave both me and my co-wife many ornaments, more than what queens possessed! A tiara for the head; heavy gold dangling earrings for the ears; *choudani*, *pith jhanpa* for the back; armlets, wristlets, anklets, *gujri pancham*, *charanpadma* and *painjorh* for the feet! But it was unseemly for Brahmins and Kayasthas to wear too much jewellery in public in those days, otherwise Europeans would smirk at us and say, who are these women—are they *sonar beney?*'

The women had been transported to a different age and partially forgotten the luxury-loving current times. They were quickly brought back to the present when a group of rowdy young boys returned home, slippers pattering, and set up a din. 'Aunties! You will not believe what we saw today! *Play!*'

'Mamima, you are a frequent moviegoer—have you seen this new bioscope show?'

Brajarani asked, 'What is the story?'

'There are these two very naughty boys. The moment their mother turns her back after putting them to bed, they get up, pick up pillows—and—and—' the boy spluttered with laughter.

'Come on, if you are going to laugh so much, how can you describe what you saw? As if you boys are not naughty enough!'

In the meantime, another younger boy had entered the room, slowly but full of cheer. Forgetting his whereabouts after a long, exciting day, he sat down near Brajarani, and mistaking her for his aunt, leant against her. He said excitedly, 'Pishima! The bioscope was so funny! I laughed but it was stupid too—it was about the antics of very naughty boys!'

This boy was used to relating everything that had happened during his day to his mother. Here, there was his Pishima. Being totally unexposed to urban society, he did not think it necessary to see who all were present around him and how he should present himself. He continued to talk in a rush, relating where all he had been and what he had seen. He leaned against Brajarani just as he would have done against his mother. She was mesmerized by this strange, lovely-looking boy with huge innocent eyes. She stared at his face, which was as fresh as the shining new leaves of spring, and her own senses seemed to cool, as though she had been immersed in manna from heaven. She wanted to hug this boy to her hungry childless breasts—it was as if her maternal feelings, so long non-existent, were fully aroused by the smell, touch and sound of this small magician (for what else was he?), as though a torrent had inundated a dry river bed! The Mother—the maternal instincts inherent in all women—awoke in Brajarani's barren life for the first time.

The boy suddenly realized his mistake and tried to retreat from the unknown lady with a small embarrassed laugh, when some of the other boys clapped in glee and his cousin taunted, 'Oh-oh! Ajit mistook Mamima for my mother!'

Another boy retorted, 'No, Mamima is much fairer and taller, and is bedecked with ornaments! Maybe, he mistook Mamima for his own mother, right Aju?'

Without thinking, Brajarani quickly clasped the hand of the boy to stop him from leaving. She pulled him gently towards herself and said, 'So what if I am not your Pishima? I love to listen to stories of bioscopes—please carry on!'

This was a totally unknown world for Ajit; he had never experienced such people in his short life. He felt like an uninvited guest who had unknowingly transgressed boundaries. But here was this grand lady who seemingly forgave him for his faults—how could he refuse her? If he didn't respond, it would only add to his humiliation and his new friends would laugh even more! So he stopped in his tracks and said shyly, 'You have seen many...'

'Yes, but not that one. It is new.'

'I heard that it has been running for four nights!'

'Then maybe I have seen it. Was this your first time in a movie hall?'

The boy raised his lotus-bud-like eyes and smiled in mortification. Brajarani was fascinated—she felt as though these eyes had lifted the sultry darkness of the night sky and replaced it with the golden hues of dawn! His thin, finely-drawn red lips curved in a smile. Brajarani deeply desired to quench her motherly yearning by drawing that face to hers; she controlled herself with difficulty. This boy was a mere child; but in Hindu households, girls were married off at that age and sometimes even became mothers. She too could have become a mother but had not, and for her to show so much affection towards an unknown ten or eleven-year-old boy was unseemly! Oh God! Why was there so much hunger in her for a child!

Ajit shook his head to indicate that he had not been to a bioscope earlier. Brajarani was about to say something, when Sarat's nine-year-old second daughter, Sarala, entered the room and beckoned, 'Ajit Dada, Maa is calling you for dinner.' And Mohitlal, Sarat's nephew and Ajit's new best friend, answered Brajarani, 'They don't have bioscopes in Burdwan, so how can he have been to one earlier? In fact, the zoo, the museum, Eden Gardens, Howrah Bridge, all these were firsts for him. This is his first trip to Calcutta—'

Mohitlal continued to talk, but Brajarani had stopped listening. When Ajit had wanted to pull his hand away from Brajarani's on being summoned, she had felt as though she had touched a live wire, and a jolt went down her spine. The sudden change did not escape the boy's eyes. For a second, he stood looking anxiously at her. The next instant, he was surrounded by the other boys, noisy and ebullient, and they all went off for dinner.

# Chapter XXVI

This unexpected meeting with Ajit had affected Brajarani deeply. Her heart was in turmoil with conflicting emotions, so much so that she ate nothing, spoke to no one and, using the pretext of a colic pain, asked her maid around midnight to summon their family brougham. Even though she had not said anything to anyone and Sarat was unaware of Braja's accidental meeting with Ajit, she intuited what had upset her. She tried to stop Brajarani, 'Why are you leaving so late at night, Bou? If you are not feeling well, we have homoeopathic remedies at home. Let my brother-in-law treat you, he is adept at homeopathy. I will arrange a bed for you, why don't you lie down?'

'I *have* to leave. Homeopathic medicines don't work on me.'

'Dada did not come, and you are leaving—'

Braja's lips bent in a small sardonic smile, 'That will make no difference to your celebrations, there are enough people around!'

Her mocking tone and smile irritated Sarat, who was already angry at her brother's absence. She retorted angrily, 'Do you think I don't know what is going through your mind right now? Go and complain to that sheep of a brother I have, and be sure to lock the doors! Don't let him out for a moment, otherwise all your spells over him will be broken!'

'You have no right to humiliate me after inviting me here! I did not come here of my own accord!' With this, Brajarani broke into tears of self-pity and quickly climbed onto the carriage, afraid that others may hear the exchange between the two. She had no desire to speak to the person she saw as her character-assassin.

After she left, Sarat, unnerved, stood still for a while. She had certainly not intended to humiliate her sister-in-law, but she told herself that Braja was not upset at *her* words—it was seeing the striking young face of her co-wife's son that had distressed her. She did not actually care whether Brajarani returned home; what mattered was that she may not allow Aurobindo to attend the wedding. Her brother had actually come for an hour early in the evening, but Ajit and his friends had not been home at the time. She had tried her best to detain him but hadn't succeeded. Aurobindo had bought a new garden house in Ballygunge. He had excused himself because of some urgent problem with the deeds which had to be resolved tonight because the wedding was the next day. Sarat was put off but hoped to arrange a meeting between father and son tomorrow. But now she was afraid that Brajarani may foil that. She also felt a bit ashamed because she had wanted to keep Ajit's presence a secret from her sister-in-law. But then, she reasoned, so what if Braja knew? Even enemies would stop and admire that charming face; and here, it had set her afire with jealousy! Oh, how unfortunate that a stepmother was so envious!

Meanwhile, Brajarani leaned on the soft leather couch of her carriage and speculated. Her blood pressure had shot up and her eyes were burning. Her mental agony was like a poisonous drug, keeping her sharply aware and simultaneously making her insentient. Jealousy and anger overpowered her— she sat up on the couch and opened the window. The horse was galloping at full speed on the empty midnight road, and a nippy breeze entered the cabin, cooling her incensed brain. She began to think clearly for the first time since the evening. What amazed her now was her own behaviour, that, in spite of the outrage she had faced, she was returning home quietly instead of striking out like a venomous snake!

But contradictory thoughts immediately arose as she considered whether she had done the right thing. Was it absolutely necessary for her to have reacted in that manner? These thoughts were again drowned by a wave of intense resentment—of course, there was enough reason! What did *she* mean by bringing *that* boy to her house? Was it for *this* reason that the sister was so concerned about her Dada's absence? And perhaps her brother was complicit in this conspiracy? Maybe the bioscope was a pretext? Maybe he was entertaining his son all this while? Who knows? Was it just the son—or? It must be! If the son had come, could the *mother* be absent? At this thought, her blood pressure rose further and she felt faint.

When she returned home, she found her room in semi-darkness, with just one lit gas lamp. The bed had not been slept in but the cover was in disarray; the mosquito net was piled atop the four-poster bed. Immediately, she was overcome with suspicion—the nasty plot against her was then engineered by none other than her husband! She remembered that when she had objected to attending the wedding since Sarat had not personally come to invite her, how vehemently her husband had reacted! How could she have known that there was so much behind the heated defence of his sister?

Brajarani's face was reflected in the room's long standing-mirror. The gas light from the opposite wall lit up her beautiful face—but whose face was this? Was it the face of pure jealousy in the form of Braja? She quickly turned away and flopped down on a Cleopatra couch and closed her burning eyes. She suddenly felt that there was nothing left for her anymore! These last few hours that she had spent—donning the carefully selected expensive diamonds and pearls to be worn with her new Varanasi silk sari that matched the latest jacket she had got especially stitched for the occasion, and then the time spent at Sarat's house—were probably the worst in her life! Despite her riches, she was like a beggar woman in torn rags that barely hid her nakedness. How could she continue with her miserable life after this?

Her maidservant, Aduri, had meanwhile woken up and entered the room. Seeing her on the couch in darkness, she asked, 'Don't you want to change, Boudidi?' Getting no response, she enquired again, 'It will soon be dawn—won't you take off your jewellery at least?'

Brajarani replied in a faraway voice, 'You take them off for me, Aduri.'

Aduri was taken aback. How would she know how to take them off? Even her forebears had no idea how the springs and clasps of ornaments worked. She tore the costly sari as she tried to unpin the diamond safety-pin that fastened Braja's hair to her sari and pulled the pearl collar around her throat so roughly that a string broke and several beautiful pearls slid to the floor. Brajarani then dismissed the maid and listlessly began removing the ornaments herself, one by one.

She lay down on the couch, half asleep, with the night's events appearing and disappearing in her mind like a story that she could neither believe nor dismiss. She felt weak, as though she had been suffering from a lengthy life-threatening disease. Without intending to, she glanced at the mirror. This time she did not turn away; she continued to stare at her tired features.

The kitchen maid, Sarada, opened the door and asked, 'Do you plan to go to Sarat Didimoni's house in the morning itself? Will Babu be eating lunch at home? Which servants will stay and who will go? Please come and take out what is necessary from the store for us to begin work. The cook has already lit two fires.'

Brajarani stretched, yawned, lay down on the bed and said in a tired voice, 'I am not going anywhere—I will not eat anything either. I am feeling very unwell.'

'Today of all days! Is that why you returned past midnight?'

'Yes.'

'Should we cook for Babu?'

'I don't know.' She wanted to ask, 'Where *is* your Babu? And where was he last night?' But she could not ask—her heart began to pound with anger at the thought! But why should she humiliate herself in front of her servants?

Sarada, the kitchen maid, guessed what may have occurred in Sarat's house and left without another word. The servants of this and all neighbouring households were quite aware that the master and mistress of *this* house had serious disputes at least ten days each month.

Brajarani closed her eyes and kept lying down. The face of the boy from yesterday—fresh as new autumn creepers washed by rain, filled with the dynamism of youth—floated unbidden before her. He was like a prince, like God Kartik without his peacock; *he* was the son of her co-wife! And people called *her*— that woman—star-crossed! People sympathized with *her* for her hapless destiny! And Braja! There was no one in the entire world who empathized with her, no one who called her 'poor girl'! *She* controlled her husband!? What a joke! And, where was that husband now? Perhaps she, Brajarani, possessed his physical body, but where was he *mentally*? The mother who bore such a beautiful son, God knows what *she* was like? Could any man who had eyes ever forget *her*?

She heard a sound that she was well acquainted with. She opened her eyes.

'Braja? When did you come home?'

Aurobindo was carrying a towel for his bath. Brajarani wondered, was it so late already? But she said nothing, and only looked at him limply as she felt anger and self-pity rising in her again.

'You must have come at dawn—we have been sitting in the outer room since early morning. I didn't see your carriage coming in!'

Brajarani answered gravely, 'I returned last night.'

'Last night? When? I didn't hear anything?'

'How could you hear? Were you home?'

'Of course, I was home! Where else would I be?'

'How would I know? Do you tell me anything?'

'That I should spend the night somewhere else, and you are not informed—has that ever happened?'

Her husband's mocking tone added embers to her anger, but she said with forced calmness, 'How long before it does?'

'Oh I see! Well, now that I am in your hands, why should that particular defamation of my character be excluded?' he turned to leave.

Braja realized she had no time to discuss the matter with him at leisure. Seeing her husband's attire, she said, 'Why are you going to bathe so early?'

'We have to go to Sarat's house, don't you remember?' He had already stepped out of the door when he heard his wife's thunderous voice from inside the room, like a bomb filled with poisonous chemicals, 'A *curse* on your son's head if you go there today!'

Aurobindo was aghast, as though a sudden, sharp arrow

had pierced his heart and incapacitated him. He turned around slowly and asked in an infinitely pained voice, 'What have you *done*, Rani? Today is Sarat's elder daughter's wedding!'

Brajarani had acted impulsively; she immediately realized the grievous wrong she had committed. But what was the point? Her whole being was livid with anger, envy and jealousy—and does jealousy know any bounds? Did it distinguish between right and wrong, good and bad? Rani would languish here at home with her sorrows, and *he* would go there! His sister had *insulted* her—and *he* would go there, eat his fill, enjoy himself with his other wife and son. Was there *justice* in that? She said in an ice-cold voice, 'I don't care! If you go there even for a moment, know this for sure—you will find my dead body when you return! I will certainly *hang* myself!'

Shocked, Aurobindo turned away and left silently.

Slowly, very slowly, Brajarani's temper cooled. But just as the turbulence of a flooded river leaves behind a particular heaviness in the muddied waters following a storm, she felt drowsy with spent emotions. She learnt from her servants later that her husband had had a quick meal after his bath, and had left for the station where he had taken the ten o'clock passenger train to Bhagalpur. Baikuntha Thakur and Ramfal had accompanied him. One of the maidservants told her, 'He had wanted to take Kartik but Kartik wanted to attend the wedding, so Babu got very angry. Babu said that he had lent money to some Raja in Bhagalpur or somewhere, but overburdened with loans, the Raja was going off to Kathmandu or some such place to evade repayment—he had to meet the collector sahib immediately about this matter!'

This was true; a Raja *had* defaulted and was leaving town to avoid legal procedures, but this was nowhere as important to

Aurobindo as his niece's wedding! What had *she*, Braja, done! She had made her husband leave the city, the state, on *this* day! When Maa and Sarat would hear this, won't they understand *why* he had abruptly left for Bhagalpur on Sarat's daughter's wedding day? She also heard from the maidservants that he had been at home last night and had slept downstairs. He had spent the entire evening with some lawyers discussing paperwork. They had left around ten o'clock—how could he have gone anywhere since they were there? And last night, the food had been cooked by Vishnu Thakur. Aurobindo had joked while eating, 'What have you cooked, Vishnu Thakur? It makes me cry just to look at it! If I had gone to Sarat's house, there would have been so many delicious dishes—but am I that lucky?'

Brajarani's heart hammered when she heard this. He was truly unaware of either Manorama's or Ajit's presence in Sarat's house! Was she setting fire to her entire universe because of her false suspicions? She felt terribly ashamed of herself! She desperately wanted to beg forgiveness at her husband's feet, take back her curse, use all her charms to send him to the wedding venue—but there was no possibility now! She also understood that if her husband had *really* wanted to, could she have prevented him from keeping relations with his first wife? She knew very well that he had always been true to the word that his father had extracted from him, despite all provocations. She realized that creating a scene, hurting others, and getting hurt in the process was like a festering disease in her. A generous wind seemed to be blowing that day—it made her accept the stark truth about herself for the first time.

Brajarani was exhausted with the bouts of jealousy and anger that had torn her apart since last night. Although the colic pain had been a pretext, sleeplessness and an empty stomach extracted their toll. When the evening prayers began, conch shells blew and gongs sounded in the nearby Sitala temple, she stared out of her bedroom window at the thin black line of the public road beyond her garden. She imagined the road in front of Sarat's house at that moment. Heaven knew how joyous it must be there now! Perhaps the groom's carriage had arrived! The road must be filled with wedding guests, bright colourful lights, the sound of the shehnai—neighbours must be spilling out of their windows to watch the festivities! And here she was, the Mami of the bride, alone in this deserted house! What was Ashima's groom like—was he good-looking? She remembered that young boy again. When it was time for him to get married, what a handsome groom he would make! Which lucky mother was praying for such a groom for her daughter—who knew?

Next she thought that if she had not come away in such a huff last night, she may have got the opportunity to get a glimpse of *her*, the beautiful *other*! There were so many women there yesterday—which one was *she*? Was there anyone so very beautiful inside? Despite racking her mind, Brajarani could not come up with an answer. She smiled to herself and thought that one should not believe all one hears; there was a saying, 'The fish that escapes the net is the largest!' Maybe *she* was not so beautiful after all! But her mind refused to be comforted. How could the mother of that moon-like child be anything but beautiful? Rani had not seen her, but *she* must have observed Rani from somewhere. Rani now realized, to her dismay, that being fair like a conch shell (which she was) was not the yardstick of beauty.

Well, what could *she* be doing now? She may have helped dress the bride and may be getting ready to welcome the groom. Perhaps she will do the *boron*? Her fate was not that of Brajarani's—she was the first wife of her husband, the *dharmapatni*, as well as the mother of his offspring! God had given her the respect and dignity due to a wife and mother, whereas she, the ill-fated Brajarani, had been burdened with so much unnecessary wealth! In truth, *she*, the *other*, was the lucky one, the one with the diamond tiara, while her own share was heavy copper ornaments! These bit into her skin like thorns and did nothing to satisfy her or make her feel beautiful!

## Chapter XXVII

*B*airagi-thakur, his forehead decorated with sandalwood paste, was doing the morning rounds, singing the dawn matins: 'You are a jeweller, but you did not recognize the jewel of old; you selected the copper and rejected molten gold!'

Manorama brought a fistful of rice to give the Vaishnav mendicant, but he stopped her and said, 'I only take rice from the baby Krishna, Gopal of this house, Maa! Where is my little boy today?'

Mano put the rice aside and said in a small voice, 'He has gone to his aunt's house in Calcutta—he is due to return today.'

'Then I will come tomorrow morning and take the rice from his hands.'

Manorama was getting tired pacing to and fro, when suddenly a carriage rumbled to a stop in front of the house. Ajit jumped down from the carriage, ran to his mother and hugged her, 'Oh Maa! My Maa! Have you been waiting here all these days? You should have come with me!'

Manorama hugged the boy, kissed him all over and said through happy tears, 'Did you miss me then?'

Ajit smiled shyly. 'Yes I did, Maa.'

The two relaxed gradually after the initial excitement, and Manorama asked, 'How was Ashima's groom?'

'Quite nice—he is much fairer than Asu-di.'

'And Ashima? Does she look like your Pishima or Pishimoshai?'

'Maa, you haven't seen Pishimoshai—how did you know that he is better looking than Pishima?'

His mother laughed and asked, 'What are all these things?'
'Pishima bought me this trunk. She wouldn't listen!'

Jagua, Sarat's servant, had accompanied the boy back home. After removing the trunk and other things from the carriage and placing them inside, he went to wash up in the nearby pond. Manorama was dying to ask her son the one question that was all-important to her, but hesitated and said, 'Go wash yourself and then eat something, Ajit!'

'I cannot eat anything now, Maa. Pishima made me eat my fill before I left. Come, let me show you all the gifts.'

'Later! Now—'

'No, you must see them immediately!' Ajit pulled his mother's hand and took her to where the trunk was placed. 'Look, this is my key!' He took out a shiny new key ring tied to the corner of a silk handkerchief from the pocket of his pink silk punjabi, showed her two old polished keys and unlocked the steel trunk with one of them.

'Oh! What has your Pishima done! She has packed the entire city of Calcutta into this trunk!'

'It is not just Pishima, my Thakuma was also there—I used to sleep with her at night. Maa, why does Thakuma cry so much? And she used to caress me all the time, even in front of the other boys—I felt terribly embarrassed!'

Manorama's own eyes filled with tears. She looked down at her feet and tried to control herself. Meanwhile, the display had begun, 'Look at these books—*Ramayana, Mahabharata, Du-bochhorer Sakha, Saathi*. This here is a book of stories called *Fairy Tales*, and this one is *Robinson Crusoe*. And look, Thakuma got her house-manager to get me these toys—red and white horses, a cycle with a spring, a steam engine, and see how this cat runs? I can't tell you how amused I felt,

Mamoni! They must have thought that I was a child! In fact, I suggested that I should gift these toys to the children, but would Pishima listen? She said, "Why, are you too old to play with toys? Let me see, do you have grey hairs already!" Didi gave me this big doll, a present from her in-laws-to-be! See, she is sleeping with her eyes closed! Now look, if she stands, her eyes open! Maa, I will give this to Nitai-mama's daughter, Khuki, okay?'

Manorama was looking at her son's childish 'wealth' with wet eyes and an amused smile. It brought back memories of the toys that her in-laws had sent at her own wedding, her own gaye holud tatwa.

'Look Ma—a silk shirt! It is nowhere near cold, but here is a light sweater. And here are a few punjabis—these are printed cotton, this one is made of serge cloth, two are gorod silk, this is an alpaca one, and this coat is made from very expensive silk! Oh my God, she has given me four dhotis with zari borders! And all these other dhotis—what will I do with so many? See, she has given me two pairs of shoes! And so many pairs of socks! Maa, you would be amazed at Calcutta's shops! Sudhi, Montu—each of them possess three or four pairs of shoes. I told them that I have no need for so many. But would they listen? See, Didi has been sending me clothes for Bhai Phonta for the past three years—they are all intact, none are torn! They were astonished when I told them that!'

'Aju, where all did you go? Where did you meet your Thakuma?'

'Why, I met her in Pishima's house. She was staying there for a few days. Now let me see—I went to the zoo, the museum, Eden Gardens, the bioscope, Gol Dighi, Garer Math, Presidency College, Mamoni! When I am older, I am going to study at

Presidency College! I will *not* study here. I am telling you right now!'

Manorama laughed. 'First, get older!'

'I will join college in less than three years! Didi-ma—have you just come home? You *knew* that I was returning today!'

'Come to me, my wealth! The house was dark without you— how could I stay indoors? What is your brother-in-law like?'

'Good. Look, my Thakuma sent all these things!'

Durgasundari immediately turned away in evident dissatisfaction and said in a grave voice, 'Show it to your mother.' Manorama looked at her from the corner of one eye and gauged her displeasure at the mention of the word 'Thakuma'. Her face was stormy; it looked like the sky overcast with the gloomy clouds of misplaced expectation. She was a mother after all; she had sincerely wished and prayed that the boy's father might have a change of heart on seeing his son; but this was a secret hope, unknown to even her daughter. Manorama therefore could not understand her mother's rage and felt mortified.

Manorama was still waiting with bated breath for a specific bit of news, but her son did not volunteer to give away any. He told her that a servant from that house, Kartik, and a maidservant, Kadam, had both gifted money when they first saw their Khoka-babu's face. Thakuma had given him a gold wristwatch and five gold guineas for the same auspicious purpose. Ajit said, 'Those people are kind of stupid; here I have been promoted to Class IX, and they still call me *khoka*, little boy!'

The old household manager had given him a few inexpensive toys, a couple of mill-made white dhotis and two rupees in cash. But the *master* of the house? Had he given him nothing? If *he* had, surely Ajit would have mentioned it by now? When his father had turned Manorama out of the house, he had stipulated that Aurobindo should not keep any relations with *her*, and Manorama had never attempted to make him break his vow. But even the revered Sri Rama had not been able to deny or neglect his sons! It was related in Kalidasa's *Abhijnanashakuntalam* that when King Dushyanta saw his and Shakuntala's son, Sarvadaman, from afar, his paternal instinct had filled him with craving, even though he did not recognize either his wife or son because of Rishi Durvasa's curse on Shakuntala. Her father-in-law could have said anything in anger; he was the patriarch and had the right to command, but did Ajit's *father* not recognize his own *son*? Would he become emotionally bankrupt if he gave this little bit, his son's right, a small dewdrop to the one begging for just a mite of recognition? Or, heaven knows, had he not been granted permission to do even this?

'What is this, son? Wrapped in tissue paper?'

'Oh, I forgot!' He unwrapped the paper and took out a photograph stuck on a bit of cardboard. Manorama's eyes opened wide in suppressed excitement as she looked spellbound at her husband's photograph. Could Manorama ever forget that face despite the changes wrought by time?

'You look so much like him, Ajit.'

'I did not see him, Maa.'

'Did not see him?'

She asked this question with so much surprise that Ajit, who had not wondered about it earlier, now realized that indeed this was something that should have intrigued him.

'On the wedding day—was he not—?'

Ajit shook his head.

Manorama's face immediately darkened. She trembled all over, 'Is he alright? Are you hiding something from me, Ajit?'

Certain things that he had overheard, some quickly

suppressed words about his father, began to coalesce in Ajit's innocent mind. Something had gone wrong—of that he was now sure. He told his mother, 'I am positive he is okay. He had to leave suddenly for Bhagalpur because of a legal emergency—that is why he could not come to the wedding.' He had believed this excuse at the time, but now he remembered that Kartik, Sarada, Hari's mother, the manager moshai, Chaturiya, Chhottu Singh and other servants from his father's house had come for the wedding; they had told Pishima that the lady of the house was unwell and the master had left for far-off Bhagalpur. Pishima had stood stunned and silent, but the others who overheard the exchange had begun to discuss the matter animatedly. Shortly thereafter, his new friend and cousin, Mohit, had cornered him and said that his father left Calcutta because he feared bumping into Ajit—there was no other reason for his departure. He had not believed it at the time and had heatedly argued, 'That is not true! Baba has a pending case in court and could not come. Do you think that he would not have come to see me otherwise?'

Although the two had become close in the course of these few days, Mohit got angry at Ajit's denial of the truth. He had been trying to open Ajit's eyes to the facts; instead, it had opened his mouth in anger! He retorted, 'Oh! Your father cannot sleep because of you! If he wants to see you, why does he not go to Burdwan?'

Ajit had answered plaintively, 'How can he go there? He has so much work!'

Mohit had said, 'You are stupid! As if fathers don't go to meet their children even if they are overloaded with work? All fathers have work! And in any case, what does your father actually do? He had a job earlier, but he left it about two years ago and now he just sits at home! He travels around the whole country for pleasure all the time! The truth is, your stepmother—'

Meanwhile, Sudhir, another cousin, had arrived. He looked at Mohit warningly and said, 'Mejda! What has mother told us all? Shall I tell Ma?'

'No, no, brother, please don't tell her! I can't imagine how Ajit has got promoted! He is tremendously stupid. You tell me that you are in the same class as I—well, let us see how you solve this mathematical question. The three medians of a triangle meet at one point—come on, let's see how you do it!'

But Ajit remained distracted. Seeing him thus, Mohit had relented and said indulgently, 'Forget it! Don't even try! Are you actually in Class IX? You are only eleven years old. I am considered a good student—but I am 14 and am in Class IX, too!'

Mohit's words kept resounding in his head. Whenever anyone commented on the absence of the bride's maternal uncle, he remembered Mohit's impish smile when he said, 'If he wants to see you, why does he not go to Burdwan? All fathers have work!'

But Manorama believed Ajit—Aurobindo had gone to Bhagalpur for legal work. She sighed in relief: 'Thank God! It was his niece's wedding, and he is her only maternal uncle—he would never have missed it if it had not been urgent! Especially because he is ever so fond of this sister and her children! For a second, I had feared the worst!' Her usual good nature and internal happiness helped her regain her composure when she heard that her husband was not ailing or ill.

## Chapter XXVIII

Sarat never visited her brother's house at Howrah after Ashima's wedding. Aurobindo, too, did not go to meet her after that calamitous day; the separation caused such a rift between the brother and sister that it squeezed out all pleasure from living; he felt like a hermit surviving joylessly in a forest. Sarat, with her incessant chatter, her kindness and generosity, and capricious admonishments had been his one source of peace, of relaxation. He had suffered much in his lifetime; just when the spring of youth had made his desires blossom, a relentless gust of hot, dry, frenzied breeze had blown through the budding flower-garden of his life and shredded the flowers before they could fully bloom. But even that seemed less cruel now, in comparison to the parting of the siblings. Aurobindo remembered Ashima, Sarat's eldest child, who had more or less grown up in their house, tended to by none other than Manorama, on whose lap she had learnt her first lisping words—that child had been the apple of Aurobindo's eyes, his living doll—and he had been prevented from blessing *her* on this first auspicious event of her life! He knew that Sarat would never forgive him. And what face did he have to ask her for forgiveness? Also, would his *mother* ever pardon her daughter-in-law, Brajarani, for her appalling behaviour? The matriarch had returned home from Sarat's house after the wedding and had not spoken a single word to either her son or his wife till today. Brajarani later learnt from her mother-in-law's maidservant that it was only Ajit who had come for the wedding, not the co-wife. While she felt relieved, she could not understand why she had reacted so strongly to the presence of such a little boy! As usual, she tried to shirk off blame and told her husband one day, '*You* always exaggerate everything! I may have said something in anger, but that doesn't mean that I asked you to *leave* the state!'

Aurobindo replied in a toneless voice, 'Oh! So, you really *meant* it when you wanted that poor boy dead! Don't you remember, you put a curse on his *head* if I went to the wedding?'

This was hitting below the belt! Brajarani flared up, 'Will you murder someone if I ask you to?'

After several days of silence, in another part of the house Aurobindo's mother called him to her room, and asked in a single breath, 'I too have a share in my husband's hard-earned property and wealth, isn't that so?'

Her son replied, 'Certainly! Half of father's property and wealth is yours.'

'Do I have the right to dispose of it, gift it or sell it?'

Aurobindo stared unblinking at his mother and said, 'Of course, you possess the right to gift it or sell it.'

His mother said, 'Baba, I don't want to live on your handouts anymore. Please give me actual possession over what I possess— what your father has left me. I want nothing from you.'

Aurobindo had never heard his mother saying anything even mildly critical to anyone, let alone him—was this the *same* indulgent, loving mother he had known all his life? He suppressed a deep sigh and asked, 'Do you want it all in cash, or do you want a portion of the zamindari too?'

'Do what is opportune. I do not wish to inconvenience you. Draw out the papers in my name in any manner that suits you.'

Two days after that, on returning from Sarat's house, she sent word to Aurobindo through the house-manager that she had heard from her son-in-law, Jagadindra, that she had no rights whatsoever to her husband's property. According to contemporary law, a mother inherited one portion of the property only if she had several sons and the property had to be divided among them. Aurobindo's mother added that she did not wish to beg for his pity—she had enough ornaments to see her through the rest of her life. She wanted nothing more.

Meanwhile, Aurobindo, weary with all that had happened, decided to visit Darjeeling along with a servant. But Brajarani began a fast and forced him to let her accompany him. The hill-station, Darjeeling, is situated high in the magnificent Himalayas and is known for its serene, misty beauty. Is there anyone in this world whose heart's turbulence is not calmed by the majesty and peace of these mountains? The many fires that were burning within Aurobindo's disturbed mind gradually cooled as he opened his being to the ice-cold mountain winds of that snow-city. But alas! Despite the momentary descent of calm and tranquillity...

Fate had yet another blow in store for him. Unknown to him, the rift between the siblings initiated at Ashima's wedding was actually the beginning of a permanent separation. At the end of spring, on a sultry evening foreboding the oncoming heat of summer, Saratsashi's eyes closed forever as the last rays of the sun faded into night.

She had been a bit under the weather for sometime, but neither the doctor nor her husband had seen any signs that her illness could be fatal. When Aurobindo, who was still in Darjeeling, got the news that she was unwell, his dearest sister was actually on her deathbed, that Saratsashi, that autumn moon as her name depicted, bright and loving like the full moon in autumn, was about to be completely eclipsed—not partial, not penumbral, but a total eclipse! It was unbelievable! But Sarat was so spent with disease that it was difficult to recognize her. Aurobindo rushed back from the hills to meet her one last time. 'My Didimoni! My dearest sister! How can you depart forever leaving this spear in my heart?'

Sarat's nature had not changed even though death hovered nearby to embrace her. She gave a slight mocking smile, which brought a hint of redness to her pale faded lips, and retorted, 'Why, are you going to fight with me about this too?'

Aurobindo was too distraught for a repartee. The doctor had announced the previous day that there was nothing further that he could do and had advised the relatives to pray to God. This, of course, was unacceptable to her family—how could they give up without trying till the very end? They had brought a kaviraj who practised traditional medicine, and he had prescribed *mriganabhi makaradhwaj* as a last resort. She had shown some minor improvement, but their hopes were soon dashed as her condition began to deteriorate.

Aurobindo had not met his sister for three months and now this! Oh, cruel laughter of fate! He hid his face on her breast. This seemed to constrict her breathing even further; her heartbeat slowed and her eyes dimmed. Seeing her fading away, her husband rushed forward. 'Chhoto-babu! Chhoto-babu! Think of the patient! Calm yourself!'

Aurobindo replied, 'Do you believe in heaven? Or have you left that nonsense far behind? Then why cry?'

Everyone was deeply affected by Sarat's untimely death. Brajarani had never been too close to her, but now she only remembered that Sarat had been very dear to her husband and he was sunk in deep sorrow. This anguished her and she was shocked into despair.

# Chapter XXIX

Aurobindo's mother had spent over two-thirds of her life in comfort and relative happiness; she got to realize the full meaning of sorrow in the remaining days of her life. She had deep misgivings that her family's current misfortunes could be the result of the heart-wrenching sighs of an innocent, wronged woman, someone whose life they had devastated. Although she was intensely afraid of the vagaries of fate, she knew that there was nothing she could do to appease providence. And Saratsashi's death had devastated her. This daughter had been special to her; Sarat too had adored her mother. She was distraught at the sorrow of her daughter's motherless children and her simple, grieving son-in-law. After returning from their house, she wept and told her son, 'I wish to give up worldly pleasures and live by myself. Please arrange for me to go to Kashi.'

She was adamant and Aru, defeated, made arrangements for her stay in Varanasi, where many Bengali widows devoted their last days to prayer and meditation. It was planned that he would accompany her on the journey. He was surprised to find Brajarani too packing her bags.

He asked her, 'What are you doing?'

Braja replied, 'I too will go.'

Aurobindo responded with a deep sigh. Braja had requested Sarat's husband to send their youngest daughter, just over a year old, with them. Jagadindra had agreed reluctantly, so this motherless baby too was part of the entourage. For once, her mother-in-law was pleased with Brajarani.

The grieving mother found some solace in prayers on reaching Kashi. They met their family *kul guru,* who resided in Varanasi. Aurobindo's mother spent her time listening to his sermons, visiting temples for nearly eight months before falling ill herself; and after about a month, she too achieved what she had come for—*Kashi Prapti*—and departed for the heavenly abode. Both Aru and Braja were by her side when she was on her deathbed. They had returned to Calcutta for a month during the pujas but came back immediately on hearing that she was unwell. Brajarani had done all she could to make her mother-in-law's last days comfortable. But she had been rather upset at hearing one piece of news from the old maidservant, Kadam: Manorama had come with her own mother and son during the puja holidays to meet her mother-in-law at the latter's insistence. Durgasundari had refused to enter the house and stayed with an acquaintance in Narodghat. Manorama, her mother-in-law and Kadam had gone to visit Durgasundari one afternoon and found her immersed in prayers. They waited for an hour, but she had not opened her eyes to even acknowledge them. Manorama had been extremely embarrassed, but there was little she could do. She herself had no such airs. The maidservant waxed eloquent on how she had cared for her mother-in-law, treating her like a deity! And what was *she* like? Manorama? She was like a goddess, way above simple human beings in looks and behaviour!

Braja listened to all this and felt deeply jealous. Whenever she went to do something for her mother-in-law, she sarcastically thought, *After being treated as a deity, will she like what I have to offer?* And of course, this affected the quality of her caregiving. But she also remembered that young boy, his bright looks, steady like the planet Mars on a clear night. Although she was very curious, she could not find it in herself to question anyone about him. However, some information came through unasked: 'Maa wanted Bouma and her son to stay on here with her. But the boy goes to school, so *they* did not agree. When they finally left, how Maa wept! As long as she had not seen them, it did not hurt her so much! People say that the interest on money is dearer than the money itself! And this boy! Is he comparable? Now if there was another child in the house, maybe it would have been different! But your husband's family has no other heir!'

Kadam was pattering on in this fashion but Braja had stopped listening. What she, an uneducated woman from another caste, a mere servant, had just said about family pride and descent rang chaotically in her ears, especially 'but your husband's family has no other heir!'

After his mother's last rites had been completed, Aurobindo did not return home immediately and instead, he travelled to several pilgrimage sites, Vindhyachal, Prayag, Ayodhya, spending a few days here or a few weeks there. It should be added that Sarat's girl-child, whom Brajarani had undertaken to bring up, caught pneumonia during the cold winter months and also departed from this earth to join her mother in the great hereafter. Braja had been overwhelmed with sorrow and repentance at the sudden death of this child—she had felt the stirrings of motherhood in caring for the little girl, and now this tragedy! She was constantly reminded of Khuki's beauty, smile and laughter, the many small accomplishments of a child learning to walk and talk—and above all, the word 'Maa' that she had begun lisping! She could find no solace anywhere. But the human mind is unpredictable—fresh hope replaces lost hope, and desire manifests itself again and again. When something new substitutes the old, the mind tries to swap old sorrows for new beginnings.

It argues with itself that the old will never be forgotten, but there is no point in weeping endlessly over something that will never return, so why should one disturb the peace of the dear departed with one's tears? Also, is it good to allow one's mind to indulge in sorrow alone without thinking of those who are still here, alive and well in this world?

∞

## Chapter XXX

There was nothing much to celebrate during the next Durga Puja. Aurobindo and his wife returned to their empty house just before the beginning of the festival. Brajarani had run into a childhood friend, Milon, who currently faced the dire circumstances of poverty, in Allahabad. Milon had a beautiful baby daughter, who touched Braja's newly awakened motherly instincts. On returning to Calcutta, she sent the child a dress and a pair of gold bangles as puja gifts. The poverty-stricken couple had declared themselves unworthy of such expensive gifts and wished to return the bangles. In reply, Brajarani had written her friend a letter:

Dear Milon,

Now I understand that love is worthless. Only the infallible strictures of societal behaviour remain. Is there any difference between you and me? You are the daughter of a genteel Kayastha family and so am I. Your husband's surname is Dutta; my husband's family surname is Basu. Both families are equal in Hindu caste status. (I have told you that I am ready to arrange a marriage between your daughter and my younger brother.) You are not lower to us in family status, caste, or in the eyes of Hindu society. The only difference between us is wealth. Why are you making such a big thing of this? What I am learning through life is that a wealthy person is the biggest wrongdoer in this world because he is rich; since people know he is moneyed, they assume that he has no need for anything else. How can I explain to anyone that if the chains binding us are made of gold, they still remain chains?

If I was the mother of a son today and I requested the hand of your daughter, Manosh, for my son, would you have refused those bangles and humiliated me? Just because God has denied me the boon of a child, you are rebuffing me and denying me the simple happiness of presenting your child with these meagre gifts? It is actually not as surprising as it seems, because it is true that she whom God has forsaken will also be forsaken by fellow humans! If only Khuku was alive today!

Yours
Brajarani

On the fifth day of the pujas, Brajarani had gifted clothes to all persons to whom she was obligated—the household servants and minor relatives. She was preparing the presents for her parental home as well as Sarat's and Usha's families when Usha arrived with her youngest son. Braja remarked, 'You have come, sister! I was about to send someone for you.'

Usha had been disturbed about something, but perked up on seeing the gifts. She picked up a sari and, realizing that it was for her, said enthusiastically, 'What a beautiful sari! Gold thread and silver border! Is it very expensive, Boudi? It could not have cost less than 200 or 250 rupees! Why did you not get the jacket stitched? I could have worn it on Bijoya Dashami.'

'I bought it in Kashi and we have been travelling. There was no time to get it stitched. I got this velvet suit for your son, Khoka—this was made in Kashi itself. Take a look—is it too large?'

'When something is *that* expensive, it is good if it is

oversized—he can wear it for a longer period. Did you get a similar one made for Didi's younger son too? Ashima's sari is just like mine! Boudi, these things cost a lot! Didn't Dada get angry?'

Brajarani became grave at her sister-in-law's words: 'Why should he be angry? Who will enjoy our wealth after us? For whom should *we* save?'

Usha was a mother and fully enjoyed the joys of motherhood; she therefore realized the agony of childlessness. She also appreciated Brajarani's circumstances and remained silent—she did not have a child, but her co-wife, the one who had been sent away deceitfully, did!

After a moment, Brajarani smiled in embarrassment and said, 'I have more or less everything under control. The guru, the priest, their dhoti–chadar are ready; all the listed items needed for the puja have been bought. I had bought similar saris for you, me and my elder sister-in-law, as usual—but this time, I will give it to her daughter. There is just one thing left—I have not sent *them* anything yet, because I do not have their address...' Leaving the sentence incomplete, Brajarani gave a slight smile.

Usha was intrigued and asked, 'Who are you talking about, Boudi?'

Brajarani hesitated before asking, 'What kind of saris and clothes should I send to Burdwan?'

Usha was astonished, 'What are you saying, Boudi? Sending clothes to Burdwan?'

'Don't you have close relatives in Burdwan?'

'*We*? Who do we have in Burdwan?'

Brajarani was getting irritated by this time. She asked heatedly, 'Why are you putting on such a farce? *You* don't know who is there in Burdwan? Your nephew and his mother live there!'

Usha raised her eyebrows, rounded her eyes, and said in a surprised manner, '*I* don't have any nephew! How will *I* know who you are talking about?'

Now Brajarani became really angry. She said animatedly, 'Don't you remember that your elder sister always sent gifts to your nephew during Bhai Phonta, and her daughter sent sandalwood paste for the ceremony? Don't you also know that last year, your mother sent for *that* daughter-in-law and her grandson when she was in Kashi and blessed them profusely? So why should *you* reject them? Your sister acknowledged that she was the boy's aunt—and if *she* was not ashamed to call him her nephew, why should *you*?'

'She revolted against our father's decision, and *see* what happened to her—she got her just rewards for disobeying him! Everyone is not like her! Have you ever seen or heard me taking *their* side in all these years?'

Usha too was losing her temper. She thought that now that her mother and Sarat were no more, Brajarani was taking out her ire on *her* for *their* 'misdemeanours'. But Brajarani became furious at Usha's words: 'Listen, Ushi! Don't you *dare* speak ill of the dead! You are still hardly old enough to be called more than a girl, and you think *you* know everything! Now *you* all decide whether he is your nephew or not, what do *I* care? Your mother and sister sent them gifts—I thought that it was my *duty* to send them presents, otherwise what are they to *me*?'

Usha replied animatedly, '*I* have no such desire—*I* have never sent them anything, *never*!' But she wanted to ease the tension and continued with a smile, 'If *you* want to send them gifts, why, go ahead!'

Hearing this, Brajarani's rage deflated into something she

herself could not understand. She sighed, 'Why should *I* send them anything?'

'But you have a reason—*you* are his mother, too!'

Brajarani gave Usha such a surprised look that Usha felt astonished. She knew that Braja was trying to convey something, but she failed to fathom what. She remembered earlier times when the very mention of her co-wife and stepson so infuriated her sister-in-law that Usha had been frightened into seeking excuses to escape from her presence. It was, therefore, not surprising that she did not now understand Brajarani's feelings.

Brajarani's face had momentarily lit up with hope at the word 'mother'; it looked like the moon's reflection undulating dazzlingly on the currents of a rapidly flowing river. Within seconds, however, that brightness was replaced by a mysterious gloom, as though the playful moon had been hidden by dark monsoon clouds. Within the course of those few seconds, a bolt of lightning seemed to have passed through her, electrifying every nerve, every sinew with violent longing, leaving her exhausted. She said in a tired voice, 'As if a stepmother is a mother! Can a dry bed be called a river?'

Why did she say this? Was she trying to convince herself or telling off Usha? Who knows? She gave a harsh little laugh after this—but was she laughing or crying? She got up quickly, wiped her eyes surreptitiously, and tried to change the topic: 'Just *look* at us! There is so much work to be done. Help me take out the pots and pans that will be required for cooking during the festival.'

But this matter did not end here. The next day was sashti, the beginning of the ritualistic celebration of Goddess Maa Durga's advent on earth, the most important religious and social festival for Bengalis. The old and young, rich and poor, men and women, all forgot their differences and joined in the prayers and festivities equally. As the conch shells sounded and the clanging of cymbals and tinkling of bells marked the ceremonious, ritualistic initiation of the goddess, and young boys from nearby houses in new clothes thronged to the site, Brajarani could contain herself no longer. She conceded defeat to herself and realized that she no longer had any desire to be mean-spirited. She repeatedly entered the inner sanctum of the house looking for her husband, but he seemed to have become a rare commodity on that day and could not be found.

Finally, she decided to go to the outer sitting room and found Aurobindo sitting alone on an easy-chair, reading a book. Before he could say anything, she hurriedly began a well-rehearsed speech without any introduction, 'Look, I have done everything that was required of me except sending gifts to Burdwan. Maybe you can tell the manager moshai what to do—the post office is open, so please send it today.'

Aurobindo was taken aback and hid his face behind his book while trying to control himself before replying, 'Why, I don't think it is necessary to send anything.' He pretended to read, testing the limits of his wife's tolerance.

She said, 'You *don't* think it is necessary? Okay, fine. My duty was to remind you and my responsibility is over, do what you think is *your* duty. But don't blame me later, any of you!'

'If nobody has faulted you for 14 years, no one will blame you today either! But one thing is certain—if someone comes in here and sees you standing without veiling your head and face, they will call *you* shameless!'

'I don't care about your antique social norms! But let me inform you that it was not *my* responsibility through these last 14 years. My parents-in-law decided who to send gifts to. But this year, it is *my* duty and *that* is why I asked. I have purchased the clothes. If you wish, please tell the manager—he will do whatever is necessary.'

'There is no need. Go inside please, Rani—Amar Mitra will be arriving soon. Chaturiya! Have the gentlemen arrived?'

Chaturiya came to the door and stood with his arms blocking the doorway, 'Yes, sir!' Perceiving that there was no way that she could talk to her husband on this topic now, Brajarani left for the inner sanctum, mentally cursing both Chaturiya and Amar Mitra for cutting short her discussion with Aurobindo. The feeling of annoyance at something she could not quite pinpoint remained, and she moved from room to room, picking fault with puja arrangements and ticking off people for imagined slip-ups, irritating others, but feeling no relief herself.

## Chapter XXXI

Ajit and his mother were among the many who had been deeply affected by Sarat's untimely death. No one from his father's family had initially acknowledged Ajit's birth; his grandfather had even questioned his credentials as Aurobindo's son. But Ajit had been blissfully unaware of the facts and most of his life was spent in misty uncertainty. And then, one day his aunt had come into his life like Goddess Lakshmi. The dilapidated house had brightened at the touch of her feet, and many pent-up painful feelings were assuaged at the touch of her hand. When the news came that his aunt was no more, his sorrow knew no bounds. Seeing him inconsolable, Manorama could not find it in herself to cry as she tried to pacify *his* grief—he was like a small creeper that had been crushed by the onset of a violent storm.

When they were summoned to Kashi by Manorama's mother-in-law during the previous pujas, she did not wish to go and had told Ajit, 'Write to them that you have to study for your examinations during the holidays.'

But Ajit wanted to go. He had just begun to enjoy the love of his father's family and was seeking any opportunity to be reunited with them. He protested, 'Mamoni, you know that I am fully prepared for the examinations.' And then, he tried to persuade his maternal grandmother, 'Didimoni! You have always wanted to go on a pilgrimage to Kashi!'

Durgasundari was tempted. She replied, 'I would love to go—but where is the money?'

Ajit was happy to finally arrive in Kashi. When he met his paternal grandmother, they grieved over Sarat for the next few days. But the presence of the boy and his mother gave her some relief in what she knew at heart were her penultimate days. The loss of his Pishima oppressed the boy, but he was after all a child, and as the days went by, he became interested in his new surroundings. Durgasundari, of course, did not stay with them; she took up residence in the house of a person from her village and soon set off to visit nearby pilgrimages with some women friends who lived in Kashi.

Following the evening prayers, Aurobindo's mother had the habit of lying down on a mat on the rooftop or the first floor veranda. Ajit, meanwhile, would have lit a lamp and sat down with a book, but he would lift his eyes repeatedly in anticipation of his grandmother's arrival. The moment he spied a corner of her pristine white sari, he would put his book away and come close to the old woman, sometimes embracing her shrunken neck with his young hands. His grandmother could hardly bear the intense happiness of the present; her voice would become heavy with the grief of the impending loss of this newly found bliss. She would sometimes mentally address her dead husband, 'Oh my dearest, do you realize what you have done! This boy is the fruit of all my prayers! *Whose* curse has deprived him of so much that he is nothing more than a wayside beggar now?' She would bless the boy with all the goodwill she had in her stock. She wanted to wipe off all his future pain, grief and obstacles as she gently stroked his hair and face. She whispered through trembling lips, 'Vishwanath! Vishwanath!' Ajit would lie smiling silently, basking in her love. Manorama used to come up to massage her mother-in-law's feet. The currents of adoration between the two brought tears of joy to her eyes.

This was the first time in Aurobindo's mother's life that she had experienced so much happiness. She had spent many afternoons with Sarat's sons and daughters but baulked whenever she tried to think of them as her own. She had, of course, felt immediate remorse and prayed to Maa Shasti, the giver of children: 'No, no, keep them safe! But it is true that when I die, only *he* has the right to give me absolution, and I have been forced to deny him! How will I ever forgive myself?' Perhaps that Great Someone up there had heard her prayers, and was granting her what was her due in her last days!

Ajit used to read the Mahabharata or the Bhagavad Gita to his grandmother on most evenings, but this was just an excuse to talk to her. He had never found such a captive listener! His maternal grandmother had listened to him when he was very young; but now, she was nowhere to be found when he wanted to talk about books! It was true that his mother was indulgent but she listened only for short durations. She would say after a few minutes, 'Oh stop! Do you think I understand all that you are saying?' And then she would smile and leave. But *this* grandmother never cut him off! Why, one could discuss any topic with her—geometry, algebra, geography! She would listen attentively and neither person would ever lose enthusiasm—one's enthusiasm to talk and the other's to admire him while he spoke! In fact, she would kiss him on his head and say, 'When did you learn all this, Dada? You are so young!' And then she would add with less fervour, 'Your father was like that too.'

She generally avoided mentioning the father to his son, but Ajit was always on the lookout for even the slightest mention of Aurobindo. If the topic of his father ever came up, the conversation went somewhat like this:

'At what age did my father pass his entrance examinations, Thakuma?'

'Fifteen, I think. You will pass it one year earlier than he did, Dadamoni!'

'Well, Thakuma, Baba received scholarships of 20 rupees on passing the entrance, 25 rupees for FA, and 50 rupees on clearing the BA examinations, right? He topped his BA examinations and received three gold medals too! He secured the highest rank in the MA examinations. Then why did he fail his law examinations three times? Maybe he never really liked legal studies? I will never study law! I will take the MA examinations and then try for the Premchand Raychand Scholarship. After that, I will do a PhD—will you like that? Baba was a good student—why did he never try for the PRS? I am sure he would have got it! It is just because he didn't like legal studies—'

His Thakuma gave a little sigh and replied, 'Yes, your father always stood first in class since he was just a small boy. He failed the first time in law, but I don't understand how he failed again... It is God's judgement!'

Ajit was intrigued by the last words—'God's judgement'—and pestered his grandmother for an answer one day. But all he got in reply were a few drops of tears, and thus never presumed to ask her again. However, he queried her about his father's medals and other achievements—which medal was how big; which books did he receive as prizes; which deserving institution had he donated his first scholarship money to? He was astonished when he learnt that this money had never been donated, and began to draw up a list of institutions to which he would donate his first scholarship instalment in case he ever got one. But he was aware that there was something that held his grandmother back—as though there was an iron hand stopping her from saying *something*. What was this *something*? Although Ajit was totally inexperienced in gauging family issues, he was intelligent and observant beyond his years. The more he got to know about his paternal home, the more he began to guess at mysteries surrounding the family. He began to suspect the cruel truth, and this threatened to shatter his childhood peace of mind. His mother had taught him to respect his father and he himself had put him on a pedestal. But now, certain niggling doubts began to gather in his mind, so much so that it was impossible to think of his father now in the same manner that he had till then.

One late evening, the two friends of asymmetrical ages had climbed onto the roof. The full moon was just two days away; the near-circular moon was shining calmly through broken, flitting clouds, lighting up the golden flag that was flying on the pinnacle of a nearby temple. The monsoon-heavy waters of the Ganges flowed by one side of the house. It was not the pure white waters described by poets; there was a touch of saffron, as though the river was an ascetic woman lying at the feet of Lord Vishwanath. Why was Maa Ganga dressed in saffron, the colour of renunciation? Was she angry with her husband and therefore drawn to asceticism? And was that why her waters were washing ashes away from the burning ghats of Manikarnika's ever-burning pyres and coating her watery arms with the dusty remains of those who had departed for the next world?

The evening cast its murky shadow on the grandmother's mood as well, but Ajit pattered on as usual. Out of nowhere, he suddenly asked her, 'Thakuma, has my father really forsaken us?' Ajit looked with unblinking eyes at his grandmother while his arms enfolded her.

His grandmother was shocked! She slipped from his arms to the ground, semiconscious. It was with great difficulty that she struggled to regain control of her senses, while Ajit called out in panic, 'Thakuma! Are you alright?'

She sat up on the rain-soaked wet floor of the roof with Ajit's help and wept like a child as she said, 'My Dada! My jewel!' She struck her forehead with her hands and cried out like a madwoman, 'Oh my husband! If only I too had died! Oh Vishwanath! Could you not have given me a mite of space at your feet, so that I did not have to answer this question?'

Ajit was stunned at the unexpected reaction of his grandmother, but it did not assuage his thirst for the truth. His desire to know followed him around like a hungry python with yawing jaws, demanding answers.

ಬಿ

## Chapter XXXII

Returning to more recent times, after the Durga Puja and Bhai Phonta celebrations were over, Aurobindo and Brajarani again left on another round of travel. Braja requested Jagadindra for another of Sarat's daughters to look after; this time, it was the pretty Bela. She had promised herself earlier that she would never ask for anyone's child ever again, but she found herself unable to keep this resolve. After all, one had to find some recourse, some reason to stay alive.

This time they found a nice house in Kashi in a narrow lane close to the Vishwanath Temple. Facing their house was a bungalow, which was always busy with visitors from morning till night. Brajarani initially speculated that it must belong to either a lawyer or a doctor, but on enquiry, she found that it belonged to an astrologer.

After further enquiry, it was discovered that the gentleman was competent at what was known as Bhrigu Shastra, based on the *Bhrigu Samhita*. In ancient times, instead of claiming expertise over a subject, men would hide behind the veil of a mysterious guru, from whom they declared that they had inherited knowledge passed on over generations through a succession of teachers; they would merge their own identity into that of *that* early patriarch, the rishi who initiated that branch of knowledge, to which successors added their own data. Some Bhargava or Bhrigu had started writing the *Bhrigu Samhita*, a book of horoscopes, and Bhrigu Shastra had emerged from that: it was a combination of astrology and *trikalajny*, or knowledge of the past, present and future that was outlined as horoscope in the ancient manuscript. The entire *samhita* or set of books had never been found—like so many of India's jewels, this set of books had disappeared under the oppressive feet of foreign rulers. This particular shastra had been recovered much later from the kingdom of Nepal. Not so long back, during the time of the Sepoy Mutiny, a Brahmin from Kashi or its neighbourhood, fearing oppression from both the attackers and defenders, fled the country; *he* had apparently been in possession of the *Bhrigu Samhita*. A portion of the book was lost while fleeing; of the sections that still remained with him, he had gifted one portion to his son and the other to his son-in-law.

Now, this gentleman across the lane was none other than the son-in-law. It was reported that his portion of the divided book contained 400,000 birth horoscopes. It was rumoured that if one took one's zodiac birth-chart to him, he would hunt through the thousands of zodiac charts in his possession and find a combination that matched yours to the letter. Apparently, munis and rishis over centuries had used their mathematical skills to draw out millions of permutations and combinations of zodiac signs, which was added to the *Samhita*. Along with that, the verses foretelling one's future course were also attached to that particular zodiac birth-chart. Important events assumed to have occurred in past lives were summarized in these verses, but the focus was on the present and the future—otherwise, how would the modern-day Bhrigu be able to target the modern man? This Bhrigu would explain the effect of the position of certain planets in the personal zodiac signs of the horoscope of the seeker of advice, which sorrows were inevitable and which could be restricted by following certain formulae; he would discuss these with reference to the *Samhita,* claiming that everything was predicted there. He would further justify through the books which misdemeanour in a past life was responsible for certain misfortunes in this present life and what means of penitence were possible for easy redemption of past faults. At the end, he would also mention whether the person concerned would go to hell or heaven, even to which exact heaven, after his death. And needless to say, the ancient Bhrigu-rishi had earmarked certain grievous sins and declared those who committed them as great sinners. In most cases, the present-day Bhrigu pinpointed these in a person's present life as the reason for certain adversities, and devised means of redemption!

Brajarani had spent a lot of money so far on charlatan palmists, numerologists and the like, but had never come across any good astrologer. Once, she had gone to visit a fortune teller in Calcutta who charged fees by the minute. He had scrutinized Brajarani's palm and given her a so-called powerful amulet that would 'redeem' her from some kind of 'imprisonment' in this life. He had also called for prayers with a sacrificial holy fire, and these rituals had cost her over 500 rupees. But did they bear any fruit? She was told that there were sacred restrictions in seeking knowledge about the effects of these pujas. So, she had no idea whether they had worked or not. Now, Brajarani wanted to consult the *Bhrigu Samhita,* and wrote to her mother, who promptly sent her her birth-chart by post. She then pestered Aurobindo to consult the astrologer. Her husband initially ignored her but finding her adamant said, 'Why are you going into these things needlessly? Heaven knows what he will say! Maybe you will lose all respect for that kind of shastra!'

Brajarani replied, 'If I lose respect for the shastra, that will be *my* loss! The shastra will not be affected! Please draw a copy of the chart and request him to examine it.'

'God knows what he will predict!'

Brajarani frowned and said, 'What can he possibly write that will be so bad?'

Aurobindo retorted, 'Bhrigu-muni is not Aurobindo Basu—why should *he* be afraid of Srimati Brajarani? Why should he not say anything unpleasant?'

Brajarani pouted, 'He will say what there is to say. If I did not have the courage to face unpleasant truths, why would I want to go to him? There is no dearth of people who speak only to please!'

Aurobindo commented with a mocking smile, 'Then you go and listen to his *facts*! I have listened to a lot of *facts* all my life!'

A copy of Braja's birth-chart was finally sent, and a brief written reply arrived soon: 'A Kayastha woman of high caste, the father—wealthy; husband—wealthier. Father—dead; three brothers presently alive and well; one of them is well-off and earning. Father-in-law and mother-in-law have expired. Childless. Husband is academically proficient and of good character. But this woman is not the only love of her husband. Husband has a living son. Because of grave sins committed in past lives, he has not seen the face of his son. There are remedies but the situation is almost irremediable.'

Brajarani read this missive repeatedly. Every time she went through it, she was filled with shame, fear and self-pride: 'But this woman is not the only love of her husband!' She knew this *truth* from her wedding day! She was well aware that the beautiful Manorama was her husband's true love; he had emptied his heart to her and now there was just a great void! Did Brajarani not realize that she had never been able to penetrate that blankness? That this was the greatest sorrow that a woman could suffer—could it be invisible to the intelligence of a great rishi? The truth was that her husband was indifferent to her;

even though the whole world may think otherwise, she was well aware of it. And those whose eyes could not be deceived, would they not know it?

But complaints or court cases were impossible under the circumstances. She had herself said that she had the courage to bear any kind of 'unpleasant truth'! She tried to console herself by thinking, *Well, what kind of love was this after all? If he loved her so much, why has he kept no contact with her all these years? Punitive measures should be taken against such love! Fie on such love! Thank God that he has not made me his* priya—*it is better to be his* opriya *than be in* her *position.*

ನಾ

## Chapter XXXIII

The day Ajit took his grandmother to the rooftop in the hope of finally satisfying his curiosity by asking her directly about whether his father had really abandoned them, he had, figuratively speaking, stepped on the head of a massive python. The damage was done and there was no escape.

He stood silently for a while, and then chose a corner of the roof where the shadow of the evening sunlight had totally faded but the moonlight had not yet penetrated. A thick branch of a margosa tree billowed onto the roof where the wall jutted upwards in a Romanesque pillar. Ajit hid his face in the leaves of that tree. He stood brooding for sometime—no thought crossed his mind; he just felt that the very foundations of his life had become unstable that day. His heart was aching with some kind of terrible, inexplicable pain as he lost awareness of his surroundings. As he gradually emerged from this state, he found himself so intensely tired that all emotions were squeezed from him. By then, the moon was like molten gold, shaped by some jeweller into a newly burnished ornament shining brightly in the distant sky. A lunar sphere surrounded the moon like a bracelet sparkling with sapphires and rubies. Galaxies of stars were also becoming visible in the distance like several multi-stringed necklaces. Ajit sat on the roof staring at this splendid sky in silence, his heart filled with a strange turbulence, the depths of which he could still not fathom. The evening bells and drums of the nearby temples began to sound, announcing the last prayers of the day; these appeared like desperate cries for help to the moon and stars in the looming sky above.

Ajit had always been a conscientious student and had gained much respect because of his academic accomplishments. The elderly men and women of his locality were captivated by the depth of his knowledge and would caress him and think, 'So young and so knowledgeable! How will he survive this cruel world?' Now, on returning home from Kashi, that same Ajit appeared to have forgotten about his upcoming examinations. He would put a book on his lap and look out of the window, seeming to scrutinize some invisible object. But did he notice anything—the small bird diving for fish in the distant algae-filled muddy waters of the pond, or the young village bride in a red-bordered green sari with a nose ring hanging over smiling red lips, her head semi-veiled, picking water spinach from the pond, did he see her? No. His eyes were blank. A spot of greyish winter sky was visible from between the window-bars. The scope and colour of his mental state were as empty and grey as that sky. Sitting there distracted, unable to focus or concentrate on his studies, he was about to reject the most precious opportunity of his life.

That day was a school holiday in honour of Jagadhatri Puja, held to honour another manifestation of the mother goddess. On entering his room, Manorama found Ajit sitting with his feet up and a book on the history of England open on his thighs. But his attention was not on the book—he was looking with unseeing eyes into the distance. Manorama called him, 'Ajit!'

The boy looked up in surprise. He picked up a pen, pretending that he had been reading and smiled. Seeing *that* face and *that* smile, Manorama's heart lurched in apprehension. His smile had always been as bright as Venus shining in the evening sky and as soft as dewdrops; his smile had made Manorama's universe sparkle with fairy lights; his laughter had sounded like birdsong at the dawn of a new day, the musical tone of the veena; it was *his* laughter that had kept the darkness of her life at bay so far! If that moon of her existence was to be devoured in an eclipse, how would the unfortunate mother survive?

Sitting down on the wooden bed, she asked, 'Have any letters arrived from Kashi, dear.'

Ajit shook his head silently. Manorama persisted, 'Your grandmother was unwell and a letter came informing us that she was getting worse! I wonder how she is.'

Ajit did not answer and instead tried to focus on his history book. Although Manorama could not see his face directly, she sensed that he was close to tears and thought that perhaps it was his grandmother's ill-health that was causing Ajit's dejection. She quickly added, 'Perhaps she is alright. You replied to her letter, didn't you?'

Ajit slowly shook his head, 'No.'

Extremely surprised, Manorama exclaimed, 'You did not reply to your grandmother's letter! Did you forget? Remember to send her a letter by first post tomorrow!'

Not getting any reply, Manorama looked closely at her son; she saw that he had clamped his mouth shut with his teeth and was staring out of the window unseeingly. Despite the cold winds of November, sweat drops had accumulated on his brow. Manorama was both surprised and hurt that Ajit was trying to hide his feelings from her! She came closer and wiped the sweat from his forehead with the corner of her pallu, and said, somewhat displeased, 'Ajit, what *is* the matter with you? Why do you stare at the sky that way twenty-four hours a day? I can see that you hardly study!'

Just as a slight breeze can start a downpour when the sky is filled with heavy nimbus clouds, teardrops coursed silently down Ajit's cheeks at his mother's words. He tried to hide his tears but big drops slipped down his shirt. Each drop struck Manorama like icy hailstones. 'Ajit! Am I no one to you! How can you push me away?'

Ajit now threw his notebook away and sobbed unrestrainedly. But—

Manorama wiped her own disobedient tears with the corner of her sari and drew him to her breast like she used to when he was a small boy. 'Ajit, my jewel! My Gopal—calm down! Oh my God, I cannot take it anymore!'

After crying his eyes out on his mother's breast, Ajit's tears did stop, but the after-effects continued for a while in the form of deep trembling intakes of breath. His mother asked, 'Are you missing your grandmother, Ajit?'

Ajit shook his head as though he was testing himself: 'No.'

'Do you wish to go to Kashi again? Your grandmother told me that she will send for us during your summer holidays.'

Just as a small boy is scared of ghosts and hides his face in his mother's lap at the mention of the unmentionable, Ajit hid his face in his mother's breast and spoke in a fear-filled voice, 'No, no! We will never visit them again!'

Manorama was surprised as well as anxious. She asked, 'Why, Ajit?'

He took a few moments to consider his answer and then spoke rapidly, 'Thakuma loves us very much undoubtedly. But that house belongs to Baba!' His voice reflected terrible hurt; his lips trembled and the colour of his face resembled the western sky prior to sunset.

Manorama was momentarily dumbstruck; she asked, 'So what if the house belongs to him?'

'Since Father has rejected us, why should we go to his

house?' Ajit had got up to leave as quickly as he could after saying this, but he was stayed by Manorama's hands clutching his. His words had stunned her; what had he learnt? She controlled herself somehow, and said in a grave voice, 'Ajit!'

Ajit was normally afraid of this familiar tone. He too controlled himself and asked in an equally grave voice, 'Maa?'

'Please listen well—*he* did not abandon us. He has only kept us at a distance because of his father's order. Do you believe me?'

Ajit's grief-wracked, tear-stained face cleared immediately and looked fresh and smooth like the dew-drenched cape jasmine bloom at dawn. He realized the gravity of his mental revolt, which he now viewed as a serious offence against his paternal family. He bent down and touched Manorama's feet—he resolved that if he ever disbelieved his mother again, may he perish from earth! He seemed to have transitioned from childhood to adulthood in the course of one evening, so striking was the change in him.

## Chapter XXXIV

That day, Manorama told Ajit the entire history of her marriage and separation from her husband. At the end, she said, 'Now that you know everything, don't let gossip disturb you into believing things that are not true. Others may be judgemental, but you are his son—for a son to be critical of his father is a grave offence. You are still a child, Aju; you will not understand what he has had to suffer as a result of his father's command. But let me bless you—may God allow you to grow up and become the father of a son; it is only then that you will understand what a terrible sacrifice it is to forsake your own son!' These words acted like manna from heaven. Ajit felt as if his mind had been freshly washed in holy water; his being was filled with calmness, which was reflected on his face like early morning dewdrops on grass. His hopes and aspirations for the future returned as he looked around him—what a beautiful world it was! How wonderful was the blueness of the sky! How dreamy was the cool breeze blowing through his heart! His mother's words acted like the perfume of heavenly flowers coursing through his being, wiping off all his mental and physical tiredness. He looked around him and saw only splendour—where was this beauty hiding all this time?

Just then, a fakir came to beg at their door, 'In the name of Allah, some rice; in the name of Muhammad, a few coins; in Khoda's name, bread—He will bless you!' Ajit immediately ran to the door to give him a coin. He returned with the fakir's blessings and a huge smile on his face.

In this refreshed frame of mind, he went out to visit Mungli and her calf Budhi, whom he had neglected for a long time, and, after caressing both, he recited an English poem to them for good measure. The old farmer, Rakhu, had died in the meantime, and Panchu Kishan had been hired in his place. Ajit met him too, and discussed his history lesson with this uneducated man, much to his consternation. He then went to the bird-cage where their pet Chandana was perching; he gave its tail a slight pull and asked it to say 'Gopikrishna' and ran away. He next visited his grandmother and made her laugh by telling her nonsensical stories—it was as if he was free at last.

The house had been engulfed in gloom since his return from Kashi. Now, it was again filled with the noise of childish song and laughter, gladdening every heart. The boy applied his new-found energy to everything—his studies, sleep, food. But something bothered him—he had misunderstood his father. Especially now that he had a sense of his quiet suffering, he felt that he had harboured unpardonable nasty thoughts about *him,* and was filled with shame. And his mother, she who had brought him back from the brink of a grievous fault, was she not worthy of devotion? That night when they lay down to sleep, Ajit hugged his mother tightly. Manorama understood what was going on in the boy's mind and smiled; then, returning to her own thoughts, she let out a deep sigh that seemed to come from the deepest core of her being.

ಬಾ

# Chapter XXXV

Meanwhile, Brajarani was extremely upset. She was seething inwardly, but just as a lightning-struck date palm smoulders inside, she remained outwardly calm. Who could she be angry with? She herself did not know who was responsible for her mental distress and the resultant hurt ego. Was it possible the Bhrigu-rishi was to blame? She read the message from the astrologer repeatedly, and the words stung her like a thousand wasps every time.

Chafing under the double burden of her loneliness and hurt self-esteem, the sorrow of which she could not share with anyone, she ran to her husband over twenty-five times a day with a thousand complaints but in vain; he remained impassive. This further increased her discontent. To assuage her loneliness, she took to her bed in such a manner that Aurobindo was finally forced to take notice. His usual routine was to spend time playing cards or chess with friends, or in what is known as *adda*—chat sessions where anything on earth is discussed—or in reading books and newspapers in the sitting room.

Here, in Kashi, he did not have too many friends; so books and newspapers were his main companions. There were so many types of books—humorous, funny, serious, religious, impious, honest, dishonest, political, apolitical; these provided company as per the particular mood of the time. But despite the companionship of books, the human mind can still suddenly yearn for the voice, the touch of a certain someone, so much so that the writings of all the great men of the world cannot provide solace.

Aurobindo had abandoned his books one day and was sitting alone thinking of his dead sister, Sarat. Memories flooded his mind with both serenity and agony. He reminisced about long bygone days. There was that day when he had accompanied Nitai to Burdwan to view a 'bride' for 'someone else', and had seen Manorama instead; he had returned and gone straight to Sarat's in-laws' house and related everything to her. He had said, 'I think you will like her very much were she to come to our house as a bride!'

Sarat had laughed and replied with typical humour, 'I will agree to act as the matchmaker, only if you promise that I will have more right over her than you!'

Aurobindo had accepted this condition eagerly at the time, barely realizing that God was going to make this promise come true—he thought of this repeatedly in later years and marvelled at it. It was true that Sarat had reconnected with them, sending gifts to Manorama's family and even bringing Ajit to her daughter's wedding, but his own hands were bound because he had given his word of honour to his father never to contact his first wife! He thought of it now and sighed in deep regret.

Then...another day...this was two years after his marriage to Brajarani, and following his third failed attempt to pass the law examinations: his father had ordered him to leave his studies and get a job, and he had moved into their paternal house in Howrah with his wife. Sarat had got annoyed at their behaviour and admonished him, 'You have made the other one miserable, and now you are head-over-heels over this one! Aren't you afraid of divine reprisals?'

Aru had laughed it off, saying, 'So, according to you, since I have caused her misery, I should do the same to this one? You are like *that* Badshah in that Arab novel—he behaved *equally* with all his wives! Marry them at night, and murder them in the morning!'

Sarat replied, 'No, no, I did not mean that at all! But if you continue to spoil this one so much, what will *people* think? Won't they suspect that you *deliberately* got rid of your first wife to marry *her*?'

Aurobindo accepted the barb in her accusation, and replied with a question, 'If I tread on this one and make her unhappy, will that help assuage the other one's sorrow?'

'No, that won't happen, but—'

'Then why add to my *virtuous* deeds by ignoring this one?'

So far, this had been nothing but light-hearted banter between the siblings. Sarat suddenly became serious, 'Dada! Please! Don't show her so much love at least in my presence!' She had started weeping by then, and stuffing her sari's pallu into her mouth, she quickly ran off.

Aurobindo recollected this scene along with so many other memories of days that he now considered the best time of his existence! But those days were over—the notebook of his past was covered with writing and it was written in indelible ink.

A cloudy sky in winter only adds to the general melancholy. The light in the room was dim and Aurobindo was, in any case, short-sighted. His thoughts became grave as the sunlight weakened. He came outside and observed the mud and slush in front of the house, increasingly depressed. He turned away to re-enter the house when he suddenly realized that he had not seen Brajarani even once since morning. It was not that he was keen to see her—she had never given him opportunity to feel her absence. Men tend to seek the unattainable; Aurobindo's second wife was far from unavailable. He had brought her home without any effort to seek her. In fact, it was just the other way around: she had come to the house as a burden for Aurobindo. That he had been able to make that burden tolerable did credit to Aurobindo's immense patience. But whatever qualities he possessed, he never had to exert himself to look after her needs. Some people are born to command and make others into slaves; Brajarani was just such a person. Whether she was given the right or not, she was able to bend people to meet her demands—and nobody had the guts to disobey her. Therefore, people found it in their interest to have a kind of treaty of friendship with her rather than revolt against her whims.

Aurobindo understood his wife well and had followed this policy from the beginning. He realized that she had great confidence in her own ability to manipulate people, and he was no exception; there was no point in protesting because she was adamant in her self-given mandate to be in charge of everyone around her. The women inside the house and men outside had both remonstrated saying, 'She has made him into a sheep!'

Aurobindo only smiled in response. But he had sometimes been desperate to avoid her and seek some lonely spot where he could be peacefully alone for a while.

Today, on this dreary winter afternoon, depressed by the sight of poorly-clad wayfarers shivering in the cold, his mind was further dejected by the cloud-anaesthetized sky stretched in gloom above. His own despondency reminded him suddenly of another unhappy resident of this house. He realized that she, who would come out of the inner sanctum at least seven times in the morning with various complaints, had not appeared even once today! He further realized that she had not been coming to the outer part of the house too often these past few days. He also could not recollect whether they had conversed much during the last four or five days. He tried to remember whether he had upset her in some way—but no, he could think of nothing. It was time to find out if anything was wrong.

Aurobindo found her lying on their bed staring at the roof. On hearing him, she looked down and smiled wanly. But what a smile! Aurobindo realized that she was more exhausted than he was. It was only extreme fatigue, physical or mental, that could produce such a smile, especially in someone who prided herself on her beauty and wealth. Aurobindo asked, 'Why are you still in bed so late, Rani?'

'Does it matter what time it is?'

'You are not feeling unwell, I hope?'

'Do barren women get sick?'

'Why are you lying down when there is so much to do?'

Rani replied in a tired voice, 'What should I do?'

Aurobindo sat down beside her, 'Is there any paucity of work? You were doing some embroidery with gold thread and tinsel—have you completed it? You were also planning to learn damask stitches, or was it satin stitch embroidery?'

Brajarani languidly threw an arm over her eyes and replied, 'What is the point?'

Aurobindo said, 'What do you mean by "what is the point"? Don't we have to furnish the new house in Ballygunge? You also spoke of going sari-shopping. When did the breeze of dispassion, which Kashi is known for, blow over you?'

Brajarani sighed and replied, 'For someone who has no one to leave anything to when she dies...' Without completing the sentence, she pressed her temple and suppressed a deep sigh. She felt hesitant to share her inner sorrow with her husband—after all, he did not belong to *her* alone! Why should he empathize? She had no offspring. How could she expect him to understand the suffering of being childless? In fact, he may even smile ironically! At this thought, she became incensed and clamped her lips together in frustrated annoyance.

However, Aurobindo had no thoughts of revenge. In fact, he understood her disappointment at being childless and sympathized with her friendless life. It was in good faith, therefore, that he tried to find a context for conversation to assuage her sense of desolation: 'You did not show me what the *Bhrigu Samhita* said about your horoscope?' Getting no reply, he tried humour: 'Okay, don't show me—I *know*! You were a queen in your past life and I was a king—isn't that so? Well, I may not have been a king, but there is absolutely no doubt that *you* were a queen! And *what* a queen—a magnificent Maharani!'

Like a lightning bolt piercing a cloudy monsoon sky, Brajarani's gloomy face lit up in a pain-filled laugh. She looked lovingly at her husband. 'What nonsense you speak! Is it possible that I was a queen if you were not a king? Maybe I was a lowly servant or sweeper!'

Aurobindo's heart skipped a beat. These same words, maybe in a different form, had been uttered by someone else on a far-off bygone day!

## Chapter XXXVI

The *Bhrigu Samhita* had suggested certain rituals involving the sacred fire, but Brajarani showed no inclination to do anything. Instead, she wrote to the *purohit* of her paternal home, who was arranging a *yagna* at the Kalighat temple: 'I think that it may not be a good idea to fight against what is destined by God. There is no need to do a yagna.' The report of the *Bhrigu Samhita* had been kept safely in a trunk. On opening it, and perhaps addressing Bhrigu-rishi himself, she muttered, 'I have no desire to conceive! If it is preordained, let my misfortune be mine alone! I do not want anyone's sympathy or blessings!'

But the message from the Bhrigu had certainly created misgivings about her destiny. One day, she rushed into the outer sitting room unexpectedly and cried out, 'Oh please send a telegram to your brother-in-law immediately! Bela has taken ill!'

Aurobindo looked up, shocked. 'What has happened to her?'

'Fever—very high fever!'

'Have you taken her temperature?'

Brajarani answered, 'Not very high, but how long does it take to rise?'

'Still, how high is it now?'

Braja said, 'It is 99.6 now. But she is also coughing!'

Aurobindo was surprised. 'That is not high—why send a telegram to Jagadindra if her temperature is just around 99? Call the local doctor, Dr Ishan!'

But Brajarani was frantic with worry. She cajoled him, 'Dear, no! Do not underestimate any illness! She is not my own daughter, I killed the other one—I could do nothing about it! God knows what will happen this time! Please send word to her father immediately!'

Dr Ishan came, examined the child and proclaimed that it was nothing but a common cold and fever. Reassured, Aurobindo went for a stroll. Past midnight, Brajarani woke him up and cried, 'The fever is rising, what will I do now? Why did I bring someone else's daughter with me again! I can't even die! God will give me no release!'

Aurobindo got up hurriedly and asked, 'Is the temperature very high? Is she restless?'

Brajarani was distraught and cried out excitedly, 'Restless? No—she is absolutely still! Please come and see for yourself!' She took her husband to the next room where Bela was fast asleep, her breathing regular and normal. A maidservant was also in deep sleep on the floor beside the cot. Only Brajarani's bed was empty. She had been sitting beside the child since evening despite the extreme cold. Aurobindo touched Bela's forehead and then counted her pulse for good measure. He straightened up and addressed his wife, 'You are absolutely mad! She has almost no fever! She is fast asleep and that is why she is still—why don't you lie down quietly and sleep? That will be good for both of you!'

'You think that I can sleep tonight?'

'Then go ahead and shiver in the cold! I am going to sleep.' With that, he left for his own room and fell off into deep slumber once more. But Brajarani continued to sit in the gloom, peering at Bela's face apprehensively while wild thoughts played tumultuously in her mind. She decided that she would send a telegram to Jagadindra in the morning requesting him to come immediately, and she prayed to whatever gods there were to keep this child alive, so that she could return her to her father; she also promised that she would never again desire to be the mother of anyone else's child. When she knew that she was ill-fated, that children may not survive under her surrogate motherhood, why had she committed this mistake again? Why had she not returned Bela to her father the day she got the message from the Bhrigu-rishi telling her the truth about herself? She failed to find answers within herself on this sleepless night as she berated herself.

An invitation letter came announcing the wedding of Sarala, another daughter of Sarat and Jagadindra. Finding her husband impassive, Brajarani took the initiative: 'You go with Bela. I will stay here.'

Aurobindo replied, 'It will be inconvenient for me to go right now.'

'Then who will escort Bela?'

'I am sure they will make some arrangement.'

Brajarani did not continue the conversation because the events accompanying Ashima's wedding were still starkly fresh in her mind. But ultimately *she* was forced to go. Jagadindra came to Kashi and reminded them that Sarala was a motherless girl; Brajarani could not refuse.

As she began preparations for the journey, Aurobindo approached her: 'Please make all arrangements for me here. I am not adept at housekeeping.'

Brajarani looked up in surprise: 'What? You will not be coming?'

Aurobindo shook his head, 'No.'

'Why?'

'I don't wish to go.'

Brajarani pretended to smile. 'I know that you want to hurt me because of what happened during Ashima's wedding.

But I have to attend for that very reason—remember, Sarala is motherless.'

Aurobindo said, 'I have not told you even once not to go.'

Perhaps no one, not even the mother who had carried him in her womb for over nine months, knew better than Brajarani about the degree of hurt and distress that was hidden behind Aurobindo's seemingly emotionless replies. Knowing how deeply he had been affected by her inconsiderate, misguided behaviour, especially because he lost his beloved sister shortly after that, Brajarani could not say another word. If she insisted on his going, he may take off for some nearby place like Sarnath for a few days until he was sure that she had left.

When Brajarani accompanied her brother-in-law Jagadindra to Calcutta for the wedding, she was as surprised at herself as were others present at the venue—she had never left her husband alone for more than a night earlier and that too only to give her parents company. However, she soon realized that sympathy for the motherless bride was not her sole reason for coming; maybe she herself did not know when this desire had entered her mind. She kept her eyes peeled and whenever she saw a group of young boys, her eyes invariably searched for someone. Her senses were aflame and she silently explored every corner of the house but to no avail. The name that she wanted to hear—why did nobody call him? *Where* was the face she so yearned to see again? That little boy, innocent as the feathers of a small bird learning to fly—if only he would appear once more, unbidden like the previous time, and satisfy her thirst!

Unable to contain herself any longer, she called Ashima aside one day and asked, 'Tell me, didn't anyone invite the Burdwan relatives?'

Ashima replied, 'Of course, Mamima! Baba went to Burdwan

himself, but Boro Mamima told him, "Ajit has his entrance examinations coming up, how will he go?" And she herself never wants to come—you know that she refused last time.'

Hearing this, Brajarani's mind was filled with gloom. She felt that the very reason for coming here remained unfulfilled. She next blamed her brother-in-law Jagadindra, who had failed to coax Manorama to come for the wedding. *So that was it! He did not get anywhere with my co-wife, so he thought of me as a second choice to help with the wedding arrangements—this is adding insult to injury!*

Following the departure of the bridal couple, she went to her parental house and told her brother to accompany her back to Kashi right away. Her mother protested, 'No Rani, how can you leave so soon? You have been in Calcutta only four days and we have not even had a good look at you!'

Braja requested in all humility, 'Maa, please let me return. He must be facing many difficulties.'

Her mother did not persist any further. She was hurt but remained silent. Her elder brother said worriedly, 'You want to go today? How can I get a reserved compartment so soon?'

Brajarani rejected that argument impatiently, 'You will be with me—we can go by ordinary carriage!'

Aurobindo did not express any surprise at Brajarani's early return. He knew her wilfulness much better than anyone else.

The construction of their new house in Ballygunge was completed by March; they decided on a housewarming ceremony at the beginning of the Bengali New Year in mid-April and returned to Calcutta. The Ballygunge house was built over a large area. It was fronted by a well-tended grassy lawn interspersed with multi-coloured flower beds; there was a lawn and flower beds in the backyard too, with a beautiful oval pond to one side.

The compound was fringed by fruit and other trees collected from various parts of the country, not normally seen in the city. The large house itself was the outcome of a mixture of Oriental and Western architecture, and it was similarly decorated in an Eastern and Western style. The lady of this beautiful house stood in the first-floor drawing room, the best-lit and most ornamental room in the entire building, feeling downcast and lonely. This was her dream house! But now, standing in the decorated drawing room, she felt that there had been no need to build it. She had embellished the house such that it was fit for a king—but where *was* that king? When she would depart from this world, close her eyes forever, who would inherit this magnificence?

She felt claustrophobic. She told her husband, 'Let us return to our house in Howrah.'

Aurobindo was astonished, 'Why? I spent so much money on this house! I have arranged to rent the Howrah house to a school.'

Brajarani replied, 'No, don't do that! Why don't you rent *this* house to someone—'

Aurobindo was adamant: 'No. I have given my word.'

Aurobindo was surprised that Brajarani did not protest any further. He was taken aback at her easy acquiescence. Was Brajarani changing?

# Chapter XXXVII

One summer day in May after a dust storm, dissatisfied with the servants' desultory dusting, Brajarani picked up a dust-cloth herself. The servants—Chaturiya, Bishana and Bihari—were dumbfounded. She had never done this before! Brajarani was well experienced in their ways. If the employer was soft on them, they certainly praised them but shirked work. Aurobindo never upbraided them even if he found them wanting. That is why the servants always praised him as the best of masters. Yet, when it came to dusting this best of masters' room, polishing his shoes or washing his towels, they seemed to be filled with fatigue and laziness. Brajarani often scolded them in no uncertain terms, but her rebukes were unable to change their character. In despair, Brajarani took up the duster herself to keep the large house tidy.

Today, she entered her husband's sitting room, and was shocked to find it in total disarray. The layers of dust had not been caused just by the storm, although the servants claimed it was so; they could see the anger on her face and slipped away as soon as they could. There was dust in every corner, cobwebs in the cupboards and dirt on the couch; books had been taken out and shoved into bookshelves anyhow, so much so that some were upside down and others had their spines sticking in. The wastepaper basket overflowed with torn envelopes, newspapers, broken wax seals and postmarked covers of journals. The strong winds of the storm had played further havoc and strewn everything around. The green felt on the writing table looked grey and the tabletop was covered with just about everything on earth. There were at least five pairs of inkpots, some empty;

there were more pens than nibs scattered all over. Brajarani did not know where to begin! She decided to first sort out the letters and put them in the letter-file. Her eyes fell on an envelope that had been redirected here from their house in Howrah. The mail bore the seal of the Burdwan post office; it had also been stamped in Howrah and Ballygunge. The envelope had been opened; she pulled the letter out and looked at it eagerly:

A million salutations and *pronam*,

> You may not have heard and therefore I am writing to inform you—I have stood first in the entrance examinations. My devoted pronams to both of you. There is no further news to convey. Everything is fine here.

In your service,
Sri Ajit Kumar Basu

After reading the letter, Brajarani stood contemplating for a while. Her mind was in turmoil. Just as the summer dust storm had turned everything upside down, hot winds seemed to be creating a commotion inside her that no one could see. That sprite of a boy had come *first* in his college entrance examinations! His face shining gloriously, he would be calling Manorama 'Ma' and no one else! And Manorama—she must be bursting with pride! This thought made Brajarani wince as she felt a redoubled emptiness in her own heart! Manorama's neighbours and friends would all be congratulating her today and calling her jewel-wombed for having borne a gem of a son! And here she was—the queen of an empty, bleak palace! Here, despite the magnificence of her home, she was a beggar!

She filed the letter away and left the room, but the words of the letter sprang out at her again and again. She castigated whatever God there was—could this child not have been delivered from *my* womb? And the next minute, she was ashamed. Someone seemed to be speaking from some dark corner within her: 'Are you not satisfied at having taken her husband away from her? What kind of a monster are you that you want to remove even his son from her?'

Aurobindo had gone to Bhagalpur for work for a couple of days. On his return, Brajarani hesitantly raised the topic, 'Ajit has come first in his entrance examinations.' This was neither a statement nor a question—it was unclear what she wanted to say. Aurobindo pretended not to have heard as he continued to eat his food quietly. Brajarani stared at his impassive face and asked, 'I suppose he will come to study in Calcutta now?'

Aurobindo answered evasively, 'There is a college in Burdwan, too.'

'That is not a good college. After having done so well, why should he study there?'

This too was not really said in the form of a question. Aurobindo did not reply and continued eating.

Brajarani had been thinking deeply about this topic, creating a spider's web of various possible scenarios. Sometimes she believed that Ajit's father would finally bring him home. And if the son came to live here, could the mother be far behind? Maybe, just maybe, Aurobindo had used the excuse of going to Bhagalpur to go to Burdwan!

What should Brajarani do in that case? Some modern novels had recently been portraying love and coexistence between co-wives—should she follow that prescription? Or, should she follow the example of the older generation of heroines and create turmoil in the family? Her mind was filled with frustration. It was normal to both hate and love with impunity when one was younger—but now that she was older, hating your co-wife was as unacceptable as loving her or living in peaceful coexistence! No, the situation was impossible! She would never be able to live in the same house with a co-wife. She knew that Manorama had a special place in Aurobindo's heart. She had contemplated many times that if her husband's mind was a material substance, something that had a shape and a body, she would have mercilessly smashed it to pieces, thus destroying that unforgettable memory forever! She was quite aware that she was not liberal-minded enough to bring her husband's beloved into her own home, to accept that *other* woman! Let others say what they liked—she would not allow her to come here.

But—but what? Perhaps she herself could not understand what this 'but' was. There was that niggling thought: on the one hand, there was Manorama, but then, there was Ajit... So, instead of being assured by her husband's silence, she felt a great apprehension hammer at her entire being. She viewed his apathy as something complex—a pretension, a plan, or was it really lack of concern towards the boy—and she became furious. She rasped, 'Have you or haven't you replied to his letter?'

Aurobindo was just about to pick up a mango fish from his plate. The anger in her voice made him look up; he was taken aback by her expression but refocused on his meal without saying a word.

But Brajarani had seen his shocked look; did *she* not know what it meant. His silence spoke volumes and she flared up like lightning in a summer sky, 'Listen, when even unknown people write to someone, he replies—have you *no* consideration? Or did you think that I would burst with emotions and die if you wrote?'

Aurobindo replied quietly, 'I have no idea whether you

would have died or not, but I am more than an unknown person to them, much more unknown, and I am sure *you*, of all people, are aware of that.'

'Your lack of acknowledgement does not change things, does it? It does not change your relationship—the whole world knows him as *your* son!'

Aurobindo remained calm. 'I don't have relations with the whole world and do not care what the "world" says.'

Brajarani took this personally and felt that he was mocking her. She felt insulted and said, 'I know that stepmothers are often evil and do harmful things! But today I am seeing that your attitude towards your son is that of a *stepfather*. I have *never* seen anything like this in my entire life! Fine, if you don't want him to succeed—what do *I* care? I thought it was your dharma, and that is why I had raised the topic.'

Having said this, Brajarani maintained a tearful silence. Aurobindo had finished his meal by then; he got up and left without another word. This subject was never discussed again.

## Chapter XXXVIII

Durgasundari was ill on the day Ajit's results were announced. When Ajit gleefully ran into the room and announced, 'Didimoni! If I bring you happy tidings, what will you give me?'

Durgasundari, recovering from a bout of breathing spasms, said with difficulty, 'Is there anyone in the world who is poorer than your Didimoni? You must have passed, right?'

Ajit's initial exuberance was slightly dampened. 'Yes, I topped the list. I came first.'

Many of his contemporaries had succeeded, but a large number had also failed. But both groups demanded a treat from Ajit. He focused on the boys who had passed and insisted, 'Brothers, you too owe everyone a treat!'

They replied, 'You call us successful! The university took pity on us and gave us extra marks! If our results were like yours, we would hold a feast everyday!'

Ajit was about to say, 'We are not rich,' but restrained himself.

Finally, it was decided that those who had passed the examinations would have to give treats serially according to their rank. Ajit had topped that year's entrance examinations and would therefore have to be the first to invite his friends. He tried to persuade his mother, 'Mamoni, I have to invite the boys for a meal—when do you think it will be possible?'

Manorama was mending a tear in an old sari. She was depressed because of Durgasundari's state of health; she said softly, 'How can we arrange a feast? Your grandmother is so ill.'

Ajit felt small, but he was in a tight situation, so he persisted,

'I have already informed them about her illness, but they won't listen! What should I do?'

Manorama said, 'In that case, I will buy a couple of rupees worth of savouries one day. Invite them for that.'

Ajit understood, but what could he do? His friends were insistent. 'They won't be satisfied, Maa. They say that I am about to get two scholarships and I should spend at least 10 rupees on them. It is just *one* day, Maa!'

Manorama replied irritatedly, 'A person is grievously ill in the house, and we don't know whether we can buy medicines or provide food for ourselves! But *you* and your friends are not ready to understand! So, do as you wish—call them home some day!'

The feast was arranged and his friends came over and ate their fill, but Ajit, realizing that he was burdening his mother with unnecessary expenses, was unhappy. Just as the dew overflows from a dew-drenched bud, Ajit's eyes often verged on tears. He had been born under the shadow of sorrow, no doubt, but had not felt the abjectness of their poverty till date. Now, Durgasundari's illness was eating away at Manorama's savings and over the last few months, their destitution had become acute. Their fields had not been tilled or looked after ever since the old peasant Rakhu died; the income from the fields had accordingly declined, and unlike earlier times, not enough was being produced to feed the family. Moreover, Manorama had recently paid the last two years' land tax to the government; after paying the daily labour who now worked the fields, there was nothing much left in the house. In fact, with no earning member, items from their household were being sold to meet the monthly expenditure. In dire straits, Manorama had been praying to all gods and goddesses she could think of, to provide money for Ajit's further education. It now seemed that the deities had heard her prayers—Ajit had received two scholarships worth 25 and 15 rupees, and this had removed *that* particular worry. Manorama felt that there was new hope now despite the burden of the debt. She had never realized earlier that poverty could be so intense. Rakhu had given his soul to the upkeep of the small farm, and Durgasundari had supervised him at every step. Whenever the need arose, Manorama had sold some of her ornaments, until none remained to serve in an emergency. Now Rakhu was dead and Durgasundari was bedridden! However, despite the penury and sadness, Manorama's spirit had been uplifted by Ajit's success. She knew that life plays tricks; the sun blazes ruthlessly at midday but cools to balminess by late afternoon.

Ajit came to see her with a freshly written letter in his hand and said, 'I have written to Baba. Should I send it?'

Manorama eagerly reached for it and said, 'Let me see! What have you written?' After reading it, she seemed to engage in a debate with herself before consenting: 'Send it.'

She had been wondering herself whether her husband should be informed but was undecided because *she* would not write to him. Now that her son had taken the initiative, she was relieved. Although circumstances had deprived her husband of the right to endow his son with his entitlement, why should the father be denied the happiness of his son's success? She kissed her son on the head and showered him with innumerable blessings.

Day after day went by. Ajit laid claim to the window in the outer sitting room from where he could look into the distance. The postman trudged down the road almost every day. Ajit's ears would prick up on seeing him as he waited for a call that never seemed to come. He would run out on some days and accost the postman, 'Na'kori, do you have any mail for me?' When the answer came, 'No, Dadathakur', he would fear that someone would see his tears of frustration. The days turned into weeks and his hopes diminished to bitterness like the slush that follows the strong currents of a monsoon flood. One day, he suddenly heard the sound of the postman's voice, 'Dadathakur! There is a letter for you!'

Ajit's heart leaped up and seemed to precede his feet onto the lane as the throbbing hurt turned into the music of hope.

But w*ho* wrote this letter? The address was written in English. When he pulled the letter out of its envelope, he realized that it was not from his father. From the manner in which he was addressed, he realized that it was from an elderly relation, and he remembered his long-deceased Pishima. The letter went like this:

My good wishes and blessings to the young scholar,

> Ajit! Please know that we are extremely happy to learn that you have stood first in your examinations. May God give you a long life and immense success! After this, you will probably come to Calcutta for further studies. Perhaps you have considered Presidency College? When will you come? I hope that everything is fine with you. I send my blessings to you. What more should I write?

Your
Chhoto-ma

There were two postscripts asking him to reply, but both had been struck off. The letter slipped from Ajit's fingers as though it had suddenly put on an unbearable weight. A long-hidden memory nagged at his mind: long ago, when he had felt embarrassed to have mistaken an unknown lady for his Pishima and spoken a lot of childish nonsense, she had tried to assuage his discomfort by pulling him towards her tenderly; the next instant, for some obscure reason, she had spurned him, pushed him away with strange loathing. He could never have imagined that a face so full of maternal love could turn into a mask of ugly detestation in so short a time. Her behaviour had then appeared mysterious, but since his mother had told him all, it was as clear as water now. That disgust he had seen on her face was nothing other than a stepmother's repugnance for a stepson. He placed his memory of that hate-filled face next to his mother's, and the difference between the two could not cheat even his inexperienced young mind. His mother was the ideal mother. Her physical beauty was further enhanced by maternal love; her eyes reflected a mother's compassion; it seemed as though God had created her to stem the hunger and thirst of the world's children! His *own* mother and *that* 'Chhoto-ma'! How could he even *think* of comparing the two?

Manorama had been noticing that her son's demeanour had become serious in recent times. Ajit had always been full of high spirits; he rarely *walked* from one place to another like other normal people. He rushed around like a steam engine and as a result, cuts, tears and small wounds were always visible on his legs and arms from tripping over obstacles. Earlier, he used to burst through doors and bang them shut despite admonishments, but now there was an unusual decorum in his movements. He had also begun to display so much respect and devotion towards his mother that Manorama simultaneously suppressed both laughter and pain. She thought that Ajit's premature adult behaviour was due to their impending separation. Perhaps that was why he was no longer interested in juvenile pursuits like flying kites, making merry with friends and generally demanding silly things of his mother. One day she asked idly, 'Ajit, that letter you wrote sometime back? Did you receive a reply?' Ajit had been afraid that his mother would inevitably ask him this question. He lowered his face to hide his pain, shook his head in the negative and quickly left the room. Just as water spills off a branch if one shakes it after a spell of rain, Manorama's question threatened to trigger the long-hoarded tears of hurt pride. He had wanted to share the happiness of his life's first success with his father—and *this* father, whom he revered over God, had turned his pleasure into bleak depression! All his life he had viewed his father's neglect not as humiliation but as something magnificent, since he had a promise to keep! How could he now tolerate this cruel behaviour? He need not have replied if he thought that scribbling a few words would have made him break his vow to his own father. Was it necessary to send a reply through his wife—*that* lady whose mind was so poisoned against him that she had withdrawn her hand from his as though he was a low-caste untouchable who would pollute her with his touch?

## Chapter XXXIX

Ajit's happy dreams seemed to float away like autumn clouds as his mind filled with the humid heat of disappointment. But he was too young to lose hope. He was still a boy, but the experiences he had gained from his circumstances as well as the knowledge he had acquired from his varied reading had transformed him into a fiery young man. The day he had tearfully parted from his mother and arrived at the gate of Eden Hindu Hostel in Calcutta, carrying bedding and a steel trunk, accompanied by Nitaicharan, his face reflected a grave resolve, unusual in one so young.

When he entered his empty, friendless hostel room, the last sight of his mother with tears streaming down her face came to his mind. He finally allowed himself to cry as he continued to meditate single-mindedly on his mother until he fell asleep. In fact, he sought sleep because his loving, beautiful mother appeared so vividly in his dreams that even after he woke up, it took him time to differentiate between what was dream and reality—this hostel where he was now lying on his cot, or what he had just seen? He had just been lying with his head on his mother's lap, or she had been combing his unruly hair affectionately after a bath—did those things *not* happen? And was *this* the cold truth—this narrow bed in a small corner room on the first floor of Eden Hostel, where he was lying listening to the silence of the night, while a regular low snore came from his roommate sleeping on a similar bed at the other end of the room? How could he survive all alone in this vast, heartless city of Calcutta, imprisoned in a strange, friendless hostel, without his beloved mother, his lifeline, for any length of time?

His treasured memories of the past twinkled brightly like evening stars in his mind. Just as minute particles attain a mammoth size under a microscope, trivial everyday events acquired importance in Ajit's memory. His mother had always plucked bones from fish before he ate. Now, while eating the unaccustomed food of the mess, he often had fish bones sticking to his fingers or throat. Life here was so mechanized—study, eat, sleep and repeat. He was so heartsick for home that his mind was always crying, 'Maa! Maa! Maa!' His mother had been his only ray of light, his buffer, the sum of his existence! Even today, despite the pain of separation, it was this very mother whose memory sparked a sense of determination in him. When his mind would rush, like a horse that had snapped its reins, towards the lane in front of their house in Burdwan, it was the thought of his mother's loving but stern eyes that would act like a whip and bring him back to his books. He had never realized that the mother who dwelled inside him could take such precedence over the mother who was far away, and be able to guide him through the homesickness of his early days in the hostel. Today he found that he was able to float the tiny boat of his aspirations on the endless sea of striving and despair by focusing on his mental image of his dear mother. If he could ever succeed in reaching the shore, he would immerse himself in the smile that would light up her face. But what if he failed? Dear God! She who had borne so much sorrow, would she be able to bear *that* grief?

In his distress, Ajit initially thought only of himself and not his mother's unhappiness. But he soon realized that her misery must be even more intense. He was busy attending classes from 10.00 a.m. to 4.00 p.m., but his mother was all alone!

He had occupied every moment of her time from the day he was born—and now he had uprooted himself and come away. How could a tree survive without the root?

This thought clouded his melancholic mind when he woke up in the morning. He remembered that in Burdwan, his mother had to call him at least seven times before he opened his eyes. Where had that deep sleep disappeared? On a stormy night, when the crash of thunder and flash of lightning made the sky look like a battlefield and the rain thundered down like the roll of battle drums, Ajit would be terrified and think of the warmth of his mother's body hugging him on such occasions at home, of the time she would hold him in her arms all night. This self-sacrificing mother—how will *she* survive?

But human nature is such that all sorrows, however grave, lose their intensity with time. The intolerable pain of separation that had crushed Ajit's heart lessened gradually as he began to accept the reality of parting from his mother. He became mentally calmer as he immersed himself in his studies. Hunger is an important factor in life. He no longer left the hostel food uneaten, however terrible it tasted. The monsoon season was over and it was almost the end of autumn. The thunder still rolled once in a while, but it no longer terrified the young boy. He still woke up at dawn, but he began to enjoy a deep sleep at night. His mother had always wanted him to get up early and study; she had told him that lessons studied in the early hours were never forgotten because of the divine splendour of the moment. His mother had consulted the family priest regarding mantras to undo planetary shadows on the boy's life and had explained the meaning of a mantra similar to that of the Gayatri Mantra, which he, as a non-Brahmin, and she, as a woman and a non-Brahmin, were forbidden to utter; she had advised him to recite this other mantra every morning. He loved his mother so much that he now began to recite that mantra at least 800 times in the morning and evenings—not to please the gods but to satisfy his mother by obeying her advice. It was a pity that she was not there to see him do this, but that was perfectly all right with him now.

As far as his father was concerned, Ajit had pulled in his own reins a long time ago. The blows that he had suffered in his short life had alerted him to the fact that there was a fear of a string of his mental veena snapping and the music becoming distorted if he thought of his father. He had, therefore, placed a stone slab on the coffin of his thoughts of his father. The picture that his mother had painted of this person, as someone shining in the majestic glory of goodness incarnate, had faded from his mind like the discoloured photograph of the young man in a graduation cap and gown that lay at the bottom of his mother's trunk. His father now appeared in the raw skin and bones of reality. However, he knew that if his mother got even an inkling of his mental revolt, she would be extremely hurt, so he kept his views to himself. Had the simple Ajit's reasoning become warped the moment he had left home and set out on the complex path of life? If this was true, fate was to blame.

The annual examinations were over and the summer holidays had begun. Ajit returned home and touched the feet of his mother and grandmother. They stared at him in amazement and exclaimed together, 'Just look at how tall he has grown! And, heavens! How thin you are! Oh Ajit! They don't give you enough food to eat?'

Durgasundari's breathing problem had improved during winter, but the summer was not good for her lungs. When Ajit asked her how she was, she replied with a wan smile, 'How am I? I am suspended like an axe between life and death! I am neither fully well nor dead—I stay alive just to bother you all!' Two drops of tears flowed down her aged cheeks. Ajit lovingly wiped them away, picked up a hand-fan and sat down on one corner of her bed. Earlier, he would have violently negated her words, but now he said nothing. Manorama thought with wonder, *My Aju has grown up so much! But I hate to see him looking so serious—my heart skips a beat!*

ಐ

## Chapter XL

Durgasundari finally left for the next world after a long illness, but the timing of her death was very unfortunate. Ajit learnt from his Nitai uncle, their Burdwan neighbour, just a day before his First Arts examinations that his grandmother's health had taken a turn for the worse. His concentration on his studies began to waver. He completed the exams somehow and rushed home on the day he finished the final paper, only to find that his grandmother had breathed her last earlier that day. The cremation was followed by days of ritual mourning culminating in the shradhha ceremony. Initially he was deeply grieved, but as with other sorrows, this too began to diminish—more so because a different anxiety replaced the anguish of her death. The golden hope of a bright future became a mirage when his results were declared: he had passed with low third-division marks and his rank was way below most of his peers.

Manorama was still mourning and was unaware when nights ended and a new day began. Perhaps she was not even conscious of Ajit who sat silently nearby, heart crunched by shattered dreams. Manorama's mother was very special to her; she had been her only solace throughout the long, extremely long, thirty-one years of her sorrowful existence, which, except for one year, she had spent in the shadow of her mother's love and compassion. After Ajit had left for college two years back, she had forgotten her heartbreak at his departure by immersing herself in caring for her ailing mother. Now she felt rootless, as if she was finally all alone in this world.

It was almost time for Ajit to return to Calcutta. He had

been unable to tell his mother about his poor results seeing her so distraught. In any case, nothing seemed to penetrate her grief-clouded mind.

Ajit finally forced himself to pick up courage and gently told her, 'I have to leave soon, Maa. The college is re-opening on Monday.'

Manorama was shaken out of her stupor; she saw the pallor of her son's face and was shocked. She caressed his head and said tearfully, 'You look terrible, Aju! Unkind fate—I have neglected you!' Then, after a while, she said, 'Take me with you, Ajit. How will I live here all alone?'

In fact, this thought had bothered Ajit for days—how would she live in this silent, empty house by herself? But how could he to take her to Calcutta with him? It was impossible, but how could he tell her that? Somehow, he turned his words around and said that if she left, whatever income came from the fields would disappear, and his circumstances were not such at present that he could afford to take her with him.

Now, Ajit's life took a new, critical turn; he had to find the means to fend for himself. His scholarships had been stopped due to his bad results. His mother had sold her gold bangles and that along with some leftover money were spent on buying essential books. He had hoped to get some tuition jobs in Calcutta to pay for his daily upkeep but lost hope as nothing was available. What then was the solution? Living in Eden Hindu Hostel and studying at Presidency College were expensive. How would Ajit be able to afford this? The fact that his mother had not even a coin to spare was evident from the string she wore around her neck instead of a gold or silver chain, and her patched-up, repeatedly repaired saris. He had assured her confidently that many tuition jobs were available in Calcutta—but where were these jobs? He also knew that many students stayed with wealthy relatives to continue their education. But did Ajit have such relations? There was Nitai-mama of course, who was not really his maternal uncle but came from a neighbouring family in Burdwan; he had known him all his life and thought of him as a close relative. But he too was very poor. He earned around 60 or 70 rupees only each month; he had to send money home, pay rent for his small house here, and take care of his wife and several daughters who lived with him in Calcutta. Ajit knew that Nitai's hair was turning grey worrying about dowries and finding suitable grooms for his daughters. How could Ajit possibly burden him further? It would be better to give up his studies!

Did he have any option? His college fee was 12 rupees; he needed at least 25 rupees more to meet the costs of his hostel room and boarding apart from necessary sundries. He therefore required at least 37 rupees to pursue further studies in Calcutta. If he left Presidency College and Hindu Hostel for a lesser college like City College and a cheap mess, maybe his expenses could be less. But poor Ajit! He was still filled with the desire to succeed! It was not really his fault that he had fared so badly in his last examinations. He had felt compelled to sit for the final paper despite the knowledge that his grandmother was dying, and had thus been distracted. Had he been able to focus only on the question paper, he would certainly have got the numbers he expected—but could he have called himself human had he ignored his grandmother's health and thought only of himself? Ajit still hoped to continue to study under able professors at Presidency College and do well in his BA final examinations, more so because the principal, confident that he could do well, had called him to his chamber and asked him to come to his house after sundown, so that he could personally oversee his studies. If he passed his BA examinations with good grades, his demand in the job market would go up. And if he did really well, Ajit hoped that he could complete the master's programme, and perhaps also be awarded the prestigious Premchand Raychand Scholarship, which would bring honour to his entire family! And this was so important to him. If he was awarded the PRS, it would be a revenge on his cruel long-deceased grandfather who had turned his mother out because she was poor—he would be able to prove that a worthy son could be born to a woman from a poverty-stricken household! If the purpose of marriage was to assure the continuation of the genetic line through the production of creditable male children, then this would be proof that wealth was *not* a criterion for that! But alas! His grandfather's castigation was now taking its retribution on Ajit. His failure to do well was not merely sad for him—it was the cause of his defeat. He had desperately aspired for success, so that the Basu family would not only acknowledge him but also feel proud that such a boy belonged to their lineage; even his father, who was known for his scholarship, donations and wealth, would feel pride in crediting the destitute Ajit with the status of his offspring! But what kind of dreams were these? Did it behove the penniless son of a beggar-woman to imagine that he could sit on a royal throne?

Ajit had recently become friendly with a new student who also came from a poor background and had secured the highest marks in mathematics in the previous examinations. One day, conversing idly, he mentioned, 'Thank God Aurobindo-babu lives close to our house. Had he not supported us, my family wouldn't have survived, what to speak of my studies!'

Ajit's heart palpitated for a moment. He looked at his friend and asked, 'They are paying for your education? That is good!'

The boy was encouraged to continue, 'Oh, they are more than good! Both husband and wife! It is not only I who has benefitted from their financial support, many other boys in schools get monetary support from them. He helps almost any student who approaches him—he only needs to know that some poor deserving boy needs money to continue his studies! His wife has also opened a school for girls. She used to personally supervise the school initially, but they have been out touring for the past seven or eight months. One does not see such graciousness and generosity in wealthy people nowadays!'

If Ajit had encouraged him, the boy would have continued showering his benefactors with gratitude, but seeing that his friend was distracted, he became silent.

Was Ajit thinking about finally presenting himself at his father's door, petitioning him like a beggar? Aurobindo Basu was after all his father. If he had to bow his head in supplication, would it not be better if he did it before his own father rather than before strangers? Well, if he could hide behind a pseudonym—Aurobindo after all donated to unknown students, and *he*, the son, was nothing better than a mendicant. But all of a sudden, the sleeping lion in the young boy's heart revolted and roared! *This* father had never accepted his paternity for a single moment—was he worthy of fatherhood? Did he deserve to be given the status of a father? Ajit felt that he could beg at every door in this huge city except for that one doorway, that of the palatial house of his father! *Never*!

Finally, somehow Ajit managed to get three tuition jobs, the first earning him 15 rupees, the second and third 10 rupees each. Since the total amount would just about meet his immediate needs, he accepted all three. He sacrificed his health and the joys of youth at the feet of his ambition to prove himself.

## Chapter XLI

The students of Eden Hindu Hostel had formed a literary society some years back. It had gained popularity as many students aspired to become writers and poets, as is common among young men of that age. The society's annual festival was celebrated with much fanfare. Gurudas-babu, a High Court judge, enamoured of both student life and literature, consented to preside over this function personally almost every year. A poetry competition was held among students during this occasion, with students being expected to contribute original compositions. A number of would-be poets took this more seriously than their annual examinations, especially because a prestigious prize was presented to the most deserving person by a panel of well-known critics.

This year, Gurudas-babu was out of town, but he was a kind and meticulous man who lived up to his commitments. He had arranged for a favourite former student to preside over the event in his stead. The students had not yet been informed about his name, but having immense regard for the judge, they were confident that any person chosen by him would be perfect for the occasion.

It was the advent of spring, and birds chirped, hidden in the new crimson leaves sprouting from young branches on the old trees of the garden outside. Ajit finished teaching a student at Potoldanga early in the morning and left for his hostel. His smile was like sunrays in the sky through light clouds after a downpour. His wide fair forehead glistened with the light of chrysoberyl—the protective stone that transforms negative thoughts into positive energy and strengthens self-confidence—

as he thought about the previous year's poetry competition. He had not won, but he had been selectively praised by a respected elderly gentleman known for finding new talent; it was said that he could recognize the worth of a tree by merely looking at a sapling. Gazing at the sixteen-year-old boy whose cheerful countenance shone like moonlight, he had encouraged him by saying that he would certainly win the next year's competition. Like the first blooms of spring, Ajit's hopes had been reawakened as he remembered the words of this mentor. The accumulated darkness and problems of the troubled past year were replaced by fresh hope as he reminisced about the encouragement he had received.

Ajit, basically a bookworm, had no experience in arranging festivals or stage decorations. He was however not timid—he had played Hamlet in the college play with confidence; whatever shortcomings his acting may have had, he had made up for that with his fluency in English and perfect pronunciation. But he had no idea how to arrange flowers or decorate pillars. In fact, he remained so distant from the preparations that he did not know there would be someone new presiding over the function—and as for who, that remained as unexplored as the North Pole! His roommate was even worse than him; he was a simple, docile fellow from a village in East Bengal, who was anxious to avoid the malicious humour of his urbane West Bengali peers and thus kept to himself. But the two did hear that this time, the boys adjudged first and second in the poetry competition would be honoured with gold and silver medals. The competitors were therefore vying with each other with renewed vigour.

The evening arrived, and so did the gentleman who was selected by Gurudas-babu to preside. The boys were entranced by his looks and commented, 'He is as handsome as a sahib!'

Another boy, who probably did not consider sahibs good-looking, frowned and said, 'Ridiculous! What do you find sahibish in him? He has perfect Aryan looks!'

Ajit, who was going to participate in the poetry competition, peeped from a corner of the stage. But what was this? The bright midday sun of hope that had been burning brightly in him dimmed to midnight darkness within a second. This person who was sitting in the presiding chair was certainly not ugly so as to repel observers; instead, his maker had given him an excellent physique, fairness of skin, and gravity in demeanour that impelled respect. In fact, the whispers around him proved that the other boys considered themselves lucky to have him with them today. But Ajit felt apprehensive—an inner voice seemed to tell him that this person had come to deprive him of *something*; maybe it was because he had replaced one of the very few people who had supported Ajit earlier? He did not know.

Gradually, the competitors recited their compositions one after another, and it was now Ajit's turn. He stood up blushing with embarrassment. He would have been totally confident had this poem not been written by him; he was adept at reciting poetry and had earned accolades at school and Presidency College several times. What bothered him today was the presence of this new chief guest, whose very sight had unreasonably drained him of all enthusiasm.

After he had read his poem once, an elderly man who was part of the panel of judges requested him to repeat it, 'Can you please recite your poem once more, young man—I really enjoyed it. I also appreciate the strength with which you recited it. Let's hear it again!'

Ajit blushed even more. He controlled his voice and began to recite as normally as he could:

### 'Maa'

Sage-accursed, you are submerged in the ocean of rejection,
Defamed by the wicked, you are the abandoned Sita,
And yet, in body, mind and spirit, you remain,
Ever faithful to your consort, and sustain,
Devotion to him, placing him on a pedestal
Like a Deity.
The ocean cannot turn back its tide,
Behold Oh Sindhu! She bears a child,
You are a mother today.
In this boy, do you see infinity,
That Divinity, your adoration, to whom you once were a bride,
That on his cheeks your kisses rain,
And you smile lovingly, gaze unblinkingly,
At your own creation?
Is that why your ambrosia you pour,
Evermore,
The nectar of your affection, on your child,
Oh Maa?
Your conjugal and maternal love's association
Is pure. It will never go astray,
It blesses your son with the boons of the Trinity.
Heaven's captive—my life's luminosity!
Greater than Heaven, this nation
Is my Maa!

'Mr Basu! The poem titled "Maa" deserves the first prize! Such a young boy—merely more than a child—what he has written reflects maturity well beyond his years! I don't think any of the other poems are comparable.'

After Ajit's recitation, the presiding guest had been unable to concentrate on any of the other poems. He looked abstracted and his eyes followed Ajit passionately like a lost traveller afraid of losing direction after getting a hint of the correct path. But when the boy lifted his blushing face and looked at him, a shudder ran down his spine as though a spark of fire, so far hidden under a heap of ashes, had been exposed. This young person could in no way be dismissed as a mere boy; rather, this youth, with his fair skin and brilliant wide eyes, could most appropriately be compared to a sharp-edged, highly polished sword. His lips, drawn in a firm line, manifested determination; his glowing eyes seemed to consider everything and everyone on earth insignificant. The gentleman felt futile sighs welling up from the bottom of his heart distracting his very being.

Meanwhile, the remaining two or three competitors completed their recitations and the elderly gentleman, mentioned earlier, had already expressed his opinion regarding who should be the winner. The chief guest thanked God that he had brought his friend along as part of the judge's panel. He looked at his friend in assent, 'Yes, that is my view too. Who do you think should be placed second?'

'Look, I have given marks to all the boys. Now, *you* decide on who will get the silver medal.' With this, his fellow panellist, Aditya-babu, pushed a paper in front of the chairperson. He looked at the sheet with approval and added his own marks next to his, and announced, 'The second place should go to Prabhatmohan, who composed the poem "Buddhadev". But let me add that two or three other poems are also worth mentioning, and one day, I am sure, these boys will join the galaxy of star-poets. I will discuss these poems shortly, but first, our duty is to present the first and second prizes to the winners. What is the name of the poet who composed the poem entitled "Maa"? The name should be engraved on the medal, perhaps there is some arrangement for this.'

Hearing that his poem had won the first prize, Ajit finally looked at the chairperson with respect. Smiling brightly, he answered the question himself, 'Sri Ajit Kumar Basu.'

The gentleman was stunned; the gold medal slid from his inert fingers and rolled to the floor.

Many boys rushed forward to retrieve the medal, but Aditya-babu picked it up and pushed it into the chairperson's non-responding fingers and said loudly, 'Oh Aurobindo, what kind of medal have you designed? There is no pin, no ribbon! How will you put it around his neck or pin it to his shirt? All right, just give it to the deserving child-poet. But why did nobody examine it earlier?'

'Aurobindo!' Just as an antelope is startled by the sudden mellifluous refrain of a flute, Ajit stared at the gentleman, eyes mesmerized, spellbound, in a dream-like state. For a moment, his heart welled up in wonder and joy as he looked at the object of his yearning, someone he had been searching for ever since conscious thought began in him. For a moment, he wanted to supplicate himself before this gentleman whom he had adored throughout his childhood. Like the light of a thousand festival lamps illuminating the moonless night of Diwali, like a million bright stars twinkling in the silent, dark sky of a new moon night, Ajit's eyes sparkled with sudden thrill and his forehead glistened like the rosy light of early dawn. But alas! The next second, just as a stormy wind blows out the candles of a chandelier, his face looked like a snuffed-out lamp as a current of revolt began to engulf him. Just then, he felt the touch of cold, trembling fingers on his hand. Willingly or unwillingly, it is difficult to say, he snatched his hand away and took two steps back. What happened exactly after that, he could not clearly recollect later. But he was aware that at Aditya-babu's repeated urgings, that trembling hand had reached out to present the medal. But like a sudden breeze makes the waters of a stream quiver, spasms shook the entire body of the gentleman called Aurobindo. Sweating profusely, the chief guest collapsed into his chair and lost consciousness. Before anyone could come to his assistance, he slipped from his chair to the floor.

## Chapter XLII

Brajarani was not home. In the evening, she had gone to attend a women's society meeting. The ladies were busy exchanging gossip, laughing at each other's jokes, and listening to songs sung by other members. Brajarani was engrossed in conversation with an old school friend from Bethune Institution who was visiting Calcutta after many years, when a bearer brought the ill tidings of her husband's condition—it was like a roll of thunder on a clear bright day!

Aditya-babu had brought the semi-conscious Aurobindo home with the assistance of a local doctor and some servants. When Brajarani rushed home, she found the doctor examining his heartbeat with a stethoscope. He looked up and said, 'No, I don't find anything wrong with his chest.'

Brajarani enquired in trepidation, 'Then what is it?'

'I think he is suffering from some kind of shock—it could be physical or mental.'

Aditya-babu had sent some students in search of a good doctor, and now they too arrived. The doctors consulted with each other, but the diagnosis was the same. Their opinion was that he got unexpectedly upset at something and crumpled to the floor, but he had also hit his head on the hard surface and injured it. But why did he fall down in the first place? Maybe he had felt dizzy, or perhaps it was simply that his feet had got entangled with the table leg and he had tripped. But whatever the reason, there was a cause for anxiety—the doctors mentioned apoplexy or paralysis but could not gauge the outcome yet. Brajarani asked the two students who had brought the doctor, 'Tell me, what happened exactly?'

The boys recounted what they knew; they also told her how earlier the students had been discussing his excellent physique. God alone knew what was in store for anyone—fate could take an evil turn at the bat of an eyelid!

One of the boys said, 'Just as he was about to give that first prize winner the medal, the boy seemed to panic, and Aurobindo-babu flopped down on his chair and lost consciousness. Indeed, the doctors are saying that he got a "shock" because he hit his head on the floor, but I think he must have been feeling unwell. Prafulla, did you notice how his fingers were trembling when the medal dropped from his hand?'

Drops of sweat dotted Brajarani's brow—she had felt uneasy from the moment she had heard about the accident; now a niggling suspicion began to gain shape. With bated breath, she asked, 'What is the name of the boy?'

'You are asking about Ajit? His name is Ajit Kumar Basu. But he is not at fault! Please don't think it was his behaviour—or the sight of him! He is a wonderful person! He cannot be blamed!'

The other boy said, 'He is very, very poor.'

The darkness deepened and their faces became obscure in the dimming light. The boys said, 'We must take your leave now. We will come again.'

They had almost crossed the veranda when they heard her voice again, 'Please—' Brajarani came closer and requested, 'When you return, can you send that boy here immediately?'

Initially they could not understand her. Then one of them asked, 'You mean Ajit? Will he come? He does not go anywhere normally. He has become a recluse ever since he fared badly in his examinations because of his grandmother's death. Besides, he does not have the time—he has to take three tuitions!'

Brajarani, however, was adamant: 'You *have* to do this for me! Once he learns about *his* life crisis, he will surely—can anyone ignore such news? I am sending the carriage with you. Please persuade the hostel superintendent to permit him!'

Had the spoilt Brajarani ever entreated anyone like this earlier? But today she felt obliged; she alone knew how deeply accountable she herself was for the present state of her husband's health. Now that she was close to losing her husband, she understood how important it was for her to give primacy to her husband's joys and sorrows, *his* feelings—this was not the time to think only of herself, her self-esteem...

She returned to her husband's room and gazed at the pale, almost lifeless face of Aurobindo in the shaded light of a single lamp; the tears that had been welling up in her chest froze completely. His motionless figure was lying supine on the bed. She stared at him like a hunter who has killed for the first time looks at his prey with guilt and helplessness—her eyes trapped, unable to look away, while a violent firestorm of emotions blew through every pore of her being. Her mind seemed to be filled with gunpowder—the slightest spark would set off a violent explosion.

Aurobindo opened his eyes and looked this way and that, his eyeballs moving rapidly, searching for a lost object. The doctor cautioned, 'Don't remove the ice bag for a moment, the patient is becoming restless!'

Someone called from outside, startling Brajarani. It was only the Tamil coachman; he had brought back a brief note from one of the boys—what was his name? Prafulla? Paritosh?

With due respect,

Ajit is extremely stubborn! He said that he will have nothing to do with rich men or their palatial houses. I feel very embarrassed to have been unable to keep your simple request. Please forgive me.

Yours faithfully,
Paritosh Chandra Nag

Brajarani returned to Aurobindo's bedside and replaced the ice bag on his forehead. He opened his eyes again; it was clear that he was seeking someone. He peered into the face of the person who was tending to him and although he still looked uncomprehending of his surroundings, a flicker of recognition crossed his eyes. Brajarani gently asked, 'Are you feeling a little better?'

After a while, a deep sigh escaped Aurobindo's lips, and he said as though he was talking to himself, 'That poem did not come out of the pen of a mere child! The picture that he painted was not in ink, it was scripted in blood—from the innards of a heartsick boy! *Who* was that boy? Please tell me—who?!'

Brajarani sat stiff, desperately trying to stop herself from crying. The doctor had mentioned some kind of mental or physical 'shock'—that word tumbled around in her head repeatedly.

The attending doctor said, 'I see that this is the beginning of delirium! But it's an improvement over the earlier senseless state.'

The night passed slowly. The early rays of dawn filtered in through the shuttered windows and cast an anxious glance at the pallor of the patient's skin. Brajarani looked at his face and her heart overflowed with painful introspection. She was filled with deep remorse; could she blame fate for her husband's current condition? She could not place her trust in prayer either, to ask the gods for his early recovery. Through her hopeless, clouded heart, a voice seemed to be thundering: 'Not the fates, not God, *you* alone are responsible for your husband's condition today! Only *you* are liable!' She wanted to scream and cry, create a scene, but not even a sigh escaped her lips. As the daylight began to strengthen, her self-loathing increased; her blood ran ice-cold as she seemed to hear a voice roaring in her ears: 'Murderer of your husband! You do not need a knife to kill someone! Now taste what it feels like to be without a husband!'

She kept staring at the floor lest she saw these accusations reflected in the faces of the doctor, servants and friends present in the room. She found it impossible to look at anyone and remained seated silently with bowed head.

ಣ

# Chapter XLIII

The sun had not quite risen and the roseate hues of dawn had not yet penetrated the interiors of the palatial houses. Its golden rays were just about caressing the high towers of the city. Semi-awake, Raghubir Prasad Choubey and a heavily moustachioed non-Bengali man stood outside the closed door of Ajit's hostel room, banging on it repeatedly and calling out in an angry sleepy voice, 'Ho Ajit-babu! There is a letter for you. Open your door!'

After a few more loud knocks, the door opened with a thud; Ajit emerged and reprimanded the gatekeeper, 'What is the matter, Raghubir! It is not yet dawn and you are hammering on my door! Whom have I robbed that you are tyrannizing me like this?'

Raghubir too was highly irritated at being woken up so early. He shouted in reply, 'How do I know what you have stolen or from whom? This man insisted on meeting you immediately— I was forced to come!'

Raghubir left muttering; first, he had been woken up at an unearthly hour, and then he had received no tips for being disturbed! Ajit had turned to close his door when Chhottu Singh held out an envelope, saying, 'Bahuma-ji has sent this letter.'

Ajit replied in Hindi, 'This must be for someone else— not me.'

Chhottu said in the same language, '*Ji*, it is for you. Your name is Ajit-babu.' He tried to push the letter into Ajit's tightly clasped hands, but on failing, flung it at him and said with folded hands, 'Please forgive this rudeness, but Bahuma-ji insisted that you must come. Babu is very unwell. He was looking for you—'

He was taken aback when Ajit shut the door on his face. He knocked several times and then waited silently till eight o'clock but did not hear a single sound from inside. Chhottu Singh finally departed in frustration. The two boys who had accompanied Aurobindo home the night before saw the *durwan* and came to plead with Ajit but to no avail. The same scene had occurred the night before; the two boys had been barred from entering Ajit's room. He had laughed derisively at their efforts to convince him and dismissed them with rough words. His roommate had gone home that day. The door had not opened once till the early morning drama. When he was called down for dinner, he said that he had a headache and did not appear. And this was a hostel after all; the cooks and bearers do not get paid to persuade students to eat! They did not disturb him further.

It was a Sunday. No one knew when Ajit quietly came down, had a quick early lunch of boiled vegetables and rice, and left the hostel hiding behind his worn-out umbrella. He walked around aimlessly till past noon, noticing nothing. When he finally stopped, he was surprised to find the road empty except for a few people and some carriages belonging to wealthy people. Instead of the bustling markets that were Calcutta's hallmark, there were huge bungalows, some semi-built, others completed, surrounded by landscaped gardens. Ajit was amazed—how had he come to this unknown paradise? Where was the heat and dust of the city that exhausted the senses? Ajit's eyes cooled at the sight of the greenery and his turbulent mind rested as a balmy breeze wafted through the silence. Instead of smoky grey skies, the majestic firmament stretched magnificently blue and clear above him. Ajit flopped down on the grass under a coconut tree by the roadside and breathed a sigh of relief.

From where he sat, an empty vista stretched to the west as far as the eye could see. As he gazed into the distance at the rays of the setting sun across the windswept grass, an image suddenly floated before him: a semiconscious man, with a face that had been bright as the sun, lying supine on his deathbed. He covered his eyes with his fingers to shut out the sight as though it was real. Immediately, another vision came to the fore: dazzling features, sharp as the noonday sun, which had become dark and lifeless in an instant. Ajit felt as though someone was piercing him with a red-hot spike; he had observed that terrible scene and yet, despite coaxing, he had not even bothered to *enquire* after his well-being! For an instant, he had longed to rush forward and call out 'Baba', to acknowledge him and be acknowledged. But he had done nothing. And he had ignored the pitiful requests from that house; he had repeatedly insulted those who had tried to persuade him. How very unfortunate he was—how very unfortunate.

## Chapter XLIV

Walking back, Ajit, astonished, stared at a board announcing that the road was 'Old Ballygunge Road'. It did not take him long to realize what attraction, working in strange mysterious ways, had drawn him to this unknown realm. Impetuously, he decided to fine-tune his hidden yearning and search for a certain building.

Ballygunge was not a small place, but in the excitement of the moment, he circled the entire area as evening began to fall. Every time he spied a garden-house peeping out from behind foliage, his heart jumped impulsively. But when he found the name engraved on a marble or wooden nameplate to be that of a stranger, he felt deeply disappointed. His circumambulations led him out of Old Ballygunge and shortly, he found himself near Ballygunge Circular Road. The moon had risen and was casting its glow on the spring blooms of the surrounding gardens, magically tinting them with dainty softness. It seemed as though the leaves, flowers, skies above, the very breeze and moonlight were transmitting pleasure as they swayed in the delight of the moment. The fragrance of the flowering mango trees, the maddening call of the cuckoo—the atmosphere was subsumed in some kind of intoxicating beauty! Some mysterious touch had caused thousands of minute flowers to spring from the soil; their charming petals spread like a glimmering veil over the grass. This mysterious touch also penetrated Ajit's unhappy heart, creating an illusory trance-like state. Exhausted, the despondent Ajit dragged his tired feet down the road until he saw a large palatial house surrounded by sculpted gardens. He slid to the ground against its high walls. His eye rested suddenly on the marble nameplate illuminated by the silvery moonlight; carved in bold black letters was the name 'Aurobindo Basu'! Ajit's tiredness disappeared immediately! He stood staring at the nameplate with desperate, ardent eyes.

As he stood gazing at his father's name, he felt that the world around him was trembling and receding from his consciousness to some far-off distance—very, very far... And his father's palatial house was descending on him like some terrifying demon with bulging, electrified eyes, advancing on him with mad, roaring laughter to drink the oozing blood from his heart! Ajit closed his eyes in fear.

The hostel superintendent considered Ajit a *good* boy; he paid no attention to some recent negative gossip and continued to hold him in high regard. Tonight, Ajit returned to the hostel around midnight. When asked to explain his absence, he remained silent and static like a flame without breeze. For the first time, a hint of a suspicion touched the superintendent's mind, but since this was a first offence, he let the boy off with a severe reprimand and a small fine, although returning after the hostel gates had closed was considered a serious transgression. If anyone had spoken to Ajit so severely earlier, he would have been totally mortified. But tonight he was in some kind of stupor and was hardly aware of his humiliation. He somehow managed to go to his room and lie down on his cot. Unimaginably exhausted, mentally and physically, fatigued with all that had happened since the previous night, Ajit sank into a deep dreamless sleep.

Days crept by. Life continued in its own wonderfully variegated way and time pursued its own set course. Ajit too followed his daily routine of tuitions, classes and study, but a lack of concentration was visible in his daily routine. As a child, his early morning laughter had brought more joy to his mother's heart than birdsong at dawn. When he reached youth and joined college, he would get up before sunrise and recite the mantra that his mother had explained to him and made him memorize. Every day, he would get up at dawn, say his prayers and set out for two tuition jobs; after returning, he would bathe, eat breakfast and proceed to college. He was so meticulous in his routine that his hostel mates could set the time on their watches by him. He took a third tuition in the afternoon, and finally, at exactly 7.30, he would sit down with his books to study.

But there was a change in this daily pattern over the past seven days; he was absent from college on two days; on two nights, he was seen walking around aimlessly in the hostel yard; and then he was found sleeping through the day instead of attending classes. On other days, he was seen in college, but as for the rest of the time? His fellow students had no idea but were suspicious, and many ridiculed him maliciously behind his back. After all, young men were attracted to all kinds of debauched places at this age and developed corrupt habits. But why blame the boys? Ajit was himself not fully aware of where he was or what he was doing, as though he was tangled in an intricate spider's web and had no idea how to free himself.

ಬಿಬಿ

## Chapter XLV

The main gate of the palatial house was locked at sundown. However, the walls surrounding the garden were not too high and could be easily climbed. After a few days of hesitation, Ajit finally jumped over the back wall and entered the grounds. He felt compelled, as though something was pulling him, forcing him to do so.

It was a dark night, with the moon completely hidden behind thick, threatening clouds. A fog had descended, adding to the gloom. The tall, sky-high coconut trees were swaying drunkenly in the strong wintry wind and the rustling palm fronds appeared to be murmuring in pain. Everything was quiet inside the house. This was mid-spring, and the seasonal nor'westers were known for their ferocity.

There was no moonlight; lights, visible from the ground and first-floor windows on other evenings, could also not be seen. Where, in this huge house, was the cherished object of his desire? How would this inexperienced thief find his way around the house? Earlier that day, he had gathered from the gardener that 'Babu' was still sleeping downstairs and had not yet shifted back to his bedroom on the first floor. This small information had given him the courage to carry out this audacious act.

A man, blanketed from head to foot, was fast asleep in the front veranda. Holding his breath, Ajit stepped by him silently and entered through an open door. The room was full of furniture but there was no one there. He spied another open door leading into a side room. The room was shaded by glossy green curtains and little could be seen. A dim light illuminated the contours of a big bedstead covered by a fine mosquito net. Ajit stood mutely by the curtains for a second, and then, determined to complete his task, entered the room. There was only a single muted night-lamp on the wall; the bulb was glowing softly through a coloured glass shade. In the soft light of this lamp, it was not difficult to spot Aurobindo sleeping on a beautiful mahogany bed at the centre of the room, the bedspread a shining white damask cloth. Ajit looked around cautiously to see if there was anyone else around. On the opposite side, he saw another open doorway into a third room; there was a similar bed there on which a woman was lying asleep—he guessed that this was his stepmother.

Ajit crept forward on silent feet like a thief and stood near his father's head. He stared at him with unblinking eyes, enraptured. He felt as though the God of gods, Mahadeva, was lying there lost in meditation, illuminated by innumerable silver rays.

When he had last seen this handsome person as the chief guest at his college function, he had not known that he was his father. After he had realized who he was, he had witnessed the horrifying spectacle of a corpse-like figure crumpled on the floor! This face had haunted him since then—bloodless beyond description. But *this* face? Although it still lacked lustre like the moon at dawn, Ajit felt that there was no other like it. Looking at his father's gentle sleeping face, his tired, sorrowful mind sensed the gentle touch of peace at long last. But he also felt small and insufficient—how could he, ignorant and filled with self-pride, ever hope to understand the greatness of the chaste devotion with which his father had carried out the promise given to *his* father? Ajit's remorseful heart wanted to wash his father's feet with tears and seek forgiveness for his wayward thoughts. Not thinking of the consequences, he moved towards the other end of the bed, clutched both his father's feet and laid his head on them; his accumulated tears burst forth and fell like monsoon rain. He failed to stem the flow and kept his head on his father's feet as he cried silently.

Maybe it was not the boy's touch but the feel of the hot tears—Aurobindo stirred and tried to pull his feet away. Unable to release himself from the grip, his foot kicked at the boy's head. The blow was soft, but Ajit felt a different kind of pain and muffled a small cry, released the feet from his panicked hands and hurriedly stood up. But that frightened low sob of pain alerted the patient and he cried out, 'Who is there? Whom did I hit?'

He tried to twist his weak body into a sitting position. Ajit was petrified as the vulnerability of his position became clear in a flash. What would he do now? Or, what should he avoid doing? He ran to the switchboard impetuously and switched off the light, casting the room in darkness, and ran out of the door. From behind him, a weak voice struck him like an arrow, 'Rani! Rani! Ramfal! Ramfal!'

He guessed that the blanket-clad figure on the veranda must be Ramfal. In the deep darkness, Ajit almost stumbled over him; he narrowly avoided bowling over the half-asleep man, deftly jumped down two stairs at a time, going towards the garden, and ran with all his might.

Outside, the night had acquired frightening proportions. The darkness stretched like a shroud, which even a needle could not penetrate, except when it was shred to pieces by jagged lightning cutting terrifyingly across the sky, followed by a roll of thunder that sounded like the announcement of the Armageddon and the total destruction of the world. And, almost as though empathizing with the pent-up emotions of the shocked boy's pained moan, the rain threw itself down on earth in torrents, flooding the ground with heartrending tears of anguish. There seemed to be no limit to the disaster surrounding him! In the tireless howling of nature, which seemed to be pouring out its immeasurable misery that night, the small sounds of everyday life were completely lost. But Ajit's newly sensitized ears picked out the shout of the doorman, 'Thief! Thief!', and the thunderous barking of what was apparently a rather large dog. His pulse raced—he felt that he was about to die! Lost, shivering, terrified, he felt that he could not run anymore—why not give up? He was not really a thief, and they would after all take him to his father! Would he believe that Ajit had come to this particular house on this appallingly stormy night, when no one dared to be outside, to *steal*? He would certainly realize the truth! But no! Nothing could be said with certainty. Looking at Ajit's forlorn figure, would he not be suspicious? Were his actions any different from that of a real thief?' And, what did his father actually know about him in any case? Why would he not assume that Ajit had been attracted by his father's wealth, the father who had rejected his mother, and had crept into his house to steal valuables?

Ajit's mind became as stormy as the hurricane around him, as opposite thoughts flashed like lightning through his brain. The flame of revolt began to burn in him again—what if Aurobindo did not recognize the son whom he had briefly seen at the function, *that* ill-fated son whom he had forsaken his entire life, and handed him over to the police? Would the humiliated Ajit then reveal his identity to him? No, never! Not even if he was sentenced to be hung! This nocturnal wanderer, this inopportune mendicant was Aurobindo Basu's son, Ajit Kumar Basu! The entire Basu family, going back to the forefathers in heaven, would shudder in shame! His father's reputation would be swept into the dust and he would sneer in contempt when *this* pitiful boy would call himself *his* son. How could his father think of this creepy worm-like creature, who had entered his house like a burglar, as his *son*? Would he not disown the boy all over again? Who knew what could happen? The police lockup—jail—deportation—oh God! Please give him that—send him to jail! At least it would be a shelter—give him a small place inside strong prison walls. Despite intense desires, Ajit would not be drawn like a magnet to his rich father's palatial house if he was imprisoned! He would spend his time doing hard labour, breaking stones, turning a grindstone—he would not find the time or energy to indulge the pain of what he had been denied. Oh Narayana! Oh God of gods! Just this trifling thing he begs of you! Will you have no pity on this boy who is asking for so little? This is the only way that the terrifying demon within him, which had been ruining his life with blow after blow, can be controlled. Take away the freedom that has abused him so much; take it away, oh Lord! He cannot stand it anymore!

Suddenly, out of nowhere, his mother's tired, beautiful face came to his mind, smiling despite her unfathomable sorrows. How very calm, soft, stable, composed and bright with the dignity of restraint! How had he forgotten his mother these past few days? Wild thoughts floated through the foolhardy Ajit's mind as conflicting memories played hide-and-seek and made him helpless with trepidation. He clutched at a big bunch of bananas hanging from a nearby tree as though it was Manorama, and cried his heart out into it as the storm raged around him.

At that very time, about twenty-five male and female servants had woken up and gathered around the doorkeeper, and a loud discussion was in progress about the thief who had run away. Ramfal was proudly declaring that thank God, the accursed thief had tripped over his body and fallen down; otherwise, heaven knew what could have happened! He had almost caught the evil fellow single-handed! But what could he do all by himself with people like Chhottu Singh as co-gatekeepers? When *that* man slept, nothing could awaken him! He had burst his vocal cords shouting for help, but did *he* get up? Did *anyone* come forward to help? He was an old man himself; how could he cling to that young, tall, huge wrestler—no, he was more like a terrorist. How could he hold him for any length of time! Even then, he would not have let go had it not been for the sudden bolt of lightning that had lit up the carved scimitar in the sinewy hands of that heavily moustachioed Bhojpuri! Oh my God! Was he going to give up his aged life to catch such a horrendous burglar who would have no qualms about murdering him with one stroke of that axe-like instrument?

Aurobindo said from inside his room, 'Why are they making such a hullabaloo? Please tell them to be silent, Rani. He was not a thief.'

Brajorani stared at her husband with astonished eyes, 'If he was not a thief, then who was he?'

Aurobindo sat silently for a few minutes and then spoke in the same tired voice that had become his trademark since his illness, 'Dream—'

'Dream?'

'Yes, dream. You know what I was dreaming of Rani? Someone with a very soft face; he was holding my feet in both his hands, and—he had laid that gentle face on my feet. He seemed to be crying. I could feel his hot tears even in my dream! Rani, will you take a look at my feet? Was it really dream, or did it actually happen?'

Amazed, Brajarani touched her husband's feet; the bottom of the feet was cool to the touch, and perhaps it was a bit moist? But she refused to believe that the wetness was due to someone's tears, be it that of a thief or a boy in his dreams, and dismissed it as sweat. She then remained silent.

Finally, Aurobindo let out a deep sigh and answered himself in a fatigued voice, 'Then it was a dream, I think.'

But Brajarani spoke up, 'If it was a dream, who switched off the light?'

'You are right!'

Aurobindo's next sigh was even deeper. It was so pathetic that it seemed that his weak heart was feebly struggling to control some unfathomable emotion.

## Chapter XLVI

The next morning when the sun peeped out through scattered clouds and looked at earth with quizzical eyes, the nakedness of the scene below in the megacity made it quickly turn away and enfeeble the dawn light. Those who had ventured out were slipping, falling, struggling through the mud that had the consistency of dirty yoghurt, which had accumulated on the broadways, not to speak of the narrow lanes that were flooded with mucky water. As the morning advanced, the scene would have become laughable had it not been for the sad plight of the pedestrians. The carriages and motor cars had all slowed down to avoid spinning out of control or getting stuck, and their wheels swished mud and sludge over those who were walking, drawing curses and shouts. The vehicles were not spared either; from shining chariots of conveyance, they became mud-splattered spectacles in no time. The drivers quietly accepted the insults because they were safe inside their vehicles; retorts would only have led to further mayhem. But those who were on foot knew how difficult and embarrassing it was to walk today; 95 per cent of the people carried their slippers in their hands instead of wearing them on their feet.

Ajit had no idea when and how he left Ballygunge and reached Upper Circular Road. Near dawn, he spied a two-storied house. Stretched to the point of total exhaustion, shivering, wet from head to toe, he curled into a ball like a scraggy street dog on its veranda and fell asleep. When he awoke, the sun was shining and he had no time to ponder about last night's happenings; he had already missed two roll-calls in the hostel and had no explanations for his absence. He knew that he was about to face a defining moment in his life. Just as last night's terrible storm had played havoc with the earth's covers, shredding it to near-nakedness in its violent fury, he felt that a similar blizzard would soon rip his future apart! What excuse did he have for his all-night absence? Would his mother be able to bear his disgrace? In the past, if he ever came second in class instead of topping it, his mother's face would lose its lovely smile and become pale. That very same Ajit, whom she had reared with her lifeblood, was now going to be an object of aversion! Ajit knew that he could tolerate everything—but his Maa?

The hostel superintendent was a man of few words; he had expressed whatever had to be said during his first warning to Ajit. Now the committee would decide on his fate, and Ajit was quite cognizant that they would recommend that he vacate the hostel, possibly right away. The hostel superintendent looked Ajit up and down with cold, unforgiving eyes—the boy had long, rough, uncombed hair, his eyes were bloodshot, his clothes were torn and muddy, there were scratch-marks with dried blood on him and his nose had obviously been injured. All these were signs of retrogression and indicated the boy's downfall. The superintendent's anger rose as he looked at the 'shameless' boy and roared, 'This is not a den for ganja or consumption of alcohol, Ajit! Boys from bhadralok families stay in this hostel! This is not a place for lowlifes; you cannot do those accursed things if you stay here! Since you have become so very shameless, I am sure you will be able to hunt out a suitable place for yourself. I hear that you don't even attend college!'

When he was finally released from the superintendent's presence and walked slowly towards the corner room that he had occupied for three years, many of his peers looked at him with sharp curiosity. He also found a crowd outside his door, but he did not react. He entered his room silently, looking neither right nor left. He knew that his dirty clothes and his wet bloodied features would be the topic of their animated discussion and derision for days to come. Two bright flames lit up his eyes—yes, his birth into the famous Basu family seemed to be finally bearing fruit! Whatever adversities and miseries were left to bear, those too had been fulfilled as a result of the night he had spent in the storm outside to meet the parent who had given him his identity. He had managed to see and feel that father for the first time only last night, even though only for an instant! He was blessed! Blessed! If the hostel authorities threw him out, let them! And if he now went to the door of an asylum and stood waiting, there was little doubt that they were sure to let him in, for what was he if not totally mad!

He heard some offensive, insulting words behind him.

'Oh, this boy has become a veritable animal, a beast!'

'He has become a degenerate, a scoundrel! Does he feel no shame?'

'I am amazed at how he became such a drunkard in so short a time! Just look at his eyes!'

'You think he is addicted to cocaine?'

'Look, he is swaying on his feet!'

'Oh, the poor son of an unfortunate widow!'

It was this last comment that struck him like an arrow—his mother, a *widow*?! It was true that Ajit was without a father, you could even call him a beggar; it was also true that his mother was worse than an orphan, deprived of her husband's home, but how could they call her a 'widow'? The thick streak of vermillion in the parting of her hair was her valued possession, her beauty, her pride! But...was she any better than a widow?

Entering his room, he found his roommate talking animatedly to another boy. Seeing him, the other boy smiled mockingly and quickly exited the room. His roommate jumped up and said sympathetically, 'They are speaking such rubbish about you, Ajit! I *don't* believe them! I was telling Kestodhan the same just now.'

Ajit suddenly felt furious. He shouted, 'Why *don't* you believe them? *Why*? When everyone believes it, why not *you*! I don't want any sympathy from anyone! Do you *understand*?'

The hungry, friendless, indigent Ajit called a coolie to carry his trunk and bedding out of the hostel into the heartless streets of the vast city. He felt afraid as he stood alone, surveying his surroundings and thinking about what to do next. But the next moment, he felt a gush of happiness at his freedom. He was finally breathing the air of liberty! Aaah! What a relief to shed the borrowed mask of genteel behaviour! His hands and feet were no longer bound in the chains of appropriateness. The burden had been heavy for a sixteen-year-old—three tuition jobs on top of the strain of his studies as he tried to pass with honourable marks; he had freed himself from these oppressions today. And far more important, he had also finally found salvation from the new drug that had intoxicated him for the past so many days—that which had drawn him to a certain house, day after day. Now he would return to his abode of eternal peace, his ever-loving mother's lap, where he was sure he would be able to regain his life's direction. Would he not be able to find himself a government job offering a monthly income of 25 rupees—meagre but sufficient for the two of them? With that, they would survive and somehow find happiness in sorrow. Why speak of sorrow? What sorrow? Thank God, all this was over!

But—but, what excuse would he give to his mother? He would not be able to lie to her, but how *could* he tell her the truth? Humiliated, insulted and thrown out like a dog, how could he tarnish his mother's dreams? How could he return home with his tail between his legs? No—no—he could not do that! The only door to Ajit's peace of mind, the shelter of his mother's welcoming arms, was shut to him forever.

The coolie was getting irritated as he stood indecisive. He muttered in a Hindi dialect, 'What kind of a babu have I got today? Sometimes he says, "Go to the station," and then he says, "No, no!" Do you have any destination in mind at all? Give me my dues—I am leaving!'

Ajit rented a small damp room in a 'mess' for the very poor in a narrow lane off Potoldanga Street. He had no money to pay the coolie; instead, he gave him his only cotton coat, which he used for attending college, as remuneration. He spread out his bedding on the dirty floor and lay down. By that time, his whole body was shivering with high fever. Every part of his body was aching...cramps travelled up his arms and legs relentlessly and an unforgiving thirst coursed through him as he cried out in desperation, 'Ma—Ma—Maa!' But no one responded. There was no one to assure him, give him water to drink, in that forgotten part of the megacity. Whimpering, he gradually slipped into a semi-coma.

When he regained consciousness, he found himself on a cot, one of the many lined up with what seemed like thousands of patients, in Medical College Hospital. He tried to open his eyes and look around but couldn't. Next, he struggled to change his position and lie on his side but had no energy to stir. He gave up and lay still; only a deep sigh escaped his lips. His mental state equalled his physical condition—he could not remember anything clearly and his thoughts got jumbled if he tried to rack his memory.

One or two days went by. Ajit drifted in and out of consciousness. When he was finally able to open his eyes, he felt someone placing a cool, wet cloth on his brow. Who was that person—surely his mother? He reached out and clasped that someone's hand and cried out weakly, 'Maa!' But no one answered. The hand, however, was not withdrawn; he clutched it harder and drew it to his weakly beating chest while he raised his eyes to look at the person and moaned, 'Maa! Maa! Maa!'

But alas, where was his mother? The emotionless face of the person standing before him was that of a professional European or Eurasian nurse. She snatched her hand away irritatedly, got up and left, saying, 'By Jove! Is this boy mad or what?'

Ajit silently followed her receding figure till the very end of the ward. Her proficient but cold touch had made him realize how desperately he was seeking his mother's loving compassion. The nurse tended to a few other patients in the same expressionless manner and left the room with measured, unperturbed steps. Lying shrouded in a blanket in a comfortless cot, Ajit's eyes filled with tears, but he was too weak and exhausted to cry.

As the days went by, he missed his mother all the more. In the past, when he had been rushing after that mirage of his father, his mother's features had faded into some distant corner of his mind. But today, when his entire being seemed to have been scorched, as if he had struggled through the Sahara Desert trying to reach a mirage that disappeared at his approach, he could only think of his mother's kind and calm face. He used all his reserves to focus on the memory of that gentle, warm face. His antics of the past few days had filled his mind and heart with venom, as though a snake had struck at him repeatedly. As he lay ill and sorrowful, the only thought that came to him was that his father seemed to have the ill impact of the planet Saturn on his life—had he not seen him at the function, his saturnine influence would not have touched his life and he would somehow have managed to continue on the path that he had chosen despite his poverty. As a result of that poisonous effect, he was now lying friendless, helpless, in the free ward of this government hospital among hundreds of beggars and other patients with unspeakable diseases. Had he been at home, his mother would have fought Death itself—it would have failed to snatch him away! And here, in this ward, Death too looked at him with contempt! In his childhood, Ajit had cried over even a dead ant, and now, he appeared to be watching the dance of Death with cold eyes, waiting for it to take him away. He was living with Death, indifferent, unaffected. Was this the same Ajit who had cried over dead ants?

# Chapter XLVII

Ajit sat up on his cot after eighteen days; he was released from the hospital after twenty-four days. He came outside and felt that he had been better off inside. He somehow managed to stumble to the 'mess' where he had deposited his trunk and bedding. He was told that they had no wish to take any responsibility for a scoundrel like him and would not allow him, a human-skeleton, to even enter the premises. What about his belongings? What did they care about those things? On the very day that they had put him on a stretcher and bid him goodbye, they had also thrown out whatever rubbish had been in his room. They had thought that he was dying and must have certainly died by now—how could they have known that he would recover and return to claim his things?

Ajit felt that he had no other option but to hang around the streets of the capital city with a begging bowl. Where would he go? Was his mother still alive? If she was, she must have heard all about his humiliation by now. Did Ajit possess the right to return home and look her in the eye? His mother had not just borne him in her womb, she had not merely nourished him with her lifeblood, she had tried to mould him into perfection through her own sense of honour and integrity! And *that* Ajit, the son she had nurtured despite her personal sorrows, was now tainted, stigmatized forever! No—no—his mother, who had lost everything in life, had now also lost her son. How could he show his discredited face to her ever again?

Suddenly—out of nowhere—was it Nitai-mama? 'Is that you, Nitai-mama? Nitai-mama!'

Nitaicharan turned around and looked at him, shocked and unbelieving: 'Ajit! Where were you all these days?! You horrible boy! You had us *so* worried. I have been hunting *everywhere* for you! Why did you go into hiding like that?'

Ajit was close to tears, but he controlled himself and replied, 'I was hospitalized.'

Nitai felt as though someone had slapped him, 'Really? That is why there was no trace of you. What happened? My God! You look terrible! But—why did you go to the hospital instead of coming to me? Wicked boy!'

Ajit could bear no more; he said tearfully, 'I did not go on my own! I was unconscious. Those people in the mess, they left me there...' The tears that he had tried to bottle up all this while began to trickle down his face.

'Please, please! Don't cry! Come with me—where are you staying? Have you eaten anything?'

It didn't need much intelligence to understand Ajit's situation after he had replied to the first question. Nitai took him to a Hindu hotel and ordered some food. After that, they took a tram to Nitai's rented house on Dharmatala Street. On the way, Ajit just asked one question, 'Uncle! My Maa?'

Nitai quickly replied, 'She had malaria—the fever was resistant and she still had it when I met her last. And on top of that, you created this hullabaloo! Just then, my mother and others planned a pilgrimage; she insisted on going with them! I thought it would be a change for her, and by the time they returned, I felt I would be able to locate you. If she stayed home all alone, she would worry her head off—'

'So, my mother hasn't yet heard of what all happened?'

'No, I haven't told her yet. My mother wrote to me one day informing me that Manu was worried because you had not written for a while. Maa instructed me to go immediately and find out how you were. I went to Eden Hostel and was shocked at what I heard! But what could I do—I was getting a letter almost every day. Manu had stopped eating and was going berserk with anxiety! I thought, let me lie. When the truth would break her heart, how could I tell her what had happened, and that you were now untraceable? I wrote—he is sitting for his annual examinations—and more such rubbish. And I began to scour the city for you morning and evening! Nobody could give me any news of you. But a shopkeeper told me that he had seen you going towards Circular Road several times over the last few days. One day, he was returning from somewhere and he saw you standing by a wall surrounding a garden house in Ballygunge. He was about to call you when he saw tears coursing down your cheeks. What happened, Ajit? Why are people saying such things about you?'

Ajit stood stiff as a pole and did not reply. He felt relieved that his mother knew nothing of his doings; the burden that had weighed him down lightened. Suddenly, he bent and touched Nitai's feet. The latter jumped in surprise and remarked, 'What are you doing!'

'I had forgotten to touch your feet, Nitai-mama!' He gave a childlike smile and took the dust from Nitai's dirty shoes repeatedly and touched it to his head.

Nitai's rented house was very small. He had brought his wife and two daughters to Calcutta and now he took the boy to his home. Ajit knew the family well and soon settled in. He began to bask in this aunt's care and started to recover. One day, he approached Nitai and said, 'Uncle, please find me a job. It would be good if it was somewhere in Burdwan. But if that is not possible, I will be happy if it is not in Calcutta.'

Nitai was astonished, 'What? You will not finish your studies?'

Ajit shook his head, 'No.'

Nitai advised, 'Why do you want to spoil your future, Ajit? At least get your BA degree! You have just one year left!'

Ajit remained silent while his eyes looked around helplessly. Then he said, 'No Mama, henceforth, I am going to live with Maa. I don't want to stay in Calcutta.'

Nitai guessed that Ajit must have fallen into bad company, and it was to avoid his corrupt associates that he wanted to leave the megacity. Perhaps he had taken the correct decision. What value would education hold if Ajit's moral character became tainted? But he kept his views to himself and said, 'Okay, let your mother return. If she agrees, then we will do what you are suggesting.'

Ajit felt reassured and that helped him regain his health quickly. Now, the focus of his anxiety was his mother. He felt that he had not seen her in aeons. Although it had only been three months since they last met, so much had happened in between that he had lost count of time.

Ajit had no work, nothing to study; in fact, he had no books of his own since the mess-keeper had thrown them all away. Sometimes, Nitai brought a few detective novels home, but in his present mental state, Ajit could not concentrate on them. He would sit for hours by the roadside watching people go by with unseeing eyes. Once in a while, he would spot someone he knew or a fellow student in the distance and quickly hide his face behind his palms in shame and humiliation. He felt resentment towards his erstwhile friends too; he had stayed with them for years, but they had made no attempt to recognize the real Ajit! But let them believe what they wished—he had no right over anyone! And when he had no rights over them, why be sorrowful? When his own father—! A bolt of lightning shot through him as he casually glanced inside the open window of a large horse-drawn landau. He knew this carriage well from his earlier trysts to the house in Ballygunge. He also recognized the pale face of the passenger inside, although he had seen him from close quarters for hardly a minute. He would have recognized him anywhere! This was, after all, his *father's* face! Curiosity, happiness, many emotions flitted through his mind in rapid succession! That instant, the humiliations and distress of his immediate past disappeared and were replaced by joyous excitement. He was so transfixed by the moment that he was quite unaware that the carriage had rumbled on and disappeared into the distance. What delighted him was that he had seen his father, whom he had assumed to be on his deathbed, alive and out, riding in his carriage.

ৡ

## Chapter XLVIII

Aurobindo's physical condition improved gradually. He took a few steps around the house and even started to go out in his carriage. But he did not regain his earlier health—that handsome physique, those charming looks. The doctors advised that he needed a change of scene. The patient had no objection, but where would he go? The doctors suggested hill stations like Simla and Darjeeling, and relatives suggested other places, but the patient had his own strange proposition. He rejected Simla, Darjeeling, Puri, Waltair, Almora, etc., and spoke of Pondicherry. Or, he would sometimes mention a sea-cruise, travelling around aimlessly, docking at unknown ports. And this is what he finally became determined to do. Brajarani was very worried at his plan; in his present state of health, how could he think of a prolonged sea voyage? Instead, why not go to Dharamshala or Kashmir? Aurobindo cut her off with a laugh and said, 'I am not a tuberculosis patient that I should go to Dharamshala! No, it is decided—sea voyage it is!'

Brajarani remained silent. She was well aware that her days of obstinacy were over. In any case, Aurobindo had always been adamantly self-willed on major decisions and flexible when it came to minor matters. But she had noticed his doggedness on every matter nowadays. Brajarani was too scared to contradict him because the doctor had said that peace of mind was necessary for his well-being. Not wishing to excite him, she, who had always had her own way, bore insults silently.

Preparations for the sea voyage started. Brajarani was extremely apprehensive about how she would survive on a foreign ship. Aurobindo had already organized for a cook and two servants. She thought he would not object to a female servant as well. Despite her unease, she decided not to say anything; what if he suddenly said, 'You need not go if you feel so hesitant.'

Then one day, her nightmare came true. Her elder brother, Satyaprasanna, by now a High Court advocate, came to visit them. Brajarani requested, 'Please come and check on the household once in a while when we are not here. You know how servants are—I am sure they will neglect the property in our absence.'

Satyaprasanna replied, 'Fine, no problem.'

Aurobindo was surprised. 'Why, are *you* planning on going somewhere too?'

Brajarani, assuming that Aurobindo's mind was wandering, said, 'I was speaking of when we leave on our cruise.'

Aurobindo asked, 'How will *you* go?'

Rani, astonished, stared at him. Her brother interjected, 'I was asking Ranu the same thing just the other day. But she got mad at me and said, "You think I will sit here in peace if I let him go alone? How could you even suggest such a thing?" Of course, your health *is* a matter of worry. But we also have to think about how *she* will live alone in this big house! Won't she go mad?'

Aurobindo looked at his wife and said, 'Then maybe you can invite Usha over for a few days? Or, you can go and stay in Bhowanipore for some time? This way—'

Brajarani was getting more and more irritated, but she controlled herself because of her husband's health. She replied with bitterness, 'You don't have to worry about *me*; I don't want anyone's charity! But if I leave *you* to the care of unknown people, will there be no lapses? If you think that you can manage on your own, fine!'

The tip of her nose reddened and her lips began to quiver. Cutting the conversation short, she quickly left by the first door that came to her sight to hide her tears. But she also did not want her husband to stay in Calcutta and go nowhere. She, in fact, had her own secret plan; as her husband's health improved and she had time for other thoughts, her nagging doubts about *something* increased.

The servants, meanwhile, continued to discuss the matter of the 'thief' who had entered the house that stormy night. She overheard something that niggled at her brain. The 'thief' grew in height and weight in their discussions. Ramfal painted him as huge and horrendous, a dacoit, a terrorist no less! But the new gardener who worked in the vegetable garden contradicted him and said that the thief was neither a terrorist nor a Bhojpuri wrestler of massive proportions; he was a babu, a gentleman! He was as thin as a stick, almost as though a gust of wind could have blown him away! He had seen this gentle-looking boy earlier, drifting purposelessly around their house on several days. In fact, one day he had asked him about Babu's health, also about where Babu slept, on which floor, and whether he slept alone, along with many other questions. He had *insisted* on details! Now, this gardener was a simple man; how would he know that Calcutta's gentlemen indulged in dacoity? He was from Puri in Orissa. Gentlemen were gentlemen there, certainly not thieves! So, in good faith, he had answered the questions of that good-looking boy, who seemed to be from a good family. But it was surely *he* who had entered the house that night!

Overhearing this debate, Brajarani was filled with wild

curiosity. She had tried to contact the boy in Eden Hostel, but Chhottu Singh's unsuccessful attempts had wiped out all hope. But when she heard the gardener talking about a waif-like boy-thief who was also a gentleman, she felt that maybe her husband had not been mistaken after all? Was that wetness under his feet actually tears? Her motherly instincts were aroused. Recalling that night's terrible storm, the repeated clap of rolling thunder, the ferocious winds scattering heavy clouds above, the resounding bellow of tumbling rain, the mad dance of trees and plants, her heartbeat took on a similar rhythm of insanity—uncontrolled, frenetic, crazy! On that wild night when the storm had spared neither heaven nor earth, when the scream of banshees had filled the world, every house and every palace, with terror, that minor boy, that child, had not been afraid to venture out and enter the closed doors of their house! What obsession had driven him to that madness? *Oh, you small boy, your poor, deprived mother's wealth! What insanity made you join in nature's dance of destruction and death? Oh, you foolish lunatic! If you had this intense yearning in your mind, then why—no! No!—False! Fake!* What was this extreme confusion fogging Brajarani's thinking? Did she not know her *husband* well enough after all these years? The boy was the *son* of that very same father! Their love knew no bounds, but neither did their pride; they could hide their emotions of love and pride deep in their hearts and live out their lives seemingly without a care in the world as though life was nothing but a game, while their very existence burnt out under the weight and burden of these emotions. The flame within them was smothered, but it ravished them like a forest fire, billowing in their innards, killing them slowly. And yet, the murderous target of their resentment was the object of their devotion! That is why that small boy had considered the storm worthless in comparison to his deep resolve to come to wash the feet of that very person who was the cause of his cruel oppression, with his precious, holy tears; and after he had completed his pilgrimage, he had left quietly without a word—a person without an identity, unknown! How mysterious he was! How amazing he was!

Brajarani's heart filled with the pain of remorse. If only her millionaire father-in-law had resisted the temptation of a few thousand rupees! If her own father had considered his daughter's happiness more important than decking her with diamond jewellery to attract her father-in-law, then today Ajit's father would not have been bedridden at this young age! And that golden boy, Ajit, would not have had to go around the streets like a beggar, a pauper! So many girls die unmarried—if Braja had died, would it have mattered? At least, destiny would not have played such a vindictive role! Was God always so unkind?

She was almost insane with worry. She called a trusted servant and sent him to enquire after the boy in secret. After being drenched in the ferocious storm, how was Ajit? The news that the man brought back sent Brajarani's heart hammering.

'Ajit was thrown out of the hostel because he has a bad character. Nobody has any news of him.' Ajit had been thrown out! His reputation had been tarnished! Brajarani's first reaction was mortification, believing the boy to be depraved. But the next minute, a great sorrow overpowered her. She realized that the boy had been expelled as per hostel rules; he had obviously been absent from the hostel the entire night and was humiliated before everyone for apparently having spent the night in debauchery. But did this mean that Ajit had actually become corrupt? *Oh God! Where are you? Do you, like us mere mortals, see only the exterior facade of a person? Is disobeying the discipline of a place a formidable offence to you too? Then why do you forgive the sanyasis, who break the discipline of domestic life, leave their wives, children, friends, wealth, everything, failing in their duty to one and all, and depart without a backward glance in search of You? How were You then complicit in the punishment of this boy who was seeking the object of his devotion? Dear God! Your heart is more pitiless than that of a stepmother!*

Ajit no longer went to Presidency College. He had not taken admission in any other college either. The one remaining hope was that he had returned to Burdwan. But no—he had not done that. Brajarani was stunned into silence; like heavy rain clouds that hover above as hidden lightning streaks the sky, her entire being was leaden with unshed tears. She did not speak of her terrifying worries to anyone lest they reach her husband's ears and agitate him. The results of her search for the boy were too shocking to even contemplate—had he, unable to live with the humiliation, jumped into the Ganges? What else could possibly have happened? She cried to herself, *Oh Ajit! The only precious thing that a pauper woman has cherished! Why did you come silently and leave behind a moment's memory like a dewdrop that disappears leaving no mark except a hint of moisture, like the thin rays of dawn that die leaving behind only a mere recollection of tender light? Oh, you proud boy! You have broken this hard-hearted woman's heart with the devoted tears you shed at the cold feet of that pitiless man! Now, your tears have sparked a flame of repentance and intense sorrow in the harsh, stony heart of this woman! Oh, why am I still alive?*

Keeping such thoughts well concealed, hating herself for her earlier callousness and jealousy, Brajarani continued to live in misery. She was mortally afraid that one day her husband may, out of curiosity, send messengers to find out about Ajit and get the news of his disgrace and subsequent disappearance. It was this anxiety that made her impatient to take her husband out of the capital city.

## Chapter XLIX

A cabin had been reserved in the ship and all arrangements were made. Aurobindo's departure date was 27 May. It was still far off, but Brajarani felt that she only had to close her eyes and *that* dreaded day would be upon them. She felt that her husband's decision was heartless, but her self-esteem would not allow her to protest. Like fire in a bale of cotton, she burnt slowly from inside. When she found it unbearable, she told herself that if he thought that he could find peace without her, then she should be ready to suffer for his sake. *Why, look at my co-wife—Manorama; how has she been able to live without him for so long? Am I that bizarre that I cannot bear parting from him for just a few days? Of course, I can!* Thinking thus, she made a list of all that she would do in her husband's absence—pilgrimages, rites and rituals, days of fasting, vows, and so on. When the list had become quite long, she suddenly picked it up and tore it to shreds and cried silently. Without her husband, everything was a big zero—life was empty! How would she be able to survive without him? Just thinking such thoughts made her knees collapse!

Her sister-in-law Usha's husband had become a *munsif*, a low-level judge at a district court, by now. She had come to see her brother once when he was unwell. Now hearing that he was about to depart on a long sea voyage, she arrived at his house along with her children. She was shocked to see her sister-in-law's face; despite being only thirty years old, she looked more like fifty; that fancy Brajarani, who was always so decked up, she whose hair used to shine so much that your own face was reflected in it, she who never wore anything less than an expensive Dhakai or Shantipur sari, *that* Brajarani was now dressed in her husband's old, narrow-bordered dhotis, and her hair was uncombed, untended. Earlier, she would change her ornaments every day to match her clothes; she would wear an extravagance of diamond, ruby and pearl jewellery every evening. Now, she wore the same few gold bangles on her forearms and a thin gold chain around her neck day after day!

Usha got angry. Not getting any response to her queries regarding Brajarani's ascetic appearance, she began to remove her own ornaments. Braja stopped her wordlessly with tears in her eyes. But mentally, she cursed herself: *Shame on me and my jewellery! It was because of these ornaments that my scheming father knowingly thrust me on this man, devastating not only him but shattering the life of one other. Had I not been the owner of these expensive jewels coveted by my father-in-law, would the boy have had to leave, so disappointed and sorrowful? I did not bear him in my womb, but how can I bear to wear my jewellery today? What if he is no more? How can I be happy? I may be extremely insensitive, but how can I forget that I too am his mother!*

Brajarani could no longer tolerate Usha's company. She now remembered Sarat with deep regret. She wondered how she could have regarded that loving, liberal, big-hearted sister-in-law with such hatred. Her daughters were married by now and lived with their in-laws; her son was studying engineering at Shibpur. There was no way that she could spend time with Sarat's children now. She wondered what had happened to those days when she had enjoyed Usha's company. Sifting through catalogues for new jacket designs and diamond jewellery, looking for new fashions, enjoying the bioscope, theatres and music concerts at Eden Gardens, gossiping about people after returning from a tea party, discussing what to wear to someone's gathering, throwing a British-style party at her own house or an Indian-style dinner when Usha came visiting—where was that time when the two friends had been happy with such pleasures? Their so-called 'sorrows' had been imaginary—wondering whether their husbands truly loved them; small fights between husband and wife. For Brajarani, perhaps it was one step more—there was the suspicion that her husband was still mentally enamoured of his first wife. This was the sum of their distress earlier. Why had God changed all that? Why could they not have continued with life just the way it had been? Usha's life had not changed, but Brajarani had never imagined in her wildest dreams that *her* life would take such an awful turn. And she had no companion with whom she could share her pain, no one who would empathize with her. She knew that she had to bear the excruciating burden of her sorrow alone. There was not a single person who would understand the torture that she was undergoing, the immense regrets, the anxiety, the fear of impending disaster.

She could not tell Usha that her days of lording it over her husband were over, that now she was more of his mental slave than his queen of hearts. So, when Usha asked her in all innocence, 'How can you let Dada go off alone?', she faked hurt pride and replied, 'Nothing serious has happened to him, has it? The arrangements in the ship are perfect—it is all the same whether I go with him or not since he will face no difficulty. Besides, I am a Hindu woman—*I* am the one who will find it tough to survive in a sahebi cruise-ship run by foreigners. I am sure they do not follow our Hindu norms for food or anything.'

There was just one week left for the ship, *Kinnari*, to sail. That day, Brajarani's elder brother, the advocate, arrived, having spent the day sorting through the will of a wealthy man who had just died. Talking about it, he said, 'After this experience, I have decided to write out my own will as soon as possible. Sons nowadays cannot wait for their fathers to die! These people have begun to fight over their shares even before the mourning period is over! Oh brother! Have you made a will? The question of your inheritance is, in any case, complicated!'

Satyaprasanna was a happy-go-lucky man. He had not meant anything serious when he spoke of a will to Aurobindo, except perhaps to alert him and also find out what was in store for his sister. Aurobindo looked listlessly into the distance at the last remaining golden rays of the setting sun. Satyaprasanna was a bit annoyed at his silence, especially since his sister's future remained undisclosed, but he was astonished when he glanced at *her* face—she looked as though someone had stabbed her with a sharp knife. She was deathly pale and was shivering from head to toe as if from immense cold. Satyaprasanna jumped up from his chair and held her, 'Rani! Rani! Are you ill?'

'Yes,' Brajarani gradually controlled herself and left the room.

Satya remarked, 'She has become weak looking after you unremittingly during your illness. I think she too deserves a change!'

Aurobindo replied shortly, 'Yes.'

Three days following this incident, Aurobindo called for Brajarani and gave her a bundle of papers, 'This is my will. Please keep it safely in the iron chest along with my other important documents.'

Brajarani stared at her husband and said calmly, 'Where is the need for a will?'

Aurobindo declared, 'Of course, there is a need. Your brother reminded us about it the other day.'

Brajarani said angrily, 'I don't think it is necessary to pay heed to what people say.'

Aurobindo smiled at her irritation and said in a slightly mocking manner, 'People see and know more than you think. Anyway, put these away now.'

Brajarani understood the innuendo hidden in her husband's words. Her eyes flamed for an instant, but she realized that there was no way that she could refute her husband's misconception of her current state of mind because she could neither disclose what she thought had transpired that night nor tell him about her fears of what had happened to the boy subsequently. Lightning, however fierce, cools once it reaches the womb of the earth. Similarly, she suppressed her anger, and when she raised her head again, there was no sign of the fury that had swept through her minutes earlier. She read through the will carefully and looked at her husband, 'Is this the original will?'

Aurobindo's eyes held a hint of satire as he replied, 'Yes, this is the original. There is a copy in the registrar's office.'

'I want that one too.'

'The rules prohibit us from retrieving that file.'

Brajarani's face flushed red as she said, 'Can you place your hand on your heart and swear that you have not written this will to shame me? It says here that in case you become immobile, your real estate as well as your other assets—about twelve lakh rupees in cash, an annuity of about ninety thousand from your zamindari, will be mine—why have you written off everything to me? Have I ever asked you to do so?'

Aurobindo laughed loudly at this; it had a peculiar, sharp, mad note to it. Had Brajarani been totally in control of her senses at that moment, that laugh would have rung alarm bells in her mind. Aurobindo continued to chortle as he said, 'Then who will I leave my material wealth to?'

Now, Brajarani was totally incensed; she cried out, 'Don't you have anyone other than me in your life?'

Aurobindo continued to laugh as he remarked, 'Yes, and that is why I had to make a will to give you total claim over everything I have. If there was no one, you would have legally inherited my property after my death. You are angry now, but you will later understand the value of money. When I die, according to law, you will get only enough to eat and clothe yourself, unless there is a will. Do you have any idea about what the law decrees?'

Brajarani felt the insult and her fair face reddened like the sun at dawn as it peeps over the eastern horizon. She looked at her husband, straight in the eyes, and said, 'My parents were enamoured of your wealth and slung me around your neck because of your money—you don't have to remind me of that every day, kicking at me with the toes of your boots. I cannot ever forget what they did and why! In fact, I am paying for their sins. My life is nothing but atonement for their transgression. But let that be—the sorrows that you have undergone because of us cannot be taken back. But do not add to the burden of your *own* wrongs! There are too many thorns in your path already on your way to the next life. If you are unable to expiate yourself while still alive, there is no reason for you to extend your enmity with them beyond this life. And however great an adversary I may be to them, I cannot allow you to do them this harm. I beg of you, don't do this to me either—don't make arrangements for me to eat a widow's meal! If I am so ill-fated that I should lose you, whatever is left from my dowry given by my father will suffice.' After this, she tore the tough paper on which the will had been written into shreds, and then rushed to her husband, fell at his feet and began to pound the ground with her head as she washed her husband's feet with tears and said in a clogged voice, 'Oh! How cruel can you be! Don't you have even an iota of pity in you? People develop attachment for even a pet bird. I have been your wife for seventeen years now—have you not developed any sensitivity towards me? If you had, you could never have hurt me like this!'

Aurobindo sat immobilized, stunned with astonishment. He could not utter even a word of sympathy.

## Chapter L

Ajit was now intoxicated with a new yearning. He would wait the entire day for a momentary glimpse of a person sitting inside a large horse-drawn carriage and feel vindicated when it passed by. But as the days went by, he was no longer satisfied with just that quick glance. He followed the trotting horse at a distance one day and found that the carriage headed towards Eden Gardens. He did this on several days, and discovered that they went to a lonely spot by the Ganges, where they would sometimes climb out of the carriage and take a walk, enjoying the balmy evening breeze from the river.

Learning of this regular habit, he began to walk over in the afternoon to the spot and wait for them under the shade of a tree, hidden from view. He could see Aurobindo's face quite clearly from there. If he spoke, Ajit could even hear a few words. How handsome he had been, what a physique he had had! And how broken he had become in the course of these few months! How pale was that golden skin now! His gait, his voice—everything was so weak! He also noticed that his stepmother was in constant attendance—she took immediate care of his every need. She tried her utmost to keep him engaged, to make him laugh. But he realized that all her efforts were in vain. He seemed to be totally distracted, immersed in himself, alarmed at some nameless thought. His smile was so pleasant, but he hardly ever smiled, and if he did, it lit up his face like fleeting summer lightning that faded into nothingness. There were times when their carriage did not come this way; on those days, Ajit's being seemed to fill with bitter poison. Nature's bounty that coloured the landscape around him in vivid colours appeared monochromatic, dry and lifeless. The next day, he would not go to Eden Gardens but sit by the wayside watching the path with unblinking eyes. His heart would jump with joy when he would spy the carriage coming towards him. The days passed by thus, stoking Ajit's sorrows with the golden touch of the setting sun and lighting up his life with a mirage. He did not realize how he was entwining his life with that of his father or how his thoughts now focused solely on Aurobindo. The few words that he had heard his father speak became his mantra. He sometimes wished that he could bring his mother here, so that she too could see him. But how could he do that? Would his mother be able to bear the sight of that other woman, who had taken away her marital rights and was now trying her best to look after Aurobindo, scrutinizing him for any sign of what he may want—would his mother be able to tolerate that look?

Sometimes, the two were accompanied by another lady whom he did not recognize. On some days, there was also a young boy with them who looked a bit like Ajit. He caught his name—Tarit. Was it possible that he was Ajit's younger brother? He was naughty but very lively, bubbling with happiness. Ajit recalled that his own childhood had been equally happy—it had gurgled and rippled like a stream without restraint. Today, thinking back, he felt that the past was a dream that had terminated. Looking at the boy, he felt an intense desire to cuddle him and fill his face with brotherly kisses. Oh, what a comely, graceful brother he had!

But there were other times when he saw the child sitting on *his* father's lap, enjoying *his* father's love—then his entire body would shake in resentment. Bitter with hurt pride, he would feel that the child had wrongfully taken away what was rightfully *his*—the boy had robbed him of the right to his father's love. The fondness that his father showed the boy, the endearing words he spoke into his ears, these should have been for Ajit, only Ajit!

One evening, the carriage from Ballygunge did not arrive, although it was dusk. Ajit reluctantly returned home and found that it was already nine o'clock. He felt ashamed to have kept his hosts waiting and quickly finished dinner. He felt Nitai's wife's eyes on him, searching for something. It did not take him long to realize what she was looking for; his reputation had been tarnished and people would always hold him in suspicion. The next day was Sunday; even though nothing had been planned, Nitai got up early and left for Burdwan. Ajit stayed indoors till 3.00 p.m. and then could not resist the urge to go and sit by the roadside. By four o'clock, he became restless and went for a walk and circled Eden Gardens; the carriage was nowhere to be seen. Then, had he left Calcutta for someplace else? Or, had he again succumbed to a disease? He waited till late into the night and again returned very late—he found that nothing had been left for him to eat.

Nitai returned on Monday morning with the news that as he was waiting to board the Down-Punjab Mail, he had seen the group of pilgrims, including Ajit's mother, getting off from that very train. Ajit jumped up in surprised joy and asked excitedly, 'Uncle, how did you find Maa? Has her health improved?'

Nitai shook his head dispiritedly and said, 'No Ajit, I think I did the wrong thing by advising her to go on this pilgrimage. She is very weak—but I did not have enough time to look properly.'

Ajit's joy vanished in a second. He stood silent for a while and then announced, 'I want to go to Burdwan today itself, Mama.'

These were the very words that Nitai was waiting for. He assented happily, 'Fine, take this money with you. And listen—until we can find something better, I have arranged for you to teach the two sons of the sub-judge, Rasik-babu, twice a day for about three hours. They will pay you 20 rupees per month. Not too bad, is it?'

Gratefulness brought tears of joy to Ajit's eyes. Twenty rupees was a handsome amount for the penniless boy. He wanted to express his thankfulness to Nitai but felt constrained—anything he said would be too little; it was better to remain silent.

Ajit bid farewell to everyone and left with every intention of going to the station. But the moment he set foot outside, he thought, *I am about to leave Calcutta for I don't know how long; I have no idea whether I will return at all. Before I leave, should I not see* him *just once more? Perhaps he is very unwell. How can I leave before I know how he is?*

Ajit turned back. He walked to Ballygunge and was astonished to see two rented coaches filled with trunks leave the house with only one accompanying person. Ajit stood and stared, understanding nothing. Then a young male servant, his hair styled in a pompadour, wearing a clean white punjabi with fashionable creased sleeves and pump shoes, carrying a walking stick, came out of the house. Ajit followed him but the servant had no time for this unkempt person with a rather large sling bag on his shoulder. He took him to be one of the hundreds of beggars who came to the house every day to request alms.

After asking several times where all that baggage was going, Ajit was told that their Babu was leaving the following day on a British steamer bound for Pondicherry or some such place. Who was accompanying him? His attending servants, Ramfal, Kanai Singh and Ashu. Anyone else? No. When would he return?

Nothing was fixed; maybe two months, perhaps six or more. Why had they not gone out for the past few days? These were rich people, did they ever consult anybody? But yes, they had left a short while back today on a drive. Which route did they take? Who knows? Oh yes, he had heard them mention that they would visit 'Didimoni's' in-laws' house.

Ajit's heart beat fast. His father was *leaving*? No one knew when he planned to return? Would Ajit *never* see him again? The boy forgot that he too was supposed to leave Calcutta today. No! No—how could he leave without seeing his father just once more?

He had no idea who Didimoni was. Did his stepmother have a daughter? Was it *her* in-laws' house? Where was this place?

Ajit waited outside the house in helpless perturbation until eight o'clock, when he finally gave up hope; he began to walk towards Howrah Station like an automaton. He realized that it would be impossible to return to Nitai-mama's house this late after having supposedly left for Burdwan in the morning. He had dismissed the opportunity of meeting his mother today in the hope of seeing his father just once more—but fate had denied him this simple wish.

He was about to turn into a small lane when, stunned, he stared at a horrific scene. There were two giant black horses; one of the harnesses that attached the horses to the carriage had partially snapped, and one of the horses, which still had the broken breast strap attached to it, was rearing up violently as it tried to run away. The other horse was following its example and rearing up uncontrollably. Although both were trying desperately to run, they could not succeed and as a result, the carriage was being ferociously pulled hither and thither. A woman's voice could be heard from inside the carriage, screaming for help. But the street was lonely, with hardly any passersby to hear her cries. The coachman had been thrown far off by the rearing horses and was lying semiconscious on the ground. Two grooms who accompanied the carriage were frantically pulling at the reins to subdue the maddened horses. If they had not been there, the carriage would probably have overturned by now.

A few poor folk had gathered around and were watching in fear and apprehension. They knew nothing of horses; everyone gave some bit of excited advice, but no one stepped forward to help. Ajit pushed his way through this crowd and somehow managed to pull open the door of the landau. He shouted loudly, 'Don't be scared—here, hold my hand tight and climb down quickly.' He was speaking loudly and ordering the person inside, something he would never have done in ordinary circumstances, but now he felt no hesitation. He could not see who was in the carriage, but there was no time to find out.

The woman did not clutch at his hand as he expected. Instead, he heard her voice again, 'Don't worry about me—*he* is unwell—how will I get him out? Please help me!'

It suddenly dawned on Ajit that these were those two elephantine black horses—and this was that self-same carriage that he waited for everyday! Yes! His heart raced with trepidation as a lightning bolt seemed to pass through his entire being. The realization gave him a new surge of energy! This thin weak boy showed unbelievable strength, presence of mind and courage as he leaped onto the carriage, picked up Aurobindo's prone body and jumped down to the ground. The lady accompanying him had climbed down without help by then. Aurobindo was conscious but shocked and silent. Ajit instructed Brajarani, 'Please sit down and place his head on your lap. I will fetch some water.'

This was a lower-class locality, almost a slum. Ajit found a genteel house in its midst and requested them for a hand fan and some water. He began to sprinkle the water on Aurobindo's face. As he watched his father's charming but bloodless face, his heart filled with both delight and anxiety.

After a while, Brajarani attempted to take the glass of water and spoon from his hand; she requested him lovingly, 'You have done so much for us already, but I have to make one more appeal—please call us another carriage to take us home.'

Ajit clutched the spoon hard and said, 'No, I can do this. You fan him please. I have already sent for a vehicle, do not worry.'

Ajit wished that he could spend the whole night with them like this. He felt he could claim that at least one night in his entire life could be called successful: he had been able to do the barest minimum for his father. But this was a hopeless wish, it was like a dwarf pining for the moon. Where was destitute Ajit—dependant for his life on food given by others—and where was this famous celebrity, feted for his education and knowledge, Aurobindo Basu, the son of the renowned wealthy advocate Mrityunjay Basu!

## Chapter LI

Aurobindo had recovered his senses by the time the rented carriage arrived. He looked here and there and then called out in a weak voice, 'Tarit!' That word meant 'lightning'. It hit Ajit like a bolt of electricity because he heard, 'Ajit!' He became faint and the glass fell from his hand. A reply had reached the tip of his tongue, but Brajarani's words stopped him short. She said excitedly, 'Tarit did not return with us this evening, don't you remember? God saved us today!'

*Oh, you wretched fool! Did you think that you were their Tarit? Did you think that your semiconscious father's mind could sense the warmth of your emotions? That he could intuit who you are through your touch? You just got a heaven-sent opportunity to serve them—that was all!*

Ajit helped Aurobindo into the carriage with great care and stood waiting at the door. His face was lit up by a ray of light coming from somewhere. Brajarani, now somewhat reassured that the situation was under control, looked at the boy's face carefully for the first time. What she saw startled her; his eyes were wet with unshed tears. But staring at those lotus eyes, brimming with wetness, she got a niggling feeling that she was well acquainted with that face, those beautiful eyes!

She had already expressed her gratitude to the boy several times for saving them from God knew what calamity. Now, seeing that his clothes were ragged and he was obviously very poor, she said, 'How can I bless you? I have no words to express my gratitude, my child. Is your mother still alive? It does not matter. I too am your mother from today! What is your name?'

Ajit was stunned. He clutched the door of the carriage and continued to stand there, stiff and silent. In the meanwhile, the coachman had whipped the horse into motion. Brajarani quickly slipped off a diamond ring from her finger and thrust it into Ajit's hand, hurriedly saying, 'This is nothing—just a token, a very small symbol of our deep appreciation! What is your name? Where do you stay?'

Ajit came out of his reverie in a flash as though he had just been bitten by a snake; he snatched his hand away and flung the expensive ring inside the moving carriage. In an anguished voice, he said, 'I cannot accept this, please forgive me! Please forgive me!' And like a humiliated, insulted, beaten animal, he fled the place mortified.

A faintly receding query came again from the departing carriage, 'Your name? Address?'

But Ajit's scampering feet had carried him quite far from them by then.

Then, Aurobindo touched Brajarani on the arm and said quietly, 'Why are you calling him, Rani? He will not return.'

Brajarani swiftly drew her face away from the window and tried to discern her husband's features in the darkness. She asked impatiently, 'Why? Do you know him then?' Her voice trembled; she was taut with concern for she knew not what!

Aurobindo was silent for a while, and then said quietly, 'Yes, I know who he is.'

Brajarani was swayed by conflicting emotions as she, too, suddenly realized who he was—that nagging suspicion... She burst out, 'Then why did you not tell me earlier?' She whipped around, thrust her head out of the window and kept shouting as loudly as she could, 'Ajit! Ajit! Ajit!'

But no one heard her. Who knew how far Ajit had reached

by this time? Brajarani's heart was in tumult. She turned to Aurobindo in fervent reproach and cried, 'You recognized him and yet you remained silent? How *could* you? Are you at all *human?*'

Aurobindo did not say anything, but it was possible that he smiled to himself in the darkness. People would think that he let out a deep sigh, but if anyone could have seen him, they would have known that Aurobindo was actually suppressing a small laugh. Brajarani knew that sound only too well. She quickly controlled herself and said with as much calmness as she could muster, 'Maybe you did not recognize him—perhaps you are mistaken. You have seen him only once, haven't you?'

Aurobindo replied, 'You too would never have forgotten him had you seen him only once. But forget this matter. I feel dizzy. I hope we can reach home safely.'

Brajarani had so far been stricken with a profound sense of guilt because she had thought that Ajit must be dead since he could not be traced. Now that she knew he was alive, she felt almost intoxicated with happiness. But this feeling was only momentary—her husband's last sentence brought dreadful premonitions of some new disaster and she became anxious as she tried to examine his features in the flitting light of passing lamps.

The path seemed endless, but ultimately they reached home. She gently helped her husband out of the carriage with the help of attending servants. After taking him inside, she gave him a prescribed tonic to help revive him and then telephoned the doctor.

Brajarani was elated on the one hand—her stepson was *alive*—but on the other, she was terrified that her husband's health was deteriorating again. Swayed by contrary emotions, she returned to her husband's side and found him lying face down on his bed, clutching his head with both hands.

His breathing was fast and irregular and his entire body shook with spasmodic breaths. A tempest seemed to be raging through his mind; a storm of agonizing sensations pitched the ship of his intellect around in a maelstrom, wrecking his mind and body. He looked like an animal in its death throes, thrashing around in unbearable pain. Was this that same Aurobindo whose normal demeanour was like that of a dormant volcano, impressive in his seriousness and calm splendour? Brajarani was appalled; she sat down beside him in silent empathy. Feeling her presence, he cried out, 'I have this terrible pain in my chest, Rani! Maybe this is my end!'

Brajarani felt as though she had been stabbed with a knife, but she hugged him with both arms and, in a voice that was like a death-cry, whispered, 'Hush! Please do not say that, dear! Oh my dear, I have no one other than you!'

She hurried off to get a lotion to rub on his chest. But when she began applying it, Aurobindo said, 'Please stop! If my time has come to depart, Rani, let me go! Bid me farewell!'

After a while, when he opened his eyes, he found Brajarani sitting immobile, holding the bottle of ointment in her hand, silent tears coursing down her cheeks. Aurobindo called her softly, 'Ranu!'

Brajarani sprang up at her husband's voice and came closer. She comprehended the long hidden eruption of deep affection, even love, in her husband's cry—she was after all a woman with women's instincts and it felt like her heart was about to burst. She laid her exhausted head close to her husband's chest and began to cry unrestrained. These were not the tears of hurt pride that her husband had become so used to, these were the undammed tears of heartbreak!

'Rani! Ranu! I will not be able to stand it anymore if you cry like that! Please sit here—I have to tell you some important things right now. No one knows what may happen later! There is an unbearable pain in my chest—put your head on my heart! Come closer—let me caress you from the bottom of my heart today! I have never been able to make you happy. You have always suspected that I have never loved you the way a husband should love a wife. But you are not at fault. I have never wished to neglect you, I have never wanted to hurt you intentionally. Please believe me! But perhaps I have hurt you unknowingly because of my terrible destiny. Why am I saying "perhaps"? If you were my only wife, if the memory of someone else—written indelibly in lines of fire in my heart and mind—did not come between the two of us, then surely I would have seen you much happier than this! I know you will say that in that case it was wrong of me to marry you. But that is not it! I married you knowing full well that I would never be able to forget her! But tell me, what escape did I have? If I had not married you, I would have pained my father deeply. I was his only son! I could not hurt him, offend him! This was written in my fate—this was preordained!'

Brajarani stopped him from speaking further and said, 'Why are you saying all this to me? How many kings give their queens as much as I have got from you? I am a witch, a *rakshashi*—false pride made me blind, and that is why I burnt with jealousy! Don't blame yourself—you are *not* at fault!'

A pain shot through Aurobindo's chest and it took him a few minutes to recover. He then continued lethargically, 'Now to come to my story—I had put my life on hold, I had dammed it up. One could say, I had pawned my life and put it aside.

But I don't believe that we have only this one life, I believe in rebirth. I was able to fill my days with the belief that everything does not end with this life—I have lived with this hope, and now my present life is drawing to its close.'

Tired after having said so much, Aurobindo fell silent. Leaning against her husband's aching chest, Brajarani's eyes were dry by now. She said in a doleful voice, 'If I had tried to understand your distress even for a single day, perhaps you would not be lying here now in such agony—'

'You are intelligent; it is not that you did not understand. But who can fault you? Let it go—all those unbelievable convolutions of our complex lives are coming to an end now! Today, let us look deep into ourselves and judge. Let me gaze into my heart and see why I was unable to give a companion as dutiful as you the happiness that was her due. There are very few people in the world, Rani, who are as unlucky as I—I request you to please remember that! And if you cannot, then please pardon me! Uff! The chest pain is gradually intensifying! No, don't worry yourself! Perhaps all aches and pains will soon be quelled! Do you want me to go through more pain? Now Ajit—my golden boy, Ajit—today I—I, the millionaire Aurobindo Basu, saw him in a beggar's guise! You have no idea, Rani, what I have been forced to bear silently without complaining, without retaliating even once! He is the only heir to Mrityunjay Basu's family name, and today he has had to suffer the consequences of his father's sins! The boy has been wrongfully stained with misdeeds he has never committed, and today he is humiliated, considered loathsome and hated! Expelled from his hostel, his college! And do you know why that happened, Rani? Do you remember that terrible stormy night when we believed that a thief had entered this room? He was not a thief—that was not a dream. He was a person who means everything to me in my life—he was Ajit! My Ajit!'

'Who told you all this? I kept it a secret from you!' Brajarani sat up as though she had been whipped.

Aurobindo laughed—that brief sad laughter that concealed all the melancholy in the world, a laugh Brajarani was well acquainted with—and said, 'I took the decision to leave the state a long time back only because of this one reason! I knew that my staying here was detrimental to his mental well-being, to his future! He has been following me around like a shadow! You would not know this—but I can recognize him by his silhouette! Have I been able to dismiss him from my thoughts even for a second, Rani? His face is chiselled into my mind, my heart, my entire being, in lines of fire! After this, do you still want me to live? This pain, do you want to know what it is? It is that fire's final extortion.'

'Oh my dear, please calm down! Tell me some other time, I promise I will listen even if it breaks my heart! You have borne so much; I too have borne a lot—I am sure I can bear much more! But now is not the time, do not get agitated.'

'No, there is nothing more. I have said what I wanted to say. But I have one final request: after my death, the boy should do my last rites. I know you have a lot of compassion in you, Rani! If you give him, who is more than what my life means to me, the right over my body after my soul has departed, our respective fathers will surely not be unhappy, will they, Rani? This will not harm anyone, will it, Rani?'

There was the sound of a car horn outside. The doctor! The doctor had finally arrived!

When the doctor entered the room, the patient was completely unconscious. He was possibly paralysed. The doctor said that the second attack was often far worse than the first. Would he live? Who could say? His heart was weak, and the pulse could hardly be discerned.

## Chapter LII

The moon loses its lustre during the Krishna Paksha, the fifteen-day period from full moon to new moon; on the thirteenth day, *treyodoshi*, it is a pale and languid sliver. Looking at his mother's listless face, Ajit was reminded of the waning light of the beautiful moon on Krishna treyodoshi. His tears flowed silently. His dry, pallid face affected Manorama and the two hugged each other and cried out their grief into each other's shoulders, their sufferings etched into their tears.

Manorama looked like a skeleton—a thin layer of skin covering only bones. She lay prone on the bed. 'Why did you go on the pilgrimage when you were so unwell?' The question was on the tip of Ajit's tongue a thousand times, but he restrained himself. Would she have been any better off had she not left Burdwan? The story of Ajit's humiliation and expulsion, followed by his disappearance, would have killed her much earlier! Why had this matricide Ajit, forgetting his ever-loving mother, scampered after his heartless father like a madman? If one leaves the shadow of a cool mountain spring and rushes after a mirage, this is the result! In helpless anger, the focus of his entire blame centred on the person who, taking refuge behind the word 'ill-fated', had absolved himself of all responsibility after bringing him most unnecessarily into this world. Ajit was a fool! That is why he had completely sacrificed his ambitions, the bright future that everyone had predicted, for that *one* person who was his enemy from birth! And now, he was about to lose his mother forever, that mother who was the pole star guiding the boat of his life, she who was a living goddess to him, much more revered than the Mother Goddess—his Maa!

And how had that *person* behaved towards his mother? Father's decree, *his* pater's command! Had Aurobindo abandoned his wife, the daughter of an indigent man, because of his father's rancour that Manorama's parents were dirt-poor and therefore unfit to be called relations, and had then remained celibate the rest of his life, honouring the memory of his wife like Shri Ramchandra, then he would have set an example to the world. He would have been a veritable God to Ajit! But what had that *person* actually done? He had heaped stigma on the one he had wed before the holy fire; he had left her helpless, without support, and married the beautiful daughter of a very wealthy man, and had lived with her happily ever after!

Shri Ramchandra, it is true, had forsaken his wife in an attempt to follow his *people's* diktat since he was a just ruler; he had sent her into exile because his subjects suspected that she had been defiled by her abductor, Ravana, but Shri Rama had refused to marry again! Instead, he had commissioned a gold statue of his wife Sita to serve as his consort. This had advertised his respect for Sita as well as his personal belief in her purity. But *his* father? Self-interest—self-satisfaction only! Were there any signs that he had been deeply affected at having forsaken his wife? *This* person was Ajit's father?!

Nitai Ghosh's mother cared for Manorama as if she was her own daughter. She brought some gruel for her, and some rice and curry for Ajit. She smiled at Manorama and lovingly told her, 'Now see, your son has returned to you, Maa. It is time for you to get well and then the two of you can live happily together.'

Manorama's wasted lips curved in a thin smile, 'I think my days are done, Mashima. I would not have been too unhappy to die if I had seen him settled!'

The elderly woman retorted, 'Don't ever speak like that! You have brought him up all these years, Manu, and now *you* have to get him married! And you have to see him placed in a good job! Only then would all the pain and sorrows you have borne single-handed be worthwhile!'

Manorama's eyes clouded over, 'Does death wait for good times, Mashima? When it is time, Death will call us and take us. But I have no issue with that. What troubles me is that Ajit will become a complete orphan; it is *that* thought that obstructs the feeling of happiness I get when I think of Death!' A few tears slid down her pale cheeks silently.

Sometime later, Manorama told Ajit, 'The fever increased exponentially after we reached Prayag. They brought a doctor who opined that my heart may fail anytime. On hearing this, they had planned to send you a telegram. But I did not want to trouble you unnecessarily—you would also have missed your classes at college. And how would you have come alone all the way? So, *I* told them not to bother you. But it would have been very lucky for me had I died in that extremely holy place, Ajit. However, how could I die without seeing you just once more? Perhaps that is why I survived! Maybe I returned to this place where the holy Ganges does not flow for that very reason, even though I almost died in Prayag, where I would have been cremated by the Ganges and gained some virtue!'

Ajit did not reply; nobody knew the intensity of his remorse! Why had he left for Calcutta to complete his graduation when he *knew* that she was so unwell? When he had come home during the puja vacations and found his mother suffering from malaria, he should have taken her to some healthy place where the air was good, found a job instead of running after his ambitions, and looked after her. He would then not have been on the verge of losing his mother forever! His sorrow knew no bounds.

The desire to see Ajit again had given Manorama unbelievable mental strength; she had hung on to life drawing on her last bit of willpower. She had undertaken the travails of the lengthy train journey somehow and returned home. Now that her son was here, her desire to see him one last time had been assuaged. She seemed to give up and her health began to deteriorate rapidly. All she could do was look unblinkingly at Ajit with thirsty eyes. Nobody knew but there was another deep desire cloistered in a secluded fold of her mind—that wish, that craving quickened her heartbeat every once in a while as she kept staring at her son.

After long moments of hesitation, Manorama placed one hand on Ajit's chin and caressed his throat with the other. She lifted his downcast face, so that he now looked at her directly, and said, 'No, don't be so downhearted, Aju-moni! My dearest! Do not make yourself ill with so much crying, my Gopal! Who will look after you? This thought worries me so much!'

Ajit could not stand this anymore. He hid his face in his mother's breast and began to cry like a child: 'My birth was futile! I have been a bad son to you! I have made you only worry for me till the end! I have not been able to do *anything* for you!'

Manorama quietly began to stroke his head with limp and powerless fingers, and said in a calm, composed voice, 'Do you really want to do something for me, Ajit?'

Ajit lifted his tear-stained face and looked at his mother questioningly, 'What do you want me to do? You just have to tell me!'

The words stuck in her throat. With great effort, Mano looked away and said in a thin, cloistered voice, 'Can you bring *him* here? I want to see him just once before I depart! Do you remember, you had given me your word one day a long time back—you had *promised* me that you will show him to me? But perhaps then was not the correct time—*now*, it is time, since I will soon be no more. Can you do this for me, Ajit?'

Ajit's senses had become languid with sorrow as he watched his mother sinking slowly, but his mind cleared in an instant at her words. A bolt of lightning shot through his large, dark eyes, just as coal lights up at the touch of fire! For a brief second, his eyes blazed! His dying mother held his hands and said desperately, 'Please, Ajit! You would have done everything you wanted to do for me in this life if you bring me my deity to see me just once! I have not seen him in eighteen years. I want to place my head at his feet and die—and *then,* my life would be complete! Dearest child, can't you do this little thing for me?'

Ajit replied to this plaintive request from his dying mother in a grave abrupt tone, 'No, I cannot, Maa!' His voice sounded like the deep rumble of thunder portending a storm of enormous proportions in a looming, cloud-shrouded sky.

If a hammer is struck on the wound of a dying person, he howls in pain. Similarly, a moan emerged from Manorama's lips, 'Ajit! Ajit!'

By this time, Ajit had almost lost his senses at the thought of the impending death of his mother. He felt that his father was the person who was solely responsible for his mother's current condition. He heaped all kinds of infamy on him, outlandish blame, and screamed, 'No, Maa! This cannot be done! How can you even think of placing your head at his feet? He is culpable for what you have had to undergo all these years! He is guilty for all that has happened to you—how can you think of *him* as your deity, your God?'

Just as one hides one's face from a ghost in fright but cannot resist staring at it in horror, Manorama continued to stare in fear and dismay at her son. She remonstrated in a weak voice, 'When I saw you for the first time after I returned home, I knew that this was not the same Ajit I had nourished through all these years! Ajit, know this, if you call God a demon, that does not make him a demon; the detractors are the ones who are most affected and remain unhappy.'

By this time, Ajit had gone almost insane with suppressed fury—his ears were ringing and he heard nothing except the roar of his own blood coursing madly through his veins. He could hardly see his mother's pale, pallid face in front of him as his vision dimmed and his burning eyes saw only the face of his worldly, rich stepmother, well established in his wealthy father's house! The mistress of riches that could only possibly be imagined as existing in heaven or in a dream! How could the man who could distinguish between his wives in such a manner that one was now a pauper and the other...how could *he* be placed on the throne of a deity?! It was impossible for Ajit to deceive his mother any longer. How could *he* be complicit in his father's duplicity? He was his *mother's* son; he could not pretend and be false to her! *He* was a God? *He* who had rejected her and not wanted to see even her face; *he* who had done her grievous injustice, so much so that she suffered not only mentally but had been physically impoverished to the extent that she was now on her deathbed? *He* was her deity! He had harmed Ajit too, but he was ready to forget that. But how could he ever forgive that person for causing his mother's untimely death through sheer starvation and neglect? *Never*! Not in his entire life! He shouted, '*Who* are you calling your God, Maa?! *I* have seen everything with my own eyes, Maa! Do you think *I* can call him a God—*he*, who after drowning you in sorrow and poverty, is *himself* submerged in opulent happiness? He has surrounded himself with such splendour and affluence that people may think he is *divine*! But how do you expect *me* to consider *him* a godhead? Look at what he has done to you!'

'Ajit! One can construct a God out of clay or stones and bestow it with divinity! Have faith in your own devotion, dear, not on external components! Have faith in yourself! You saw only the outer embellishments of material affluence, but could you see the emptiness inside? Sitting here, I have been able to experience his internal lonely and perpetual pain—the relentless ache in his heart, day and night! I feel it in my inner being constantly! Oh Ajit! I had never imagined in my wildest dreams that *you* could break my heart like this when I am on my deathbed! Baba Vishwanath, oh Shiva! Oh Maa Annapurna! Mother Goddess! I left you and came back here to die blinded by love for my son. I am getting my due punishment! You are castigating me for straying from the path of spiritual devotion!'

Meanwhile a lady, wearing a sari with a multicoloured border, her entire body wrapped in a large thick bedsheet, descended from a hired carriage and entered the house. Peeping into various rooms, she now entered the room where the mother and son were locked in misery. She stood still, shocked at the sight before her. The room, which still showed signs of its previous glory in its size and inbuilt mouldings on the walls, was now bereft of all decorations and looked totally destitute. On a grimy bed lay an incomparably beautiful woman whose face was now lustreless like the fading twinkle of a star in the grey light of dawn. A young distraught boy was desperately crying at her breast, his arms flailing as he tried to hold her hands, her face, any part of her body. He was howling in lament, 'Maa! Maa dearest! Oh Maa! Maa—'

The lady stood stunned as though struck by lightning and

then quietly wiped her eyes with the corner of her sari. She came closer and touched Ajit's hand and said, 'Will you be able to wake your mother by crying like that? Go fetch some milk or water.'

Ajit obeyed like an automaton. When he returned, he found that the unknown lady had sat down on the bed and pulled the exhausted, limp head of his beloved mother onto her lap, and was fanning her face with the end of her sari. With bent head, she was murmuring into her ear in a mellifluous loving voice, 'Didi! Didi!'

She looked up at Ajit's terrified face and said, 'Don't be afraid, Baba. Your mother has simply fainted—she will recover soon.'

Having said this, she turned back to Manorama and began tending to her single-mindedly. Her hands were quick and experienced, full of care and love. Ajit was first surprised, and then filled with wonder and deep respect.

Within a few minutes, Manorama stirred and took a deep trembling breath and turned on her side. After a while, as she became conscious of her surroundings, her lips, which were now like the petals of a white rose, fluttered open, and a thin, quivering voice emerged, 'Ajit...'

'Maa, Maa! I will never hurt you again! I promise! Please forgive me just this once—' Ajit again burst into loud moans. He clutched his mother's thin feet that were already losing warmth and washed them with his hot tears. At this, a shiver ran through the unknown lady from head to toe.

'Didi! Didi! I had come here to seek atonement for my grave sins—to seek forgiveness! Will you not give me any opportunity to repent, my sister?'

'Rani! You have not committed any sin, my sister! What repentance are you talking about? No, no, please don't cry like that, sister! I have no anger in my mind, no resentment. God will bear me out. I have never felt any kind of hatred or bitterness towards you! Today too, with my last breath, I bless you, however little my blessing may be worth. May God make you into another Savitri, who brought her husband Satyavan back from death's door!'

Brajarani could not stop her tears from flowing. She held a spoon of water to the dry, dying lips of her co-wife. Overcome with sorrow, she cried, 'I had come with such high hopes but all my hopes have been dashed! Let me at least be blessed with the dust of your feet! Will I be able to keep him alive after he hears of your condition? Don't you know that his mind and spirit are all yours? You are everything to him!'

'Rani! My dear sister! I am sure he has shared his love with you—he has never been unjust, he would never have treated you with inequity!'

Brajarani let out a troubled sigh. This seemed to cleanse her soul. She said with admiration: 'Didi! Now, today, I fully understand the difference between you and me! Today, I can say wholeheartedly, and God is my witness, if there is an afterlife, if rebirth is true, then your husband will forever remain yours and yours alone through all future lives, through transmigration of souls! A million Brajaranis will not have the strength or power to take him away from you! Not ever! No, sister, whatever fate has in store for me will happen—but I do not wish to share your husband with you ever again! Let me not repeat what I have done in this life ever again!—I want this assurance from you!'

As she spoke, tears coursed down her cheeks uninhibited. Her husband, after all, had been everything to her—she had dedicated her life to Aurobindo! Her life had been, however, bereft of reciprocal love. She felt that her existence was unnecessary, not only in this life but pointless and redundant forever and ever, as she made this supreme sacrifice. Nothing seemed to be left to her after this, neither in this life nor in any other.

Manorama sensed her emptiness, her depression. The suffering in Brajarani's beaten eyes found an empathetic resonance in the dying eyes of her co-wife, who seemed to struggle with death as she tried to express her sympathy and affection for the unfortunate woman in front of her. She gathered enough strength and spoke with difficulty, 'Why are you feeling disturbed, my sister? Why are you perturbed? What had to happen in this life, what was fated, has already happened! I have decided that from now on, we two sisters will care for his two feet together, equally. Now, I have a responsibility for you in the years that you have remaining. Here, take your son, make him sit on your lap and care for him. I want to see you do that before I close my eyes forever. Ajit! You have not paid obeisance to your younger mother, your Chhoto-ma, yet! You have not touched her feet?'

Ajit had turned to stone; stunned and shocked, he came closer. Brajarani immediately reached out and clutched his hand. 'No, no obeisance, no touching the feet, no pronam now! If you can ever forgive this demon-mother, this rakshashi Maa of yours, this witch of a mother, then call me mother, just once—Maa! Ever since I saw you first seven years back, I have been rushing around madly, just wanting, waiting to hear you call me "Maa"! I have been desperate!'

Ajit knelt down in front of her slowly and touched her feet with his head. Then, in a voice filled with emotion, he called her 'Maa!'

## *Acknowledgements*

At the end of a happy journey, one is always grateful to so many people and places for having made their expedition, especially into uncharted waters, successful, but there are some people who stand out particularly, and here, I wish to express my gratitude to them.

First, I am deeply indebted to my parents, Asoka Nath Banerji and Subrata Banerji, who helped shape me into who I am and who would have been the happiest today had they been here to see the completion of this book. My father always wanted me to read Bengali literature, something I was reluctant to do, being 'Bengali-compromised', never having had any formal education in the language; he used to say that I would be impressed at its depth and variety—and I appreciate that now. My mother always had faith in me, in whatever I did, and encouraged me to believe in myself. She is the one who told me the most interesting stories about my grandmother, Anurupa Devi, and got me hooked on women achievers of the early nineteenth century, who fought against all odds in subtle ways and paved the path for women's empowerment in present times.

I am sincerely grateful to my sister-in-law, Sharmistha (Ray) Banerji, and my brother-in-law, Gautam Bhattacharya, for having patiently read the draft, which I imposed on them, and encouraging me to complete it. I am especially indebted to my friend, Prof. Surabhi Banerjee, for not only volunteering to go through the entire manuscript meticulously but giving me the confidence to publish it. I also thank M.J. Akbar, who had a quick look at the draft and vetted it.

I am thankful to the editors at Rupa Publications, particularly Sakschi Verma and her team, for doing an excellent job with the editing of the manuscript. I also thank Dibakar Ghosh, editorial director, and Kapish Mehra, managing director at Rupa Publications, for having faith in me. I must mention the cover of the book—it is after my heart; I am deeply thankful to the artist for capturing the essence of the storyline.

And finally, I have to acknowledge my appreciation for my husband, Niranjan Bhattacharya, who has given me enough space, time and encouragement to pursue my varied and numerous interests, with the greatest of good humour. Without his constant support and encouragement, this translation—which I always wanted to do but had little confidence to pursue as it is so far from my usual writing activities, and also because of my limited knowledge of my own mother tongue—would never have been completed.

# Glossary

| | |
|---|---|
| *Aghran* | Bengali lunar month, which falls between mid-November and mid-December; also spelt as Ograhoyon or Agrahayan |
| *Akalyan* | Harm |
| *Ashar* | Bengali lunar month; falls between mid-June and mid-July |
| *Athhe kathe chorena* | Bengali saying that a pregnant woman is not supposed to sit or climb onto anything wooden (*kaath*) in the eighth (*aath*) month of pregnancy |
| *Attar* | An Indian perfume |
| *Bagdi* | A Hindu low-caste person |
| *Bagdidni* | A woman from the Hindu Bagdi low caste |
| *Barandala* | A metal or wooden plate containing auspicious items, like a lamp, vermillion, turmeric, flowers, betel leaves, paddy, etc., used on special occasions by married women to ritualistically welcome and bless special guests or family members |
| *Bhadralok samaj* | A society of gentlemen or genteel people; can be interpreted as the educated middle class |
| *Bhai Phonta* | Also called *Bhatri Dwitiya* (*Bhai Dooj* in Hindi); falls on the second day following the new moon of Kali Puja/Diwali, when sisters pray for their brothers' well-being and good health, chanting mantras while putting sandalwood paste on their brothers' forehead. This is normally followed by celebrations that include a feast. |
| *Bisti* | An Indian board game |

| | |
|---|---|
| *Bonidi* | Belonging to a well-established and distinguished family or lineage |
| *Boron* | To welcome ceremonially |
| *Chadar* | Shawl, scarf, sheet |
| *Chamar* | The contextual meaning refers to a heartless and unfeeling person. |
| *Charanpadma* | An ornament for the feet |
| *Chiranjibeshu* | 'May you live forever'; a phrase used to address someone in letters |
| *Choudani* | An ornament |
| *Daan* | Donation; to give |
| *Dewan* | Chief treasury official |
| *Dhoti-chadar* | Traditional Bengali dress for men involving a set of two pieces of cloth |
| *Dom* | Low-caste cremation ground attendants |
| *Durwan* | Doorkeeper; guard |
| *Dustu* | Naughty |
| *Ekadashi* | The eleventh day of the waxing and waning lunar cycles of the Bengali calendar month |
| *Ganga prapti* | To have one's ashes immersed in the holy Ganges after cremation; Hindus consider it helpful in achieving salvation after death. |
| *Gaye holud* | A pre-nuptial ritual where both the bride and groom are smeared with turmeric paste before a ritual bath; while this is considered auspicious, turmeric also helps to add a glow to the skin |
| *Golum-chor* | A card game that is played with 51 cards; it is called Jack Thief in English, the 'golam' being the jacks. |
| *Gujri pancham* | An ornament; possibly two ornaments: *gujri* and |

| | |
|---|---|
| | *pancham*. These are mentioned in some books of the eighteenth and early nineteenth centuries but are now obsolete. |
| *Jahannam* | Hell (in Islam) |
| *Jamai Sashti* | A traditional feast prepared for the son-in-law of a household on the sixth day of the month of *Jyestha* of the Bengali calendar (mid-May to mid-June); a ritual meant to honour the son-in-law and strengthen the bonds between him and the wife's family |
| *Jestho* | The elder sibling or family member not merely in age but also in status |
| *Jora maash* | In the Bengali calendar, some months in certain years are considered to be *jora* or sick as per astrological calculations. No auspicious events are conducted in those months. |
| *Joshti* | The hottest month in the year, the second month of the Bengali calendar; falls between mid-May and mid-June; also called *Jaisthya* or *Jyestha* |
| *Kasai* | Butcher |
| *Katla* | A type of South Asian carp |
| *Kaviraj* | A person who practises traditional Indian medicine |
| *Khaja* | A dry fried sweetmeat made from flour |
| *Kul Guru* | Family priest for several generations |
| *Kulin* | Upper genteel class belonging to a higher caste (Brahmin or Kayastha), which has maintained its family status for generations through marriage with families from the same caste |
| *Kush* | Reed; a species of grass |
| *Lila* | Divine play or playful nature of the Divine; |

| | represents the essence of liveliness and joy |
|---|---|
| *Madur* | Reed mat |
| *Maina* | The Indian Mynah (*Acridotheres tristis*) |
| *Malsha* | Round earthen pot |
| *Motichoor* | A ladoo (a circular sweetmeat) made from chickpea flour |
| *Mriganabhi makaradhwaj* | An Ayurvedic medicine prepared from a combination of herbs and minerals used for treating various health issues, including tuberculosis and pneumonia |
| *Muchi* | Cobbler |
| *Nikah* | A Muslim wedding contract necessary for a couple to be legally wed under Islamic law |
| *Opriya* | The unloved one |
| *Paan* | Betel leaf |
| *Painjorh* | An ornament for the feet |
| *Pallu* | The usually decorated end of the sari that is thrown over the shoulder and hangs loose |
| *Para* | A neighbourhood or locality; in earlier times, paras evoked a strong sense of community |
| *Pith jhanpa* | An ornament that covers the back of the blouse or jacket; currently obsolete |
| *Potol* | Pointed gourd; a vegetable also called *parwal* |
| *Priya* | Loved one; dearest |
| *Pronam* | A respectful salutation that may involve touching an elder's feet or folding of hands in greeting |
| *Punjabi* | Dress with long, loose sleeves usually worn over a dhoti in Bengal |
| *Purohit* | A priest versed in Vedic rituals |
| *Saadh* | A ritual where a pregnant woman is given the |

| | choicest dishes to eat and gifts of saris shortly (normally a month) before her baby is due |
|---|---|
| *Sandesh* | A Bengali sweet made from curdled or thickened milk |
| *Sanyasi* | A religious ascetic who has renounced the world |
| *Sarkar* | The family accountant; also a kind of housekeeper |
| *Shehnai* | A clarinet-like musical woodwind instrument |
| *Shraddha* | A Hindu rite or ceremony performed by the immediate family for a departed person to express one's respect (shraddha) and pray for his soul to reach its eternal abode |
| *Sitabhog* | A milk-sweet; a specialty of Burdwan |
| *Sonar beney* | A Hindu caste with the occupation of dealing with gold; also called *subarna banik* |
| *Sravan* | A month in the Bengali calendar that covers the period from mid-July to mid-August |
| *Talshansh* | A sweetmeat made of hardened curdled milk with a core of sweetened water or liquid jaggery |
| *Tatwa* | A ceremonial custom of exchange of gifts between both families at a Bengali wedding; these are a kind of exchange of blessings for the bride and groom and for their families |
| *Tulsi* | Holy basil; tulsi is considered a sacred plant and its leaves are essential in most religious ceremonies |
| *Vaikuntha* | The celestial abode of the Hindu deity, Lord Vishnu |
| *Yagna* | A Vedic ceremony involving a holy fire, oblation and sacrifice |